HUNTED

EDNAH WALTERS

SPENCER HILL PRESS

ALSO BY EDNAH WALTERS

Writing as E.B. Walters

The Fitzgerald Family Saga
(Firetrail Publishing)

Young Adult

The Guardian Legacy Series

This book is dedicated to my sisters, Meb and Singh,
who instilled in me the love for books.
I could never thank you enough for your love and patience.

A SELECTED GLOSSARY OF TERMINOLOGY

Fallen angels: Angels sent to earth by God to protect humanity who strayed and intermarried with humans.
Nephilim: Children descended from the union of fallen angels and humans.
Guardians: Good Nephilim.
Cardinals: Guardians with the ability to control energy, solids, water, air, time and psi/mind.
Civilians: Guardians with limited abilities who support the Cardinals financially and by monitoring demonic activities.
Hermonites/demons: Nephilim who can choose to be good or bad.
Primes: Powerful demons with the ability to control energy, solids, water, air, time and psi/mind.
Souled Demons/Neutrals: Demons and children of demons who have given up their evil ways and/or have no interest in hurting humans.
Neteru: Nephilim who don't have the ability to shift into other beings, form or sprout non-human body parts.
Nosferatu: Vampire Nephilim.
Werenephil: Shape-shifter Nephilim.
Lazari: Werenephils that can shift into smoke-form.
Nephling: Nephilim with one human parent or grandparent.
Nature-benders: Nephilim with the ability to manipulate nature.
The Brotherhood: Short for the Brotherhood of Guardians—Souled Demons who live in a closed community with their own chosen leaders, are peaceful, and don't side with Guardians or demons.
Chosen One: The most powerful Guardian, prophesied to unite the Nephilim.
Kris Dagger: A powerful dagger the Chosen One uses to channel and direct his or her psi energy.
Psi or psi energy: Psychic energy channeled byNephilim.
Alrunes: soul mates.
Tartarus: The abyss where fallen angels and evil Nephilim can be sent.
Alphas: Energy balls created by Cardinal Energy Guardians.
Omegas: Energy balls created by ordinary energy demons.
Omnis: Energy balls capable of great destruction, produced by powerful demons. Only one person can destroy them—the Chosen One.
Teleport: Move from place to place by dematerializing and rematerializing.
Telegate: An energy pathway left behind when someone teleports.
Medium: A human psychic who channels communication between humans and Nephilim.
Mimic: To shift and copy another being.
Athame: a powerful dagger used by demons.

PROLOGUE...

In the middle of the Pacific Ocean, an island rose from the sea like a partially submerged moss-covered rock. Short rivers and streams drained into its waterfalls and bays. Waves sloshed the base of the hanging cliffs and curled away as though pushed back by an invisible force.

A girl stood on the sandy beach along the coast of the island, midnight-black hair cascading down her back. Dressed in white pants and a white tank top under a matching, gauzy duster, she appeared oblivious to the lush tropical vegetation or the pristine blue waters cresting under the gentle breeze. In her hand was a dagger with a wavy blade chiseled with red inscriptions, rays of sun reflecting off the wicked red stone on its guard. She lifted her hand and pointed the dagger upward. A streaming red light shot from the blade and tore through the air, piercing the sky to the east, west, north, and south.

"Come to me," she whispered, and angled her head as though listening to a response. She searched the sky even though not a single cloud, airplane, or bird drifted across the heavens.

"I command the dagger now, therefore I command you," she ground out, her brilliant blue eyes glittering with annoyance. Her pupils dilated, swallowing the iris until the whites of her eyes disappeared. Black bottomless orbs remained, catching the light bouncing off the ocean water. "Now!"

A burst of black flakes appeared in front of her, swirling faster and faster like a swarm of bees. They coalesced until a woman in black pants, with matching shirt and trench coat materialized. She dropped on one knee and pressed a fist on her chest before standing. Next came a man with silver hair, in an expensive designer suit. More followed, until there were twelve of them, a mixture of men and women. Most were youthful with eyes full of optimism, a few had eyes filled with wariness, but they each bowed to the girl with the dagger.

"It's time for the summoning," she said, studying her followers.

"Are you sure about this?" a man with wavy bronze hair, graying at the temples, asked. "This could be catastrophic if we are not careful."

Without answering, the girl pointed the dagger at him. The man started to shake, his mouth opening and closing as though he was silently begging for mercy. His skin shrank, his eyes became sunken, and his hair changed color and texture until he looked like a thousand-year-old mummy. He dropped onto the wet sand, his brittle bones snapping.

The girl looked at the silver-haired man, who grinned as though the demonstration of power was a joke. He lifted his hand and an energy ball materialized above his palm. The core glowed red, yellow and orange flames leaping from its edges. He threw the orb at the body. In seconds, nothing was left.

The girl didn't look at the others and her voice was deceptively soft when she asked, "Anyone else that thinks we shouldn't summon *it*?"

- 1 -

FIRST CONTACT

"The boys were amazing tonight," Antony Mancuso said in a regretful voice, referring to the punk group he promoted.

"There's no reason why they can't continue touring," Bran said.

Mancuso shook his head. "No, we had a good run. I don't care what you said. No one plays around with his soul and gets away with it." He puffed on a cigar, smoke drifting toward the ceiling.

Mancuso was a heavyset man with heavy jowls and sad, beady eyes. He didn't offer us seats despite the comfortable leather sofas scattered around the room. That was okay. We didn't want to sit anyway. Our presence made the damned uncomfortable. We, on the other hand, despised them for selling their souls for material gain and fame, but we needed their cooperation.

"What do you want me to do?" Mancuso asked.

Bran pulled a rolled-up scroll from the inside pocket of his trench coat, and a dagger from the belt around his hip. The scroll was dark-brown and thin like animal skin, the edges darker and uneven as though cut by fire. He unrolled it to reveal a list of names. The letters glowed fiery orange against the dark background.

"Antony J. Mancuso," Bran read.

A contract appeared out of thin air. Square and made from the same material as the bigger scroll, the words written on it were in the ancient language of Nephilim and angels. The only recognizable words were Mancuso's name.

Mancuso watched Bran with shiny eyes as though he was fighting tears. He snuffed off the smoldering tip of the cigar on an ashtray. "How long do I have after I cancel the contract?"

"You'll get your soul back right away," Bran explained.

"I meant my health, the reason I gave up my soul."

"Nothing is going to happen to you," Remy said impatiently from where he stood by the door. "Because of us, you are about to cheat hell."

"No one cheats hell." Mancuso picked up his cigar and placed it between his lips with shaking hands. "Or death."

"Stop puffing on that garbage and you'll add ten more years to your life," Kim added bluntly, blue eyes flashing.

That was Kim for you. She spoke her mind, damn the consequences. Mancuso didn't even look at her despite her nasty tone. Instead, his gaze kept swinging between Bran's face and the contract.

"Give me your finger," Bran said, gesturing to Mancuso.

Mancuso heaved forward and extended a chubby finger. No one spoke as Bran pricked his finger and blood pooled from the punctured hole then dropped onto the parchment. It smoldered at the wet spot then burst into flame, leaving behind nothing.

"Why don't I feel different?" Mancuso asked.

"You had a massive stroke, Mr. Mancuso," Bran said. "You couldn't talk, eat, and walk before you signed with me. You are talking to us."

Mancuso stretched his arms and wiggled his fingers, a smile flitting across his round face. "Yes, I am. So David Lee's voice…?"

"Will be okay even after he cancels his contract," Bran finished patiently. "We'll be back after he's done with his last song."

Mancuso was the promoter at Zone, the hottest new club on Union Square in New York City. He was famous for plucking garage bands out of obscurity and turning them into overnight teen sensations. But his most successful band, a punk rock group called Hellboys, weren't young. They had had their time in the limelight in the late nineties. Then their lead singer, David Lee, lost his voice to drugs, until two years ago when he 'found it' and the group had an amazing comeback.

No one knew how David Lee's voice recovered. Doctors called it a miracle. Fans didn't care. The truth was known to a select few. Us. The Cardinal Guardians, children of the Nephilim, whose sole existence was to rid the world of demons.

David Lee had sold his soul to Bran when Bran used to collect souls for a demon queen. Mancuso had introduced them to each other.

We filed out of Mancuso's office and headed upstairs to the VIP lounge. We had a clear view of the dance floor and the stage, where David Lee was singing his heart out while sweaty bodies writhed and arms flailed in a rhythmic daze.

I felt the urge to sway to the pulsing beat, but we weren't here to dance. All of us—Izzy, Kim, Sykes, Remy, Bran and I—were dressed in black hunting clothes, which blended well with the Gothic outfits most of the clubbers wore. Anonymity was everything in our line of business. No one was supposed to know we existed.

Across the table, Sykes turned his chair and started whispering in the ear of a giggling human girl. Next thing, the girl slid her fingers through his blond hair, gripped his head and whispered something back. Somehow he always found time to flirt or make out with some girl even in the middle of a mission.

Remy, seated next to him, drummed his fingers on the table, oblivious to everything and everyone, his gray eyes staring into space. He'd been acting weird the last couple of months. Sykes insisted Remy needed to get laid. I think dealing with humans on a daily basis was getting to him.

The "girls", as I often called Kim and Izzy, wore bored expressions though the two were critiquing the outfits the women at the neighboring tables wore. Kim, golden blonde hair professionally styled and makeup impeccable, and Izzy, with skin a shade of brown that attracted light in ways that defied description and a dark curly mane, lived and breathed fashion. Unfortunately, they could be so catty sometimes. Even though they wore black shirts and trench coats like the rest of us, their black leggings and designer thigh-high boots were not standard Cardinal Guardian issued. But the boots were very handy when hiding the special weapons we used when hunting demons—knives, daggers, and sickles.

Bored with eavesdropping on their conversation, I went back to studying the dancers. Dry-ice smoke rose like the Lazari from the stage as the band started their next number, an old favorite that sent the predominantly teen and twenties crowd screaming. I tried to block the noise, their thoughts, which were loud, and their emotions, which were varied, but couldn't completely do it.

How long do we have to wait? I asked Bran. The club was too loud to have a normal conversation.

An hour or so, he answered calmly as if we had all the time in the world and the clock wasn't ticking on his soul.

Bran's story was complicated, but then he was a complicated guy. Coronis, the most powerful demoness of all time, had kidnapped his grandparents and forced their only son, Bran's father, to marry an alpha demoness. As a result Bran had grown up among the demons and like every faithful follower, he'd moved into the soul-collecting business when his powers appeared at the age of sixteen. A year ago, he found us, the Guardians, his grandfather's people, and switched sides. To save his soul, he had to cancel every contract he'd ever enticed a human to sign.

Three months ago, we'd acquired a list of Damned Humans who'd sold their souls to demons in the last several millennia, Bran's included. As a result, we'd given up beach time to chase Damned Humans. Looking at Bran, you couldn't tell he was worried. He was cool like that. Being the oldest in our group might have something to do with it. He'd just turned twenty. The other Cardinals were nineteen—they all had summer birthdays—and I would turn seventeen in three weeks.

Like most Nephilim, Bran was startlingly handsome, with an angular face, wavy, shoulder-length black hair, broad shoulders and a tall, masculine body. His most striking features were his emerald green eyes, which now reflected the strobe light flashing around us. I caught the gaze of a girl at our neighboring table and smiled. She glanced away but within seconds, she was back staring. Even though Bran never seemed aware of it, he attracted more attention than the rest of us wherever we went. Something about the way he carried himself was mesmerizing, like he could chew you up and spit you out without losing sleep over it. He was a badass when badassness was called for.

You are tired, he telepathed, giving me a probing glance, then he tucked a lock of my hair behind my ear. Such a simple gesture, yet it showed his gentler side.

I shrugged. *It's almost midnight and we still have one more stop to go.*

Then go to sleep. I'll wake you when it's time to leave. He angled his solid body and pulled me closer.

I couldn't sleep if I tried, not with the noise level. Still, I rested my head against his broad chest and closed my eyes. Despite being seated upstairs above the bar, the rotating strobe lights still reached us. I hated strobe lights. They messed with my mental focus. As a Psi Guardian, having a calm mind was everything.

Bran's psi energy gently brushed mine, and I sighed. He always knew what to do to relax me. Smiling, I drifted away from the noise and the lights.

It's time, Bran telepathed later, pulling me out of a pleasant dream of a world with no demons.

We got up, left the balcony and headed for the stairs, which led to the back of the club and Mancuso's office. The security guards saw us coming and stepped aside. Mancuso offered us seats this time, but no one wanted to sit down. The sooner we were done, the faster we'd head to our next target.

The door burst open and we all reached for our weapons. The security guard froze. I was sure facing six teens dressed like Val Helsing and carrying deadly, medieval-looking weapons wasn't something he did every day. We had removed our glamour when we entered the room because we weren't supposed to hide our identities from the humans we dealt with.

"What is it, Joey?" Mancuso asked.

The security guard dragged his gaze away from us. "David Lee is gone."

"What do you mean 'gone'?" Mancuso bellowed, heaving to his feet.

"He slipped out for a smoke and took off."

Mancuso's face grew red. "Didn't someone go with him? What am I paying you for? Find him and bring him to me or you are all fired." He dropped back on his seat, his chest heaving. He shot us an apologetic look. "I explained everything to David Lee after you talked to him earlier, and he seemed okay with canceling his contract even though he believes he'll lose everything. You know, the money…his voice… I just never thought he'd run."

Cowards! I hated Runners. One would think we were handing them death sentences instead of their souls.

"We'll find him," Bran vowed then shoved his knives in the sheaths around his thigh and glanced at me. "Finish it."

As the Cardinal Psi in our group, it was my job to erase memories after each cancellation. Mancuso watched me curiously as I walked toward him. Human Psi energy was easy to breach, but changing human perception of past events was a bit tricky. We didn't want them dreaming about demons and Guardians, or having déjà vu sneak up on them to remind them of the past. Some tended to see a shrink to learn the root cause of their unexplained feelings and dreams, so I had to give them something to find.

"What's going on?" Mancuso demanded as I stopped beside him.

"I'm going to make you forget you ever gave up your soul or dealt with a demon, Mr. Mancuso. Would you like that?"

He nodded, his jowls shaking. "Oh yes."

"Good. Look at me."

I had gotten better at mind-blending. The first time I tried it, I'd gone a little crazy. I got inside Mancuso's head and went to the beginning—his first meeting with Bran. They'd met at a concert of one of his other clients. We always discussed the fake memories before leaving HQ. Instead of a collector, Bran could be a young, talented singer Mancuso had tried to represent and whose career tanked. Thoughts of Bran and the feeling of doom accompanying them would become regret. Last, our presence in his office and the purpose of our meeting wasn't to cancel a contract. We were Hellboys' number-one fans and had backstage passes to meet with David Lee. I went over the new memories and his perception of each image, then broke the mind-blend.

Mancuso blinked as though prodded into awareness. His eyes narrowed as he heaved to his feet. "Damn groupies. Out of my office."

"Chill, old man," Sykes said. Bran was already out the door. "We just wanted David Lee's autograph."

"Do you see him in here? Out…out." He waved his pudgy arms. "Security!"

We were laughing by the time the door closed behind us. We exited the building through a side door and entered the alley.

"Let's get some lattes and frappes before we head to our next stop," Kim suggested.

"I'm in, but let's not forget we've added another Runner to our list," Izzy said. "That makes…what?"

"Fifteen," Bran said.

"How can you be so calm about it? We want to help and they run, damned cowards," Kim grumbled. "Why aren't there consequences to selling a soul anyway?"

"Because Master Haziel said there weren't, and he's the wisest and oldest Guardian," I said. He was also our master trainer. "I'm more worried about what Mancuso is going to say when David Lee returns and brings up the subject of damned souls and us. I did what I could, but we've never canceled one soul when two humans signed together."

"I'm sure they'll consider it a miscommunication. You know how humans get. 'I'm sorry I bailed out on you, old man,'" Izzy imitated Lee's raspy voice. "'Oh, that's okay, Lee my boy. It's all forgotten. Just head back to the stage and sing your heart out. You'll have them eating out of the palm of your hand again,'" she added in Mancuso's deep baritone. "'Are you sure, Mancuso? I thought they'd be mad and come after you.' 'They love you, David Lee. Just don't ever run away again in the middle of a concert.'"

Perfect improv. We were laughing by the time she finished.

"I don't care whether Lee brings it up or not as long as another name disappears off our list," Sykes said. "It's been a long, boring summer."

Bran chuckled. "I agree."

"No way." Sykes moved closer to Bran and dropped an arm around his shoulders. "Finally, we agreed on something."

"Let's also agree to keep personal space." Bran pushed Sykes' arm from his shoulder.

"Why?" Sykes pretended to sniff his armpit. "I showered before we left."

Bran just shook his head. Sykes' antics used to bother him, but not anymore.

"You have issues, Llyr." Sykes jabbed a finger in his direction and smirked as we exited the alley.

The alley opened onto the Union Square, an oasis in the middle of the concrete jungle that was New York. Lovers strolled hand-in-hand near the green center of the Square, and late-night bingers nibbled on snacks from a nearby coffee shop.

A chilling scream came from the back of the building. The people on the Square didn't appear to have heard it. I scanned psi energies.

"It's a human," I said, already turning.

"Oh no, you don't." Kim grabbed my arm.

"He's terrified and in pain, Kim." I tried to free my arm, but her grip tightened.

"I'm sure he is a hobo. It's not our job to heal and help every suffering human that crosses our path. Where are *you* going?" Kim asked when Izzy took off.

"Going to see if we need to call an ambulance, Ms. Anti-hero," Izzy retorted.

Like me, Izzy could never walk away from a suffering human being. She was the healer of our group, a rare ability which was handy when our wounds were too serious to self-heal. Healing humans was easy for her, but she needed me to make them forget the incident.

I wrestled my arm free from Kim and followed. Curses came from behind us, but I knew the others would come. The guys might complain, but they always came through. Kim was the typical anti-hero, a Guardian who couldn't stand people depending on her.

"It's David Lee," Izzy called out from beside a blue dumpster. "He's strung out on something."

I ran to join them. David Lee was on the ground, arms punching an invisible enemy, legs kicking and spittle shooting from his mouth to his beard.

"Go away…leave me alone…leave…me…alone…" he screamed.

Calm down, I tried to use my power of persuasion, but he only kicked harder. He was going to hurt himself. I lifted my hand above him. *Freeze.*

He froze with his arms and legs curled up like a child throwing a tantrum. The others joined us and we studied the frozen rock star in silence. Up close he looked smaller and older. His sleeveless jacket, as well as the jewelry on his wrist, neck, and pants, were all studded. What I'd believed was a long-sleeved shirt was actually tattoos.

"Unfreeze him," Bran said then squatted beside David Lee, who'd gone back to battling his imaginary foe. "Hey, Lee!" Bran reached for his arms. "Snap out of it, man." He pinned David Lee's arms while Sykes grabbed his legs.

Lee bucked and twisted until he realized he couldn't escape. He went still, opened his eyes and studied us with unfocused eyes.

"Where…where's the thing that attacked me?" His eyes darted around.

"What thing?" Bran asked, letting Lee's arm go while Sykes released his legs.

David Lee shook his head and winced. "I don't know. There was a bright light and thick smoke, then terrible sounds and pain inside my head. I was in hell, man. There was fire everywhere, people crying and begging for mercy." He looked up and shuddered. "It came from up there."

Maybe he'd imagined a meteor. August was meteor month, and New York was one place you'd expect a spectacular display. We followed his glance and reached for our weapons. Instead of streaming lights shooting across the sky, a large, fluffy cloud blocked our view, lightning churning in its core as though struggling to burst through.

"What in Tartarus is that?" Sykes mumbled.

"It looks like a volcanic plume," I said.

"There are no active volcanoes within a thousand miles from here," Izzy said. "It looks like a Lazarus demon, but I've thoroughly studied demonic books and there's nothing about Lazari using their abilities while in smoke form."

"Okay, so it's another new fiend," Sykes murmured. "Big deal. Let's nuke it."

"Not so fast," Izzy added. "I think we should trap it and identify it first." She pulled out six crystals from her coat pocket.

The crystals, smooth and colorless, usually released light and formed a cage around a demon. Ever since we'd defeated Coronis, demons of mixed breed kept appearing and blindsiding us. Some weren't bad. Like the Souled Demons and Neutrals we knew and left alone because they had no interest in hurting humans or collecting souls. This one was obviously one of the bad ones since it had attacked David Lee.

Per our rules, demons didn't attack humans. They might possess them, make them sign contracts for their souls, use them to further their diabolical plans to take over the earth, but they never ever directly attacked humans. This was a first. "Let's finish here, then lure it away from the city," Bran said. "There are way too many people around here. All it takes is one person seeing past the glamour without our knowledge and we'd be exposed."

"Lure what?"

We all turned to glance at David Lee. We'd completely forgotten his presence until he spoke. He struggled to his feet with Sykes' help.

"Thank you, man."

"Did you get a proper look at the thing that attacked you?" Bran asked.

David Lee shook his head. "Who are you? Cops?"

"We are Guardians." Bran nodded to indicate all of us. "We talked to you and Mr. Mancuso earlier."

"Mancuso?"

"Your manager," Bran reminded him.

David Lee scowled. "You must be confusing me with someone else, man. I don't know any Mancuso."

Bran's eyes narrowed. "Is this is an attempt to get out of canceling your contract, Lee?"

"Is that my name? Lee?" David Lee asked.

Humans often came up with every excuse in the book to delay canceling their contracts, but no one had ever faked amnesia before.

"Your real name is David Leonard Birtwhistle, but you use David Lee," Bran said. " You were singing at Zone here in New York City."

Surprised flashed across Lee's face, then he glanced down at his leather pants, studded jacket, bracelets and the many rings with skull heads on his fingers. He grinned. "I sing in a band?"

"No, dude," Sykes said. "You *are* the band. Concerts in every continent, fans chasing you, hot babes in your bed wherever you go." He shrugged. "I read it in *Rolling Stone* magazine. I'm not a fan, okay? That was pure research."

"I made *Rolling Stone*," Lee mumbled.

"Just a minute here." Bran raised his hand. "Are you saying you lost your memory after you were attacked?"

Lee frowned. "Attacked? What are you talking about?"

Bran pointed upward. "You said that thing…" His voice trailed off as though he'd just remembered David Lee couldn't see the demon. Not that there was anything to see anymore. The demon was gone. Bran's hand dropped to his side and he took a deep breath.

"What's the *last thing* you remember?" Remy asked impatiently.

"Leaving the family farm in Oklahoma with my guitar and big dreams of being a star."

"Those are lyrics from your first hit." Sykes shrugged when we glared at him. "Hey, the dude can write amazing lyrics."

"Are you saying you don't remember him?" Remy snapped, pointing at Bran.

Bran reached in his inner coat pocket, pulled out the list of names and read out, "David Leonard Birtwistle." The contract appeared. Bran snatched it up and shoved it at Lee. "You signed this contract and gave up your soul to revive your singing career after it tanked. We need you to cancel it."

David laughed. "You're kidding. I might not know what's going on here, but I know I'd never sell my soul. That would be nuttier than a crapper at a peanut festival."

"Yet you did," Bran said through gritted teeth. As though he realized he was losing his cool, he finger-combed his hair. When he glanced at me and spoke, his voice was calm again. "Confirm it."

I stepped forward and Lee eyed me curiously. "Who are you, sweetheart? If I'm really a rock star and not someone you're trying to con, where are my bodyguards? Did you kidnap me? How much money—?"

"Shut up," Kim snapped, elbowing me out of the way. "If you want to get out of canceling the contract, just say so and stop wasting our time. If that thing that attacked you screwed up your memories, she," Kim jabbed a finger in my direction, "is the only one who can confirm it. Get it?"

David Lee blinked as though Kim had reached out and slapped him. "Okay, sweetheart. No need to get antsy."

Kim's eyes flashed and for one brief moment, I thought she'd slap him. "Don't you ever call me sweetheart."

David Lee swallowed, "Yes, ma'am."

Times like this, I was happy Kim was on my team. She could be so scary sometimes.

"You asked who I was," I started, and Kim rolled her eyes. She hated it when we explained who we were, but rules were rules. "I'm a Guardian. We all are. We fight demons, like the one we believe attacked you and messed with your memories. Right now, I'm going to see what you know. Okay?"

He hesitated. Despite having the abilities to teleport, use telepathy, manipulate the elements, time, and the mind, we couldn't force humans to do anything against their will because they had something called free will—a lifetime pass to screw up as often as they liked and get away with it. And we knew how many of them did just that.

"David Lee?" I asked gently, wishing I could tell him the truth—that the soul of the guy I loved was at stake too.

He stole a quick glance at Kim, then nodded.

I was in and out of his mind in seconds. "There's nothing there but mucking stalls and hauling horse manure. It's like he hasn't done or seen anything in years."

"Can I leave now?" Lee asked.

"Sure, David Lee," Kim said sweetly. "As soon as you cancel the contract you signed or the demon that attacked you will come back and drag you to hell."

"Kim!" we all protested.

She shot us an annoyed look. "I'm tired of babying them. We would be done with this if we were honest with them." She glanced at David Lee. "Sometimes the demons send hellhounds. You know, dogs the size of a calf that can rip you in two with one bite, fangs dripping with drool, red eyes, smelly breath…"

"Where do I sign?" David Lee asked quickly, moving away from Kim.

The process went smoothly after that. I felt bad erasing the memory of our meeting from his head because of what the demon had done to him. We escorted him to the side door of the building and handed him over to security.

"That was brutal," Izzy said, glaring at Kim.

Kim shrugged. "But effective. Don't say I forced him because I didn't. I gave him his options."

"One option," Bran corrected her. "Do you still want that latte?"

Kim made a face. "No. That demon left a bad feeling in my stomach."

Bran nodded, but he continued to search the sky as though he expected the demon to reappear. "Let's go."

We appeared inside a gated beach home in Myrtle Beach, a South Carolina coastal city. After the noise of downtown New York, it was nice to hear the calming sounds of waves washing the sands and smell the salty air. Lights blazed behind the windows, indicating the owners were home.

"What is their story?" I asked as we crossed the well-tended lawn.

"I met Mrs. Watts at a hospital two years ago. Her little girl had bone cancer and was in the last stages of the illness. Mrs. Watts wanted her daughter healed."

"Cases like hers are so heartbreaking," Izzy muttered. "When we started, I assumed we'd meet selfish, greedy, and fame-seeking scumbags like David Lee."

"Most of them are," Kim told her.

"Yeah, but sprinkled among them are the selfless husbands and wives, mothers and fathers willing to do anything for their loved ones," Izzy added defensively.

"How old was the little girl?" I asked, interrupting what could escalate into a heated discussion.

"Six," Bran said. "Mrs. Watts was pregnant and already had two twin boys. At first, I dealt with her. It wasn't until after her daughter recovered that she contacted me and brought her husband. They wanted success and power, so I gave them another deal—his soul for a lucrative business as a real estate agent. Within six months, they moved from their modest home to this." Bran stopped in front of the entrance and pressed on the doorbell. Through the window, we could see the foyer with a high ceiling, fancy chandelier, and a grand staircase.

A woman opened the door with a brilliant smile on her lips. Her eyes widened when she took another look at Bran, the smile disappearing from her face. "You? It can't be. You…I…is it time? You said I'd have twenty years."

"Calm down, Mrs. Watts. I'm not here for you. We just need to talk to you and your husband. May we come in?"

"No," she said in a horrified voice then stepped forward, closed the door behind her, and pulled the sweater tightly across her chest. Swallowing, she studied us nervously. "He's not here. We are getting a divorce."

"I'm sorry to hear that," Bran said.

"There's no need to be. He changed, became a jerk." She glanced at us again before focusing on Bran. "If you are not after me, what do you want?" she asked rudely.

"We are here to give you a chance to cancel the contract you signed with me and get your soul back," Bran explained, speaking slowly so there was no misunderstanding.

"What's going to happen to my daughter if I cancel?"

"Nothing." Bran reached inside his pocket for the scroll with names. He read her name and the contract appeared. Putting the list away, he pulled the dagger from the sheath at his waist. Mrs. Watts took a step back, her eyes wide.

"It's okay," Bran said reassuringly. "All we need is a drop of your blood on the contract and you can go on with your life."

She shook her head.

Bran sighed. "Mrs. Watts—"

"I can't. If I cancel, Michele is going to be sick again. She just celebrated her eighth birthday this evening." She hugged herself. "I don't want to lose her."

I tuned out Mrs. Watts and the others when I felt a sharp tug on my psi. I looked around and found the source. *Guys, look up.*

They stepped away from the doorway and looked up, everyone reaching for their weapons. Unlike in New York, the demon darted around as though eager for some action.

"Get inside the house, Mrs. Watts," Bran ordered.

The woman had stepped from the door to see what held our attention, but from her confused expression, she couldn't see the demon. She opened her mouth to speak, but Bran snapped, "Now!"

She scurried inside and bolted her door.

As a Cardinal Psi, I can see psi energies of anyone and anything, yet I couldn't locate the demon's energy. The special Xenithian jadeite core of our protective amulets didn't glow either and my dagger wasn't vibrating as it usually did in a demon's presence. The jadeite emitted light that was harmful to demon, so all our weapons were forged from it. The blade of the Kris Dagger contained the purest form of the jadeite, the light from it deadly to demons. Maybe the clouds and the lightning shielded the demon's energy from reaching us or something.

"We can't fight him…her…whatever it is while it's up there," Izzy griped.

"Get down here and face us, you coward," Sykes yelled, energy balls appearing above his palms.

"I'm going after the bastard," Bran said, stepping away from us, two daggers in his hands, wings lifting.

"No," we all protested.

"You can't face an unknown demon on your own," Remy said. "Only Lil's lightning bolts can reach that far."

"And if that fails…," Bran vowed.

"Then I'll use the Kris Dagger," I answered firmly.

The others nodded. Bran took his time, but he finally jerked his head in approval. "Spread out and stay linked," he instructed.

We moved apart, so if the demon attacked it wouldn't get us all at once, but we stayed visible. I pulled out the Kris Dagger from its sheath, the ancient text racing up my arms as we linked. The jolt that shot through my body was exhilarating, the pain still there but insignificant.

I'm ready, I informed the others, then willed lightning bolts from thin air. They zipped through the air like heat-seeking missiles.

The demon battled lightning with lightning, the explosions lighting up the sky like it was the Fourth of July fireworks show. I pointed my dagger upward.

Attack!

Green, bright light shot from the blade and headed straight toward the cloud demon. It would have been a clear hit, but the demon did something to bend the light, changing its trajectory to outer space.

That's impossible, someone ground out.

No demon had ever survived an attack by the Kris Dagger. But whatever the demon did, he or she forgot about the lightning bolts. They converged in its crackling core, causing it to expand. The resulting explosion was blinding. Then there was nothing but clear blue-black sky. No screaming. No smoking demon plunging to the ground.

"What in Tartarus was that?" Izzy asked.

"A new breed of demons," Kim answered. "They don't even scream anymore."

As the others dissected what just happened and joined me, a strange feeling coiled my insides. As it spread, I realized what it was: panic. The Kris Dagger was the most powerful Nephilim weapon, and a demon had just bested it.

"You did it?" Bran said coming to stand beside me. He must have read my emotions.

"The demon deflected the dagger's death rays, Bran. What are we dealing with?"

"I don't know. Let's finish with Mrs. Watts and go home."

But Mrs. Watts had her doors and windows locked tight and lights turned off. Our knocks went unanswered. Or maybe we didn't try hard enough. We were more concerned about the demon that could block the rays from the Kris Dagger.

- 2 -

BE CAREFUL WHAT YOU WISH FOR

"I hate not knowing what we're dealing with," Izzy griped.

"Me, too," I added.

A week had gone by since we killed the crackling-cloud demon. We each told the senior Cardinals our version of the events leading to that confrontation then we'd gotten our new orders—no more leaving the valley. No more canceling the remaining contracts.

Luckily, we weren't too worried about them. We only had fifteen more to go, and all of them were Runners. The Security Team was trying to track them down. I recalled Grampa's earnest expression when he'd said it. It was the lamest excuse in the book for putting us on a weeklong lockdown. Of course, no one had yet to admit that the senior Cardinals were busy trying to find the den of this new demon on their own. Even Bran wasn't allowed to hunt with them anymore.

"The senior Cardinals have started a record of all the new demons we've encountered since Coronis got her one-way ticket to Tartarus," Izzy said. "I saw it yesterday at the library. It's growing fast."

"Did they add ours?"

"Ours?" Kim asked scathingly. "You two are pathetic. We've been forced to hide in the valley for an entire week while the senior Cardinals chase their tails hoping to meet another crackling-cloud demon, and now that they've concluded the fiend was a lone hybrid and we can finally leave the valley, you sit here and yap about the same, stupid demon."

"You've got to admit it spooked everyone," I said.

"Whatever. Look at the guys," Kim continued. "They don't seem to care. They're having fun."

The sweaty, shirtless Guardians were slamming a ball over the volleyball net. We had decided to celebrate our freedom by joining the students from the Guardian Academy on their first vacation. The island crawled with excited teens sunbathing, swimming, or watching the game, their teachers and the Security Guardians from Xenith, but it was private and away from prying human eyes. The security shield and glamour covering it were impenetrable, and reached far into space. Located at the center of churning dark-blue waters of what humans called the Bermuda

Triangle, Pearls Island was the last stop for Guardians teleporting home to Xenith. The portal was in the middle of the forest inside a lake.

My gaze swung back to Bran just as he looked my way. I smiled when he winked, dimples flashing. At six-foot-three, with massive raven-black wings and matching hair which had grown longer over the summer, he stood out even among the gorgeous Guardians.

"Stupid game," Izzy continued. "It's nothing but a chance for them to show off their powers to the students." She lowered her sunglasses to glare at her boyfriend Rastiel, who was home for the holidays. "He's neglected me since we got here. Maybe I should make out with someone else."

"Maybe you should give him a reason to ditch volleyball. You too, Lil. Get up, walk right past them, and take a dip in the ocean. There's something to be said about the power of a wet swimsuit. Just remember to keep your chins up and push your chests out. Especially you, Lil. You slouch."

Not bothered by the criticism, I giggled, visualizing myself waddling like a goose with my butt sticking out and my modest chest straining against the bright-blue bikini top. My usual one-piece swimsuit had finally been traded for a skimpy bikini in the name of looking hot for my boyfriend. Bran didn't care what I wore. He never had, but I was beginning to learn the meaning of peer pressure.

Izzy had pushed and scolded me until I gave in to a makeover. The manicure and pedicure were nice enough. The electric-blue nail polish matched my bikini. But I'd hated the hours at the salon while a stylist washed, trimmed, and tried to tame my unruly red hair—until I looked in the mirror. The partial French braids held back half of my hair and the rest tumbled down my shoulders in glorious curls, making me look exotic.

A collective gasp drew my attention back to the game. Bran was up in the air, chasing the ball. He turned and sent the ball flying with one giant sweep of his wings. The ball jetted downward to the other side of the net. A crack filled the air as a teacher tried to block the ball and ended up with a broken arm. A collective "ooh" came from the spectators. He disappeared in mid-air and someone else took his place. He wasn't the first player to get hurt. Guardian volleyball was brutal. One of the Civilians had set up a healing room inside the resort's main building to take care of injuries.

Guardian beach volleyball was crazy and weird. The net was five times as wide and high as the ones used by humans, the play area huge, and bets were off on the use of powers. Good thing the island was private, its location unknown to humans.

Bran looked at me and grinned when they scored.

You are amazing, I telepathed him.

Thank you. He made a flamboyant bow, which made Remy and Sykes tease him.

"Rastiel's team sucks. The only students cheering for them were Celeste and her friends," Izzy mumbled.

Celeste, Bran's sister, would cheer for the underdogs just to be contrary. It was what made her so interesting. Rastiel, Izzy's boyfriend since her early teens, had the ability to control air. He might not have had enough power to become a Cardinal Air Guardian like Kim, but he had enough for a mean game of beach volleyball. Rumor had it that he planned to teach at the Academy when he finished college.

"They didn't stand a chance to begin with," Kim said with indifference then she raised the brim of her beach hat and lowered her sunglasses to peer at the shirtless guys. "But who knew the Academy had such hot teachers?"

"You wouldn't," I said, knowing how often she changed boyfriends.

Kim shrugged. "Why not? I'm single."

"Not for long," Izzy said in a sing-song tone.

"Shut up." Kim imitated her tone.

"You'll have to tell them some time," Izzy added in a serious tone.

"I don't have to do anything," Kim said firmly.

Izzy made a face then raised her hand. A frozen pink and yellow drink with a tiny umbrella, courtesy of the Civilian cabana boy behind us in the beach snack bar, floated into her hand.

I wondered what the stilted conversation between Izzy and Kim meant. The two were pretty tight, so being in the dark wasn't something new to me. As the youngest in our team of junior Cardinals, I'd been reduced to little sister status, privy to only what they chose to share.

"I think you should tell them to back off," Izzy insisted. "Their attitude is archaic and so last millennium."

"They're my parents, and I don't want to discuss this anymore," Kim snapped.

"Suit yourself. I'm going for a swim." Izzy plucked her wide brim hat and her sunglasses, and threw them on top of her bag, her attention shifting to her boyfriend. "Maybe I'll turn into a siren, lure Rastiel into the water and drown him."

She crossed the sand with a gentle roll of her hips, drawing the attention of the players. Rastiel almost got bludgeoned by the volleyball when he continued to watch Izzy until she dove under a wave.

"Idiot," Kim murmured.

"Rastiel?" I asked.

Kim hesitated, then she removed her hat, finger-combed her long blonde tresses and sighed. "Izzy. They had a fight, but it means nothing. Rastiel is nuts about her, and their families approve of their relationship."

"You think they'll be mated?"

"She hasn't said anything, but she's eighteen now and can choose him if she likes." Her tone was neutral, but my empathic senses picked up envy.

Why would she be jealous of Izzy? Kim hooked up with different guys all the time, two in the past year, strung them along then dumped them. I wanted to ask her what was wrong without appearing nosy, but I wasn't sure how to go about it.

"It's interesting that we…women…get to choose who we mate with," I said.

She shrugged. "That was Goddess Xenia's way of dealing with male arrogance. She saw how our forefathers abused their power by taking many mates."

"So do you have someone in mind for a mate?" I asked tentatively.

Kim bit her lower lip, and for a brief moment I was sure she wouldn't respond.

"Why don't you go for a swim too instead of interrogating me?" she said.

"Nah," I said, shaking my head. I'd done enough scuba diving. Bran and his ability to trap pockets of air under water made scuba diving quite an experience.

"I suppose you and Bran will have a *pactus* when you officially choose him," Kim asked with a mocking smile that usually bugged me. Not today though. Beach times had been rare this summer and I wasn't about to let her spoil it for me. "I guess so."

He was my soul mate, or to use the ancient term, my *alrune*. I was attracted to him the moment we met even though I thought he was from the loony bin at the time. He was confident and fearless. But his most admirable quality was his loyalty to his family, even to his brother, who didn't deserve it. Falling in love with him had been inevitable. Mating with him was something I'd assumed was a given, not that I needed to think about such things now. I had about a year to go before I could ask him to be my mate.

Frowning, I studied him. Would he say yes? Just because women did the asking didn't necessarily mean men said yes. I'd never attended a *pactus,* the mating ceremony performed in the temple of Goddess Xenia in Xenith—the Guardians' homeland. Nephlings weren't allowed in Xenith, and since I was one, thanks to my human grandmother, that meant Bran and I would not be mated there.

"I'm going to read in the cabana for a while." I nodded toward the one set aside just for us Cardinals.

"Remember, we're leaving in less than hour," she reminded me.

"I know." I reached for the book in my tote bag, my hand brushing against the strap of my dagger's belt. Even on vacation, we carried weapons just in case demons attacked. Not that they would dare come after us on Pearls Island.

A shadow fell over me, the silhouette of the wings reaching Kim. Squinting, I looked up at Bran and fought a blush when he studied me with heated emerald eyes.

Water droplets glistened like diamonds on his tanned chest, the scar of the Guardian amulet light between his pecs. Funny, I had once thought the scar marred the perfection of his golden skin. Now it was a reminder of how much he'd sacrificed to leave the demonic world and join us.

"Done showing off?" I asked, smiling.

"For the moment," he answered cockily. "You okay?"

"Yeah." He must have felt my brief moment of sadness when I was thinking about Xenith. It was great to have a boyfriend so in tune with my feelings.

Izzy appeared behind him. "If you want to drool over the new and improved Lil, take her away from here and do it in private."

"I second that," Kim said with a bite in her voice.

Bran ignored them. He offered me his hand, pulled me straight into his arms and wrapped a possessive arm around my waist.

"New and improved?" he asked, his right eyebrow arcing as he glanced at Izzy.

"You know. The hair, new swimsuit, the whole makeover. She looks hot. Told you he'd drool," she added, winking at me.

"I don't drool," Bran protested though half-heartedly.

"Do too," Izzy retorted.

"I don't need to. Lil always looks hot in anything she wears," he added, smiling.

I hugged his arm. He said the nicest things ever. I kissed him.

Izzy made a gagging sound. "You two are nauseating."

Kim pointed toward the cabana and added imperiously, "Go. You're messing with my tan."

Bran grinned. "We're going, but not because you ordered us to. I've something else on my mind."

"Yeah, we know," Kim quipped.

"Thank me later," Izzy teased.

"Shut up." I still wasn't used to their teasing. *Let's go to the lounge,* I telepathed Bran.

No, we're heading up. He scooped me up like I weighed nothing, then he teleported with me.

We materialized in the air, his wings beating fast to stabilize us. Below us, the Guardians looked like ants on the powder-white beach. The Bahamian colonial-style houses of the resort blended with the palm trees and the pristine turquoise waters lapping the shores of the island. Admiring the view from the air wasn't what I had in mind, but at least we were alone.

He shot up, aiming higher. Over his shoulders, the islands grew smaller. A few miles away, several cruise ships drifted in the darker, deeper waters. Not a single cloud marred the perfection of the sky.

Bran did a couple of loop-de-loops, then steadied us, his dimples flashing and emerald-green eyes sparkling. He was happiest when flying.

"What do you think of the view?" Bran asked.

"Beautiful." I looked into his eyes. "I think you deliberately brought me up here because you were losing."

"Losing?"

"The game where you'd look at me then pretend not to." I tapped his nose. "You're not that sneaky."

He chuckled and brushed his lips against my temple. "I could never ignore you, Sunshine. You're my chosen mate."

"I haven't decided on that yet," I teased, trying not to laugh when shock registered in his expressive green eyes.

"Take that back or I'll drop you." He removed his arm from under my knees. I tightened my arms around his neck and scrambled to wrap my legs around him.

"That wasn't funny," I scolded him. "I could have fallen."

"I'd fall with you." He dropped a quick kiss on my lips this time. "In life and in death, Lil Falcon." He pressed his forehead against mine and added softly, "This lifetime is not enough for the things I plan to do with you."

"Me, too."

His arms tightened around me. "Then choose me as your mate," he said, his voice low. "Make it official."

I giggled. "I can do that after I turn eighteen, silly. *Pactus* must be performed in front of witnesses. It's the Guardian tradition."

"On Coronis Isle, we didn't have a temple. *Alrunes* made their own vows." His eyes grew intense. "Let's make ours right now, with the elements as our witnesses."

"Bran—"

"Do it," he added softly, daring me.

He was worried. How ridiculous. I'd never choose anyone else. "I love you, silly, and if you want this, then let's do it." I took a deep breath and looked into his eyes. "I vow right here and now that you, Bran Llyr, are my chosen mate. With the sun, the stars, the waters, the air, and the earth as my witnesses, I will love you through eternity."

"In flesh and ascension," he added.

"In flesh and ascension," I repeated.

"Yours always, mine forever."

"Yours always, mine forever."

He repeated the vows, then grinned. "Let's seal it."

He kissed me, his touch igniting fire in my blood so effortlessly, making me feel wanted and special at the same time. Our breaths mingled and hearts pounded in perfect rhythm. His kiss deepened as our energies blended. We shifted to a different plane. Fates sealed. Souls united by our vows and kiss.

He forgot to flap his wings and we dropped suddenly, forcing ours lips to part. My arms tightened around his neck. Laughing, I stared into his eyes, which had darkened to a stormy green.

"You can never take it back," he whispered, studying my upturned face.

His intensity told me this was important to him. I stopped laughing and my arms tightened around his shoulders. "I'd never want to."

"Good. So, what do you want for your birthday?"

"You," I said without hesitation.

Bran smiled, or at least I felt his lips curve into a smile against my temple. "You already have me, Sunshine."

"You know what I mean."

He chuckled. "We have fifteen contracts to go. Imagine that. Fifteen." He whipped around while laughing, forcing me to hold on to him tighter. He moved faster and faster until everything blurred except his eyes, which flashed with merriment. "Then I'll be free. Free to do anything, to give you whatever you want."

His laughter was contagious. I flung my arms out as he continued to spin and screamed with glee.

Then something blocked the sun. Probably his wings, was my first thoughts, but then a chill crawled up my spine like icicles grazing heated skin. Bran must have felt it too, because he stopped, turned, and looked around.

The crackling-cloud demon moved leisurely toward us, looking bigger and more ominous in the day than against any night sky. The edges swelled like a thousand, fat worms, the core so bright the sun paled in comparison.

My stomach sank and my heart started beating fast. For a week, I'd dreaded this moment. Dreaded and felt ashamed, because as a Cardinal I wasn't supposed to be scared of demons. I reached for my dagger then realized I still wore my swimsuit. I had left the Kris Dagger behind in my bag.

- 3 -

THE VOICE

Lightning shot from the cloud's core and speared through the air, speeding toward the ocean. Another plume appeared beside it as though spat by the air. They drifted apart, darting around like scavengers searching for food or…victims.

"They're acting like hunters," I whispered.

"Yeah. The question is, what are they after?"

"Us."

"Or the portal. The one in Myrtle Beach didn't fight back. It must have a different agenda."

Nothing could penetrate the glamour and the shield the Circle of Twelve placed around the islands, but when it came to these demons, nothing we knew mattered. Below us, the Guardians looked tiny and defenseless. "We must warn the others."

"Yeah. Go." Bran squinted at me. "I need to study them, see if I can find a weakness. Tell Remy the students should head to the portal. Teleporting back to the valley will only leave telegates."

I frowned. "Are you sure about staying up here?"

"We are still inside the glamoured and protected zone."

Bran liked to take chances, which could be a problem when we were dealing with these particular demons. "Don't cross the boundaries or let them sense you."

He chuckled. "Aye, aye, captain."

"I'm serious, Bran."

"I know." He stopped smirking, nudged me forward, and added, "Ride the wave until you can see a safe landing spot."

I didn't know what he meant, until something cold and wet lapped my feet, and I looked down. A gush of water snaked from the ocean surface like the tongue of a lizard. The top hardened into an iceberg surfboard. Having a boyfriend with water abilities, who also knew I was clumsy when I teleported, had its perks.

"Thanks." I let go of him and steadied myself on the icy board, knees slightly bent. I loved to surf. "Don't stay up here too long."

"I'm right behind you."

The bite of the wind on my skin was brief and quickly forgotten. My mind was on the demons and how they'd found us. Even Coronis had never known about Pearls Island.

Closer to the ground, I found an empty spot on the beach and teleported. Brushing sand off my hands, I looked around. Everyone's attention was on the demons, including my team of Cardinals and the Security Guardians, who already held their weapons.

Remy? I telepathed.

He waved me over.

The students need to head to the portal and Xenith. I ran toward my tote bag.

Why? he called back.

Going to the valley will leave telegates. Bran said the portal is secure. I grabbed my dagger, motioned the students closest to me and pointed toward the forest. *Go!*

The other Cardinals echoed my orders. Students took off at a run. We were trained to stay calm under pressure, which inspired confidence in others, but a demonic attack wasn't something to be taken lightly. Especially not when we had about fifty students and teachers with us.

Led by the Security Guardians, they disappeared into the forest where the portal was located. Some paused to glance at the angry, lightning-spitting demons before they disappeared inside the shadowy woods. They were first-year students, sixteen-year olds with new powers who had never met a demon, and probably wouldn't since most of them weren't powerful enough to become Cardinal Guardians.

I strapped on my dagger and joined the others.

"How can he stay up there when we don't know what those demons are capable of?" Izzy asked in disbelief.

"Because he can," Sykes said in an envious whisper. "I could kill for wings right now."

"I'm right behind you," Bran had said. I should have known. My gaze shifted from him to the large masses moving across the sky, looking more like a volcanic plume wrapped in lightning. One changed directions and appeared to head straight for our island.

"They've located us," Izzy whispered.

"No, they haven't," Remy said. "The shield is holding."

From the corner of my eyes, I caught Sykes' fingers flex. Two *alpha* energy orbs materialized above his palm, the blue core coiling with energy. "What are you doing?"

"Getting ready to kick ass," Sykes said with a smirk. "I don't care what books say about the shield around here. Do they mention nature-benders? The Specials? Fire demons up there? I. Don't. Think. So."

Bran was flying higher and getting too close to one of the demons. My hand tightened around my dagger, as I seriously started to question his sanity.

Get down, I yelled just as the demon released a lightning bolt. My heart nearly stopped as I watched the bolt zip through the air not too far from Bran and hit the water. Thankfully it was outside the shield. Then Bran disappeared and rematerialized beside us without losing his balance, despite the massive wings.

"Did you learn anything, Llyr?" Remy asked.

Bran nodded. "There's a something inside the cloud. The cloud and the lightning are just covers."

"The cowards. I say let's just nuke them," Sykes said, bouncing the *alpha* energy balls as he would basketballs. Kim was ready too, stance wide, hands open and extended. The air above her palms churned so fast it distorted the images seen through it.

"If we do it from here, we'll give away the location of the island and the portal," Remy said.

"So let's use maneuvers 24a followed by 35d from *Battle Strategies II*," Bran said.

Remy scowled, then nodded. "It might just work."

"Whoa, slow down," Sykes interrupted. "What in Tartarus are 24a and 35d?"

"Create a decoy and lure away from target then attack," Izzy said absentmindedly while adjusting the arrows on her crossbow. "Seriously, do you ever read *Battle Strategies*?"

"No, Miss Judgmental." Sykes made a face. "I believe in learning from experience." He glared at Bran. "Next time just say 'the move we pulled in the Bayou'. So how are we going to do this? We're in the middle of the freakin' ocean."

"I'll create islands of icebergs," Bran said.

"I'll cover them with rocks and sand for traction," Remy added.

"And I'll move them around and create confusion, so the demons won't pinpoint our exact location," Kim threw over her shoulder. Her wind tunnel had picked up moisture from the air and was now visible.

"That's right," Bran added. "We'll teleport from island to island as we attack."

"Great." The energy balls fizzled out and Sykes rubbed his hands. "Get moving, pronto. Lil got lucky but we haven't kicked serious demon butts in weeks. I need my fix."

"What can we do to help?" a man asked from behind us and we turned. The Security Guardians were back from leading the students to the portal. They were five of them, two women and three men, all packing daggers.

"Guard the portal," Bran said. "If they get past us, leave and seal the portal from your side."

"You can't do that," Kim snapped. "It's the only portal left."

"This is the standard protocol, Kim," Remy said impatiently.

"Go," Bran ordered the Security Guardians, then made eye contact with me. "Distract the demons."

"Got it." My lightning bolts didn't originate from my fingers like most demons, or above my palm like Sykes' energy balls—I willed them with my mind. With the shield and glamour on, the demons wouldn't be able to pinpoint my location.

I turned to face my target. Focusing, I took a deep breath, drew strength from within, and let the demon have it. Lightning bolts appeared around the white mass west of us and blasted it from all directions. It rocked, rose higher then suddenly dipped.

Bran grinned when our gazes met. He always got a kick out of watching me fight, until the demons got too close and his protective instinct took over.

"You'd better leave," I told him. "I don't know how long I can fool them."

"How are we going to do this?" Remy asked, sounding doubtful.

"From underwater. Don't worry, I have your back." The two waded past the shallow stretch of the beach and dove in.

In the sky, the other demon changed directions and went to the rescue of the first one, ribbons of lightning criss-crossing the sky as they returned fire with fire. I caught the second one unaware, cutting across its path.

"Tartarus pit! We have a third one," Sykes said.

Chaos followed as the demonic clouds moved left and right. The new arrival kept teleporting and reappearing in different parts of the sky.

"How long can you keep this up?" Izzy asked in a worried voice, a hand on her forehead as she shielded her eyes from the glare of the sun.

"Not long." A dull ache was quickly building on my temples. My vision blurred and dizziness washed over me, all signs that I was overusing my powers. I grasped the hilt of the Kris Dagger. A surge of raw energy pulsed through me, replenishing my psi energy. The headache disappeared along with the dizziness, and my vision cleared.

"It won't be long before they realize there's no one out there," Kim warned.

"They just did," Izzy said in a worried voice as the annoying third one shot downward and into the ocean. She angled her crossbow. "That one must have spotted Remy and Bran."

My stomach dipped. I scanned for Remy and Bran, found their psi and pinged them. "They are okay."

How is it going? Bran asked.

There's a demon in the water. Watch your back. Flares appeared from the corner of my eyes as *alpha* energy balls materialized above Sykes' palms again. The wind picked up behind me as Kim's wind tunnel grew bigger.

We've created four. One more to—

A sharp tug on my psi energy cut off our communication. I tried to block it, but a link was already formed. The pressure in my head shot up, forcing me to stop attacking the demons in the air. Shouts came from the others but I couldn't make sense of their words. My skull felt like a nut in a nutcracker, white-hot pain seared across my head.

I opened my mouth to tell the others what was happening to me, but my mouth couldn't open. My arms grew heavy and my breathing became shallow as though someone cut off my air supply. Everything became blurry then white. Finally, darkness crept in and chased away the light.

The clang of metal hitting metal pierced the air and mixed with screams, hisses, and screeches. Thuds shook the ground, each like a slap at my psyche.

I tried to move and search for the sources of these sounds, but my body stayed frozen. My arms and mind were at odds too. I tried to reach for my dagger with little result. Frustration roiled through me. My toes curled and sank in the sand, the only proof that I was standing at the beach, that all of this was real. My eyes moved too, thank goodness.

Still, I couldn't tell where I was or whether the others were with me or not. The shadows pressed heavy on my senses. After months of drawing strength from energies around me, I was being sucked into a hole where nothing existed. No matter how hard I tried, I couldn't see a single energy. My fear of darkness returned.

I closed my eyes, resorting to my old way of sensing things. Nothing.

Sighing, I opened my eyes and searched through the darkness for hope, anything. I opened my mouth to call to the others, but either the din swallowed the sound or I couldn't produce any. Maybe I didn't even open my mouth.

A movement appeared from the corner of my eyes then something shiny reflected light as it sliced the air. More appeared, the sound of metal against metal growing louder. Squinting, I studied them and realization dawned. There were weapons, swords and daggers thrusting and slicing. A battle raged around me and all I could do was watch, helpless and confused.

Bran? Remy? Sykes? Izzy? Kim? What's going on? Can you guys hear me?

Once again, my telepathic questions went unanswered. I squinted, trying to see if my friends were among the fighters, but I couldn't see faces, just silhouettes against a starless sky. *Who's out there? Where am I?*

My senses threatened to explode from the echoes of pain and death. Bodies fell from the sky. Something sticky dripped on my arms, my head and face. Blood. Even in the darkness, I knew it. I smelled it. Swallowing, I tried to move again. *Somebody help me,* I screamed.

Tiny flakes fluttered down from the sky and fell on my head and on top of the bodies on the ground. No, not snowflakes. Feathers. Downy ones and larger ones, like the ones covering Bran's wings. Guardians were being slaughtered.

Bran? Remy? I called to them again and again, but it was useless.

They are here and you must stop them, a woman's voice, faint but sweet, broke through the murkiness. With it came light so brilliant I closed my eyes against the glare.

Who? I asked, opening my eyelids and squinting.

The Tribe.... The deafening resonance swallowed the rest of her words, yet I still couldn't see anything, not the source of the voice or the light.

Tribe? What tribe?

Faint words followed. I strained to hear her with little success. Then her voice grew audible. *Fight back or they'll win again.* There was a familiar lilt to it, yet I couldn't place it. *Don't make my sacrifices be for nothing.*

The screams, now jarring chords like a choir singing out of sync, rose again. More dead wingless bodies floated to the ground, arms flailing, the thuds as they landed on the ones already on the ground sickening. I watched helplessly as a black hole appeared on the ground and sucked them away. It beckoned to me, offering solace and refuge. Just one step and I'd be free of this nightmare. Just one step.

Fight, my child. Fight. The familiar voice returned, more insistent and authoritative.

How? I begged. *It hurts to think.*

No, it doesn't, she snapped. *They make you feel a pain that's not there, a sorrow that's forgotten and a nightmare that never ends. The power is within you to stop them. Reach deep within and find your strength. Use it to fight back.* The voice grew faint.

Don't leave me, I screamed.

Always with you, Lilith. Remember what I said...stop them...find the Summoners or...my weapon.

For a moment, I was too confused to react. She had called me Lilith. Only demons used my given name. I recovered and yelled, *I didn't hear everything you said. Who are the Summoners? And what do you want me to do with your weapon?*

But she was already gone, leaving me in the endless nightmare. The screams reached fever pitch. It hurt to think. To focus. To breathe. The false comfort offered by the dark pit tugged at me until I found myself weakening, begging for it to swallow me.

I had never thought I'd die paralyzed in place like some stupid statue. I was meant to grow old with Bran, hunt, love and live until it was our turn to ascend together. Even as the thoughts crossed my mind, I searched for him in the inner recesses of my mind. Memories of the two of us together bathed in light floated out of the darkness. Memories of Grampa, Aunt Janelle, my fellow Cardinals, Kylie…

Their love, laughter and happiness penetrated the horror and drowned out the screams. The echoes of death receded as peace cocooned me in its arms like a warm blanket on a wintery night. I tried to open my eyes, but couldn't.

"Come on, Lil," a female voice urged.

"I think she's coming around," a male voice said.

I lifted my eyelids. At least I thought I did. There was nothing but blinding whiteness. I strained until the blue sky and faces inked in. Unfamiliar faces. Two women and one man. Their eyes were filled with concern as they stared down at me. Beside them were familiar faces—Bran, Grampa and Aunt Janelle, Kim, Izzy, Remy, Sykes and Kylie, but they began to fade.

"No, don't leave me," I cried out and reached out for them.

"Not so fast," one of the unfamiliar women warned and pressed my shoulder down. "You had a nasty fall."

I struggled against her hand and sat up. Black dots appeared in my eyes and a sharp pain radiated from the back of my head. I closed my eyes until the dizziness passed, then raised a trembling hand to my head. There was a huge bump the size of an egg, and my skull felt like someone was hammering it with a blunt object.

Squinting, my gaze moved from her to the other woman, then the man. They all wore black pants and matching shirts, a uniform of some kind, and had daggers in sheaths strapped around their waist and their thighs. I'd never seen them before in my life, yet they watched me with such concern.

I inched away from them and noticed I wasn't dressed like them. I wore a bikini and was lying down on a towel. Frowning, I took in our surroundings. We were on a grassy patch by a pond in the middle of a forest. The trees were so tall and curved in such a way that was unnatural.

It was like they deliberately curved to block the skyline or hide the pond.

Why couldn't I remember where I was or how I got here? What was my name?

My gaze moved back to the woman squatting beside me. I wondered whether to ask her these questions, but survival instinct stopped me even though I didn't feel any negative vibes from her.

I scooted backward and realized my grip was around a dagger. Intrigued, I studied it. It had a clear, wavy blade and green stones on its gilded hilt.

Seeing the dagger switched on something inside my pounding head. Memories of places and people rushed back—I saw myself entering a booth in an arena, where a familiar man with red hair called me his daughter; attempting to escape a dark-haired woman who claimed to be my half-sister; a huge black man with soft brown eyes helping me, and another with short-cropped blond hair swearing allegiance to me…

If my head wasn't pounding, I would have laughed with triumph. My name was Lil Falcon. I was a Psi Cardinal Guardian within the Northeast Sector, and I hunted demons.

Going by my memories, we must still be on Jarvis Island. I glanced around again. The strangers continued to stare at me with worried expressions. They weren't demons, which was a relief. Still, I didn't know them.

Gripping the Kris Dagger, I staggered to my feet and almost fell over when dizziness washed over me. The three strangers took steps toward me, then froze when I pointed the dagger at them. "Who are you? Where are the Cardinal Guardians?"

"We are Security Guardians. I am Evangeline," the woman with black hair and pale skin answered then she pointed at the man, "That is Javan and she," she pointed at the other woman, "is Irin."

Security Guardians guarded Xenith. Maybe we weren't on Jarvis Island after all. "Are we in Xenith?"

The three looked at each other, obviously surprised by my question, then Evangeline said, "No, we are on Pearls Island. We guard it and the portal, but Cardinal Llyr ordered us to bring you here and keep an eye on you until they get back. If they don't make it, we are to take you to Xenith with us and seal the portal."

Panic washed over me. "Seal the portal? Why?"

"They are fighting powerful demons," Evangeline said. "One of them attacked you."

"I must help them!" I looked around.

"Cardinal Lil, you can barely stand, let alone face a demon," Javan protested. Evangeline and Irin nodded.

They were right. Something was wrong with me and it wasn't just my pounding head. My heart beat fast like I'd just sprinted and my skin felt like a thousand ants had crawled under it. And the fear from these three slammed into my senses. I tried to raise my shield but nothing happened. The demons didn't just mess with my memories, they'd messed with my powers too.

The Security Guardians were telepathing each other, but I followed their glances and my stomach dipped at what I saw. An ominous cloud hovered in the air to our right, lightning churning in its core and around it. There was something vaguely familiar about it. As I watched, it exploded. Demons usually burned bright orange as they fell, not exploded like fireworks.

"What was that?" I asked.

"A new breed of demons," Javan explained.

"One of them attacked me?"

"Yes. We were in here guarding the portal." He waved toward the pond. "So we didn't exactly see what happened, but Cardinal Llyr telepathed us to go and get you. Cardinal Sykes said you fainted while you were attacking the demons."

None of what he said sounded familiar. A quick search of my memory didn't help either. I glanced down at the Kris Dagger. It was supposed to protect and heal me, yet my head still hurt. There was something wrong with it and different about it, yet I couldn't pinpoint what.

"How are you feeling?" Javan asked.

"I'm fine. I need to join my team."

"No, Cardinal," he insisted. "We have a direct order to keep you here."

Before I could ask who had given the order, Bran appeared with Sykes, Remy, Izzy and Kim close behind him. They were all wet, the men shirtless and in their swim trunks while the girls wore bikinis. Their triumphant grins disappeared when they saw me.

"Why is she up?" Bran demanded, closing the gap between us, the Security Guardians giving him room.

"She wouldn't listen to us and there's something wrong with her memories," Evangeline said. "She didn't recognize us or know anything about the demons."

"Or where we are," Javan added.

I wanted to tell them to shut up, but Bran was already in front of me, cupping my face, his worried gaze searching my face. "What did you forget?"

My throat closed and tears rushed to my eyes. I refused to cry or say anything to make him and the others worry even more. "Can we discuss this later, please?"

The rest of the Cardinals moved closer, bringing with them waves of worries. Once again, I tried to raise my shield and form a barrier, but it didn't work.

"The fiends stole her memories like the one in New York did to David Lee," Izzy said.

I frowned. "We've battled these demons before?"

"Yes, a week ago," Bran said. "One attacked a Damned Human in New York and stole his memories too then followed us to Myrtle Beach, but you got him."

"Or her," Kim added. "They don't come out of the cloud even during battle, so it is impossible to tell what they are. The one in New York deflected the rays from the Kris."

This was worse than I'd thought. No demon should escape the rays from the Kris Dagger. Once again, I raked my memory, trying to connect the words with what I knew and came up blank. I was afraid to ask how long it had been since we were on Jarvis Island.

My gaze connected with Bran's. His emerald eyes were narrowed, a frown between his eyebrows. The others continued to stare at me as though they expected me to keel over again or something.

How bad is your head? he asked.

I couldn't hide anything from him if I tried. Times like this I wished he wasn't in tune with my emotions or felt my pain. *Please, don't tell the others. Let's just go home.*

Okay. "I'll take Lil home," he said louder.

I don't know if I can even teleport, I telepathed, feeling both useless and angry. I hated feeling helpless.

Don't worry about it. He put both arms around me and nodded to the others. "I'll see you guys in a few minutes."

"What about the icebergs?" Remy asked.

"We don't want humans noticing them this far south and starting to panic about global warming and melting icecaps," Kim added.

"I could melt them, but I might end up frying sea creatures around here," Sykes added. "I can make sure Lil makes it home safely," Sykes added, starting toward us. "Izzy can watch my back in case the cloud demons are keeping tabs on us and decide to follow our telegate."

I didn't want to leave with Sykes and Izzy. It would be so humiliating if I couldn't teleport. I felt bad enough a demon got the better of me, but the extent of my injuries was something I wanted known to only to Bran and me for now. I didn't voice my reluctance, but Bran felt it.

"Thanks for the offer, Sykes, but I have her." Bran put his arms around me.

"Some of us should go with you and watch your backs in case the fiends pull a fast one," Sykes insisted.

Bran paused as though considering it, then he nodded. "Good idea. Remy?"

"I concur. The two of you," he nodded at Sykes and Izzy, "go with them. Kim and I will start working on those icebergs. We'll move them closer to the island and away from any cruise ships out there. I may not be able to melt them, but I can keep them submerged."

"About the things the students left behind," Bran said, looking at the Security Guardians. "Could you take care of them?"

"Of course, Cardinal," Evangeline said. "But when you return, we have to discuss what to do about the students and the teachers."

Bran nodded. "We'll check with Mrs. D at HQ about that."

Listening to them made me both confused and angry all over again. I had no idea why they were discussing icebergs, students and teachers. The portal to Xenith was on Pearls Island, which was in Bermuda, hardly the region for icebergs. After facing Coronis, the Queen of Demons, and battling hordes of demons in back alleys, fighting demons didn't terrify me as much as when I first started hunting. Having one screw with my memories and powers was something new, different and bad. I was scared to learn just how much memory I'd lost and what abilities I couldn't control anymore.

- 4 -

LIES

Relief raced through me after we left the island and appeared on top of some building. No demon followed us. I mentally checked off teleporting on the list of 'possibly screwed up abilities' as we looped our route, even though something was different when I was in this energized state. I wasn't sure whether that was good or bad.

The house was quiet when we appeared inside my bedroom. Bran leaned back and grinned, dimples appearing on his cheeks. *You did great.*

His smile was forced and tinged with worry, but I pretended not to notice and gave him a toothy smile. *I know.*

Let me take a look at your head. He walked around, parted my hair, and searched for the bump. I exchanged an uneasy smile with Sykes and Izzy, who had followed our telegate and were watching us from the doorway with worried expressions.

It is not healing, Bran added, his hand gentle and cool on my throbbing bump. *See if Izzy can take care of it.*

I didn't like that suggestion—I didn't want Izzy and Sykes to know something was wrong with my dagger and my powers. Like all Guardians, I self-healed most superficial wounds, but the dagger usually enhanced that ability. I still gripped the hilt, hoping for a miracle or a tug as we linked. So far, I felt nothing. Nothing was bad.

"Lil?"

From Bran's scowl, it wasn't the first time he'd tried to get my attention. Izzy and Sykes also continued to watch me. They'd eventually know the truth. Besides, my head was killing me.

I shoved the Kris Dagger in its sheath. "Izzy, could you take care of my head?"

She nodded and entered the room then gasped when I turned and Bran showed her the swelling. "Lil, this is huge. It should be gone by now."

"My powers are off."

I felt rather than saw her hand hover near my wound, then there was warmth and the pain disappeared. The pounding inside my head didn't go away though. Refusing to panic, I made eye contact with Bran, who looked like he wanted to punch something. Once again, I wished he couldn't feel my pain.

"Is that better?" Izzy asked, drawing my attention away from Bran as she entered my line of vision.

"Yes, thanks," I lied smoothly. "Thanks for the escort too, guys, but I'd like to rest now."

No one made a move to leave, making me feel worse. I hated being the cause of their worry. Unfortunately, something always happened to me to give them a reason to worry. This time, there was nothing they could do about it.

I glanced at Bran. *Please. They won't go unless you leave.*

"Could you guys head to HQ and tell Mrs. D what happened?" Bran asked. "I'll join you shortly.

"Sure, but first, I have something to say," Sykes said as he sauntered to where the three of us stood and elbowed Bran and Izzy out of the way. "Give me room."

He gripped my shoulders and looked me straight in the eye as if trying to read my thoughts. Thankfully, he couldn't. His love and concern flowed to me though and I bit my lower lip to stop myself from saying something reassuring. Bran was in the room, watching Sykes with annoyance. Sykes had never bothered to hide the fact that he loved me. Maybe not as passionately and completely as Bran, but he loved me in his own way.

"You are going to be okay," Sykes vowed.

"Of course she is," Bran retorted.

Sykes ignored him and added, "You remember me, right?" He peered at me. "The guy you secretly have a crush on."

I giggled.

"Don't believe anything they," he jerked his thumb to indicate Bran and Izzy, who were shaking their heads at his antics, "tell you about me. Remember this face." He pointed between his eyes and turned his head left then right to give me side profiles, blond hair sweeping his broad shoulders. "This is the face of your number-one fan."

I chuckled and immediately regretted it. "Thanks, Sykes."

"See? She remembers me." He smirked.

"Of course I do, silly."

The smile disappeared, his hazel eyes darkening. "As soon as we come back here, we're going after the fiends that did this to you and making them pay. No one hurts one of us and gets away with it. Meanwhile whatever you don't remember, I'll be available for mind-blends, memory retrieval, or whatever you want so you can relive everything you've forgotten through *my* memories. Okay?"

Tear prickled the back of my eyes, but I managed a nod. Bran snickered, but this time I shot him a censuring look. He wore that arrogant look that said the gates to Tartarus would open before he let Sykes mind-blend with me. Ignoring him, I hugged Sykes. "Thank you."

"Okay, no slobbering over me." He teased, then leaned back, shot Bran a defiant look, and planted a kiss on my forehead. "Let's go, Izzy." He added in a gruff voice and teleported.

Izzy gave me a tiny smile. "He was really worried that you wouldn't remember us. David Lee lost most of his adult memories."

"Who's David Lee?"

"The Damned Human the demon attacked in New York."

"I could never forget you guys, Izzy." I hugged her too. "Your voices pulled me out of that dark, horrible…place." The words poured out of my mouth, yet when I tried to grasp the memory to support it, all I got were white-hot slashes of pain across my skull.

"You remembered something?" Bran asked urgently, his eyes searching my face.

I tried again to search for the shadow of the memory and winced at the pain on my temples. "I don't know. Maybe."

"How much have you forgotten?" Izzy asked.

Bran shook his head. "Let's discuss that later, Izzy. She needs to rest."

She shrugged and left. I released a breath I didn't know I was holding, sat on my bed and glanced at Bran. "What kind of demons are we dealing with?"

"We don't know." Bran settled beside me and covered my hands with his. "Today was the second time we met them. First encounter was a week ago. We told the Cardinals what happened. Something about the demon bothered them enough to put us on a lockdown while they searched for them. You picked up on their unease right away, though." Bran tucked a lock of my hair behind my ear and tilted my chin. His emerald eyes were shadowed. "How much have you forgotten?"

"What year and month are we in?"

"August. You're turning seventeen in about two weeks."

I'd lost about four months. "The last thing I remember is entering Valafar's booth on Jarvis Island."

Surprise flashed across Bran's face. "That's not bad."

"Compared to the guy Izzy said lost most of his memories, I guess I am lucky. Still so much has happened. Are Kylie and I still friends?"

"Yes. You grandfather didn't erase her memories yet, so you two do *stuff* whenever we're not busy."

"Stuff?"

He grinned. "Girl stuff—you know, shop, talk, watch movies. We've even double-dated."

"Really?" Only Bran could put up with Kylie's incessant chatter for me. Kylie was my best friend, but our friendship almost got destroyed when I froze a cup in front of her then tried to B.S. my way out of telling her the truth by claiming it was a Gypsy trick. In the end I had to tell her who and what I was when we learned she had the ability to channel our energies and thoughts, and hear our telepathic communications. Humans called people like her psychics. We preferred the term 'mediums'. Humans weren't supposed to know about our existence, but her case was different.

Something else occurred to me. "Did we get the List?"

He smiled. "Yes, and we've canceled most of the contracts. We have fifteen more to go and those are all Runners."

"Runners?"

"Humans who'd rather run than cancel their contracts."

"Why would they do that?"

He chuckled. "Because they can. We'll discuss all that later. Right now, I have to go." He cupped my face and gently brushed my skin with his thumb. "I know your head still hurts, so rest until we get back. Maybe you might get more fleeting memories like you just did."

I hoped so. "Okay."

He pulled me into his arms. "We'll find out what's wrong with you and fix it, Sunshine. I promise."

That was something about the men on my team. They always believed they could fix everything. Maybe this was something I had to fix by myself. "Are we going after the demons?"

He shot me a determined look. "Oh yeah."

Panic followed his words and I immediately felt terrible. No matter how strong or evil a demon was, I'd never been scared of hunting until now. Not knowing what I could or couldn't do didn't help either.

"About mind-blending, I was going to suggest it before *he* did. You will blend with me. Not Sykes or anyone else. I don't know what crazy crap they've been up to this summer, especially him. He still changes girlfriends every week."

I wasn't too sure about the mind-blend thing either, but I wanted him gone so I could take inventory of my powers. "Okay. No one but you."

"You are giving in without a fight?" he asked in disbelief.

I smiled. "No, I'm trying to get rid of you."

He chuckled. "You wish."

"So I can rest," I finished.

As soon as he left, I set out to confirm something I thought I'd seen when I teleported, something that had me a bit worried. Visualizing the kitchen, I willed myself there.

My teleport was definitely different. I could slow down and see other psi energies around me while I was in my energy form. I studied the kitchen. The energies pulsed and grew stronger until I recognized objects. Two cups sat side-by-side inside the sink, indicating Grampa and Aunt Janelle had been home earlier. Flowers on the kitchen counter and dining room table filled the air with their fragrance. A new garbage can was by the garbage disposal. I couldn't identify it until I materialized. It was a blue recycling can, probably put there by Aunt Janelle. As an Earth Cardinal Guardian, she loved nature and was big on saving the earth.

As I teleported back to my room, I slowed down again. Moving through the wall felt weird and ticklish. Something was different about my bedroom too. I hovered near the ceiling and drew from my old memories until something clicked—I had moved my furniture around. I materialized and walked around, noting the changes. The lime and lemon cover was new and so were the dresser, lamps, and the draperies. I even had a DVD/ VHS player. A digital frame sat on my dresser, the photographs changing every few seconds. One showed my mother laughing, then another of her with a baby with a mop of red hair. Me? I lifted it up and studied the pictures. I must have received Valafar's present.

Mom appeared happy in the photographs. Valafar too. In fact, they looked like normal, doting parents. Not that I knew anything about regular parents. Grampa had raised me by himself and he was a demon hunter.

Putting the frame back, I pulled the dagger from its sheath and placed it on the bed. *Come.*

It didn't move. It usually obeyed me.

Extending my hand toward it, I recited the words I used when I'd first commanded the dagger. *By the Order of Goddess Xenia and the Principalities, I command you, Kris Dagger, to come to me.*

Nothing. My dagger, the most feared and coveted Nephilim weapon, just sat there like an ordinary kitchen knife, the link between us gone.

Refusing to panic, I moved on to my other abilities. Placing the computer chair at the other end of the room, I stepped back. Just a small lightning bolt to melt the leather seat, something Remy could fix later, I told myself.

Several large bolts appeared from thin air, zipped across the room and incinerated the chair with a blinding explosion, leaving behind a giant hole on my bedroom floor. Oh, crapola. That was too easy and over the top.

A pounding came from the front door, causing me to jump. A psi scan told who my visitors were—Security Team. I raced to answer the door. A man and woman stared at me with scowls. "Yes?"

"The psi-dar detected an energy surge in your house, Cardinal Lil," the man said, "Is everything okay?"

My face warmed, but I tried to give them a relaxed smile. "Oh yeah. I had a little accident, that's all."

"Do you need our help?" the woman asked.

Then the entire enclave would know about it. I didn't think so. "No, thanks. It's nothing. Really. I already took care of it."

They didn't look convinced, but nodded and apologized for disturbing me, then left. Exhaling, I closed the door and headed back to my bedroom. For a moment, I just studied the charred carpet. I could see the guest room under my bedroom through the gaping hole. Those were some serious bolts. Giggling, I mentally checked off energy abilities.

Moving on, I lifted things around the room, starting with lighter then moving to heavier objects until I finished with my bed. Once again, the entire exercise was effortless. All my abilities were heightened, but my connection with the dagger was gone. It didn't make sense.

I got a wad of sticky notes from my desk drawer and quickly scribbled what I could and couldn't do, how many months of my memories were gone. On the last pad, I added what I'd told Izzy word for word. Just in case I met the same demons and more of my memories got erased, I'd have these notes for reference.

Feeling better, I went to my closet to get a fresh towel. As I turned to re-enter my room, the box tucked away on the top shelf caught my attention.

Instead of heading to the showers, I grabbed it and sat on the lounge. Two manila envelopes were wedged between layers of white packaging foam. A memory teased me, but it disappeared fast, before I could grasp it. I pulled from the last envelope pictures of me with my parents. They were the same pictures that were on the digital frame on my dresser.

I reached for the second envelope. It had VHS tapes inside, which explained the VHS player. Popping one in, I pressed play and watched, smiling at some of my antics, frowning at the others. I was a healthy baby with riotous red hair. Who would have guessed Valafar loved to read to me when I was a baby? But my favorite part was when he videotaped me asleep in my mother's arms while she read. She had a beautiful voice, yet I couldn't remember hearing her voice before or watching these movies.

"Hey," Bran said from my bedroom doorway. In his hand were my beach bag and flip-flops. "I brought your stuff."

"Thanks." I pressed the remote control to pause the replay as he dropped the colorful bag by the door and met him across the room. He still wore his swim trunks and no T-shirt. He was all muscles, lean and hard. Beautiful.

"You're not ready?" he asked.

"I was rediscovering my room, which I obviously changed."

"So as not to remind you of the one Valafar kept you in on Jarvis Island," Bran explained. "We repainted the wall, and you even insisted on changing the car…whoa, what happened?"

I winced at his shocked expression. "I tested my powers to see which ones were still working. You think Remy might fix it before Grampa gets home?"

"Sure." Bran walked to the edge of the hole and peered below. "That's a big hole."

"They were big lightning bolts."

He cocked his right eyebrow at me. "What else?"

"My dagger is not responding to me yet and my other abilities are on hyperdrive. The bolts appeared too easily. I can also slow down my teleport, which is both cool and weird. While we were at the beach, I tried to raise my shield and block emotions from you guys and failed. I think my empathic abilities are over the charts too."

"That is strange," Bran said then joined me. "When Solange's minions attacked you, your powers were drained."

"And I was okay within twenty-four hours."

"Maybe that's all you need for your powers to stabilize. How is your head?"

"It's getting better, just at a snail's pace." I waved toward the TV screen, where the replay was on pause. "Did I ever watch that?"

Bran chuckled. "Over and over again the last few months."

"And the digital frame?"

"I got that for you and scanned the pictures a couple of months ago. It was a surprise. You loved it."

Another precious moment gone. "I want my memories back," I griped.

"You will get them back," Bran vowed, wrapped his arms around me and held me close.

My heightened senses picked up on everything—the way his warm skin felt against mine, his pounding heart, his scent. But it was more than that. I tapped into his inner feelings without meaning to. He was worried about me, but his love for me shone brighter and purer than anything I'd ever felt. My senses leaped in response.

"We should head to HQ," he said, leaning back.

"Not yet." I cupped his face, leaned forward and kissed him. "We need to make some new memories."

"Lil, we…" his voice trailed off as though he forgot what he was about to say. We kissed, breathing impossible as we got lost in sensations.

How many moments like this had I lost? Would I ever get them back?

Something snapped inside me and I threw my arms around his neck, making him lose his balance. He landed on the lounge with me on the top.

"Sorry," I whispered.

"No, you're not." His eyes went to my lips. "You got me exactly where you want me."

"You don't have to sound so tortured about it," I teased. "I'm making things easy for you."

"The opposite." Then he kissed me. Really, really kissed me without holding anything back. The kiss mushroomed into something both scary and exciting. Heat surged through me like a giant wave. I wasn't sure whether what I felt was my reaction to him, his reaction to me, or a combination of our needs. My wacky empathic senses just soaked it all in until I thought I would explode.

Heat followed his hands across my skin, making me squirm and press against him. Then he tugged the string holding my bikini top and we both froze. Confusion flashed in his eyes as though he wasn't sure about what we were doing and how we got on the lounge.

"I should go." He spoke slowly, his breathing uneven against my skin.

"Why?" I whispered, feeling hot and cold at the same time, wanting him to kiss me again, to make me forget all problems, even for just a moment.

Emerald eyes met mine and begged for forgiveness. "Because we shouldn't be doing this now, not when you got hurt and your powers are off."

"I don't care."

"I do."

"*You* have memories of everything we did the last four months, Bran. I don't. It's unfair."

"I know." He reached behind me and retied the strings of my bikini top. "You can mind-blend with me and retrieve them whenever you like. We will create more memories. I promise."

I blew out air, closed my eyes then rested my cheek on his chest. His heated skin smelled so good. Of sun and sea. And it bugged me that he was so rational. Why couldn't he ever let his emotions rule his head? I know he loved me, wanted to be with me in every way. Worse, he was right this time. We couldn't make out until we were sure about the extent of my injuries, the damage the demons did to my Psi energy. Even the thought of mind-blending with him scared me. What if whatever the demons did to me was contagious and I passed it on to him?

I lifted my head off Bran's chest and sat up, forcing myself not to stroke his bare chest. He was pure muscles, six-pack, and warmth.

"Are we really going after the demons?" I asked.

"Yes." A smile filled with anticipation curled Bran's lips. "Vengeance is the only thing demons respect. We want to catch them while they're still celebrating and with their guard down."

A hollow feeling settled in my stomach. Fear was fast becoming my constant companion and it sucked. If facing those demons would help me overcome it, I was in. "Okay. Let's do it."

Bran grinned. "I'll tell the others. They weren't sure you'd want to come with us."

I bristled. "Why wouldn't I? I'll be fine, but we can't mind-blend."

A frown chased the smile from his lips. "Why not?"

"The demons probably contaminated my energy, Bran. If I mind-blend with you, I could do the same to you."

He tucked strands of hair behind my ear. "Don't worry about me. I want to do this. You recovered in twenty-four hours when you blended with Lottius. If it makes you feel better, we can give your mind a couple of days to recover then give it try."

I opened my mouth to argue, but he put a stop to that before I uttered a word. He cupped my chin and ran a thumb across my lips. His emerald eyes heated and his head dipped as though to kiss me. Then he stopped, confusion flashing in his eyes.

"I have to go." He disappeared and reappeared by the door. "Change and head to HQ. Mrs. D is expecting you."

I shook my head. I should be empowered that I had that kind of effect on him. Usually, I was. Now his behavior just annoyed me.

I took a quick shower, then pulled on the standard hunting clothes—black pants and a matching T-shirt. Inside the bathroom, I studied my reflection. Nothing was out of place. Same slanted green eyes stared at me. Same multi-colored red hair. My skin, inherited from my gypsy grandmother, was more tanned than usual. I couldn't see any changes to explain my heightened powers.

I hated feeling out of sorts, hated not knowing what surprises my body hid. My father was a nature-bender with unknown lineage, so there was no telling what blood flowed in my veins. Maybe one day I would turn into smoke like a Lazari, grow horns or a tail like a Werenephil, or worse, start craving blood like a Nosferatu.

Hating the direction of my thoughts, I splashed water on my face and teleported to HQ.

"I already dispatched several members of my security team to the island." Mrs. D, the head of security and my former English lit teacher, said as I entered HQ's main office. She and Remy frowned when they saw me. I gave them a weak smile, which only made them frown harder. "They'll keep an eye on the portal in case the demons return. As for the students, I'll confer with the chairman and see what he decides to do about them. Come here, sweetheart," she added, beckoning me forward.

She cupped my face and peered at me from above her rhinestone glasses, her colorful bangles jingling. "I was told you fainted while fighting demons."

I shrugged.

"Shrug all you want, but fainting and memory loss are symptoms of something serious," she scolded. "How are you feeling?"

"Okay. The bump is gone." The headache was still there, but no one needed to know that. Remy continued to stare at me with a weird expression.

"And your memories?" Mrs. D asked.

"They are coming back." It wasn't exactly a lie. I remembered a dark place.

"Were you holding the dagger when they attacked?"

"I was and now it's not responding to me."

"Leave it with Master Haziel."

I sighed. I didn't want to be grilled by my trainer yet. He could smell my lies a mile away. At the same time, I couldn't disobey an order from Mrs. D.

"Where did you say the others went?" Mrs. D asked as I walked away.

"To the library," Remy said. "They are trying to figure out the words Lil yelled after she fainted."

"I said something?" I asked, turning to face them.

"Bran and I were creating the fake iceberg islands and weren't there when you were attacked," Remy explained. "Sykes said you fell and started talking in the ancient language, but even they can't agree on what you said. They hoped the librarian might help decipher the words."

"Ms. Laylah is very knowledgeable and will do whatever she can to help," Mrs. D said. *Laylah had better not give them anything on the Tribe.*

Not sure I'd heard Mrs. D's thoughts correctly, I studied her expressionless face. I didn't usually hear others' thoughts unless I eavesdropped, yet her thoughts had floated to me as clear as though she'd telepathed them to me intentionally.

The Tribe. Why did that word sound familiar? I racked my brain for an answer and only made my headache worse. And why would Mrs. D pretend she didn't know the identity of the demons, or 'the Tribe' as she called them?

Civilians in the inner rooms also continued to look our way instead of at their computer screens or the clairvoyant images they were communicating with. Their wariness streamed my way, the distance not lessening the intensity. I raised my shield to shut them out, with little success. Instead, their thoughts trickled through.

The junior Cardinals should be told the truth...

We should go back to Xenith until this blows over...

If the Cardinals don't find the Summoners, we are in trouble...

Summoners. The word echoed in my head like a distant memory too. Going on a hunch, I asked, "Have we found the Summoners yet, Mrs. D?"

She blinked. "Excuse me?"

"The Summoners. Have you found them?"

She frowned. "Where did you hear that word?"

"It just popped in my head. The other word is the Tribe. I know I've heard them before, but I can't remember from where. What do they mean?"

Her eyes narrowed, the pupil slitting like a cat's. "I don't know. When you remember where you'd heard them, let me know. Now run along and take that dagger to Master Haziel."

Liar, I wanted to yell. "So you and the senior Cardinals haven't identified these demons even though one attacked us a week ago."

She frowned at my combatant tone and for one brief moment, I thought I'd given myself away. I smiled, but I must not have been very convincing, because she continued to stare at me suspiciously.

"No, we haven't. With Coronis' minions on the loose, there's no telling what new breeds are out there. And yes, the Cardinals have taken to naming new breeds of demons in order to differentiate them from each other. Maybe that's where you heard those words." She glanced over my shoulder and added quickly, "Ah, there you are, Cardinal Bran. What did Master Haziel say?"

"He said we can go," Bran said as he entered the room. He had changed into jeans and a black T-shirt. "But first, he wants to see Lil."

Mrs. D opened her mouth as though to speak, then humphed. *The Cardinals are not going to like this. I must inform them at once.* "Okay. We tracked down four Runners, including Mr. and Mrs. Watts." Her gaze touched the three of us, lingering on me, before it settled on Bran. "Stop by the security room for the crystals."

I waited until Mrs. D left, then grabbed Bran and Remy's arms. "Come with me."

"What's going on?" Bran asked at the same time as Remy said, "Where are we going?"

"I need a favor. I have a giant hole in the middle of my bedroom that I accidently created," I explained as I led them out of the office and down the hallway toward the tunnels then stopped. "Do you think you can fix it for me, Remy?"

Remy eyed me with his brow furrowed. "You don't have accidents, Lil."

"Okay, my powers are messed up and I had a little mishap. Ask Bran. He saw the damage."

"Little? Half the floor is gone. You could watch TV from the basement," Bran said and grinned.

I elbowed him. "Very funny, but the hole is not why I brought you guys out here." I glanced toward the office and did a quick scan. No one was eavesdropping on us. "I didn't want the Civilians to hear us. They are in on something."

"In on what?" Bran asked, eyes narrowing.

"Mrs. D and the Civilians know the identity of the demon that attacked me," I whispered. "She referred to them as the Tribe."

"You eavesdropped on her thoughts?" Remy asked reproachfully.

"Not intentionally," I said, shooting him an annoyed look. "My powers are off, so I hear and feel everyone's emotions even when I don't want to, even with my shield or theirs up. I faked knowing the Summoners and the Tribe after I heard Mrs. D and the Civilians' thoughts." I quickly explained everything I had heard while inside the office. "The words sounded familiar, so I asked her but she denied knowing them. Have you guys heard of the Tribe and Summoners before?"

They shook their heads.

"Then we should ask Mrs. D about them and force her to tell us the truth."

"No," Remy and Bran said at the same time, horror on their faces.

"Why not?"

"We are going after the demons, and she *will* stop us from leaving if she knows. She might not be able to read your mind, but she can read ours," Bran explained. "Right now she thinks we're going after the Runners to finish canceling the contracts."

I frowned. "She doesn't agree with Master Haziel's decision and is trying to find Grampa and the senior Cardinals to stop us from leaving the valley. I heard her thoughts before she left. "

Bran and Remy exchanged a glance.

"No one is stopping us from leaving, but having a name will make it much easier to locate them," Bran said. "Lil, go and see what Master Haziel wants while I get the crystals." He glanced at Remy.

"I'll fix the hole in Lil's bedroom and get the others," Remy said. "Let's meet at my place ASAP."

- 5 -

THE POWER WITHIN

According to my scan, Master Haziel was at the library, as were Izzy, Kim, and Sykes. The hallways usually buzzed with students, but now they were eerily silent. It felt weird. Like a tomb.

I hurried toward the entrance, the massive doors gleaming under the lights on the walls. For some reason, the scenes of ancient battles between Guardians and demons etched on the wooden panels and frames seemed so real.

I waved a hand and the massive doors flew back and creaked on their hinges. I cringed. Having too much power had its drawbacks. Lucky for me, the door was sturdy.

Like the hallways, the Academy's rotunda, with its soaring columns, torch-like glowing crystals on the wall, and leather benches along the walls, was empty too.

I paused in the middle of the foyer and glanced up at the painting of Goddess Xenia on the dome-shaped ceiling. In a white, flowing robe, her huge white wings raised, glorious red-hair tumbling down her back and the Kris Dagger in her hand, she looked infallible. I was the failure who had let the demons break the bond between me and the dagger.

"I promise, I'll bond with it again," I vowed.

"Talking to yourself, Lil?" Ms. Laylah's cheerful voice called out.

She stood in the doorway of the library, the only room with blazing lights, her graying hair braided and wrapped around her head like a crown.

I pointed at the ceiling. "I'm talking to her."

She glanced up at the ceiling and chuckled. "She can hear, you know."

Then hopefully, she would know the dagger problem wasn't my fault.

"If you're looking for your friends, they are downstairs in the archives," Ms. Laylah said.

"No, I'm here to see Master Haziel."

"He's in there somewhere." She stepped back and beckoned me forward. "Not having the children around is turning this place into a mausoleum, but he enjoys the quiet."

He would. He was so eccentric. I went through the main room, checking niches where student often hid while making out. He wasn't in the main room. I entered the quiet, reading area in the back and saw him at the end booth, his nose buried in a book, white hair peeking above the top. The brown, leather cover had the same picture of Goddess Xenia as the painting in the foyer. He lowered the book, revealing his bearded, ancient face. As usual, he wore an off-white linen tunic shirt.

"I expected you to bring the dagger to me as soon as you arrived in the valley," he scolded.

Yeah, well, we don't always get what we want, do we? I wanted to retort, but I couldn't bring myself to be rude to him. He was the wisest Guardian and best trainer I'd ever had. And he took such pride in my accomplishments.

"Sorry." I removed the sheath holding the Kris Dagger from my waist and placed it before him. "What's wrong with it?"

"Sit down, Lil." He placed the book he'd been reading face down, then pulled the dagger from its sheath and studied it, his lips puckering in thought. "Interesting."

I frowned. "What?"

"Things that were meant to happen have come to pass," he murmured.

I hated it when he went all cryptic and mysterious. "What things?"

"Prophesies fulfilled, some too soon and others too slow. Do you notice anything different about the blade?" he asked, extending the dagger toward me.

I was still trying to read the meaning behind his words and scowled. The blade was clear, the etched ancient scribbles gone. No wonder it couldn't bond with me. The demons had destroyed the means through which I linked with the dagger.

"The writings are gone."

"Yes." Then he looked up and studied me. "Remove your coat."

"Uh, excuse me?"

He gestured impatiently. "Coat. Off."

Sighing, I stood and shrugged off the trench coat.

He took my hands and held them in pace, his gaze running up to where my T-shirt hugged my upper arms. He lifted my arms to check the underside. "Hmm. Turn around and lift up your T-shirt."

"Master Haziel," I protested.

"I want to see your lower back," he said. "

Sighing again, I turned and lifted my T-shirt. There was silence. I tried to twist around and look, but I couldn't see a thing. "What are you looking for?"

"The writings from the dagger," he explained. "The demons did not destroy them. They were transferred to you."

"What?" I screeched. No matter how far I twisted, I couldn't see them. "Why?"

"There is no need to panic. If the prophesy is right, this is the dagger's way of protecting itself and you. When the writings from the dagger were transferred to you, its powers were transferred too. You are now our Goddess Xenia's weapon."

"Weapon?" I blurted out then frowned as the echoes of that same word resounded inside my heard, like I'd heard it before. Pulling my shirt down, I sat. "Have we had this discussion before?"

"Not with me." Then he did something strange. He reached across the desk and placed his gnarled hand against my temple. "You are warm and your pulse is racing."

"Yeah, it's called a panic attack."

He scowled. "Guardians do not have panic attacks. How is your head?"

"Fine."

"Telling lies is beneath you, Lil Falcon," he reprimanded.

Wasn't he just full of sage advice this afternoon? "I have a headache. How did you know?"

"I just do," he said mysteriously. "The memory loss is because of the attack, but the effect is temporary because of the dagger's power inside you. Your body is adjusting and that is why you have the headache. You will be physically fine once the power moves back to the dagger."

It was only temporary. Great! "When will that be?"

"When the Goddess decides you and the dagger are safe."

The certainty in his voice was reassuring. Still, I frantically searched my arms. There was nothing. Maybe he was wrong about the transfer.

"Keep the dagger with you at all times. When the writings appear on your skin, grip the dagger and see if they are transferred back. Come and see me immediately. Take the book too." He pushed the book with the picture of the Goddess toward me. "You might learn a thing or two."

I wrinkled my nose. "I don't have time to read."

"Make time." When I hesitated, he added, "It is merely fifty pages. I will quiz you in a few days."

"Quiz? You're kidding." Even as the words left my mouth, I knew the answer. He never joked. "It's not fair. I was attacked today and my memories were wiped out… and…and I just learned I'm a freaking weapon. I don't need homework. I need to know how to transfer the power back to my dagger before the Tribe attacks again."

He scowled. "The Tribe?"

"You know, the demons that attacked us. Were they summoned by the…*Summoners*?" I angled my head and tried to listen to his thoughts, but all I heard was static. I guess having lived for eight hundred years meant he'd learned a thing or two about keeping his students out of his head. On the other hand, he couldn't block his emotions. He was shocked by my words. "You know about them, don't you?"

Instead of answering, he studied me intently. "Where did you hear these words?"

"From Mrs. D and the Civilians' thoughts, but the words sounded familiar. You know, like I'd heard them before."

He pursed his lips with disapproval but I refused to feel guilty.

"Who are they? Or are you going to deny you know them too?" I challenged. "Like Mrs. D."

He chuckled. "No, Lil, I am not going to lie to you. I did not approve of the senior Cardinals' decision to keep you children in the dark. Yes, demons summoned the Tribe. Find these demons, the Summoners, and force them to send the Tribe home. Do not go after the Tribe. You are not ready to face them, not until you are in control of the Kris Dagger. With the Tribe, you only get one chance." He raised one gnarled finger.

Ominous. "And where's home? Tartarus?"

He shot me a look I couldn't read, then said, "Go on. Your friends are waiting. Remember, do *not* go after the Tribe."

I grabbed the book he'd given me and my coat, and got up.

"I will see you and your friends first thing tomorrow morning at seven o'clock sharp."

I frowned. "What's happening at seven in the morning?"

"We will start a new training regimen. You need to learn how to use your new powers until they are transferred back to the dagger." His eyes twinkled as though he looked forward to our next session.

I wanted to scream that I didn't want to be a weapon, whatever that meant, but it would be pointless. Grinding my teeth, I deliberately broke one of the Academy's rules—I teleported from the library.

The guys were at Remy and Sykes', but I detoured to my house first, dropped off the book, and undressed. There were no other markings anywhere on my body except for my birthmark. I should be relieved, but I wasn't. Being me just sucked more than usual.

I yanked my clothes back on and teleported to the guys' place.

Everyone looked up. Bran got up and walked to my side. "What did Master Haziel want?"

"He said we can't go after the Tribe. We should find the Summoners instead."

"Why?" Bran asked.

I shrugged. "Taking down them is complicated and we are not ready."

"That's bull," Sykes retorted. "We are."

The others nodded. Bran didn't. His gaze stayed locked on my face. The others were running on emotions while he…he was thinking things through, plotting.

"We are also pissed," Remy added. "The senior Cardinals know the identity of these demons and didn't tell us. I'm sure you don't remember this, Lil, but they had us on a lockdown while they tried to locate the Tribe's den. Didn't exactly go well for them, so it's now our turn."

The others nodded again.

Bran wasn't ready to jump on the bandwagon. "Why does he think we are not ready?"

"Because my powers are off." I explained everything Master Haziel told me about the dagger's powers transferring to me. "I hope he's wrong."

Silence followed as they studied my hands.

I extended my arms and rolled up the sleeves of my coat. My skin was still clear. "He said the ancient markings will appear soon, but my body is still adjusting to the power surge from the dagger. That is why I have this crazy headache."

Everyone started asking questions at once.

I raised my hand. "I can't answer all your questions because I'm still trying to understand what is happening to me. The headache started when I gained consciousness on the island. Yes, I tested my powers and created a giant hole on my bedroom floor." I glanced at Remy. "Thanks for fixing it. My teleporting is different and my Psi abilities are off the charts. I can hear your thoughts and feel whatever you guys are feeling, whether my shield or yours are up." Their expression became guarded. "I know you hate hearing that, but believe me, I'm not too thrilled either."

The first time they'd learned about my empathic abilities, they'd reacted the same way—with revulsion—except Bran. I had had to promise never to read them. Their thoughts drifted to me and I sighed.

"No, Remy, I don't hear and feel stuff all the time. Like my headache, one minute I'm bombarded with thoughts and emotions, the next it's blissfully silent and calm." I glanced at Kim. "No, my powers haven't shown the same instability. As for you two," I glared at Sykes and Izzy, "don't feel sorry for me or I will go off on the both of you."

Another silence, with grimaces and uneasy smiles, followed. If possible, their worries shot up a notch. "I mean it, guys. Ixnay on pity-fest. Can we leave now?"

"We must discuss this first, Lil," Izzy said. "I don't care that you can hear my thoughts and read my feelings, I've nothing to hide. But, I need to know if you are now exactly like the Kris Dagger. Can you sense demons?"

"Shoot out the dagger's special rays?" Sykes added.

"What if your powers ebb when you are fighting a demon?" Kim added,

"Come on, guys," Bran protested. "Leave her alone."

"It's okay," I reassured him. "If my powers disappear, Kim, I can still fight. If that fails, you guys can protect me just like you did on the island, just like I would protect you if something were to happen to your powers." Kim made a face. "But if my presence bothers you, I can stay at home."

"No," several voices protested.

Bran cocked a brow. "Kim?"

Kim glared at him then the others. "I didn't say I wanted her to stay behind." She smiled at me. "I'm used to having you and the dagger as our safety net. It's a bit weird to go out knowing that net is gone."

Surprised she hadn't said something mean, I smiled back and patted the hilt of the dagger. "We might not be able to link, but we are both here."

Everyone laughed, and tension leached out of the room.

Bran stood. "Okay, let's do this. We'll start with our first stop." He pulled a clairvoyant blue crystal from his inner coat pocket, placed it on the table and activated it by waving his hand above it. An image shot from the core and hovered above the table. "We usually do this before we leave so we can choose entry position," he explained, glancing at me.

"Have I been here before?" I asked while studying the medium-sized house with overgrown lawn and weedy flower beds. "I don't recognize it."

"No, this is where Mrs. Watts is hiding. She was reluctant to cancel her contract when we visited her a week ago in Myrtle Beach. That was the night we first encountered one of the Tribe demons. We couldn't see her again after that because of the lockdown. Mrs. D's team found out she'd moved and just located her this morning."

"She's definitely slumming," Izzy said, nodding at the holographic-like image.

"She didn't want to be found." Bran's gaze swept everyone. "I know you guys would rather skip going after her and the other Runners and just start searching for the Summoners, but Mrs. D expects a report."

"And the Watts will be off our list," Sykes added with a knowing smirk.

"True," Bran said with a slight smile. "But I also want to see if seeing Mrs. Watts triggers Lil's memory. Any question?"

I couldn't wait to leave. Being cooped up in the room with the others was slowly driving me crazy. What part of "don't feel sorry for me" didn't they get?

- 6 -

MRS. WATTS

We appeared behind a walled fence. A barking dog alerted an elderly couple walking down the narrow street of our presence, and they eyed us suspiciously. Six teens in trench coats in the middle of summer in L.A. were bound to draw attention.

Ignore us, I projected into their thoughts.

They continued with their walk, but when I turned around, the others were watching me like they expected me to do something crazy.

"Will you guys think of something else? The Summoners, demons, Mrs. Watts, anything," I said through clenched teeth. "Just stop stressing about me. Look at them," I pointed at the couple. "I just told them to ignore us and their heads didn't explode."

Bran's energy brushed against mine and I exhaled. No matter how much I loved that he could excite or calm me down with a touch, he really shouldn't allow his energy near mine until my powers were stable.

Squinting against the sun, I started up the slabs leading to the front entrance of Mrs. Watts' home. The clairvoyant image had been kind. Plywood—or possibly cardboard—covered some of the windows, as though she was in the process of boarding up her house for a hurricane or tornado. A lone hose snaked past untrimmed rose bushes and shrubberies, crossed the dry grass and ended in a plastic pool filled with dirty water and dead bugs. A van, its windows shattered, stood in the driveway.

My senses picked up a familiar energy. The more I tried to identify it, the more elusive it became and the harder my head pounded. As we got closer, I realized that most of the windows had no covering. Our boots crunched on shards of glass littering the porch.

"What's with the glass?" Kim murmured.

"It's from the windows." Remy pointed at the jagged edges of broken glass bordering the windows. He picked up a large piece, turned it over in his hand, then glanced through one of the windows. "Every glass surface in the room is shattered, even the TV screen. It's like a gas explosion or something."

"Yet there's no evidence of fire," Sykes said.

"No, this is the work of a demon." Bran stepped forward and pressed the doorbell. "Strong wind can shatter glass, right?" He glanced at Kim.

"And everything in its path," Kim said. "This is something else."

"Sound is more selective," Izzy said. "But sound demons don't exist."

"I don't know about that. I knew several Banshees on Coronis Isle," Bran added, ringing the doorbell again. "They were funny."

Izzy rolled her eyes. "Ha-ha funny or hey-you-are-about-to-die funny?"

The energy was stronger now, but not enough to get a reading. Even our amulets didn't glow in response to it. It bugged me that I couldn't identify it. Running footsteps resounded in the air and drew closer. Bolts clicked then the door was flung open.

A petite freckled-faced woman squinted at us. Her eyes were red-rimmed, her hair sticking every which way, and her pajamas, a wrinkled one-piece, had wet blotches. There was no sudden rush of memories as I stared at her.

"Finally," she said with relief and indicated we follow her.

No one moved.

Why is she being so nice? Izzy telepathed.

Yeah, Runners usually slam the door in our faces, Kim added.

"Mrs. Watts, we are here to—" Bran said.

"I know," she said, interrupting him then gestured that we follow her. "This way. Mind the glass. It is everywhere and on everything. Vandals broke in last night and destroyed everything." The living room wooden floor had an area rug littered with toys and more shards of glass. "The children are in the bedroom," she added.

Bran gripped my arm. "Do you remember her?"

I shook my head.

He muttered a curse, then looked at his watch. "Okay, let's find out why a demon was here, then get out of here. The perfect time to pay demons' dens a visit is during lunch, when their guard is down. Come on." He led the way inside the house.

"What's that smell?" Kim asked.

"Smells like Lazari," Izzy mumbled. "You think some did this to her home?"

"I never heard of Lazari with the ability to break glass," Bran said. "Whatever did this might still be here. Do you sense anything, Lil?"

"Yeah. Something gooey." I rolled my eyes when they all stopped and reached for their weapons. The way they blended in at school, I often forgot they hadn't grown up around humans, but instead spent their first sixteen years in Xenith. They all grew up in Xenith until they got their powers at age sixteen. "The scent is not demonic, it's puke," I explained.

"As in partially digested food?" Kim asked, her expression dubious, one hand covering her nose, the other holding her knife.

I nodded. "Yes."

"How do you know?" Sykes asked.

"I've been around sick humans." From their expressions, they didn't believe me. I shrugged. I had enough on my plate without trying to convince them of something so mundane. "Whatever, but you need to put those weapons away before Mrs. Watts sees them and concludes we're here to hurt her."

We continued along a narrow hallway, following sounds to a medium-sized room. The windows were boarded up with cardboard, so the only light came from a bedside lamp on top of a dresser. The room had two twin beds and a crib.

Two boys about six shared one bed, Mrs. Watts mopping the brow of one of them as he threw up into a bucket. An older girl about eight lay curled up in another bed. She looked so pale, her psi energy weak. The youngest child sleeping in the crib was hardly breathing.

"Mrs. Watts," Bran called out.

She looked up from her boy and frowned.

"Why are you just standing there?" she asked, refolding the wet towel and cleaning her son's face. "Help me. They need treatment."

"What happened to them, Mrs. Watts?" Bran asked.

"I don't know. They were perfectly fine when we went to sleep last night," Mrs. Watts said in a tired voice, "but they woke me up at four in the morning crying and running high fevers. I gave them over-the-counter medication and they seemed to be doing okay several hours later. They even had some soup. Then their fevers returned and they couldn't hold down anything. I can't drive them to the hospital because the same people who vandalized my house also broke into my car, so I called you guys."

Bran frowned. "The broken windows happened last night?"

"Or this morning, I don't know. I woke up and the glass was everywhere and my children were sick."

"We'll take the children to the hospital. In the meantime, come with me." Bran extended a hand toward the woman.

"I want to ride with them to the ER."

"You will," Izzy reassured her gently. "As soon as we figure out what's wrong with them."

Mrs. Watts hesitated, a haunted look entering her eyes.

Go with him, I projected into her thoughts. *Everything will be okay.*

She allowed Bran to lead her out of the room. Sykes lifted the cell phone from the dresser and showed it to us. It looked like road kill.

"Unless the demons were here *after* her kids got sick, I doubt she used this. I'll check the houseline." He threw the phone to Remy and left the room.

Remy's ability to manipulate solids came in handy at a time like this. Within seconds, the cell phone was whole again. He flipped it open and checked the calls.

"There's no record of a call to the emergency room," he said.

"So the demons were here *before* the kids became ill," Kim said.

"Let's not jump to conclusions. Maybe this is the result of food poisoning." Izzy placed a hand on one of the twins' chest. She moved to the next child, then the older girl and finally the baby. "Forget I said that. They're dying."

"Of what?" Kim mumbled. She stood close to the window as she tried to breathe the fresh air from outside.

"Bone cancer," Izzy said. "The same illness the oldest had before their mother sold her soul. Why is this happening?"

No one answered her, but my mind started racing. What were the chances of an entire family coming down with the same cancer overnight? Nil. This could be an attempt to scare Mrs. Watts against canceling her contract.

"Can you heal them, Izzy?" I asked.

"I could try." Izzy placed a hand above the baby's chest. A glow started in the middle of her palms and spread until her fingers sparkled. Tiny electrical bolts shot from her hands to the baby, filling her and making her skin iridescent under the pink blanket.

A movement to my right showed Remy getting busy too. He pressed a hand on the plank covering the window. The wood shimmered and grew light and transparent as it transformed from wood to glass. He opened the glass windows to let the stale air out. He moved to the next window.

Sykes appeared in the doorway. "Her phone's working. She made a call about an hour ago."

"The paramedics should have been here by now," Kim murmured in a muffled voice, hand covering both mouth and nose now. "I have to do something. I can't breathe." She lifted her hands, creating a soft gust. It swept the stale air out of the room and through the window. Air scented with wild roses drifted inside.

My gaze moved back to the baby Izzy was healing. Color appeared to be returning to his cheeks.

Guys, you need to come to the living room, Bran telepathed us.

What is it? Remy asked.

Mrs. Watts doesn't remember us. The demons who jerked her house wiped out her memories too.

Only one kind of demon did that. We looked at each other and hurried out of the room. Izzy stayed, her focus on the kids.

Mrs. Watts' voice reached us before we joined her and Bran in the living room.

"Why should I?" she said, sounding frustrated. "I'm good with faces, and I'm telling you I've never met you before. Or them," she waved toward us as we entered the room. "What does remembering you have to do with my children? Are you the paramedics or the police?" she studied our outfits. "Your uniform is…is…who are you?"

My headache got worse as I listened to them as they tried to convince Mrs. Watts they were the good guys. Then Izzy walked into the room with her youngest.

Mrs. Watts jumped to her feet and plucked the baby from Izzy's arms. She touched her forehead. "Her fever broke."

"Izzy healed her," Bran said and indicated the couch. "Please sit down, Mrs. Watts. We need to finish our talk."

"Are the others okay?" His gaze clung desperately to Izzy's face.

"They will be when I'm done with them." Izzy answered confidently. She glanced at us. *Lightning demons did this to her?*

We think so, Bran said.

Why? She asked.

We are still trying to figure that out, Bran said. *Why don't you finish with the other children while we figure out how to deal with this?*

"I'll take care of the broken glass while you guys deal with her," Remy said, drawing our attention.

From her confused expression, Mrs. Watts didn't understand what Remy meant, until some glass bits lifted from the floor like weightless crystals, while others raced across the floor as though they'd grown legs.

Mrs. Watts screeched and moved back, her little girl clenched in her arms. The child laughed gleefully and wiggled her pudgy fingers, wanting to play with the moving things. The shards coalesced into mirrors, vases, cabinet doors and picture frames. The cracked TV screen shifted and flowed until it was whole again while the discarded toys pooled in the middle of the room.

Bran had explained that we often demonstrated our abilities to convince Damned Humans that we were the good guys, but Mrs. Watts wasn't impressed. She was totally freaked out.

It's okay, I reassured her. *We're not here to hurt you. We wouldn't heal your child if we were bad.*

"I'll take care of the other rooms, then your van," Remy said. *She's all yours, guys,* he telepathed as he left the living room.

"How did he do that?" Mrs. Watts whispered, her gaze following Remy, her arms tightening around her child.

"We already explained who we are, our abilities, and why we are here," Kim snapped. "Make up your mind already." She left the room to join Izzy.

"What my friend meant to say was we can't force you to cancel your contract, Mrs. Watts," Bran said, leaning forward and flashing his signature, charming smile. He reached inside his coat, pulled out the contract and unrolled it on the coffee table. "You get to decide whether you want to or not."

She still hesitated. This was taking forever. How in Tartarus had we canceled hundreds of contracts when it took forever to convince one human to make up her mind?

"Mommy!"

Mrs. Watts whipped around as Kim entered the room with the twins. They let go of her hand and ran to their mother. Mrs. Watts fussed over them, touching a cheek here, a nape there, kissing their foreheads.

"Their fevers are gone." Tears filled her eyes and streamed down her face. "Thank you. Thank you for healing them."

"My friend healed them, Mrs. Watts, not me," Kim said.

The woman craned her neck and looked expectantly behind Kim. "Where's my Michele?"

Kim indicated the hallway. "Izzy's working on her."

"Stay here," Mrs. Watts told the twins, then jumped to her feet and ran from the room. The children followed her anyway. The two year old continued to play with her toys, oblivious to the drama.

"How bad is her daughter?" I asked.

"Bad. Izzy can't heal her, but you know Izzy. She'll keep trying, until she exhausts her powers." Kim brushed something off the arm of the sofa and gingerly sat on the edge. She picked up the contract from the table. "She refused to cancel again?"

Bran nodded and scrubbed his face.

"Does it always take this long to convince them, or is her case just special because of her lost memories?" I asked, not masking my frustration.

"It takes this long," Kim said.

"It doesn't always," Sykes countered. "Do you guys think the lightning cloud demons are going after our humans and reversing their deals?"

"Oh yeah. But why now?" Kim asked. "Why not last month, or when we started after Jarvis Island? Are they after the ones who haven't canceled or the ones who already did too?"

"Let's not jump to conclusions yet." Bran's expression grew thoughtful. "We need to confirm this first. This is only one case."

"Two if you include David Lee," Remy said, entering the room. "Someone needs to talk to Izzy. She's determined to heal that child when it's obvious it's not going to happen. I think we should either call an ambulance or drive Mrs. Watts to the hospital before we check on the others."

"Call the ambulance," Bran said and got to his feet. "Where's her phone?"

I didn't like the calm way they were taking the woman's refusal. We were doing the woman a favor. Besides, we had already healed her kids.

"No," I interjected, getting up.

Everyone turned to look at me.

I stared right back at them. "I don't know how we've done things before, but we are not leaving. Remy, don't fix her van. We are not doing anything more for her until she cancels that contract."

Uneasy silence followed my outburst.

"Lil," Bran warned, closing the gap between us.

"Red, where did that come from?" Sykes asked.

"Yeah, you're usually the voice of reason," Kim added. "You and Bleeding Heart Izzy."

"It's time we stopped being nice and make them face the consequences of their actions. Izzy already healed three of her children, and you and Remy restored her house. It's time she did something for us."

"I'm liking this new you," Sykes said, smirking.

Bran scowled. "We can't."

Sykes squinted at him. "We can't like the new Lil, or can't blackmail Mrs. Watts?"

Bran glared at him. "We can't blackmail or coerce Mrs. Watts. Remember free will? Lil will erase her memory, then we will leave and revisit her some other time."

"I'm not erasing her memory. Let her have nightmares for all I care." I teleported to the bedroom before anyone could respond.

Mrs. Watts knelt by the bed, her boys watched from her side, while Izzy worked on Michele. The girl's eyes were closed, her expression peaceful as though she were asleep. Izzy, on the other hand, was a mess. Sweat dotted her forehead and her hands trembled. I checked her psi energy. It was dimming, which meant she was growing weak.

"We are leaving," Bran whispered as he walked past me. He put his arms around Izzy and said, "That's enough, Izzy."

"No," she protested. "I healed the others. I can do this."

"Her situation is different," he insisted, his voice gentle but firm. "There's nothing you can do for her."

"Of course there is," Izzy snapped.

"You healed her brothers and her little sister, Izzy," I added. "That's plenty enough. We need to get out of here and focus on the de…" I remembered Mrs. Watts' boys. *Go play outside.* I waited until they filed out. "We need to confirm that the lightning demons are messing with our humans, not waste our time and energy on something we can't change."

Bran threw me a warning look, then turned Izzy around. She was shaking so badly, she stumbled. He pulled her into his arms and murmured, "It's okay. You did your best."

Watching them reminded me of why I loved Bran. It wasn't just his looks. It was moments like this, when he showed his loving, caring side. The thought that there were demons trying to stop us from canceling all his contracts filled me with rage.

I picked up the cell phone from the dresser, where Remy had placed it, and thrust it toward Mrs. Watts. "Call for an ambulance to take your daughter to the hospital."

"Why? Your friend will heal her."

"No, she will not," I snapped.

"Why not?" she asked, looking confused.

"Because you are ungrateful," I snapped.

"Lil!" Bran and Izzy said at the same time.

I ignored them, my gaze not leaving Mrs. Watts. "She's already healed your other children and she's so weak she can't even stand." I took a step closer and thrust the phone toward her. "Take it and do it. Now."

"Lil!" Bran barked again.

I ignored him. Mrs. Watts swallowed, glanced at him then me. Something in my expression had her snatching the phone from my hand. She ran out of the room. When I turned around, both Bran and Izzy were staring at me with shocked expressions.

"What?" I asked.

"What's gotten into you?" Izzy asked.

"Reality."

"You are being cruel," Izzy snapped. "Deliberately cruel. That's so unlike you."

"Oh, yes, this is so me. The new me." I refused to look at Bran, but when I turned, I did it so fast the room swam. I thought I heard Bran said something, but I had already teleported.

"You have to cancel it before the paramedics get here, Mrs. Watts," Kim said as I hovered above them in energized state.

"Will my Michele get better?" Mrs. Watts asked.

"No, she'll not," Kim said impatiently. "There's nothing we can do about your daughter's cancer."

I thought of a way to make Mrs. Watts cancel the contract. Through the window, I could see Remy's psi energy next to the children near the van.

Bran and Izzy entered the room, then left. They were probably searching for me.

"So why should I cancel the contract?" Mrs. Watts insisted. "What is the benefit to me?"

"Uh, you'll get your soul back," Sykes said. "You know, that thing inside you that makes you human, that makes you have compassion, kindness and—"

"Can I sell it back to you again to save her?" Mrs. Watts asked, cutting him off.

"We. Are. Guardians," Kim said through gritted teeth. "We're *not* in the business of buying and selling souls."

"But I signed with one of you before," Mrs. Watts insisted, desperation in her voice.

I materialized beside her. Surprised, she took a step away from me, tripped on a toy and plopped on the couch behind her. "What part of 'he doesn't work for demons anymore' didn't you get?" I asked.

"But—"

"Mrs. Watts," I said, getting in her face and forcing her to lean back. "My friends have the ability to heal and restore things, but there's a lot more that *I* can do. A lot more and a lot worse."

My hand shot up and everything in her house lifted off the ground, including her TV console. Her eyes widened. I wiggled my finger and tiny bolts of lightning zipped between the bobbing things.

"You see, my friends here are pure Guardians. I, on the other hand, have demon blood in my veins and a massive headache that's refused to go away, so you do not want to mess with me. Those three children Izzy healed can easily become ill again like that." I snapped my fingers. Everything came back down with thuds, a few missing their places and crashing to the floor. "Then I can do things to your head that you'll beg me to kill you."

Mrs. Watts swallowed, his gaze swinging from me to my friends. "Can she…?"

"Oh yes," Sykes said, grinning.

"Don't encourage her," Kim snapped. "She's not herself."

I glanced at Kim and chuckled. "Actually, Kim, I am." Turning, I studied Mrs. Watts. "So what is it going to be, Mrs. Watts? One sick child or four?"

She swallowed.

"You're wasting our time, Mrs. Watts," I snapped.

"That's enough, Lil," Bran said.

Mrs. Watts looked at him with relief.

"Don't look at him. He's not going to help you."

"Lil!"

I glared at Bran and for one brief moment, my sight blurred until all I saw was a shadow where his face had been. Dizziness washed over me again. His thoughts, along with the others', crashed into my psyche, but they were jumbled and didn't make sense. My knees gave away.

I've got you, Bran telepathed me just as he pulled me against his chest. *You are okay.*

Calmness settled on my mind as his psi energy blended with mine. Cool hands touched my forehead and voices echoed in my head as though filtered by a mist.

"She's burning up," someone said in a distorted voice.

"We'll finish here, then take her home," another added.

My vision and hearing cleared. The headache was slow to react.

"She'll be fine," Bran reassured them.

"She fainted, Bran," Kim insisted.

"And her eyes glowed just like they did on the island," Izzy added.

"I'm fine," I finally spoke, but my eyes stayed locked with Bran's. I tried to disengage our energies but he wouldn't let me. I could have pushed him out of my head, but I might have ended up hurting him. I wiggled, hoping physical distance would do the trick, but he refused to let me go. *You can't do this.*

Says who?

You're sharing a burden that's not yours, I insisted. *You'll get my headache and mess up your powers.*

So what? You and I are mated for better and for worse.

I frowned. *We are?*

Yes, so sit back and let me take care of you.

Reasoning with him was getting me nowhere. It was time to lay on the guilt. *You are draining my energy, something you swore you'd never do.*

He grinned. *Nice try. When we are done here, I'm taking you home, where you'll stay until your powers stabilize.* He severed the link. *Can you take care of Mrs. Watts' memories without turning her into Mrs. Hyde again?*

I rolled my eyes, but at the back of my mind I kept hearing "Mated." When? Another lost memory? Leaving that for later, I turned to see the contract burst into flame. Mrs. Watts let out a screech.

Amazed at how much better I felt, I approached her. "One last thing, Mrs. Watts."

She cringed, "Stay away from me."

Don't be afraid. I won't hurt you. I could feel the others' stares, knew they worried about me dealing with Mrs. Watts fairly. *Don't worry, guys. I won't blow up her head.*

"That's not funny," Izzy said then added softly, "Are you sure she should do this?"

"She can handle this," Bran answered.

"What did you do to her? Kim asked.

"I drained some of her energy."

Silence followed. I shook my head. He really shouldn't blurt out things like that. Only demons drained energies, and it was usually to enhance theirs.

"Dude, that's messed up," Sykes said.

"And demonic," Izzy asked tentatively.

Bran shrugged. "So? She's stable now."

From the smile on his face, he was getting a kick out of shocking the others. Cupping Mrs. Watts' face, I stared into her eyes and meshed our minds. Snapshots of her fake memories zipped past, most of them of her children, women friends. The most recent showed her eating dinner with her children, then waking up and finding her children sick.

Was that how my memories were? Hours of nothing mixed with a few treasured moments? Bran and I were mated. How could I forget that?

Focusing on Mrs. Watts, I let my thoughts flow into her head. *When I let go of your face, turn around and walk out the door to your van. Wait there with your children until the ambulance arrives to take Michele to the hospital. Forget you saw us or that we were here. Forget your broken windows. Only your oldest daughter is ill. She was okay for a long time, but now she's ill again.*

When I let her go, she turned around and walked out the door without glancing left or right. She walked to the van with even, measured steps. When Remy held the door open for her, she got in without looking at him.

"What in Tartarus did you do to her?" Izzy asked.

"I just erased her memories and told her to wait outside for the ambulance."

"But the people usually talk to us in confusion and ask who we are, what we're doing in their home, office or wherever. They don't walk away like zombies."

"It doesn't matter," Bran cut in. "What's done is done." He walked to my side and touched my forehead. "You're still feverish and—"

"Nothing." I didn't want to hear another lecture about going back home. "I'm fine now. We should teleport to our next stop."

Bran frowned. "I'm not going to force you to do anything you don't want to do, but you cannot treat humans like you just did Mrs. Watts."

"She was being impossible."

"I know, but you must control your anger and frustrations or they'll control you."

I rolled my eyes. "I'm not responsible for what's happening to me. Are you forgetting the transfer of the dagger's powers into me?"

"I'm not. But I know you, Sunshine. I know what you are capable of. You can control anything." He studied me intently, love and utter belief in me shining in his emerald eyes. His hair, shorter on the sides, swung across his cheeks as he peered at me. "You *can* control them."

Of course I could…would with time. I reached out, twirled the lock of his hair around my finger and smiled. "Yes, I can."

He took my hand and pressed his lips into my palm. When he stepped back, my gaze met with the others. I'd completely forgotten their presence.

That was intense, Izzy telepathed me.

I just shrugged. My gaze met with Sykes and it was hard to describe the look in his eyes. Annoyance? Jealousy? A combination of both. I just couldn't deal with him and his feelings.

"Okay, let's do this." Bran removed his clairvoyant stone and activated it. Light shot up from the core of the stone and projected a holographic image of a house. "This is Mr. Watts' new place in Palos Verdes. The roof is flat, so let's teleport there."

"What happened?" Remy asked when he joined us and saw the mess on the floor. "I just cleaned this place up."

Sykes pointed at me like a child tattling. "Lil did it."

I laughed, happy to see him bounce back. I was also thrilled I could laugh without wincing. "But Mrs. Watts canceled the contract."

Remy's eyes narrowed. "You forced her?"

"Of course not," I said. "I couldn't see or hear a thing when she agreed to cancel it."

Remy looked confused. "What?"

Sykes slapped Remy on the back. "Long story, dude, but the EMT is here. We need to disappear."

The ambulance pulled up outside Mrs. Watts' van. We dematerialized before the EMT reached the house.

- 7 -

GAVYN'S AGENDA

A yellow police tape wound around Mr. Watts' broken door and window like a bad bandage dressing. His neighbor eagerly informed us that Mr. Watts had been having a "noisy party last night and was cooking something in the early hours of the morning when an explosion blew out his windows."

No one spoke after we thanked her. We headed to our next destination. After several more stops, we materialized on the roof of U.S. Bank Tower, the tallest building in California with a rooftop helipad. Lucky for us, it was empty, giving us enough space and privacy to vent.

"We're so screwed," Sykes said, pacing.

Shut up, I wanted to yell. He'd been saying that for the last thirty minutes and driving me nuts. My powers and headache were on the upswing again after leveling off at Mrs. Watts' but I didn't want to get catty with my teammates. The glances Bran threw my way told me he knew I was close to losing it again.

"So freaking screwed," Sykes repeated.

"You can say it a gazillion times, Sykes, it won't make anything better," Kim snapped. "And it's not us who're in trouble, the humans who made the deals and canceled are."

"But we helped them," Izzy said.

"No one forced them to sell their souls in the first place," I cut in.

"Lil!" Izzy scolded me.

"She's right, Izzy," Kim said. "No one put a gun to their heads."

It didn't matter whether the humans had canceled their contracts or not. All the ones we visited had similar stories— they had no memory of what had happened, yet their homes had broken glass everywhere and an accident had occurred that had reversed their fortunes. Bran made sure I didn't get anywhere near them.

A man whose daughter sold her soul after he was hit by a car and broke his spine was now brain-dead. He and the daughter were in a head-on collision with a truck yesterday. She was now the one with the broken spine while he was on life support.

A couple who couldn't have children, and had twins after the husband gave up his soul, was in the hospital with carbon monoxide poisoning.

Their children didn't make it and the husband, who had done the signing, was in the ICU.

A music mogul's club caught on fire, killing several people and leaving most of his body with third-degree burns. Lawsuits were already piling up because the doors had been jammed for some reason. Not only was he ruined financially, he was being held liable. By the time the lawyers finished with him, he would be penniless.

"Not only are they losing their ill-gained wealth and fame, they are being punished." I glanced at Bran. He hadn't spoken since we left Mrs. Watts, except to choose our next location. He was frustrated and kept forking his fingers through his hair. Even now, he stood near the edge of the roof and stared down at the city, anger surging from him in giant waves.

"The weirdest thing is that these misfortunes started while we were stuck in the valley," Izzy said.

"Let's be honest here," Remy cut in. "They started *after* we sighted the first lightning demon. Mancuso was right and Master Haziel was wrong."

I shook my head. "Master Haziel is never wrong. Who is Mancuso?"

"David Lee's manager," Izzy said. "Mancuso said no one could get away with playing with their soul without consequences. Master Haziel had said nothing would happen."

"And we haven't heard anything about David Lee," Sykes said. "We need to find an Internet café and see how he's doing."

Kim gave an unladylike snort. "Enough with the bromance, Sykes. I'm sure David Lee's voice is gone. It is obvious the demons are targeting the humans to get their souls back. I'll ask again, why now? Why not four months ago when we started canceling their contracts?"

"Maybe it takes a special kind of demon to harvest souls," I said.

"Like Reapers?" Remy asked then glanced at Bran. "What do you think, Bran?"

"Reapers don't hurt humans or exact retribution," Bran said. "They are Neutrals. The Tribe is made up of something else, and they were summoned to do one thing—stop me from getting my freedom."

"Why would you think that?" I asked, not liking the certainty in his voice.

"Because I know who is behind the summoning."

We converge on him, every said asking, "Who?"

"Gavyn," Bran said.

There was silence, then everyone started talking at once.

"Your brother?

"How do you know?"

"Why would he do this?"

Bran pinched the bridge of his nose and sighed. "He's the only person who'd go to extreme lengths to stop me from canceling my contracts. He wants me to take my rightful place as the leader of the demons because I won the battle on Jarvis Island. He asked me about it during Darius' party at the Brotherhood's compound."

"What did you tell him?" Remy asked.

"What do you think?" Bran snapped. "I wasn't interested and I'm still not. He didn't stop asking and pushing. The last time I saw him, we had a fight about it and he stormed off."

That was the Gavyn I knew, throwing tantrums when he didn't get his way. Every time I thought there was hope for him, he pulled some crap that made me hate him.

"I know how my brother thinks," Bran continued. "Waiting until my freedom is within my grasp then pulling a fast one is straight out of our mother's book." He paused, his gaze locked with mine a moment longer before moving to the others. I knew everything about his past—or, at least, I had known it. "Our mother did exactly the same thing when our father tried to sneak us out of Coronis Island. She knew for months what he'd planned, but waited until the night we attempted an escape. We were in a cave on the way to collect the Kris Dagger when she and her Lazari warriors surrounded us." He chuckled, though there was no humor on his face. "It's actually a brilliant strategy if you want to punish someone."

"Evil and mean-spirited," I said dismissively. "Gavyn is—"

"My brother," Bran said and gave me a sad smile. "He's not thinking straight."

Oh, he was. Gavyn only ever thought about one person—Gavyn. He was conniving and power-hungry. To think I'd offered to heal him when a demon drained his powers. That was one memory I would have loved to forget.

"Why didn't you tell us earlier?" Kim asked. "You know, after we visited the fourth or the tenth Damned Human?"

Bran shrugged. "I wasn't sure. And part of me didn't want to believe it."

"Doesn't what you want count for anything in his stupid plan?" I asked.

Don't worry, his plan won't work, Bran reassured me. "Gavyn doesn't know that my psi energy is purified despite the Runners' refusal to cancel. We should do something to help the humans. The Tribe got a head start on this, but we must catch up and stop them. Remember, we only canceled my contracts."

There was silence, but we were all thinking the same thing—this might be bigger than we'd thought. When Bran won the battle on Jarvis Island, he'd gotten hundreds of thousands of contracts. While we'd focused on canceling his, the other junior and mid-level Cardinal Guardians from the other sectors around the globe had gotten the bulk of the other contracts. If the Tribe was punishing humans for canceling contracts and getting their souls back, their reach might extend beyond our sector.

"Sorry, dude, but your brother is a douchebag," Sykes said.

"Please, don't insult douchebags," Kim said. "Now what?"

"We tell Darius to kick Gavyn out of the Brotherhood compound," Izzy snarled. "He doesn't deserve their hospitality if he's back to his evil ways."

Bran shook his head. "Gavyn left the Brotherhood the day after the party four months ago, but I know where he stays and works. I'm going to find him and have a long talk."

"We are all going," Remy corrected him. "He's going to tell us how to send the Tribe back to Tartarus or whatever hole they crawled from."

Bran actually smiled. "He runs a private club at Ritz-Carlton, L.A. Live. Demons only. He also lives there. Follow me."

The room we appeared in was done in white and black, and had floor to ceiling windows with an amazing view of the city, the mountains, and the ocean in the background. Gavyn wasn't home, but it was obvious why he had left the Brotherhood, with their homey stucco houses, for his old life. He was living in a lap of luxury, the latest electronic gadgets beside clairvoyant crystals projecting holographic motion images of him, his sister Celeste, and Bran.

"How very domesticated," Kim said with a sneer.

I wanted to rip the place apart.

"The restaurant is several floors below us." Bran said and glanced at his watch. "He's probably there."

"Just a second. My powers are peaking and I need release." I pulled out a knife from the sheath inside my boot, walked to the couch and stabbed the edge of the cushion. Slowly, I moved across the white upholstery, from one end to the other, the fiber filling spilling out. I did the same with the back and the arms.

The surprised expressions on the others' faces when I looked up didn't bother me. I grinned. "I'm starting to feel better already. Remy, could you change the white walls into green mixed with gray and whatever ugly color you can think of? Too much white makes my headache worse."

Without batting an eyelid, Remy pressed his hand on the nearest wall and murky green color spread from the point of contact. It spread over the walls.

"Hmm, I've an idea," Sykes said as energy balls appeared above his hands. He dribbled them on the white carpet as one would a basketball, leaving behind blotches of scorched surfaces. Smooth moves. He leaned back and smirked. "How's that headache, Lil?"

"Getting better by the second." I cocked my brow at Kim and Izzy.

Laughing, they joined in. Bran chuckled, but he didn't try to stop us. Izzy helped me remove the down inside the pillows and cushioned stools, while Kim blew them around, along with other knick knacks off the tables and shelves.

Gavyn's place had three bedrooms, and from the décor and the displayed images, one was supposed to be Celeste's and the other Bran's. While Sykes continued to bounce his energy balls from room to room, Remy changed the shapes of anything he could touch, including electronics, which Gavyn appeared to collect. Bran gave up trying to stay uninvolved and turned on water in every bathroom and kitchen, flooding the floors and carpets.

Trashing the place was childish and we knew Gavyn would get the place fixed in seconds, but it felt good. We were all laughing by the time we finished.

The hallways were quiet when we left, no humans or demons, but the demonic energy hung in the air and our amulets warmed. They lit up when we teleported to several floors below us.

'Hermonite Lodge,' written in white, looked stark against the dark-gray wall. Underneath them were the words 'Private Club and Restaurant'. There was a set of double doors to our right. Bran placed his palm against the door and pushed. It didn't budge.

"Allow me." Grinning, Remy pressed his hand against the door. The door shimmered and flowed, as though it was alive, until it became a doorway.

Let me do the talking, guys, Bran telepathed us. *But stay vigilant. If anyone attacks, take them down.*

The others grinned. They were eager to take down demons as payback for the attack on the island. I was more cautious because once again my powers were off and I had the hated headache messing with my head. I dragged my feet as we followed Bran into the club. Remy took the rear and transformed the doorway.

We were in some kind of an entryway with chest-high walls to our left and right. Behind the walls was a sunken floor packed with customers dressed in expensive suits and dresses, their perfect hair nicely groomed. The club looked like any exclusive club for the rich and wealthy—heavy curtains and paneled ceiling, comfortable leather seats and subtle lighting. A wrap-around bar dominated the center of the room, and further on, there was a lounge area facing glass windows and the patio. But the similarity to a human club ended there.

Menus hovered above the table from clairvoyant stones. Drinks floated from the bar to patrons' hands in an orderly fashion without spilling, but the aroma of food, leather, and wood mingled with demonic scents. And even though the diners used forks and knives like any civilized being, their diet made me want to gag.

Werenephils, who loved their food raw, sliced and chewed on bloody meat. The ones who preferred bugs scooped them by the spoonful or forkful. To our right, two Nosferatus buried their fangs into the necks of two scantily-dressed humans, who didn't appear to mind. They lifted their heads, dabbed their lips, and went back to sipping wine while their lunch supply got up and disappeared behind a curtained door only to be replaced by two more. Probably dessert.

A demon dressed all in black blocked our path before we entered the main floor of the restaurant. An upper-level demon, going by his psi energy. Behind him stood two security guards, who looked like they could bench-press the Rock of Gibraltar. Their energies weren't noteworthy.

"Your kind are not allowed in here," the head honcho demon said.

"And you are?" Bran asked rudely.

"The assistant manager."

"Well, Mr. Assistant Manager." Bran casually reached out and flicked imaginary dirt from the shoulder of the demon's jacket. "We are here to see my brother. So why don't you run along like a good minion and fetch him?"

Confusion flashed across the demon's face but he recovered fast. "Your brother?"

"Tall, gray eyes, silver hair…otherwise known as your boss. Meanwhile, we would like a table for," Bran glanced at us and grinned, then faced the demons and added, "six, preferably away from the Nosferatus. My friends have a problem watching them feed."

The demon's eyes changed from gray to red. "You cannot be in here. Take your friends and leave, before someone gets hurt."

"And guess who that someone will be. You or your minions." Bran turned his head and surveyed the customers seated to our left then those on the right before adding, "or them. Tell my brother we are here." He nudged the demon out of his way and the other two stepped aside. He waited for us to walk past him, then he joined Remy in the rear. "We'll start with some drinks, please."

We headed to the bar, a heavy silence falling over the restaurant. Bran was spoiling for a fight. From the smirks on Sykes and Remy's face, they were feeling exactly like him.

The customers around the bar abandoned their stools when they saw us coming, even though only four of us sat. Sykes and I flanked Kim and Izzy. Remy and Bran remained standing, and faced the assistant manager and his bouncers. We watched the room through the mirror behind the bar, our bodies tense, eyes not missing a thing.

We were not wanted here. Hatred twisted their faces and flowed to me.

"Your brother is not here," Mr. Assistant Manager said between clenched teeth. "He's on Mount Hermon."

Mount Hermon? The cluster of mountains in the Golan Heights in the Middle East? When the Principalities rebelled against their directive to guard humans and chose to marry human women instead, they met on Mount Hermon. Was it really the same one?

"Then we'll wait while you send for him. May we see the menu now?" Bran asked, his voice carrying in the quiet room.

"I don't know where Mount Hermon is located," the assistant manager snapped. "He told me he was headed there a week ago."

We looked at each other. Gavyn hadn't been seen in a week and we first saw the lightning demon a week ago.

"Find him," Bran ordered.

The assistant manager dismissed his minions with a flicker of his fingers.

"Hey," a female shouted, drawing our attention to the left side of the room. "You have some nerve showing your faces here in our club after you kidnapped our brothers and sisters."

"We haven't kidnapped anyone," Bran called back. "We haven't even bothered you for months. You should be thanking us."

The female hissed, a row of teeth like a shark's elongating from her gums. Her male companion gripped her arm as though to calm her down, then he said, "Her sister disappeared last week. Who else could have taken her except your people?"

Bran shrugged. "She must have done something really bad to be dispatched to Tartarus. Unfortunately, it wasn't by *us*."

"She's not in Tartarus," the female retorted, the shark teeth sinking back into her gums. Her voice shook, then she added, "I'd know."

Bran frowned. "How?"

"We are twins and I've been able to feel what she feels since we were children. She's alive. What do you want with her?"

We glanced at each other.

"Sorry, we can't help you there, lady," Bran said with indifference. "We didn't touch her. Now if you'll excuse us. We'd like to eat lunch in peace."

"You won't be served until we get some answers," a male voice snarled and slowly got to his feet. Dressed in an expensive suit, his eyebrows connected above the bridge of his nose. His lunch partners got up too, and the four of them left their table and closed in on us. "My two sons were taken two days ago from their apartment."

"My neighbors' daughter is missing too," his buddy on the right added.

"There will be no fighting in here," the assistant manager yelled. "You know the rules."

"To Tartarus with the rules. They are kidnapping our children for some secret agenda and we are supposed to let them?" Uni-brow lashed out in an angry voice. He jabbed a hand in the direction of the assistant manager. "And now you let them walk in here like they own the place."

"I didn't," the assistant manager protested. "They just appeared."

"Why would we kidnap your people?" Bran asked.

"To turn them into Guardians the way they turned you," Uni-brow added.

"No one turned me," Bran snapped. "I chose to be a Guardian."

"Then you are a traitor," Uni-brow yelled.

"Traitor," his buddies echoed.

The room erupted as more voices joined them. A prickly feeling of imminent danger shot up my spine and I whipped around to see a knife sailing toward me. I froze as it inched closer and closer as though someone had slowed down time. It stopped a few inches from my face. The room grew silent, eyes on me and the knife. Then Izzy appeared beside me.

You okay? she asked

She had just saved my life by stopping time. Unlike humans and inanimate objects, Nephilim didn't freeze when time stopped.

No, but thank you. I reached out and gripped the handle. There was a collective gasp around the room as though I'd done the unthinkable. It was beautifully crafted, the black blade gleaming under the artificial light, the handle curved perfectly for a small hand. A woman's weapon. I'd never held a demon's blade before. A strange energy vibe came from it.

The thing about my heightened senses was I didn't just feel others' emotions, I could separate them. There was so much hatred toward us in the room, but mingled with it were guilt and fear. I weeded through the emotions until I locked onto the guilty party—three of them—father, mother and son. My gaze locked with the boy's. He looked young, probably early teens, maybe a tween. His mother gripped his arm as though to keep him in his seat.

The father stood. "I threw the knife."

"No, you didn't," I said, speaking slowly. My hand tingled. The ancient writings appeared around my wrist and the back of my hand. The lettering was faint, but whatever power that accompanied them was strong enough to ignite the knife. I opened my hand and let go of the flaming knife. By the time it reached the floor, there was nothing left but a pile of ashes. "Your son did."

"I will take his place and fight you," the father said, starting toward me while the son struggled against his mother's grip.

"No. I don't want to fight you. We are here on personal business. Like my friend said, we *have* not taken your friends and relatives, and fighting us will not bring them back. When we finish our business here, we'll leave. Oh, good luck finding your missing friends and family."

The demon didn't mask his surprise. Slowly, he moved back to his chair and sat. Murmurs rippled across the room. Even demons seated on the balcony moved inside and inched closer.

"What business could you possibly have with one of us?" someone asked.

"We are looking for the Summoners," I said.

The murmuring stopped.

"We know that some of you summoned the Tribe, malevolent minions who love to hide inside clouds and play with lightning, break rules and hurt humans," I added.

Two things happened simultaneously—there was mass teleporting from the restaurant and thuds came from behind me. I turned and blinked. Bran, Remy, and Sykes were fighting Uni-brow and his men. They weren't using their weapons, just open-hand strikes and well-aimed kicks guaranteed to cause maximum pain.

The assistant manager, sprawled on one of the chairs, watched them with a defeated expression on his face as they broke tables, plates and glass, spilled leftover food and spilled drinks.

"I guess no one wants to discuss the Summoners or the Tribe," Izzy said.

"I guess not. You think they'd want to gloat. Demons can be so weird sometimes. Should we help them?" I asked, nodding at the guys.

"No, they're having fun," Kim said.

"How did you ignite the dagger?" Izzy asked.

"I don't know. It just happened." I checked my palm and the back of my hand. The writings were gone. I winced when Uni-brow landed a blow on Bran's chin. He staggered backward, recovered and went after the demon with a kick, followed by a well-placed jab between his neck and shoulder. The demon dropped to his knees.

"We might as well get something to drink while we wait for them to finish," Kim said and teleported behind the bar. She got three glasses, made eye contact with the assistant manager and added a fourth one.

A groan drew my attention back to the fighters. They all had bruises on their faces, more on the demons than our guys. Bran was so caught up in the moment he'd forgotten I could feel his pain. Two more minutes was all I would give them, then I was stopping the fight. It was one thing to let out steam and quite another to pound each other into pulp.

"Here you go," Kim said.

I accepted the red liquid in a wine glass with a lemon wedge on the edge. "What is it?"

"Cranberry juice for you and something else for us." She took a sip of her drink and looked at the assistant manager, who had moved to the bar. "So, do you have a name, Mr. Assistant Manager?"

Kim grilled the demon about the Summoners and the Tribe, threatening him with instant decapitation if he lied. When she realized he was clueless, she changed the subject to managing a restaurant. I shook my head. Kim was a class act.

The guys staggered to the bar, bruises and broad grins on their faces. The demons teleported one by one while Kim passed out drinks. I touched a cut on Bran's forehead and froze when the cut just closed up and healed without leaving a mark or redness. I looked at my hand and frowned. The writings weren't there, yet I'd just healed him.

"You okay?" he asked, peering at me.

I opened my mouth to tell him about the markings and what just happened, then decided against it. "Yeah. You?"

"I feel great." He glanced at Sykes and Remy. "Guys?"

Remy stopped dabbing a cut on his lip and grinned, his eyes going to Kim. I'd noticed the way his eyes kept straying to her when we were at his place. She, on the other hand, seemed oblivious. Could he be into her? Sykes stuck up his thumbs, his knuckles red, showing off as usual.

"Liars," Izzy retorted. "You look like something Tartarus spit out. Do you want me to take care of your wounds or what?"

"We'll be fine," Remy said. Sykes nodded.

Bran was busy fingering his forehead as though he just realized I had healed him. He caught my gaze and cocked his right brow. *Did you…?*

Don't ask, I shot back.

His expression said he intended to discuss it later. "Anyone hungry?" he asked.

Everyone nodded.

"But not the food from here." Kim exchanged a knowing look with Izzy. "Let's go to Kieran's."

"Again?" Remy asked and scowled.

"It's the only place you can walk in looking like a road kill and get a hero's welcome," Izzy said.

"And waitresses inspecting our battle wounds," Sykes added with a grin then tried to bump fists with Remy. Remy glared at him. I had no idea where Kieran's was, but it sounded like a Guardian restaurant, which shouldn't bother Remy. What was his problem?

"Kieran's it is," Bran said then glanced at the assistant manager. "Tell my brother we're looking for him. We'll be back."

- 8 -

A NEW ORDER

We materialized inside a large office, where a Guardian was hunched over a computer while telekinetically pounding on the keyboard. On the screen, two warriors dueled with swords, a Werenephil and the other, going by the halo above his head and the self-righteous smirk on his face, an archangel.

He's Keiran, Bran telepathed me, then added aloud, "You know the real thing is nothing like that," Bran said mockingly.

The Guardian lifted his middle finger, then he rotated his chair around and studied us with a lopsided grin. "Cardinals, nice of you to drop by looking so…presentable."

"Just open the damn door, Keiran," Bran said testily.

Keiran ignored him. Tall and slender, Keiran had a dimpled chin, chiseled features and wavy brown hair with highlights. Alchemy Gothic earrings looped around his ears and a silver full-finger armor ring gleamed on one of his fingers. But his most striking features were his eyes. They were a deep shade of violet. They twinkled as his gaze swept us and zeroed in on Kim, a slow smile curling his lips.

Kim blushed.

Interesting. I'd never seen Kim blush before.

His smile deepened as though her blush pleased him, then he got to his feet, waved and a door appeared on the wall beside his computer desk. Bran, Remy, and Sykes made a beeline for it. "I'll start charging."

"You already do," Bran said. "Your food is outrageously expensive."

"That's because it's the best in town." He turned and smiled, his gaze locking with Kim's again. "What is it going to be? Something heavy or light?"

She smiled. "We had lunch in Bermuda earlier."

"Light it is. The usual Lil…Izzy?"

Izzy nodded, and so did I, even though I had no idea what my usual was.

"I'll see to it." He teleported to the door, opened it and winked at Kim. "You want to sample something new? I know you like variety and I saved something just for you."

Kim sashayed to where he stood by the door and whispered as she brushed past him, “And here I thought you couldn’t surprise me anymore.”

As the door closed behind them, I turned and faced Izzy. “Is Kim…?”

“Dating him?” Izzy finished. “Oh yeah. I thought it was the excitement of a forbidden love, but I think she might actually be in love. Don’t tell the guys though. It’s supposed to be a secret.”

“Why? They wouldn’t care.”

“Her family would if they found out. He’s a member of the Brotherhood, hardly what her family considers ‘suitable’. Her parents want to choose a mate for her.” Izzy rolled her eyes.

“That’s so archaic and…” my voice trailed off when her glance shifted to the guys as they re-entered the room. They were blood-free, the cuts on their faces and knuckles already healing but still visible.

“Are we eating in here or out there?” Izzy asked.

“Out there,” Sykes said, cutting across the room. “I’m starving.”

Remy and Izzy followed him.

“We’ll catch up,” Bran called out and walked to where I stood. He pushed his hair away from his face.

I touched the bruise on his lower lip. It closed up nicely. Funny, I was used to being awed by Izzy as she healed us, yet because of my new, temporary powers, I could do it too.

Bran touched his lip and smiled. “How’s your head?”

“Not so bad.”

He cupped my face and studied my face as though searching for something.

“Don’t do that, please,” I whispered.

He cocked his right eyebrow. “Do what?”

“Look at me like I’m, you know, different.” Then a thought occurred to me and I reached up to touch my forehead and hair. “I *am* the same, right? No horns or weird things growing out of my head?”

He chuckled and pressed his forehead against mine. “Of course you are the same…physically. Your psi energy is off the charts. I can take care of the headache if you like.”

Doing it once was enough. “No, I’ll be fine. The writings appeared on my hand when I touched that boy’s knife.”

He checked my hands to see if they were back. “So that’s why it caught fire. Master Haziel was right.”

I made a face. “It’s kind of scary not knowing what they can do.”

Bran gripped them and pressed them against his lips. “We’ll deal with them as they come,” he whispered. “Come on, I’ll escort you to the others.”

We walked down a broad hallway toward double doors. Before we reached them, they swung open and Kieran walked out. He was alone.

"You are at your usual table," he said. "Cook has his orders, so the food should be there soon."

Bran stopped. "Are you very busy?"

Keiran gave him a lopsided grin. "That depends on what you want, Llyr. I'm on level eighty-two of a new game."

You bragged it was faster than the humans' best system and that you have programs that can get you in and out of places undetected."

Keiran chuckled. "What I have are mad skills, Llyr. And yes, it will take humans a decade to catch up. What do you want help with?"

"I'll explain when I come back. Right now, I need to show Lil where the others are seated." He pushed the double doors but Kieran spoke.

"Just one second." I thought Keiran would ask why I needed to be shown to our regular table, but all he said was, "Tell your friends to stop hitting on my girls. I'm tired of mediating fights every few weeks because they keep flirting with them."

Bran laughed. "Sure, but do you really want to get between them and women?"

Keiran's expression became thoughtful then he made a face. "I guess not. Who am I to kill some girl's dream of mating with a Guardian? Not that you guys have anything we don't have."

"Uh, we travel in style," Bran said. "We have a license to kill and we make black look good." Bran stared pointedly at Keiran's pants, matching shirt, and studded boots.

Keiran rolled his eyes. "I was rocking this look way before you were born, Llyr, so don't even go there. Your favorite dish is coming up, Lil. Extra cheese?" He touched his brow in a salute and turned.

"Yes. Thanks, Keiran," I said. Bran groaned. *What?*

Do you even know what he's talking about? he asked as we cut through the busy kitchen.

No. What is my favorite dish?

He laughed. *You'll find out soon enough.*

"So? What do you want with his computer? You once told me you had no need for modern technology because you keep everything in here." I tapped his head.

"You don't remember our *pactus,* but you do the day I was being a jackass."

"I know I said I didn't want to mind-blend, but that's one memory I want back."

"We can mind-blend when we get home. As for Kieran's computer, I want to track down Gavyn and to do that I have to find Mount Hermon."

We entered the main floor of the restaurant, which was L-shaped, and wove our way past booths and couples lost in their little worlds. With the menu from clairvoyant crystals, floating drinks and beautiful décor, it looked like Gavyn's restaurant, except it was spacious and hatred-free.

Bran led me past a set of doors and onto the balcony. The view of downtown L.A. was spectacular, but my eyes were drawn to Kim, Izzy, Sykes, and Remy. They were having a heated discussion at a corner table. Six glasses of water with bobbing chunks of ice sat untouched before them.

"No, no, the senior Cardinals must know what's going on because the Tribe has been going after Damned Humans since last week," Kim said as we got closer.

"You can't know that," Izzy protested. "You think the worst of them all the time."

"Are you listening to yourself? Fact, ever since we started hunting, they've hidden things from us. Case in point," she jerked her head toward me, "they knew about Valafar's existence and never told Lil. When Bran's feathers started to fall, they never told us. They've known about the Tribe since last week, maybe even longer, but once again, they…never…told us. They keep treating us like children," Kim added through gritted teeth. "We face demons every day, just like them. We should demand equal access to information."

"On with the revolution," Sykes said, waving an imaginary flag. "Downtrodden junior Cardinals demand equal access to intel and a pay raise."

"Pay raise?" Izzy asked.

Sykes shrugged. "I need a new car, preferably a new model of—"

"The Mustang you totaled last year," Izzy cut him off and shook her head. "We know. You've been singing about it the entire summer. Your obsession with fast cars is senseless. Now if you don't have anything to contribute to the discussion…"

"Lil made a demonic weapon catch fire and spooked an entire restaurant of demons," Sykes said then spread his arms to indicate the table. "Discuss."

All eyes turned in my direction. I kicked him under the table.

"Ouch!" He glared at me, then spoiled it by smirking.

"I'll be in Keiran's office," Bran said and squeezed my shoulder.

"Why?" Remy asked before Bran could leave.

"Keiran is going to help me find Mount Hermon, which could lead us to Gavyn and the Summoners. I'll fill you in when I get back." Another gentle squeeze of my shoulder and he added telepathically, *if that headache is still bothering you when I come back, I'll take care of it.*

"You still have the headache," Remy asked after Bran left.

"It's nothing," I mumbled, picked up a glass of water, took a sip, and pressed the cool glass against my throbbing temple.

Remy frowned, "How bad is it?"

I shrugged, hating that everyone's attention was on me and that I could once again hear their thoughts. "It comes and goes, and 'going home so I can rest', as some of you are thinking, will not make it go away."

"Are your powers on and off, too? Is that why you didn't stop the knife when that child tried to kill you?" Izzy asked.

"See? I knew we'd come back to the knife," Sykes said, smirking. "Glare at me all you want, Lil, but something is happening to you. You've held demonic weapons before and never destroyed them. And your eyes glowed like they did when you fainted on the island. *And* you healed the cut on Bran's brow with just a touch."

"She did?" Izzy asked.

Did he spend time watching my every movement? "What else can you do?" he added and leaned forward. The others leaned forward, too.

I sighed and put my glass down. "I don't know. My powers and new abilities come and go." I covered Sykes' hand with one of mine and waited. When I lifted my hand, the red bruises on his knuckles were still there. "See? I can't do it now. The writings from the Kris appeared on my hand just before the knife went poof. I healed Bran afterwards, but there were no ancient writings on my skin then. They must come out when I'm in danger."

"Should we test that theory?" Kim pulled out a dagger from inside her boot.

"I think she meant danger from a demon." Remy glanced at the Brotherhood men and women at the nearby tables, then added, "Let's talk about something else."

"Like what?" Izzy asked but her gaze was on my hands, as if staring at them would force the markings to appear. "This is much more interesting. It's like having a human Kris Dagger."

"Lil the lethal weapon," Sykes added.

I winced at the word "weapon". My gaze connected with Remy's. He was scowling.

"Seriously, guys," he warned sharply. "Change the subject."

The others didn't mask their surprise at his sharpness.

"Okay, let's talk about Bran's brother," Kim said, "And how I'd like to send him to Tartarus piece by piece."

"Brutal," Sykes said, smirking.

"Don't you want to see him suffer?" Kim asked.

I tuned them out as they discussed everything they hated about Gavyn Llyr. Finally I couldn't take it anymore. Gavyn was Bran's brother, and whether he should be sent to Tartarus or not depended on Bran.

"You know there's no proof he helped summon the Tribe," I said when there was a pause in their rant. "We can't just jump on the bandwagon because Bran thinks he's guilty."

"Why are you giving that fiend the benefit of doubt?" Sykes asked. "He's never done anything to deserve it. Come to think of it, Valafar would not have known of your existence if it weren't for Gavyn."

"I don't understand why Bran keeps hoping he would change," Kim added.

"Gavyn wasn't always evil," I said.

Sykes faked shock. "You mean he wasn't born with a trident, horns and a red skin?"

I laughed. "Before his father tried to escape with them from Coronis Isle, Gavyn was your typical big brother. He watched out for Bran and Celeste. In fact, he was the family jokester. Their mother hated being mated with a Guardian and took it out on them." I explained everything Bran had told me about their upbringing, then the attempt to escape with their father and what happened afterward. "Their mother torched the Guardian amulet Bran wore and tortured them for weeks."

"You mean the scar…" Izzy touched her chest.

I nodded. "You asked about it before, but I couldn't say anything because you guys weren't exactly crazy about him joining the Guardians, but things are different now. He's one of us."

"What did the mother do?" Remy cut in.

"She kept Bran in a shack somewhere in the forest and made sure he couldn't self-heal, so that the burn scarred." I'd never forget Bran's pain when he'd narrated the story. "Celeste found him, sneaked him food and nursed him. Gavyn wasn't so lucky. Their mother and her guards kept him somewhere underground and tortured him. Before, he had black hair like Celeste and Bran. When they finished with him, it was all white."

There was silence.

"He became a carbon copy of his mother after they finished with him," I continued. "Cold and ruthless. Bran sees the brother he once was, not the soulless jerk he's become. That's why he will do everything in his power to help him."

"Poor Bran and Celeste," Izzy said.

"I'll try to be nicer to her from now on," Kim added.

"As long as you don't feel sorry for Gavyn too," Remy said in a hard voice. "He's had a chance to change and chose not to."

Keiran appeared beside our table, a weird expression on his face.

"Where's the chow, man?" Sykes asked.

"Food will have to wait. There's a situation in my office that needs your attention."

We exchanged glances and pushed back our chairs to get back. I did a psi scan. There was a demon with Bran, his psi energy familiar.

"What situation?" Remy asked.

"Just follow me," Keiran said.

Remy grabbed his arm before he could teleport. "Not that we don't trust you or anything, but—"

"You're acting like it." Keiran yanked his arm from Remy's grip.

"When it comes to Cardinal business, we have a response protocol." He glanced at me. "Psi scanned the office yet?"

"Already did. Bran is not in any danger," I answered, feeling bad for Keiran. He didn't understand we didn't rush into situations in case of an ambush. "He's with a demon. Someone with familiar psi energy."

"Gavyn," someone murmured.

Our weapons were drawn when we materialized inside Keiran's office. But instead of Gavyn's lithe body and silver hair, a tall black guy with diamond studs glistening in his ears stood in the middle of the room. His eyes narrowed on our weapons.

"Is this the welcome we get after braving Keiran's overzealous guards to reach you?" Dante asked in an annoyed voice.

"You didn't hurt them, did you?" Kim asked.

"Of course not." Dante sounded insulted. "We compelled them to go to sleep. Kael is keeping an eye on me, just in case." He bowed toward me and touched his chest. "Lilith. It's nice to see you again."

Memories of everything he'd done for us after my father kidnapped us rushed through my head. They seemed so fresh, like they happened yesterday. Deciding to give him a hug, I pushed my dagger in its sheath and moved toward him.

"Where have you been?" I asked, hoping we hadn't seen him for a while.

"Here and there, trying to make a liv—" Dante doubled over as I got closer.

"Are you okay?" I asked, touching his arm.

Dante hissed and yanked his arm away from my hand. He staggered backward, putting as much distance between us as he could, his face wreathed with pain. He clutched his arm where I'd just touched.

Kael materialized beside him. "What is it?"

"It's nothing," Dante insisted, his eyes not leaving mine.

Kael's eyes narrowed. "What's going on?"

For a moment I was confused, then everything fell into place. My gaze flew to my hand. The ancient writings covered the back of my hand. I pulled back my sleeve. The writings snaked up my arm like tattoos. Horrified, I checked my other arm.

My gaze collided with Dante's as Bran pulled me away. "I'm so sorry."

"It's not your fault," Bran insisted.

"What did you do?" Kael demanded.

I shook my head, feeling terrible and helpless. "I'd never knowingly hurt Dante, Kael. You know that. I was going to hug him but…but…I guess I can't."

Bran's arms tightened around me. The silence in the room stretched.

"Can someone explain to us what is wrong with Lilith?" Kael demanded.

"Excuse us, Kieran?" Remy asked.

Keiran hesitated. "My guards?"

"We'll awaken them before we leave," Kael said impatiently.

Remy didn't speak until Keiran teleported from the room. "Lil was attacked by demons."

"Who?" Dante asked, sounding outraged.

"When and where?" Kael added.

"A few hours ago," Remy said. "Do you know anything about demons that hide inside a cloud and shoot lightning bolts, shatter glass but leave everything else intact?"

Dante shook his head. "Shatter glass? Banshees can use sound to break glass, but they are all in Tartarus. At least the ones we knew existed were sent there by Coronis. Did Banshees attack Lilith?"

"We don't know, but the demons use sounds and get inside your head and mess with your memories." Remy paused long enough to telepath us. *Do we tell them everything?*

Yes, we all agreed.

We're going to need all the help we can get, Bran added.

Just don't mention the island by name, Izzy chimed in.

Of course not. "We were relaxing on an island when the demons attacked," Remy said then went on to explain my memory loss and Master Haziel's theory that the powers of the dagger had been transferred to me. "We didn't believe him, but her powers are now tied to the ancient writings on her skin, which are similar to the ones that used to be on the dagger's blade."

Kael and Dante studied my hands, which I lifted for them to see without getting too close. The writings were still there, which meant my body considered Dante and Kael as threats even though they weren't. Shouldn't I be able to control these powers and how they reacted?

"I'll learn to control them," I vowed. "What happened when I touched you?"

Dante shook his head. "It doesn't matter, but now I understand how you destroyed the knife at the Club."

"How do you know about what happened at the restaurant?" Remy asked.

"Word spreads fast where she is concerned," Kael answered.

"The customers said you were looking for a fight when you arrived," Dante added.

"We were looking for Gavyn, not a fight," Bran corrected him. "You don't happen to know the location of Mount Hermon, do you?"

Dante frowned and exchanged a glance with Kael, then they both shook their heads. "No, but we can find out," Dante said. "You think your brother is hanging out with these demons?"

"We think he summoned them," Bran explained.

Dante frowned. "Why would he do that?"

This time Bran explained his theory about what happened to the humans. "We have no idea how two of them managed to survive. One is a woman with children, so we assumed the demons either felt sorry for her or decided to punish her by making all her children ill."

"Demons don't show mercy," Dante said.

"Really?" Sykes asked, then he pressed a fist against his chest, imitating the gesture Dante and Kael often made whenever we met. "I always thought you two were the picture of gallantry."

Dante ignored him. "I have not heard of a demon capable of doing what you just described."

"What if the Tribe is a breed of demons from somewhere else?" I asked.

Dante's eyes narrowed. "The Tribe?"

"We think that is their name—the Tribe. What if they were summoned from, say, Tartarus?"

Telepathic communication between Dante and Kael happened so fast all I caught was 'Summoners' and 'no way', then silence.

"If you know something, tell us, please," I cut in, my eyes moving back and forth between the two nature-benders.

Dante's expression grew thoughtful as though he was debating how much to tell us. When he spoke, he did slowly. "It is possible to summon powerful beings into this world, but it's never been done in my lifetime. It takes special circumstances to do it and the consequences are never pleasant. Hermonites and Guardians have a system in place that keeps the balance between good and evil. Bringing in more powerful beings could tip that balance, so summoning is very rare."

"Besides," Kael added, "summoned demons don't look anything like us. They come back with rotting flesh and stink."

I heard their words, but I focused on what they weren't saying. "You know about the Tribe."

"We knew something was going after your humans and tried to get in touch with you last week, but whenever we responded to Guardian energies, we always found the senior Cardinals." Dante's glance swept us. "From the aggressive way they went after your humans, I think the Order might be involved."

"The Order?" Sykes asked.

"The new Hermonite High Council," Dante explained.

"It's made up of representatives from each house," Kael added.

Someone cursed. I reeled with shock. The demons had planned to select a new ruler during the mortal combat battle on Jarvis, but we'd foiled their plans when Bran won. Obviously the crafty demons had found a way to come together after all.

"Who's their leader?" Remy asked.

"What makes you think they're involved?" Bran asked at the same time.

"We don't know their leader because we're out of the loop since…" Dante glanced at me then away. I had a feeling he meant to say since my father was defeated. "But the council has been holding secret meetings since the combat on Jarvis Island. Like clockwork, they met every Friday night until a week ago. Something happened to stop them from meeting. The day after, young Hermonites began to disappear from their homes. No one knows why. At the same time, your humans were being targeted. That kind of efficiency means a lot of demons working together under a single directive."

"The ones at the restaurant believed we were behind the kidnapping," I said. "How do you know so much when you are out of the loop?"

Dante shrugged.

Bran chuckled. "You have someone on the inside."

Dante didn't deny it, but neither did he admit it. Instead, he bowed toward me again. "We will contact you once we get more information on the Tribe and Mount Hermon."

"May I see, uh, your arm?" I asked before they could leave.

Dante looked ready to argue, then he pulled back the sleeve of his coat. He had a nasty burn on his skin. Kael scowled.

"Can you self-heal or do you have someone to heal it?" I asked.

"I do. I'll be in touch." He bowed briefly.

"What if I want to contact you?" I asked before he could teleport.

He hesitated, his eyes narrowed. I was tempted to telepath him that I knew he and Kael had lied to us. They knew more than they'd told us about the Tribe, but with my crazy powers, I could hurt him worse than I already had.

"Use your powers and we'll find you," he said then dematerialized.

"Now that we have those two in our corner once again, let's eat." Sykes patted his stomach and started for the door.

"I don't know if they're really 'in our corner' as you put it, Sykes," I said. "They know more about the Tribe than they told us and what they know scares them."

Sykes groaned. "Damn. Now you've ruined my appetite."

- 9 -

THE CONFERENCE

Mrs. D was waiting for us when we arrived at HQ, her glasses dangling on the tip of her narrow nose.

"Where have you been?" she demanded, eyes slitting like a cat's. "We've been trying to contact you for hours. "Return your weapons and head straight to the conference room."

"What's going on, Mrs. D?" Izzy asked.

"Ask the Cardinals. Don't keep them waiting," she snapped.

We looked at each other. No one spoke, but we were thinking the same thing—we were finally going to get some answers.

Inside the conference room, the senior Cardinals sat at one end of the large circular table, their expressions unreadable. My grandfather, the Cardinal Psi Guardian, waved us toward the empty chairs. He wore his "leader of the Cardinals" face, not the indulgent, loving Grampa I saw around our house. Like the other Cardinals, he wasn't dressed for hunting, which was strange. He studied me intently as though searching for something. I gave him a brief smile, which he didn't return. Not a good sign.

"How long have you had that headache, Lil?" he asked in a soft voice, though the vibes from him indicated he was angry.

"Since the attack on the island."

"Yet you still left the valley?"

Confused, I glanced at my friends. They wore bewildered expressions, too. "Master Haziel said it was okay."

"Is he also the one who said you could take the dagger instead of leaving it behind to be examined?" Grampa barked.

"Yes. Didn't he explain?"

"He is not here to explain anything, but I'm sure he gave you a reasonable explanation for allowing all of you to leave the valley after an attack and with a dagger that is practically useless." He pinned me with a glare.

I made a face and glanced at the others. All the junior Cardinals looked down without speaking. Bran was the only one staring at Grampa as though he'd lost his mind. This wasn't what we'd expected. I couldn't tell them Master Haziel hadn't approved of the way they'd kept the secret about the Tribe from us.

"You have nothing to say? Could it be that the decision to leave the valley didn't really come from Master Haziel?"

"That is correct, Cardinal," Bran said, leaning forward. "Master Haziel didn't suggest it. I did, and he supported my decision. I thought seeing Mrs. Watts might trigger Lil's memories, especially after some words we'd mentioned caused her to remember a few things."

"Did it?" Cardinal Seth asked sharply, speaking for the first time.

Bran shook his head. "No, but we learned something else while in L.A. Demons visited Mrs. Watts, wiped her memories just like the ones that attacked us wiped Lil's. Even though they also made all her children ill, we thought we might be dealing with the same demons."

The Cardinals didn't look surprised, confirming our suspicions that they already knew about the attacks.

"Why didn't you come right back home once you realized the same demons were out there attacking humans?" Grampa asked.

Bran's eyes narrowed. "We had to confirm that the attack on Mrs. Watts wasn't an isolated incident. You told us to always confirm things before bringing them to your attention, Cardinals."

Grampa's eyes flashed. "That is beside the point. Lil had just been attacked, her memories wiped *and* she had no control over the Kris Dagger—"

"She could handle herself, Cardinal," Bran snapped.

"You do not tell me what *my* granddaughter can or cannot handle."

Bran sat back, hands fisted.

"You have no idea what's at stake here," Grampa continued, "the danger you put all of them in."

"That is not my fault, Cardinal," Bran shot back. "She would not have been attacked if we'd known what we were dealing with in the first place, how to fight them and protect ourselves. She should have been prepared. We all should have been prepared."

"No one can be prepared—" Grampa paused then added, "Where did she go?"

Until he asked the question, I hadn't realized I had dematerialized. I hovered near the ceiling, so angry I wanted to zap them both. It hurt to watch them tear each other apart because of me. Worse, they were fighting over something they couldn't change.

Lil, Bran ordered, looking directly at where I hovered as though he could see me. *Get back down now!*

Don't talk to me in that tone.

He sighed. *Please.*

No. I refuse to sit there while you two continue with your stupid and senseless fight.

"It is not senseless when you and your friends' safety are at stake," Grampa snapped.

He heard me? Of course, he could. He was a powerful Psi. *It's not Bran's fault, Grampa. He gave me a choice to either stay behind or go with them. I chose to go.*

"Where are you?" Grampa looked around the room, then he zeroed in on my location. "Since when can you control your movement in energized state?"

Since the Tribe's attack.

"The Tribe?"

The shock in his voice got me to return to my seat. Heads turned when I rematerialized but I ignored them and focused on Grampa. "Yes, the Tribe, Grampa, as in the demons who attacked us. We also know they were summoned by other demons you call the Summoners. We went searching for them."

Instead of surprise or anger, the feeling I got from the senior Cardinals was relief. Weird.

"Permission to speak, Cardinals?" Remy asked.

"You don't have to ask permission, young man," Cardinal Seth said sharply.

"The decision to go after the Summoners was not Master Haziel's or Bran's, Cardinals," Remy said, glancing at the seniors. "We all decided to go, so if you want to yell at someone, yell at all of us."

Sykes, Kim, and Izzy nodded.

"Now can we just be honest with each other?" I asked. "Not knowing what we are dealing with is scary. Seeing what they can do is even scarier."

Grampa opened his mouth to interrupt.

"Please, let me finish," I added. I glanced around at the faces around the oval table before stopping with Cardinal Moira. She might be the quietest of the senior Cardinals, but she had a way of making them stop acting like a bunch of dictators and listen to our opinions. She nodded, an encouraging smile lifting the corners of her lips. "I got lucky because of the Kris Dagger. If they'd attacked one of my friends, the effect would have been worse. We are on the same team and shouldn't keep secrets from each other. Oh, and Bran is right. Whatever is happening to me, the headache and the heightened powers, I can deal with them now that I know their cause."

"Their cause?" Grampa asked.

"Master Haziel said that the powers of the Kris Dagger were transferred to me. He said it was the dagger's way of protecting…" My voice trailed off when Grampa got up, an expression of utter horror on his face. "Me," I finished.

Cardinal Janelle gripped his arm and shook her head. She waited until Grampa sat down before she got up and moved to my side. "Show me your arms, *Luminitsa*."

I shrugged off the hunting trench coat and extended my arms. There were no writings on my skin. I glanced at Grampa to reassure him, but he was scowling so furiously. Aunt Janelle beckoned Cardinals Moira and Hsia, who pushed back their chairs and joined us.

"Turn around," Cardinal Janelle instructed.

After my meeting with Master Haziel, I knew what was coming and balked at being examined in front of the others like a freak. *No. Let's do this at home, Aunt Janelle. Please.*

Cardinal Janelle glanced at her friends, then they nodded and we teleported.

"Remove your top," one of them said as soon as we arrived in my bedroom.

My face hot, I pulled off my T-shirt and turned around. Someone touched my waist, then my middle and upper back. My embarrassment changed to puzzlement when cool air touched my neck as they lifted up my hair.

"Are they there?" I asked, turning my head to study their faces since I couldn't see anything.

"Yes, from your lower back to the base of your skull. See?" Cardinal Hsia gave me a portable mirror and turned me so my back faced the larger one on the dresser.

Markings dotted my back like tattoos, spreading along my waist, up my spine and disappearing under my hair. I lifted the hair out of the way. They actually looked pretty. Like some ritualistic markings I should be proud of instead of fear.

"Here you go, love," Cardinal Hsia said, handing me my T-shirt.

Cardinal Moira cupped my face and studied me intently. As usual, her hands were hot. "Do they hurt or tingle?"

"No, though I felt a slight tingle when they appeared on my hands."

She nodded. "That's good. You will be able to know when you are about to use them and therefore will learn to control them. It's not going to be easy, but you can do it."

"Master Haziel said the switch was temporary."

The Cardinals looked at each other again.

"Of course," Cardinal Janelle said. "Let's go back. Your grandfather will want to know we've confirmed it."

"Why was he horrified when I said the powers had moved from the dagger to me?"

The Cardinals exchanged glances again. I was beginning to hate their glances, especially since they weren't accompanied by thoughts I could listen to.

"Your grandfather loves you and worries when anyone, demon or otherwise, targets you," Cardinal Janelle explained. "He'll be fine once this mess with the Tribe is over."

Back in the conference room, my eyes sought Grampa's as soon as we materialized. He looked like he'd aged a century. Something about having the powers of the Kris Dagger inside me bothered him.

Master Haziel said it is only temporary, I telepathed him.

He smiled, but his eyes were sad. *Of course it is.*

"The marks appeared on her arms when someone tried to hurt her with an athame," Remy said, answering a question from one of the Cardinals. "She touched the blade and it caught fire. They appeared on her arms again when we met with Dante. He couldn't get close to her without feeling pain."

Cardinal Seth studied me thoughtfully. "So you reacted the way the Kris Dagger would react to a demonic energy."

I gave him a tiny smile. "Yes, but the power switch is only temporary. Master Haziel said so."

Cardinal Seth nodded, though I had a feeling he didn't agree with me. His focus shifted to Remy. "Did her powers ebb with her headache?"

Remy glanced at me. *Do you want to tell him?*

No. I didn't like the way they reacted whenever I insisted the power shift was temporary. Besides, Cardinal Seth often treated me like I was a child who needed to be told what to do. In my mood, I might make a snarky comment. I studied the other senior Cardinals instead. I couldn't shed the feeling that they were operating at a different level from us. They were keeping secrets and only talking to us to get information. They hadn't shared anything new.

"We visited a few more humans, whose contracts we'd canceled months ago," Remy said, answering another question. "Their stories were the same—they had no memories of ever seeing us and their fortunes were reversed. We don't know how widespread it is."

"It is worldwide," Cardinal Hsia said.

"Anything else you'd like to add?" Cardinal Seth asked impatiently, focusing on us.

"I think my brother might be one of the Summoners," Bran said.

"Why would you think that?" Grampa asked, not masking his shock.

Bran explained his theory then added, "I'd like a chance to find him and talk to him."

"Not now," Grampa said firmly.

"Can you at least tell us about the Tribe and how to fight them?" Bran asked.

"We've never dealt with them before, but Master Haziel suggested we find the demons who summoned them and reverse the summoning." Cardinal Janelle glanced at the other Cardinals, who nodded, then she continued, her expression earnest. "We spent the last week searching for them. When we heard rumors about the humans getting hurt, we went to investigate. Hsia treated some, but the majority of them were beyond help. However, it was too soon to conclude that the demon you encountered on the island and the one hurting humans was one and the same."

"Since we didn't meet any, we were beginning to doubt your account of what happened," Cardinal Seth added.

"After today, we believe you," Grampa said. "We owe you an apology, because their reappearance today confirms they are here and we must stop them."

They are here and you must stop them… the words echoed in my head.

"Say that again," I said urgently.

Grampa scowled. "Say what again?"

I rubbed my temple as I tried to grasp the elusive memory. "I've heard the words 'They are here and *you* must stop them' before. But they were spoken by a woman. Why am I getting snippets of conversations I'd never heard before, or are they from my lost memories?"

"Maybe your mind can provide us with some answers." Grampa stood and Bran gave him his seat. "Lil, you know that when we mind-blend, psi energies tend to mix."

I nodded. Earlier in the year, they'd refused to let Bran and me link, out of fear that his energy might contaminate mine.

"At times, memories and thoughts are left behind too," Grampa continued. "They could tell us the Tribe's plans. Also, if we find residual energy, we can feed that energy to the Psi-dar and try to locate their whereabouts."

Psi-dar was a pool of the purest form of psi energy that Civilian security teams used to monitor demonic energies around the globe. I heard the energy came from the residual auras of millions of Guardians who'd ascended. Being around the Psi-dar was like being in a room full of ghosts, smart ghosts all thinking together.

"Is it safe? I mean, what if I contaminate your energy? Remember, I couldn't link with Bran before because he could contaminate mine."

Grampa chuckled. "I've been doing this a lot longer than Bran, so I'll be okay. What's the last thing you remember?"

"Walking inside Valafar's booth on Jarvis Island," I explained.

"That was four months ago," Cardinal Janelle said, coming to stand behind me. She placed her hands on my shoulders and rubbed them reassuringly.

"Then we have a point of reference." Grampa cupped my face. His hands were clammy as though he was nervous, which didn't make sense. Grampa was invincible. I studied the others, hating the way they were watching me as if I had all the answers. "Look at me," he added.

I tensed.

"Relax," he said, his voice reassuring. "I'll be quick."

I only grew tenser. Some of my recent memories were very private. Would Grampa blame Bran for what almost happened in my bedroom this afternoon? Did it matter? A hand wrapped around mine. Bran.

Exhaling, tension leached out of me and I let Grampa take over. At first, I didn't feel a thing even though I knew the moment our energies overlapped. There was slight pressure in my head, but it quickly passed. After a few seconds of studying his calm expression, heat crawled up my face. He was seeing everything I'd done the last few hours, including how mean I was to Mrs. Watts and everything I'd said and done with Bran.

The pressure continued to build up on my temples and I forgot about being embarrassed. He was staying too long. My eyes watered as the pressure increased. I squeezed Bran's hand and was probably hurting him and whoever was holding my other hand. The pressure kept going up until my head felt like a nut between pliers' teeth.

Grandpa, I protested.

A few more seconds, he responded, his inner voice harsh.

My vision blurred. A dull throb radiated from my temples, slowly building momentum like a train taking off from a station. It grew in intensity, until I thought I'd go mad. A scream echoed in my head and mingled with the searing hot pain.

The pain stopped, leaving behind echoes of it and a buzzing sound. The pressure on my temples eased. Arms wrapped around me and pulled me against a warm chest. A blend of leather and pine scent filled my senses. Bran. I clung to him, my body shaking, tears racing down my face.

"Is she okay?" someone asked.

I strained to see through the white mist covering my eyes until I saw the faces of those around me. Their gazes kept volleying between me and something to my left. I followed their gaze and gulped. Grampa was a heap on the floor, his eyes closed, skin pasty white. Cardinal Janelle cradled his head and spoke softly to him.

I tore away from Bran's arms and ran to their side. "What happened, Aunt Janelle? Did I…hurt him?"

"He went deeper than he should have and stayed too long. Your mind did what it did to protect itself," she said reassuringly.

"Grampa." *Wake up, Grampa. Please.* This was my worst nightmare—hurting someone I loved. I touched his cheek, searched his psi energy. It was so weak. The Kris Dagger should replenish his energy. My hand flew to my waist for the Kris Dagger before I remembered that all its powers were transferred to me.

I pressed my hands on his chest. *Heal him.*

Nothing happened.

I clenched my teeth, my body shaking with fear. *Heal him, damn it!*

Nothing.

Tears filled my eyes. Maybe I was doing this the wrong way. Master Haziel always told me the strength of the dagger depended on the wielder—me. I was scared now, afraid of what I'd done. Fear weakened me, therefore weakening the powers of the dagger. I needed to find my source of strength.

Source of strength? Another familiar expression.

Closing my eyes, I let images of Grampa over the years flash through my head. Grampa cooking in the kitchen with Aunt Janelle, laughing at something I'd said, on stage at the Circus performing a trick, teaching me to sword fight, wiping my tears after I fell off a bike…

The more the images, the stronger I felt. The love I felt for him flooded my body. A tingle spread from my back to my hands. When I opened my eyes, everything was white, yet I knew everything would be okay. I pressed my hand against his chest again. *Heal him.*

Then Grampa's voice reached me. "I'm okay now, sweetheart."

"I know." I blinked and my vision cleared. My hands glowed like a thousand-watt bulb, green light shooting from my palms to Grampa's chest, the dark ancient writings stark against the glow that snaked up my arms. I clenched my fist and the writings ebbed as they disappeared under my skin. The light dimmed.

I got up, giving Grampa space. Color returned to his cheeks, but the silence in the room was eerie. Slowly, he stood too.

"I didn't mean to hurt you, Grampa. I would never do that."

He smiled and patted my cheek. "Of course not, sweetheart. I was desperate for answers and went deeper than I should have."

I searched his face. "What did you see?"

He shook his head, his hand gripping my wrist. "There's quite a bit of residual energy left, but it's unfamiliar. Tomorrow, I'd like you to link to the Psi-dar."

Lucky me. I hated that pool of ghost energies. "And the memories?"

"I heard a woman's voice though the words weren't clear. I stayed longer, hoping to understand her words. If you remember anything at all, however small, tell me or Bran. Now I want all of you to go home and rest." He glanced at the other senior Cardinals. "We have much to discuss and decisions to make."

If it weren't for my heightened senses picking up signals from him, I would have left without arguing. He was trying to get rid of us. "The woman you heard in my head, could she be the demon that attacked me?"

"I don't know, but I'm sure the Psi-dar will give us answers." I opened my mouth to ask another question, but stopped when he pinned me with a stern look. "We are not speculating about the identity of the owner of that voice, Lil. Now go home. You, too," he added, glancing at the rest of the junior Cardinals.

"Did they say we can't leave the valley?" Sykes asked as soon as we left HQ offices behind and headed toward the tunnels.

Remy chuckled. "Nope."

"Want to hook up with the waitresses?" Sykes asked. He walked backward, hazel eyes twinkling, the meeting in the conference room all but forgotten.

Remy shrugged and the two bumped fists.

"You had time to make dates in the middle of that mess in L.A.?" Izzy asked.

"Hey, no one is stopping you from ditching Rastiel and hooking up with someone now and then." Sykes wiggled his brow suggestively and pointed at his chest.

Izzy laughed. "In your dreams."

"You don't know what you're missing," Sykes added, smirking.

Bran chuckled. "You're losing your touch, Sykes."

"I'm just warming up." He interlocked his fingers and snapped his knuckles.

"Am I the only one who feels the Seniors gave us the runaround back in there?" I asked when we stopped by the tunnel leading to my house. "The Cardinals' behavior was weird."

"I think they have no idea what's going on," Bran cut in "Master Haziel is the one with the answers. We need to come up with a plan to make him talk to us. He's proven to be more cooperative that the seniors."

The others thought it was a brilliant idea. I just wanted to crawl in bed and sleep even though it was only four in the afternoon. "Master Haziel will only tell you what *he* thinks you should know. Nothing more and nothing else."

"You don't have to deal with him if you don't want to," Bran said.

"She must," Kim insisted. "He has a soft spot for her."

"He doesn't," I protested. "He yells at me the most. I'm definitely in. Are you guys really sneaking out tonight?"

"Maybe," Remy said.

"Yes," Sykes corrected him.

Telling them not to go would be like waving a red flag at a bull. "Be careful. If you haven't noticed, the Tribe only appears when *we* are out there."

"We'll be fine," Sykes said confidently.

"Watch your backs," Izzy warned them, then she and Kim teleported.

I shook my head as Remy and Sykes headed toward their house. "They are so reckless."

Bran chuckled, taking my hand. "Sykes is. Remy just goes along to make sure Sykes doesn't do something stupid."

No surprise there. Sykes tended to break rules with no thoughts of consequences. Yawning, I sighed. "What did we do last week when we were on lockdown?"

"We hung out and practiced. Kylie stopped by a few times. Come on. I've been saving something special for your birthday, which drove you nuts because you wanted to see it so badly," he grinned, dimples flashing, "but I think you should see it now."

I hated reminders of my lost memories, but surprises from him were always fun. They usually involved teleporting somewhere, though I doubted that would be the case this time with lockdown and all. "What is it?"

He rolled his eyes then pulled me back into his arms. "Always impatient."

"Okay, where to?"

"My room."

"Oh. I like it already."

He chuckled. "It's not what you're thinking."

I blushed, though I refused to be embarrassed for loving him and wanting to spend time alone with him. We dematerialized and reappeared in his room. The house was quiet without Celeste. The seniors had never said when the students would come back from Xenith.

Bran's room looked more lived-in than I recalled. The iPod on a docking station and the laptop were new, as was an armchair and the rug on the floor. Two canvases were flipped to face the wall. Near the window sat a table with pencils and sketch pads. I knew he sketched, but he'd never shown me any of his work.

Or maybe he had and I'd forgotten. The urge to cry washed over me.

"You are worrying again," he whispered against my temple.

"No, I'm not."

He leaned back and studied my face. "Yes, you are."

The urge to cry increased. "I'm trying not to, but I hate that everything is different and new because of my messed-up memories. My room. Your room. Keiran is a stranger to me when he shouldn't be. Dante can't come close to me without getting hurt."

"Then mind-blend with me and relive the last four months."

Stepping away from him, I shook my head. "No. Not after what happened to Grampa. I could hurt you too, or worse."

"There's a difference. He was searching for—"

"No, I won't do it," I insisted.

"Fine. It's okay." He pulled me in his arms again until I calmed down, then took my coat and threw it on the bed. "Sit. I'll get us something to drink. Don't move or touch anything."

I scooted against the headboard and curled my legs under me. It was hard to get over how different his room was. I picked up his iPod and browsed through his music library. Classic rock, some heavy metal, alternative rock. I smiled when I saw some of my favorites.

"Didn't I say not to touch anything?" he scolded.

I wrinkled my nose, took the can of cream soda from his hand and put it down. I looked at him with anticipating. "I'm ready for my surprise."

"So am I." He rubbed his hands as he walked backward to the first canvas and slowly turned around with it.

It was a painting of the sunset from Haleakala in Maui, our special spot in Hawaii. I hopped off the bed and went to kneel in front of the painting. The colors were vibrant. He'd even included the rock he and I had sat on, except it had our initials and a heart.

"Did we do that?" I whispered.

"You did."

I traced the initials, remembering our vow to always meet on that mountain if something catastrophic happened and we were separated. How many times had we visited it since that first day?

I blinked back a sudden rush of tears and glanced up at him. He was such a gifted artist. "Thank you. It's beautiful."

"You think so? I thought I could add more color here," he pointed at a section of the sky, "and make the clouds fuller here."

"It's perfect." How could it not be? He'd painted it. For me. I stood, took the painting from his hand and propped it against the wall. But when I turned around, he was holding the second canvas—a painting of me. A breathtaking me. A perfect me.

I wore a Gypsy skirt and top, charm bracelets and anklets, and my feet were bare. I didn't recognize the beach, but the radiant smile on my face said I was happy and in love. He'd caught my slightly slanted green eyes, made my skin more flawless, my chest…bigger. I think. I looked down, then back at the painting. I guess his perception mattered more than mine, and my hair had never been that beautiful.

"Is that how you see me?" I whispered.

He put the painting aside and smiled, closing the gap between us. "No. That is who you are." He ran his knuckles down the side of my face. "Beautiful," he murmured against my temple, then moved lower and pressed his lips near my ear and whispered, "Smart." He moved lower and nuzzled my neck. "Impossible." His breath was hot against my skin, sending a shockwave through my flesh.

I'd stopped breathing at "That is who you are." All I could think about was his lips against mine. When he turned his head, eye blazing, I knew my wish was about to come true.

We kissed. Pure, refined heat warmed my insides while goose bumps spread on the surface of my skin. I pressed against him, seeking his warmth, needing to forget all my problems in his arms. His fingertips flitted down my back until they reached the curve of my hip, where my shirt met my pants.

He muttered something under his breath, lifted me up and carried me to his bed, his emerald eyes intense as they met mine, his movements gentle as he lowered me down.

I leaned up and tried to pull him closer, but he resisted. Laughing softly under his breath, he ran his fingertips up and down my arms, making me tremble. Turning his head, he pressed his lips along the sensitive skin on my wrist, then moved toward my shoulder, then my neck. A few more teasing nibbles then our lips met again.

Time lost meaning. My problems melted away, by his kiss, his touch, his love. We were wrapped in our own little world, where nothing else mattered, but us and the feelings swirling around us.

But somewhere in the back of my mind was a niggling warning not to fully let go. A blend of our energies could seriously hurt Bran. Reduce him to a catatonic state worse than Grampa earlier. If I could hurt a powerful Psi like my grandfather, the things I could do to Bran could be worse.

"Thinking about the Cardinal while making out is a total ego-crusher," Bran whispered.

I blinked, my mind slow to process what he was saying. "What?"

"I could hear your thoughts."

I covered my face. "I'm so sorry."

"Don't be." He pulled strands of my hair from my forehead and tucked them away. "I needed to chill anyway." He scooted off the bed and walked to the table by the canvases and came back with two sketch books. With an uneasy look on his face, he gave them to me.

"Why are you looking at me like that?" I asked, still wishing we were making out.

"I sketch a lot." Color rushed to his cheeks, dimples flashing. "Since you won't mind-blend with me, I'm going to bare my soul to you by letting you see my work."

Wanting to know why he was blushing, I pushed aside my raging hormones and flipped the cover before he curled beside me. A sketch of me baking a cake leaped at me from the page. I never cook. In fact, I hated cooking with a passion.

"That's you taking lessons from Remy. You insisted on baking me a cake on my birthday." He chuckled, enjoying a private joke.

"And?" I asked.

"It was pitiful."

I believed him. "So you had a cake-less birthday?"

"No. You and Kylie had already ordered one from a local bakery, just in case. FYI, I'm a better cook than you."

I elbowed him, then flipped the page, then the next. His blush made sense. The pages were filled with sketches of me, some going back to when we first met. Since I had never posed for him, he must have sketched them from memory. Seeing myself through his eyes was the most beautiful gift ever, and I'd never felt more loved.

- 10 -

NIGHTMARES

Screams echoed in the dark, yanking me into consciousness. I thrashed against the restraints around my arms. Strands of my curly hair stuck on my sweaty forehead and blocked my vision, adding to the images tumbling through my mind—wings and feathers floating to the ground, daggers flying through the air, swords clanging. A rational part of me told me I was in my room and that the arms wrapped around me were Bran's, yet the nightmare paralyzed me.

"It's just a dream," he whispered over and over, running a hand through my hair, pressing my head against his chest.

I clung to him, my screams becoming whimpers. What was happening to me? It was bad enough I had to deal with headaches while awake. My nights were filled with dreams I couldn't explain.

"Is it the same nightmare?" Grampa asked from somewhere inside my room, my bedside lamp turning on at the same time. Concern knitted his brow as he stared at us. If he was surprised to find Bran in my room, he didn't show it.

"I don't know, but she woke up faster this time." Bran squeezed my shoulders and asked, "Do you want me to get you a wet cloth?"

"No, I'll get it." I got up and staggered to the bathroom, Bran following me as though I'd collapse or something. At least he stayed by the doorway as I splashed water on my face. Then I stared in horror at my reflection in the mirror.

Three straight nights without sleep, four if I didn't catch some shut-eye during what was left of tonight, had turned me into the girl from The Grudge. Dark shadows clung to my eyes. My hair was wild and untamed. My usually glowing skin looked pasty and grey. I needed uninterrupted REM cycles.

The nightmares had started on Saturday, the night the demons had attacked me. Grampa and Bran had teleported into my bedroom at the same time, both thinking I was being attacked. Though I'd like to think I wouldn't scream like a demon on its way to Tartarus. We Guardians were tougher than that.

Grampa had left after Bran reassured him he'd stay until I fell asleep. And he had. The night after, he hadn't left after I woke up screaming again. Just as well. Immediately after I'd fallen asleep, the dreams had started again.

It was terrible fighting what you couldn't see, being surrounded by a dense fog while lightning speared the air around you. Then there was the carnage, the cacophony of sounds. Shrill, brain-numbing, ear-piercing screams.

By the third night, Bran hadn't even bothered going home. Grampa never slept. He came and went during the night, so I knew he was aware of our new sleeping arrangement. That he didn't say anything said just how worried he was.

Voices came from bedroom and I realized Bran had disappeared from the doorway. They were talking in low tones, but I heard them anyway.

"I don't like it," Grampa was saying. "Maybe a long break might be better."

Don't like what? I angled my head to catch more.

"She has shadows under her eyes and looks so fragile," Grampa continued.

"You shouldn't ask her to stop, Cardinal. The only times she doesn't feel the pain is when she trains," Bran said.

How dare they discuss me? I opened my mouth to protest and closed it without speaking. Lack of sleep was making me cranky. I splashed more water on my face, then dried off.

"What does Master Haziel say?" Grampa asked, his voice fainter. "He and I haven't spoken since he started the new regimen."

"He wants her to control the powers and pushes her hard, but she likes that, which is very unlike her. It's like she craves it. She and I train between group lessons, too."

"Interesting," Grampa mumbled. "I wonder if the adrenaline rush helps her block the pain."

"Endorphins," Bran corrected.

Endorphins? When his energy soothed mine, it eased my headaches. Making out worked wonders, too. If they were talking chemicals, I'd vote for dopamine. I derived some pleasure from training with him. He was a better fighter than me, but because of my new powers I'd acquired more stamina and went toe to toe with him. Izzy called it foreplay. Too bad it never led to anything.

Walking back to my bedroom, I waved my hand and turned off the bedside lamp, then slipped under the blanket. Sleep wasn't going to come easily. I turned my head and buried it in a pillow. It had the woodsy scent Bran favored. I smiled, but that soon changed to a scowl.

Why was I having these nightmares? Were they residual memories from the attack, or something the dagger's powers induced? Considering how many demons it had killed over the millennia, there was no telling what was stored in the writings that usually covered the dagger's blade. All I knew was that they were somehow connected to the powers of the dagger.

"You still haven't found Gavyn, Cardinal?" Bran asked.

Grampa and Bran's voice grew stronger or maybe hearing Gavyn's name pulled me out of my funk. If there was a demon I wanted to hurt, it was Nitwit Gavyn.

"I'm afraid not. Without him, tracking down the Summoners is impossible."

"You should let us give it a try, Cardinal. I know you said you didn't want us out there, but—"

"I still don't. As long as the Tribe is on the loose, waiting to catch you young ones unaware, I want all of you inside the valley."

"What if I went alone? I work faster and I promise to be discreet. Gavyn is also more likely to come out of hiding when he hears I'm looking for him without the Guardians."

I held my breath as I waited for Grampa's verdict. He wouldn't dare let Bran go. Surely, he couldn't be that desperate.

"I'll discuss it with the Cardinals and Master Haziel."

Unbelievable. I jumped out of bed. "What is there to discuss, Grampa?"

"Lil—"

"He's not going out there, period. What are you trying to do? Use him as bait?" Grampa closed the gap between us as I continued. "If you haven't noticed, the Tribe only comes out to play when *we* are out there. They don't want you. They want us. Maybe it's Bran they are after. Or maybe it's…me." My voice broke just as he pulled me into his arms.

Grampa didn't speak. He held me as I cried, something I'd avoided doing since the attack. Lack of sleep had reduced me to a whining ninny. Of course he would never use Bran as bait. Grampa had integrity. He was likely to use himself first before sending anyone else.

He leaned back and studied my face.

I swiped my cheek and gave him an uncertain smile. "I'm sorry. I'm exhausted and not thinking straight. You'd never do something so despicable."

He smiled and kissed my forehead. "No, I wouldn't. So? How are you feeling?"

"Like Tartarus swallowed me whole then spit me out."

He chuckled. "What do you remember of your dreams?"

I frowned. "Why? Do you think there's a reason I'm having them?"

"I don't know, sweetheart. The Psi-dar didn't give us anything to work with." He let go of me and pushed his hands inside his coat, making me realize he was dressed for hunting. He must have either just arrived home or was about to leave when I screamed. "I'm trying to understand what is happening to you."

That made two of us. "The fog appeared out of nowhere, then the lightning and the sounds."

"And the woman's voice?" Grampa asked.

"I still can't understand what she says. The sounds and the screams always swallow her words."

He touched my clammy forehead. "I don't know what is going on, but you can't go on like this forever. Bran says training is good for you, but—"

"No," I protested. "I need to train. It burns off the excess energy."

Grampa sighed. "Okay. We're going to have a joint conference of High Council members and senior Cardinals from all the sectors starting tomorrow, to discuss our next move. The High Council members love wasting time listing useless diplomatic solutions where a pre-emptive strike is needed. I will be in and out as usual, just not as often. Will you be okay?"

I nodded, then a thought occurred to me. What if they were attacked during the meeting? The attack by the nature-benders had decimated the Guardians. Having the High Council and senior Cardinals in one place could be disastrous if the Tribe attacked them.

"Where are you meeting?" I asked.

"Rio, headquarters of the Southwest Sector." He pulled out a pocket watch from his coat pocket and glanced at it. "It starts in exactly twenty minutes. It might be 5 a.m. here, but it is eight in Brazil. Since I'm opening the meeting, I think I'd better head out."

"Could you change venues every few hours?" I asked.

Grampa frowned. "We could. Why?"

"All those psi energies in one place are bound to draw attention and make you guys sitting targets."

"Sweetheart, every High Council has an impenetrable security created by its Psi-dar," he reminded. "No demon can breach it."

"Yet the Tribe found us in Bermuda despite the high-security shield," I said.

"She has a point, Cardinal," Bran added, coming to stand by my side. "The Tribe might not have known the exact location of the island, but they were drawn to our combined psi energies. I think you should do as she suggested."

Grampa's frowned deepened then he palmed my face and pressed his lips to my temple. He reached out and gripped Bran's shoulder and nodded. "I think we'll do just that. Now try to rest. Both of you. Help her go to sleep."

"Of course, Cardinal."

Grampa patted my cheek then teleported. I glanced at Bran. "What did he mean by help me go to sleep?"

"He knows that my presence calms you down."

Ah, the curse of having a powerful Psi as a grandfather. Nothing ever escaped him. Bet he'd know when I finally lost my virginity. I cringed at the thought. Or maybe now that I was a stronger Psi, I could compel him *not* to read me. I turned and eyed Bran. Maybe I should practice on him. We had two hours before the training session with Master Haziel.

I took Bran's hands in mine and looked into his emerald eyes. *You must do my bidding without questioning me.*

"What are you doing?" he asked, scowling.

Compelling you to do my wish. Come with me.

He chuckled, dimples flashing. "Nice try. Do you want to head to the pit for an early workout?"

"How come I can't compel you?"

Bran tapped my head. "I hear your thoughts, Sunshine. And the calculating gleam in your eyes told me you were up to no good before you spoke. Come on, change into your gym clothes and meet me at the pit in three minutes."

I pouted. "You are no fun."

"I don't mind being your guinea pig, just not now. Training will get your mind off seducing me. Not that you need to. The first person at the pit gets to choose the first weapon," he added, then teleported.

I made a face. Lack of sleep might make me cranky as a hellhound, but he wasn't beating me.

Being able to see psi energies had its perks. I noted that Bran wasn't in the pit before I materialized. Although lights were on in the Academy's rotunda, the pit was in total darkness. I willed the light crystals to turn on as soon as I arrived.

I was choosing a wooden staff when Bran arrived.

"I won," I said with glee.

"I should have insisted on proper dress code," he said, staring at my feet.

I glanced down and grimaced. We all had several pairs of lightweight leather martial arts shoes, in black or black and red, for use in the pit. He wore all black. Mine didn't match.

"Nitpicking, sore loser." I threw one stick to him.

He caught it and rotated it while moving, already anticipating an attack. "We'll see about that."

"After the sticks, we'll use knives then swords."

"Bloodthirsty this morning, aren't you?" He teased, circling me slowly, knees bent and feet angled away from each other for stability, eyes on me. While I held the long staff with two hands, knuckles up, he rotated his in one hand.

"Scared?" I asked.

"Shaking in my shoes." He rushed me.

Ducking, I blocked, twisted my stick and disengaged it from under his and attacked, aiming for his feet. He teleported out of the way and appeared behind me, but I'd anticipated his move. I turned and knocked the staff from his hand.

He caught it and cocked his right eyebrow. "Very good."

"I know."

Next time around, I wasn't so lucky. He had me on my back in five moves.

"Stop goofing around," he scolded, offering me his hand. "Don't *ever* let me get inside your head and anticipate your next move."

I hated it when he talked to me in that superior tone. Ignoring his hand, I teleported to my feet and swung, aiming for his ribs. He blocked, shifted his weight and leveled a kick at my exposed side. I ducked and jumped back. Anchoring the stick down on one end, I swung on it and caught him in the chest with both feet. He staggered backward and grinned.

"Could be better," he said.

There was no pleasing him, so I pushed harder. There was no more talking as we tried to outmaneuver each other with moves and counter-moves, the sounds of wood hitting wood echoing in the pit. Adrenaline pumped in my veins and euphoria buzzed through me. Soon we were both breathing hard and sweating.

We stopped for a water break and a change of weapons. Bran's gaze shot to mine as he reached out to take his dagger from my hand. I had kicked his butt in the last round.

"Don't worry," I said. "I promise to go easy on you this time."

Smirking, he took the dagger and flipped it around. The blade gleamed as it whipped in the light. He flung it in the air, then grabbed it backhand and lunged for me, the blade directed at my throat. I batted his arm away and surged toward him.

He used my weight and threw me over his head, but I teleported and reappeared on his side. He was waiting for me and I barely managed to block his attack. Another bout of strikes and counterstrikes followed and it seemed like forever before I tackled him and had him at a disadvantage. I loomed over him, my pulse quickening.

"You are enjoying this?" he said.

"Oh, you have no idea." I pressed the edge of the blade to his skin, loving the way his eyes widened. I could never hurt him and he knew it. Still… I nicked him. He sucked in a breath.

"You're playing with fire," he warned in a voice gone suddenly husky.

Heat pooled like warm honey low in my belly as I responded. "What are you going to do about it?"

He grinned.

"This." His free arm looped around me and pulled me on top of him. Eye locked with mine, one hand skated along my arm while the other reached for my face. He pried the dagger from my hand before I realized his intention, then he pressed both blades against my neck. "You are dead."

"You don't play fair," I protested.

"You lost focus."

"You cheated." Giving him an annoyed look, I jumped up and went to get swords. I handed him one and willed a second one from the wall. Using a move Master Haziel had taught me, I focused on the powers inside me, willing them to move.

Heat shot from my lower back, up my spine and spread through my core. The ancient words raced to my hands, making them tingle. I grinned. We'd practiced controlling the Kris Dagger's powers, but I didn't know I could bring the powers forth without being attacked.

"How was that?" Bran asked.

"Effortless." I removed wet strands of hair from my sweaty forehead. "Should I be worried? I don't want to get comfortable with them."

"I'm sure the headaches will continue to remind you they don't belong inside you. Ready?" He attacked.

We moved across the floor, thrusting, cutting, and parrying. Bran was a better swordsman, and he didn't cut me any slack. He pushed me hard, landing blows several times when I messed up, but I got him several times too. Luckily, the carbon steel training swords didn't have sharpened edges despite having the balance and weight of real swords.

"Slowing down your teleport has made you a better fighter," he said during another water break.

"Praise from the master, yippee."

He rolled his eyes and looked at his watch. "It's six-fifty. Do you want to stop or move to hand-to-hand combat?"

Gutter fighting involved lots of body contact, which was both exciting and frustrating, because he distracted me way too easily. Not needing another lecture on self-control, I plopped down on one of the mat and stared at the crystals on the ceiling.

"Nope. I'm done," I declared

He squatted beside me. "Come on."

"No," I said with a pout, then saw Master Haziel near the entrance. How long had he been watching us? "We have an audience."

Bran followed my gaze, got to his feet and wished the trainer good morning.

"You could not sleep again?" His ancient face scrunched up with concern as he studied me.

I nodded. His scowl deepened.

"I wanted you to try something different this morning, but it can wait. Go home and rest." He glanced at Bran. "Stay behind."

"But I'm not tired," I protested.

"You look tired, and your responses a few minutes ago were slower," Master Haziel said. "Have you had time to read the book I gave you?" he asked pointedly.

"Uh, yeah. I'm out of here." I jumped to my feet and teleported.

After a shower and breakfast, I curled up on my bed with the book on the Goddess. Boring couldn't begin to describe it. Half the book was things I already knew. My eyelids grew heavy. I must have dozed off because the sound of my cell phone woke me up. The clock said it was quarter to nine and the streetlight fell into my room through the window. My stomach growled.

I'd slept the day away without having a nightmare. A quick scan told me Bran wasn't in the valley, but Grampa and the Cardinals were at HQ. They weren't alone, which meant they were still having the conference. Izzy and Kim were at the guys' house.

I picked up my cell phone and chuckled at the text message from Kylie. She had an emergency and needed my help. I texted her back, promising to be at her place in a few minutes.

I got dressed and checked my cell phone again. Kylie hadn't texted me back, so I slipped the phone in my pocket and headed to the kitchen for food. I chewed on an apple as I warmed leftover lasagna. I hated eating alone. Usually, I ate with Bran. Where was he?

I checked in with the others as I ate. *What are you guys doing?*

Talking Guardian business, Remy said. *Happy you are awake. Now get here ASAP. and bring Bran. We need his input.*

Guardians business always came first. Kylie would have to wait. *Dran is not in the valley.*

Then join us, Sykes added. *We stopped by your place twice, but you were asleep. You looked cute, Red. No drool or anything.*

You watched me sleep? I screeched

Just for a few minutes. You don't snore, just in case you were wondering, he teased.

I'm going to kill you, Sykes, I vowed.

He chuckled and broke the link. I teleported to their place and was met by raised voices.

"Oh, come on," Remy was saying.

"No way," Sykes retorted. "I'm not changing my routine because of new roommates. I love free Sundays."

"What's free on Sundays?" Izzy asked.

"I am. It's laundry day." He saw me and waved me over. "Hey, Red. Rocking that Gypsy outfit. Did I mention you were smiling while you slept? Must have been dreaming about me."

I shot him a mean look.

"Don't listen to him. We stopped by your place but you were out. How are you feeling?" Izzy asked.

I shrugged. "Better, I guess."

"Back to the subject," Kim said, snapping her fingers in front of Sykes' face. "Why are you free on laundry day?"

Sykes smirked. "Use your imagination, Goldie."

"He walks around naked," Remy said.

"That's so…so…" Kim couldn't think up a word.

"'Liberating' is the word you are searching for," Sykes said, still smirking.

Izzy made a disgusted face. "Does he really?"

Remy nodded. "I usually just ignore him, which is not easy because he's a morning person and often wants to recap everything that happened the day before while I make breakfast. Thank the Goddess for kitchen counters."

I imagined the scene and laughed.

"Come here, Red." He patted the seat beside him. "Knock some sense into their heads. Tell them it's wrong and unfair to move in with us. I don't want to watch chick flicks and forgive snippy comments at a certain time of the month."

"That's insulting," Izzy said indignantly.

"Who's moving in?" I asked, my gaze volleying between the girls.

"Izzy and Kim," Remy said.

Sykes gave a mock shudder. "Don't you mean Miss Rules and Miss Stuck Up? The things that go on in this house stay in this house. My women won't, uh, you know, be themselves with you two around."

"What women?" Kim said in a disparaging tone. "Don't you mean the poor human *girls* parading in and out of here like it's a cheerleading camp?"

"We can have our bedrooms upstairs," Remy continued. "You girls can take downstairs."

"We get upstairs," Izzy corrected him. "*And* we get to redecorate the living room." She and Kim laughed and high-fived each other.

"You two are actually thinking of moving in?" I asked, sitting on the bench by the TV. "With them?"

"My parents are bending the rules again to suit themselves," Kim explained, a defeated expression settling on her pretty face. "When Cardinal Guardian trainees turn eighteen, which I did a month ago, they are supposed to get places of their own. My parents insist there are no houses available, yet Kenta's house is empty."

Kenta was our disgraced former master trainer. He had betrayed us by feeding my father information about me, and been banned from our Council.

"And even if his house wasn't empty, it takes Guardians…what? A week to build a house?" Izzy rolled her eyes. "Hardly a reason to keep us under their thumbs."

Izzy had lived with Kim's family since her family moved back to Xenith. "You too?" I asked.

Izzy shrugged. "They can't allow me to move out and refuse Kim, so I'm being punished too. Worse, they're trying to find Kim—"

"Don't," Kim snapped and slapped a hand over Izzy's mouth.

Izzy teleported and appeared beside me. "A mate."

Kim growled. "You need to mind your own business, Isadora Salazar."

I expected the guys to burst out laughing because it was absurd. No one arranged marriages anymore. But everyone went quiet, their expressions serious. Immediately after joining the Guardianship program, Izzy had told me something interesting about Kim's family—the Larsons had a history of arranging marriages to produce powerful offspring and future Cardinals, which was why every generation of Cardinals included a member of their family.

"That's messed up," Remy said, frowning. "You can pretend to choose one of us to get them off your back."

Kim smiled. "Thanks, Remy, but there's no need for that. Can we discuss something else?"

"I second what Remy said," Sykes added, his expression earnest. "It might mess up my rep with the ladies, but we're friends and friends help each other out. So, yes, count me in for as long as you want me." He stretched and pretended to check Kim out. "But if you want to upgrade it by adding benefits, I'm calling first dibs, bro."

Kim laughed and leveled Sykes a mocking glance. "You couldn't handle me."

"Try me," Sykes said, then he winked.

"So? Should we rearrange the rooms for you guys?" Remy's glance bounced between Izzy to Kim as he spoke.

"Whoa, slow down, dude. We are still in the maybe-it-might-happen-depending-on-the-ground-rules stage." Sykes pointed at Remy, then tapped his chest and indicated upstairs. "Let's go."

They disappeared upstairs.

"Are you guys *really* thinking about moving in with them?" I asked, not buying it.

"Do you have a better idea?" Izzy asked.

"I can talk to my grandfather. As the head of the Cardinals, his ruling trumps Kim's father when it comes to Cardinal Guardian business. Because of him, you guys lived with your parents when you moved here from Xenith, instead of rooming with members of the High Council like the new students."

Kim studied me with narrowed eyes as though thinking about my suggestion.

"There was no 'Academy' at the time and parents weren't willing to send their kids to this High Council after the demonic raid, which, your father led, princess," Izzy teased.

I stuck out my tongue. "It was just a thought. Don't call me princess."

Izzy shook her head, her ponytail whipping left and right. "Princess… princess…princess…"

She could be so annoying sometimes. I waved a hand, and a pillow from one of the gaming chairs shot toward her. She caught it and flipped it back at me. I stopped it before it reached me and sent it her way again.

"Stop it, you two," Kim snapped, then nodded at me. "Do it."

I blinked. "Really?"

Kim arched her right eyebrow. "You offered. Let's see if Grampa really *is* putty in your hands, princess."

With a lift of my chin, a pillow shot up and flew toward her. Air shot past me as the pillow reversed directions with a whoosh. The guys came back to find a pillow fight and giggles.

Sykes laughed. "Now this, I can live with. Saturday night strip poker and pillow fights are a must for roommates." He ducked when four pillows flew toward him.

"We'll pass for now," Kim said. "Lil will talk to her grandfather about getting us our own place."

"Now, or after this Tribe mess is over?" Remy asked.

Just like that, the playful mood disappeared. The discussion moved to the Tribe.

"They're still discussing what to do?" Izzy asked, outraged.

"From what my grandfather said, the Cardinals would like us to face the Tribe head on, but the High Council prefers diplomacy."

"I wonder what the CT has to say about all this," Kim murmured. "Do they even know what's going on?"

"It's been four days since the attack and Academy students and their teachers are still in Xenith," Remy said. "Someone must have explained their presence."

"Meanwhile we train without knowing the Tribe's weaknesses and strengths," Izzy added.

"Master Haziel knows something but he's being so close-mouthed," Kim griped.

"Did Bran tell you what they discussed this morning?" Remy asked. "It seemed intense, but they were both grinning like they'd found the Holy Grail."

I shook my head. "I haven't seen Bran since our morning training session."

"You trained this morning?" Izzy asked.

"Around five o'clock," I said.

Kim reached out and rubbed my arm. "The nightmares again?"

Surprised by the gesture, I nodded. "I agree with Remy. Master Haziel knows something. Remember how he pointed out a passage on the book on Mediums before we knew Kylie was a medium? He gave me a book…" My cell phone dinged. I fished it out of my pocket and read the text.

Is Bran with you?

I typed. **No. Why?**

When I pressed the send button and looked up, the others were staring at me with annoyance. Making a face, I put the phone back in my pocket. "Sorry. It's Kylie. Uh, where was I? Yeah, Master Haziel gave me a book on the Goddess and he keeps pushing me to read it." I shrugged. "So are we going to continue hiding and waiting?"

"We should sneak out and do our own investigation, beat the senior Cardinals to the punch like we'd planned before," Sykes said. "Like we did with Coronis *and* on Jarvis Island."

Silence followed his announcement, then everyone started talking at once.

"I don't know, guys," Izzy said.

"Live a little, Izzy," Sykes said with a gleam in his eyes. "We can round up demons and torture them until they talk."

"Or ask Darius and the Brotherhood to help us," Remy added. "The problem is how to contact them without the senior Cardinals knowing about it."

"Don't worry, Keiran and his friends *will* help," Kim said confidently.

"How do you know that?" Sykes asked then he smirked. "Ah, I forgot you two are joined at the hip now."

"We're not," Kim protested.

Everyone laughed while she blushed. My cell phone dinged again. I reached inside my pocket and muted the phone.

"Dante and Kael might help too," I said, "if they don't hate me for hurting him."

"The big guys can handle pain," Remy said dismissively. "They're nature-benders. Who wants something to drink?" He got to his feet.

Everyone nodded. While he went and got sodas, my phone dinged again.

"Give me that," Kim snapped and stuck her hand toward me.

I cocked my brow. "What?"

"Your stupid phone keeps making that annoying ding," she explained. "I know you and Kylie are tight, but she can't monopolize your time. She's always calling with some cockamamie excuse about needing your help or…"

I tuned her out, pulled the cell phone out of my pocket and checked the last text. Kylie was desperate. Her 'get here now' had exclamation marks. I powered it off. "Are we done? Because I've got to go."

"Did you hear anything I just said?" Kim asked.

I grinned. "No. See you guys tomorrow morning."

Izzy gripped my arm. "Wait a sec. Do you know that Kylie's family moved?"

Another lost memory. "When? To where?"

"Beginning of summer. They live in Nibley now. I'll show you. We've had to drag your behind from her house a few times in the past few weeks."

- 11 -

TRUTH AND LIES

A big dresser stood in the middle of Kylie's bedroom and I would have bumped into it if I hadn't slowed down my teleport. Izzy wasn't so lucky.

"Dang it, Kylie. What's this doing in the middle of your room?"

Kylie looked up and grimaced. She had been watching something on her laptop while lying on her bed. She sat up, a frown on her face. "Sorry about that."

"Never mind. Gotta go." Izzy glanced around and whistled softly. "Nice décor. You two have fun."

Kylie wore a confused expression. "What was that about? I mean, what was she doing here?"

"Long story. But seriously, what's this," I pointed at the dresser, "doing in the middle of your room?"

Kylie wrinkled her nose. "Dad had it repainted and brought it in an hour ago. I tried to move it, but it weighs more than I do. What time is it?"

"Nine-thirty-ish," I guessed without looking at my watch, my gaze on the Celtic symbols all over the dresser. With the black background, the squiggly drawings popped. Her new bedroom was spacious and beautifully decorated. "This is beautiful."

"I know." Kylie stood and stretched, her tank top hiking up to reveal a tattoo on her hip. "It's perfect. Matches my curtains, don't you think?"

"*And* your tattoo." Kylie was a petite five-foot-four with a pixie face, grey eyes and brown hair—her natural hair color. Before, she'd dyed it black during her Gothic phase.

"So what took you?" she asked. "I texted you, like, an hour ago."

I laughed. "What took me? Who do you think I am? Your servant?"

"Clark Kent to my Chloe Sullivan, faithful sidekick and best friend ever." She grinned when I scrunched up my face. Still grinning, she walked to where I stood beside the dresser, hands going to her hips. "You're not just the Chosen One, you are Lil *Fáthaig*. That means—"

"Lil the Mighty, I know."

She made a face. "I hate that you can speak, like, a gazillion languages."

"Okay. From now on I'll pretend I don't know Gaelic."

"Don't bother, smarty-pants. Anyway, when I need heavy lifting, you're the one I text. When you need R&R from Guardian biz and computer research, I'm your girl."

I made a derisive sound. "You can't be Chloe. You suck with computers."

"Nitpicking, and not my fault. My parents gave all the smart genes to my brainiac brother." She pouted. "It's so unfair. You can find me any time and any where, while I have to send a stupid text."

"Texts," I corrected her. "As in five of them. What is the emergency anyway?"

Kylie frowned. "What are you talking about? I sent you *one* text message because of this," she waved at the dresser, "not four."

"Four *more* after the first one. My cell phone kept vibrating while I was in the middle of a conference."

She searched for her phone "That doesn't make sense."

"What?"

"I texted you once."

She was getting pissed. "Forget it. It's not important."

"Is too." She marched toward the door, her frown fierce. "I'm going to kill the slimy worm."

Before I could ask her what she meant, Kylie had yanked open her door and stomped to the one down the hall. It had a quantum physics poster and a picture of Albert Einstein. She banged on it with her fist. "Jesse!"

No response.

"Open up or I'll break it down!"

The door jerked open to reveal her brother, pimpled face red, a mop of curly brown hair falling over his forehead. He wore a T-shirt with the writing *Schrödinger's Cat, Dead and Alive*, and a drawing of cat in a cage. Two of his friends appeared behind him and stared at Kylie with wary expressions, video game controllers clenched in their hands.

"Break it down?" Jesse asked. "Physically impossible since you are only five-three and weigh about one—"

"Shut up, you freak," Kylie snapped. "You took my cell phone again! Where is it?"

"I don't have it," her brother protested. Then he saw me and smiled. "Hi, Lil."

I gave him a tiny wave.

"Don't talk to her. Just because she's played a few video games with you doesn't make her *your* friend. You can't pretend to be me and text her."

His brother shook his head. "I didn't touch your stupid phone, Kylie. We've been in here playing video games all evening."

"Liar! My phone is missing and you've been bugging me for days to ask her to come over." She thrust her face forward and hissed, "She's got a boyfriend, you loser."

Jesse glanced my way one more time, face redder than before, then whispered through clenched teeth, "Ask Mom. She'll tell you we haven't left my room for hours. Maybe your witches," he wiggled his fingers, "took it."

"Goddesses," Kylie snapped. "Celtic deities."

"Get a life." He slammed his door.

"I have a life," she shouted through the door. "And it's not in some online gaming world."

Feeling bad for Jesse, who'd had a crush on me since the first time Kylie had invited me to their home, I retreated into her room. He was a year younger than her, tall, gangly, and going through the zits stage. The few times we'd played video games, I had had fun, though.

"I swear my parents found him in a crashed spaceship," Kylie snapped when she re-entered her bedroom. "He's so weird."

"I'm sure he just wanted my help with a game. Where do you say you wanted the dresser?" I asked, hoping to distract her, but I shouldn't have bothered. She continued to search for her phone while muttering under her breath.

"I'm telling on him, the worm."

"It's no big deal, you know," I said, trying to calm her down.

"Is too. He's always stealing my phone to text his friends. It's not my fault he lost his."

I stopped trying to help and studied her room instead. It was done in black and white, from the bed cover to the draperies; the only colors were the wooden floor and colored pillows on her bed. Celtic spirals and knots dominated everything. It was beautiful and so Kylie.

"Okay?" she asked.

I raised my brow, feeling a little guilty for ignoring her rant. "What?"

"I said, let's move the bed first from this wall to that," she pointed to the wall adjacent to the window. "Then the dresser to where the bed is. This way, the mirror can reflect the window and give an illusion of more space."

"Move out of the way," I warned. I waited until Kylie stood by the door, then moved her bed to the adjacent wall. The books shifted a little but didn't fall. Next, I put the dresser where the bed had been while Kylie issued orders like a drill sergeant.

"A little to the right…not too much…an inch or two to the left," she said. "Perfect. Thank you. Look, I found my phone." It was inside the top drawer of her new dresser. "And it's dead. I swear if catch him with it again, his DS is mine." She placed the phone on the dresser, jumped on to her bed, scooted over and patted the area beside her. I moved the pillows behind me then flopped on my back and stared at the ceiling.

"Start talking," she said.

I frowned. "About what?"

"What the Guardians have been up to…what I've missed. Duh. I haven't seen you in over a week. You promised to keep me in the loop and I look forward to hearing about your escapades."

"Escapades? We've been canceling contracts. Hardly exciting."

"Not from the way you often tell it, and there was also the meeting with that lightning demon that blocked the light from the Kris Dagger. So start talking and don't leave anything out," she warned.

Obviously, I'd shared everything with her. "I'll start with why Izzy came with me to your place. I was attacked on Saturday and lost months of memories, including those about your new home."

Kylie sat up, her eyes round. I started with the attack and the more I talked, the more frantic she became—surprise giving way to worry then panic.

"Powerful demons are after you and you waited for nearly a week before telling me?" she screeched.

"Four days," I corrected her.

"Whatever. And your powers…do you have a headache right now?"

I shrugged. "Just a dull throb. Sleeping this afternoon helped. But, I've learned to live with them."

"Have you taken something for it?"

I cocked my brow. "Something?"

"Headache meds. It doesn't have to be prescription strength. Just over-the-counter ones."

I shook my head. "What?"

She rolled her eyes. "You are part human, so maybe, just maybe Ibuprofen or Aleve might take care of your human side of the headache." She hopped off the bed and disappeared in the hallway. I was still staring after her in disbelief when she returned with a bottle and water in a glass.

"You think over-the-counter meds will cure me?"

"What do you have to lose?" She read the label, opened the bottle, and removed two pills. She pushed them in my hand, then offered me water. "Take them."

I stared at the oval-shaped gel. "They look like miniature hellgels."

"These have chemicals that stop headaches and whatnots. Swallow them whole too, no biting or chewing."

I chuckled, then placed the gels on my tongue and washed them down with water. "Now what?"

"Now let human technology work its wonders. It will be absorbed into your body. Could I, you know, see them?" She indicated my back.

"Why? They look like tattoos. No big deal."

"Thanks for spoiling the surprise for me. Now turn around."

For such a tiny girl she could be so bossy sometimes. "I swear to Goddess, if you say anything mean…" I stood, turned and lifted my shirt.

For a moment, Kylie didn't speak. Then she said, "Uh, Lil, there's nothing on your skin."

I frowned. "What do you mean? They cover my spine, from the base of my neck to my lower back."

"Not anymore. See for yourself."

My heart pounding, I pulled off my top and studied my back through the mirror. Kylie was right—there was nothing on my back. Not sure what it meant, I pulled my shirt back on. "That's weird."

"Weird good or weird bad?"

I shook my head. "I don't know."

She sat back on her bed and continued to study me like I was some alien she was trying to figure out. For a brief moment, I was tempted to read her thoughts, but I resisted. I had a rule about not getting inside my friends' minds.

"Tell me what we did this summer," I said instead.

She chuckled. "Funny, I'm usually the one with the questions. Okay, don't give me that look. I'll answer you, but first, do you really think Gavyn is behind this?"

"It doesn't matter what I think." I scowled at the ceiling, remembering the look on Bran's face when he'd told us about a possible connection between his brother and the Summoners. "What matters is Bran and what this would mean to him if it's true. Sometimes, I wish I had the power to spare him pain."

"Having Gavyn for a brother totally sucks. Makes me appreciate mine."

It didn't seem like that a few minutes ago. "Makes me happy I'm an only child," I said.

"Uh, you're not an only child."

"Thanks for reminding me." Solange's perfect face, gorgeous hair, and body like a swimsuit model flashed in my head. She was only my half-sister and about as evil as Gavyn. "Every time I think Gavyn has changed, wham, he does something stupid. If he deliberately summoned these powerful demons to stop Bran from canceling his contracts, we'll have to deal with him."

"Send him to Tartarus?" Kylie asked.

Bran would have to let go of his brother before we could do that. "I haven't thought that far yet, but yes."

"What if it's not Gavyn? Don't look at me like that," she added when I scowled. "What if it's…Solange?" She raised her hands in mock surrender. "There's that look again. You told me Solange vowed to come after you."

I frowned, trying to remember. "I did?"

"Yes, the night of your party. You know, after Jarvis Island and the mortal combat. You came back and threw a killer party. The students talked about it the rest of the semester. You're officially, the party—"

"Yeah, that's nice," I said impatiently. "Tell me about Solange."

"You told me you called the number Valafar had given, but she was the one who answered it. She vowed to make you sorry."

I sat up and scrunched my face. "Why would I call Valafar?"

"You wanted proof that he was dead or something like that."

"Tell me everything I told you. Bran tried to fill me in on what we did, but that only covered what *he* and *I* did."

"I helped with his birthday party, so if he said the cake you baked was scrumptious? He lied. It was terrible."

I threw her a disgusted look. "He told me the same thing. Now back to filling in the blanks."

She talked about everything I'd told her about Valafar and my doubts about whether he was really in Tartarus or hiding somewhere until he healed, then she moved to the party, our mutual friends, and the things we'd done together since school closed. McKenzie, my other human friend, was visiting relatives in England. Basically, when I wasn't out with the Guardians or with Bran, I spent time with Kylie watching reruns of her favorite TV programs online or went shopping at the mall, except for the weeks she and her mother visited her aunt in L.A. and went to the Celtic Arts Center. A door slammed shut somewhere in the house, followed by laughter. I looked up and frowned. "Your parents are home."

Kylie shrugged. "So? They love you. Mom thinks I'm discovering my Celtic roots because of you and your Gypsy background. According to her, you are the perfect friend."

Perfect? If only she knew. "So you're never going to tell her about your special ability?"

"No way." She shook her head. "Not until I have to. Despite her excitement over all this," she waved to indicate the Celtic symbols in her room, "she'd freak out."

There was a light knock at the door. "Sweetheart, are you asleep?"

"Still up, Mom," Kylie yelled.

Her mother said something, then her dad's deeper voice answered. "Can we come in?"

Kylie looked at me and cocked an eyebrow in question. I shrugged.

"Sure," Kylie responded

The door opened and her mother peeked inside the room. A smile lit up her heavily made-up face when she saw me.

"Hey, Lil. I didn't know you were visiting. Jim, look who's here," she called out and opened the door wider. Kylie's dad moved from Jesse's doorway to his wife's side. He was the lumberjack type, tall and big-boned with a hearty laugh. He topped his petite wife by at least a foot.

"Howdy, Lil," he said with a broad grin. "We haven't seen you around lately."

"I've been working. I mean, I have a summer job," I fibbed, my face warming up.

Kylie rolled her eyes. "Daddy, I told you she works with her grandfather."

"So you did." He looked around the room and frowned. "Did you two move the furniture around on your own?"

"It was nothing," Kylie said.

"Jim," her mother scolded, giving her husband a censuring glance. "You didn't move it for her? They shouldn't carry such heavy things on their own. They could have gotten hurt."

Kylie smothered a giggle.

"They're fine, Charlene." He dropped a kiss on her temple then leveled us a stern look, "No hauling heavy things behind my back, you two. I didn't see your truck outside, Lil, so if you need a ride home, let me know." He whispered something to the wife, turned and ambled down the hall toward the living room.

Kylie's mother smiled at us. "Do you girls want something to drink or eat? We brought some takeout."

Kylie glanced at me. I shook my head. She grinned at her mother. "Thanks, Mom. We're fine."

"Then I'll leave you alone." She glanced around and smiled. "The room looks amazing."

"I know," Kylie called out before the door closed.

I groaned and gave her a resigned look. "I can't teleport home now and Bran is still not back to pick me up."

"Leave it to me," was Kylie's mysterious response.

We hung out until a truck pulled up outside their home, music blaring and disrupting the tranquility of the quiet Nibley neighborhood. She peeked out the window and smiled.

"Stay away from the window." She raced out of the room, closing the door behind her.

I lay on her bed and closed my eyes, picking out energies in the house. Then, I scanned the valley. The Cardinals and their guests were gone.

Bran hadn't returned yet, and Izzy and Kim were no longer at the guys' house.

Voices drifted from the hallway, interrupting my telepathic searches. The engine of the truck revved, then the music grew faint.

Kylie slipped inside her bedroom, a broad grin on her face. "I just escorted you to your grandfather's truck."

"What did you do?"

She plopped beside me on the bed. "That was the older brother of one of Jesse's friends. Mom saw me walk toward the house after I talked to him, and I told her your grandpa's truck was behind theirs. You can teleport now. Text me or come over whenever. I want to know what happens next, and if I can help."

"You don't want to get mixed up in our mess again," I warned, giving her a hug.

"Last time I had no choice," she reminded me. "This time will be different."

I'd never knowingly use her. "We'll see. Later."

I dematerialized.

The lights were still on in my room, just like I'd left them, but the rest of the house was in total darkness. Grampa and the Cardinals weren't back. Since the attack, they had always made sure two senior Cardinals stayed in the enclave while three left to search for the Summoners. Bran was still not back either. I was starting to seriously worry about him.

My headache was gone, but I wasn't fooled. It could be back. Then a thought occurred to me and I chuckled. Maybe the meds Kylie had given me actually worked. I changed into my pajamas, brushed my teeth, and crawled into bed.

I was on a beach, the sun shining bright in the clear blue sky, waves slapping against the sands, students frolicking in the water, throwing Frisbees, or sunbathing. A shirtless group of Guardians played a mean game of volleyball to my right. I recognized Bran, Remy, Sykes, Izzy's boyfriend—Rastiel, and teachers from the Academy.

I stood on the beach next to Izzy and Kim. We were laughing about something when a shadow fell over us and we looked up. Lightning demons were everywhere, spreading darkness over the island and the surrounding waters. We didn't get a chance to react before they attacked.

Screams split the air. Feet pounded the ground. I tried to move but I couldn't. I called out, shouted, begged, but no one came to help us as Guardians screamed and the clang of metal filled the air. Wings and feathers fell around me and on me, making it impossible to breathe or see. My screams mingled with the echoing screeches, but when I tried to cover my ears, I couldn't move my arms either.

Then a woman's voice rose above the din. She sounded familiar, yet I couldn't place her voice. Her words didn't make sense, but I tried to do as she instructed.

I woke up gasping, my heart slamming hard against my ribs. I sat up, then realized I wasn't alone. Two figures in long coats stood over me my bed. A scream rose from my throat.

"It's okay, Lil," one of them said, reaching for me. "It's us—me and your grandfather."

Aunt Janelle. Relief washed over me, and I started to shake. She pulled me into her arms and for a moment I clung to her, my breathing harsh in the silent room. Someone turned on the bedside lamp, and I sat back and squinted, pushing back the hair that was plastered with sweat to my forehead and neck.

"Are you okay, sweetheart?" Aunt Janelle asked.

"No…yes," I mumbled. "They killed Guardians. So many of them and I couldn't help. I couldn't move. There were screams and bodies, but the woman said it wasn't real. How is that possible? I saw them fall. Feathers…wings…" I shuddered.

Aunt Janelle rubbed my arms, then took a wet cloth from Grampa and mopped my brow. I hadn't even noticed him go to the bathroom. After a moment, I took the cloth from her and pressed it against my neck.

"Why didn't you wake me up?" I asked accusingly, my gaze bouncing between the two of them. "I was terrified."

Grampa sat on my other side, his brow furrowed. "Your mind blocked what happened to you on that beach, and we knew that seeing the dream—"

"Nightmare," I interjected.

"The nightmare in its entirety would provide you some answers." He swept unruly strands away from my face and peered at me. "Can you tell us what you saw?"

Hearing the concern in his voice, I forgot about getting mad. "I was at the beach with the others and the Academy students when the demons attacked us," I said, my gaze volleying between them. "Everything went black. They were killing Guardians and I couldn't help. Something held me back. Paralyzed me. It was awful. You should have woken me up, you know," I added peevishly. A quick psi scan confirmed Bran was still not in the valley. "Bran would have woken me up."

"That's true. He thinks with his heart and not his mind where you are concerned."

"So?" I became aware of something I'd missed because of my nightmare-clouded mind—Grampa and Aunt Janelle wore ceremonial robes, white with burgundy lapels and bulbous sleeves. I'd only seen Grampa dress like that once—when he was going to meet with the Circle of Twelve in Xenith to petition them to allow Bran to join us.

"Lil," Grampa snapped, drawing my attention to his face. He'd shaven. "Tell us about the woman. What did she say?"

Aunt Janelle touched his arm and added in a softer voice, "Take your time."

I closed my eyes and the images sprang into my head. My eyes snapped open. "She said I must stop the Tribe, or they'll win and make her sacrifices be for nothing. She kept urging me to fight back, but it hurt and I didn't know what to do." I blew out a breath.

"Go on," Grampa urged.

"She said *they* make you feel a pain that's not there, a sorrow that's forgotten and a nightmare that never ends, and the power to stop them was within me. What did she mean? I tried to focus but it was useless. In the end, I reached for my memories of you guys and Bran and the others, then I woke up."

"She didn't say anything else?" Grampa asked.

Why was he so interested in what the woman said? "Uh, just before I woke up, she said find the Summoners or something about her weapon."

Silence followed, but their disappointment hung heavy in the air. When they exchanged a glance, I pounced. "Did I just relive what happened on the beach last weekend? Who is she? Why would she want to help me? Is she the reason the dagger's powers shifted to me?"

Aunt Janelle rubbed my arms and smiled. "Yes."

"Who is she?"

Grampa and Aunt Janelle looked at each other and stayed silent.

"Tell me, please. From your expressions you know the answer. Who—"

"The Goddess. She is known to guide us from time to time when we face formidable enemies. She chooses a conduit and relays her message through him or her. In this case, that conduit is you. It's an honor."

Something the librarian had said about Xenia listening and answering flashed into my head. Then there was Master Haziel giving me a book about her, and Grampa searching my mind for residual energy. Her energy?

"So you knew she was the one who did this to me on the island?" I asked.

Grampa shook his head. "No, she didn't attack you. She helped you deal with the attack."

"But you knew. All this time you knew and didn't say anything?" I yelled.

"We suspected," Grampa said calmly.

Sometimes they made me so mad I wanted to scream. "Why is she talking to me?"

"Because you are special," Grampa added.

"Special? That's the kind of answer you give a three-year-old, Grampa. Were you searching for her energy or the demons' when you blended with me?"

"Her's. Other than you, she's the only one with the ability to control the powers of the dagger. As soon as you told us what Master Haziel said, we suspected she must have made contact with you." Grampa glanced at Aunt Janelle then added, "We couldn't tell you the truth until we were sure. That is why we didn't wake you from the nightmare tonight."

I wanted to yell at them again, but it wouldn't change anything. "But she didn't tell me anything we don't already know. I mean, you already knew about the Summoners."

Grampa smiled, though there was no humor in his eyes. "Master Haziel has vast knowledge of our world and how it works. Unfortunately, he only tells us what he thinks we should know. As for the Goddess, we expected more." He stood, Aunt Janelle joining him. "But we now know that the images the Tribe project in our heads are not real, and the way to stop that kind of invasion is to focus on happy memories. That is what you did when you focused on us, Bran, and your friends. Love got you out of that nightmare."

I got up too, the wet facecloth still clenched in my hands. "What about the dagger's powers? If thinking of you helped me, what were the powers of the dagger doing inside me? And why are they gone?"

"Gone?" Aunt Janelle asked.

I turned around, and lifted the back of my pajama top, then glanced at Grampa and Aunt Janelle over my shoulder. Their expression was unreadable, but they couldn't hide their puzzlement. "They *are* gone, right?"

"Were you holding the Kris when it happened?" Grampa asked slowly.

"No. The Kris is with Master Haziel. I use it during training and leave it with him. I didn't realize the writings were gone until last night. What does it mean? And please don't lie or say you don't know. I don't care if it is a theory, just tell me. Not knowing only drives me crazy. Please?"

"It means that the Kris Dagger has completely bonded with you. Do you still have the headache?" Grampa asked, his expression unreadable.

I shook my head. "It's gone. I thought Kylie's…never mind. Completely bonded with me? What happened to 'it's only temporary'?"

Grampa sighed. "I don't like it either. The powers were supposed to move back to the dagger. They always move back."

I blinked. "So this is not the first time this has happened to its wielder?"

"No." Aunt Janelle rubbed his back gently. "I'm sure there's a reason for this, *Luminitsa*. Maybe Master Haziel has an answer or the Goddess will let us know what it means."

Yeah, I had a question or two for the Goddess. Like why was she screwing with my head? I couldn't do my job when I was busy worrying about my powers.

"You know what? I don't care anymore. I don't have the headache, so I'm fine with whatever *this* means. How was the meeting?" I asked in an upbeat voice and pointed at their priestly robes. "Did everyone wear those?"

Grampa frowned. "We reached a consensus, which we plan to convey to the elders. Lil, about the dagger—"

"I'm not going to discuss it anymore, Grampa." I rubbed my arms as goose bumps spread fast on the surface of my skin. The sleeveless pajama top and shorts weren't exactly warm, but the chill wasn't brought on by cold. "When you say elders, do you mean the CT?"

He nodded. "Yes. The final decision rests with them."

"You can't leave now," I protested, hating the panic coiling inside me. "The CT takes forever to decide on anything. It took them days to sanction canceling contracts, yet they knew Bran's soul was at stake."

Aunt Janelle chuckled. "Mass canceling of contracts is not something we've done before and they had to weigh the pros and the cons."

What were the cons of canceling contracts and Bran getting his soul back? Senile old goats! They made it so easy for me to hate them.

Grampa dropped a kiss on my temple. "Now go back to bed. We'll be back by the end of the day. Cardinals Seth, Moira, and Hsia will keep an eye on things while we are gone. Don't forget to tell Master Haziel about the missing ancient texts first thing in the morning."

Talking about them wasn't going to change a thing.

- 12 -

SECURITY GUARDIANS

I couldn't sleep. Maybe I was too used to falling asleep in Bran's arms, or the worries about the Tribe, my wacky powers, and the fact that Grampa was in Xenith got to me. The other three senior Cardinals were around, but having my grandfather in charge often made me feel safer.

Whatever the reason, I tossed and turned the rest of the night until I gave up on sleep, turned on the lights and picked up the book Master Haziel had given me.

Starting from where I had previously stopped, I scanned the pages for clues, read captions under drawings, and scrutinized the pictures. There was nothing about transfer of powers from the dagger to its wielder. About to give up, words leapt out at me when I turned the next page and saw the subtitle.

'Vessels'.

I sat up with excitement and read.

"To communicate with her people, Goddess Xenia used Guardians as vessels from time to time. This practice allowed her to interact with her people on a physical level even though the bodies she chose were not hers. The Guardians got the chance to hear her voice and even see her mannerisms manifested by her vessels. It was considered an honor to be chosen as a vessel. Unfortunately, the effect of possession by the more powerful Goddess often proved detrimental to the chosen Guardians. The vessels…"

My heart pounded with dread as I turned the page.

"…often ascended as soon as the Goddess left their bodies. Even though the ability to ascend was and is still a coveted achievement among the Guardians, the Goddess stopped this practice after several millennia. She did not think it was right for the chosen vessels to sacrifice their physical lives for her. Also, most of her vessels were Cardinals, which deprived them of their primary objective, which was and still is to defend humanity and help the remaining Guardians get their glory back."

My admiration for the Goddess went up a notch.

"Instead, Goddess Xenia chose to telepathically link with her people in their time of need. Until a more powerful Cardinal is born to be the Goddess' vessel, the Guardians must be content with telepathed words from our Goddess. Even though such messages are often misunderstood, it is better than completely severing ties between the Guardians and their exalted Goddess."

A more powerful Cardinal? Like the Chosen One, or a Cardinal with the dagger's powers inside her perhaps? I didn't want to speculate, yet I couldn't help myself.

I changed and was ready to go training by seven before I remembered Master Haziel's instructions not to go to the pit until eight. I pinged him anyway.

Can I come and talk to you? I asked.

Now is not a good time.

Why? What are you doing? I mean, you are not training us or anything, and I really need to know something.

He chuckled. *Always impatient. Okay. What is it, Lil? Is it your headache?*

My headache is gone. The writings are gone too. Am I the Goddess' vessel?

There was silence then, *Lil—*

Just give me a yes or no answer, Master Haziel. I tried to stay calm but my inner voice rose. I hated losing control and the hollow feeling in my stomach just kept growing. *Am I or am I not her vessel?*

Yes, you are. You were not ready, but the arrival of the Tribe caught us unaware, so the Goddess did what she could to prepare you. That is why the powers of the dagger moved to you. I was not sure whether your body would reject or accept the powers.

I blew out a breath. *You knew from the moment we were attacked, didn't you?*

No, I knew from the moment you were born that you were the one. Do you think the Fates decided you should survive the dangers that have dogged your steps since your birth? Guardians were strategically placed to ensure your survival. You might not have seen them, but they were there. I am but a humble trainer, destined to prepare you. As the Chosen One, your duties will be many and varied. Some of them, like being the Goddess' vessel, are happening sooner than we had expected, but you will rise to the challenge just as you have risen before when the Cardinals needed you.

I swallowed, not sure whether to be scared or furious. *Do I have a say on whether I want to be her vessel or not?*

Of course you do, but being her vessel is an honor. If you have a problem with it, tell her.

Yeah. Right.

It is true. Just because she is the Goddess does not mean she gets her way all the time.

He was nuts. *How do I talk to her?*

When she links with you again. After all, this is not the first time she has appeared to you, is it? According to the Chronicles of the battle on Coronis Isle, she helped you retrieve the Kris Dagger.

No wonder she'd sounded familiar. I would have died in that cave if it weren't for her. Not sure how to feel, I asked, *How many surprises should I expect from her?*

All will be revealed to you, Lil. Be patient. I will see you at eight. Come prepared to train. And no more doubts about your destiny. I believe it. The Guardians believe it. We will need to rally behind you, but we cannot if you are not a believer.

He broke the link before I could come up with a response. I hadn't asked to be given all these powers. They came with responsibilities and pain. Pacing, I fought the urge to scream, my heart pounding. Could one really refuse a Goddess? I was a nobody, a teen still exploring her abilities, while she was the Goddess, daughter of Azazel—one of the leaders of the Principalities. She was stronger, powerful and older, while I was…me. Worse, I could still ascend once she was done with me.

Ascend. I had never known that word would fill me with so much fear. Unfortunately, I couldn't outrun my destiny. Like Master Haziel had said, the responsibilities of the Chosen One were many and varied. Grampa always told me to face my problems head on, even if it meant death. Ascend, death, same thing.

The acceptance didn't mean I liked it. Neither did it take away my fears. Sighing, I laid on my bed and stared at the ceiling until it was time to head to the pit.

Lights from crystals blazed in the hallway and the offices. The morning shift employees were visible through the glass panels on the doors, holographic images in front of them. The whirring of ellipticals and treadmills filtered into the hallway from the Civilian gym. The High Council provided everything for its employees.

Surprisingly, the lights along the hallway leading to the dorms were also on. Could the students be back? I entered the rotunda of the Academy to find Sykes and Remy slouched on one of the benches.

"Cutting it close, aren't you?" Remy said, looking at his watch.

I glanced at my watch. It was three minutes to eight. "You guys coming?"

“No, not yet,” Sykes said, teleporting to my side and draping an arm around my shoulders. He led me to the bench. “Sit. We’re waiting for Kim, Izzy, and Llyr.”

“Bran is not in the valley.” I slouched lower and sighed. “He never came home last night. What’s going on?”

“We need to make an entrance,” Sykes added, finger combing his messy hair.

“Don’t listen to him,” Remy cut in. “Master Haziel was waiting here in the rotunda when we arrived. He told us to wait for you guys. What’s wrong with you?”

“Nothing. Why?” I finally removed Sykes’ arm from my shoulder.

“You look like you want to punch someone,” Remy said.

“Yeah,” Sykes added, dropping beside me on the bench. “Didn’t you sleep?”

“Sleep has nothing to do with it. My life sucks.”

They stared, not masking their shock. I tended not to whine about stuff, except to Bran.

“That’s extreme. Did you and Llyr have a fight?” Remy asked.

“Want me to hunt him down and beat the crap out of him?” Sykes added.

“Everyone but me,” I snapped. “Why is that? Is it a conspiracy?”

“What?” Sykes asked.

“When did you find out?” Remy asked.

I explained everything that happened. “So the bottom line is I’m completely bonded with the most powerful weapon in the universe, so I can be the Goddess’ vessel.”

The massive doors to the rotunda closed with a thud and we whipped around. Kim and Izzy walked it. Kim’s usually gorgeous hair was a mess and her eyes were red-rimmed.

“Please tell me he canceled,” she said hopefully.

Sykes laughed. “Nope. What happened to you? And don’t say you couldn’t sleep because your life sucks. Lil called dibs on that first.”

“I’m too exhausted to argue with you,” Kim mumbled.

“Let me guess.” Sykes smirked. “You went back to L.A. to visit a certain violet-eyed Brotherhood Guardian and spent the night tangoing between the sheets?”

Kim opened her mouth to respond, and closed it without saying a word.

“She was up late last night helping her mother pack, and this morning dealing with her tears,” Izzy explained.

“Pack? Why?” I asked.

“Most Civilians have been ordered back to Xenith,” Izzy explained. “They will stay there until we finish with the Tribe.”

Kim looped her arm around Izzy's. "And the sooner we send them packing, the faster things will return to normal around here."

"Lil is the solution," Remy said, causing the other two girls to stop and glance my way. But before they could speak, Remy gripped their shoulders and turned them toward the pit. "We'll explain later. Right now, Master Haziel is waiting."

"You can't just drop that bombshell and expect us to forget it," Izzy griped, digging her heels in.

"The power of the dagger didn't just switch to Lil temporarily; she bonded with it because she's the Goddess' true vessel," Sykes said.

I shook my head. He couldn't keep a secret if his life depended on it.

I ignored the questioning looks from Kim and Izzy as we left the rotunda. Already, the noose of responsibility and of everyone's expectations was tightening around my neck. How could I train and mentally prepare myself to fight the Tribe with thoughts about the Goddess and being her vessel hanging over my head? When would the Goddess need me?

As we got closer to the pit, we could hear thuds and voices. We glanced at each other without saying anything, but we were all asking the same question—who was with Master Haziel?

Kim, still in the lead, pushed open the door and stopped, forcing us to stop too. We stared. There were at least sixty men and women, all dressed in black sweats and tank tops like us. Unlike the gold six-sided star on the breast of our uniform, their insignia looked like a rising sun. From their sweaty skins and the wooden staffs in their hands, they'd been practicing for a while.

Were they new trainees? Most of them looked older.

"Come on," Master Haziel called out impatiently from somewhere in the back. "Grab a stick and step forward."

Propped on the wall by the door were six wooden staffs. We grabbed them. When we faced the new trainees, they had split and created a path between them.

"Come forward, please," Master Haziel called out. "No need to be hesitant. You are among your peers."

You'd think he would have warned us we had visitors, Izzy griped.

Where did they come from? I asked as we walked forward.

Remy chuckled. *Xenith, of course.*

I made a few eye contacts and received nods and smiles. *How do you know?*

They are SGs—Security Guardians trained to defend Xenith. I recognize a few hotheads from the Institute, Sykes said. *Don't worry, they love us. They consider us heroes.*

My hand tightened on the staff. Master Haziel had a wacky way of doing things, but parading us before these Guardians just didn't seem like him. Unless…

Guys, get ready, I warned. We were in the middle, nearly surrounded by them.

Ready for what? Sykes asked, smirking and nodding at the SGs he knew.

An ambush, I said.

They rushed us from all sides just as I finished speaking, two against each of us. I raised the staff, ducked and blocked, and counterattacked. The flurry of movements kept me from being hit. Two sticks came at me, their movements so fast they were a blur. I teleported and reappeared, knocking the attackers off-balance from behind. I delayed rematerializing until I saw an opening, over and over again.

The SGs meant business, and as soon as two went down, two more replaced them. They got time to rest, we didn't. My gaze connected with Sykes'. *Hero worshipping, huh? Nice red carpet.*

He smirked. *I know. Incoming. Nine o'clock.*

I turned and parried, then attacked. Switching to autopilot, I went on offense. I anchored the staff on the floor and swung on it, using a split kick to stop my two attackers at the same time. More replaced them. Sweat ran down my face. My lungs hurt with each breath and my arms grew tired and heavy. How long was Master Haziel going to let this go on?

"When outnumbered, go for the unexpected," Master Haziel often said. But we were out to defeat these guys, not kill them. Still, the unexpected came in many forms.

I locked on some of the psi energies and telepathed one message. A woman was in the air, aiming a kick at my side. In a fraction of a second, she adjusted the arc and caught the man on my other side instead. The man responded. Grinning, I blasted them with my power of persuasion. The ones in the periphery joined the fight, first one by one, then in droves. In seconds, the floor was filled with fighters, all more interested in each other than in us.

I teleported to a booth on the upper level of the arena, settled on a seat and watched the mayhem below.

What are you doing? Kim yelled.

Resting.

She materialized beside me, her breathing labored, and gave me a high-five. "Nice move."

"Thanks. These guys mean business, don't they?"

"Yep." She leaned forward and studied the booths below. "Where did Master Haziel go?"

"Home. He's probably having potato soup for breakfast," I said. "Ready to go back?"

She gripped my arm. "Not yet."

We grinned and watched the fight.

"They're good," I said. "I'd like to see their sword skills."

"They are just as good as us. Master Haziel trained them. But if we used our powers, we could take them out in seconds." Kim winced when Izzy got hit. "That was some mind control you pulled."

I was beginning to feel bad. I watched a girl trying her hardest to beat Remy into the floor. She was totally focused on him, which might explain why my mojo hadn't worked on her. "Do you know some of them?"

"No. My family didn't allow me to associate with other students before or after I joined the Institute."

"Friends?"

"No time," she said airily, as if it didn't matter, yet she sounded regretful.

"I'm not buying it," I said.

Kim shrugged. "Mom kept me busy. I had a private tutor, private trainer, movies, and computer games from Earth for entertainment."

I frowned. "I thought Xenithians despised earth things."

"We do, but my parents knew I'd be joining the Academy, so what better way to prepare me? Dad brought the gadgets home; Mom selected appropriate DVDs and games whenever she visited him. I grew up watching Veronica Mars, The O.C., Gossip Girl, 90210…even Buffy."

I grew up on Earth and yet never watched any of these programs until I'd met Kylie.

Izzy dropped on a seat on the other side of Kim. "Bitches, you should have telepathed me."

Kim laughed. "You were having so much fun."

"Fun?" Izzy elbowed Kim.

Watching them, I now understood why Izzy's friendship meant so much to Kim. She was her first and only friend.

"You did that?" Izzy asked, jerking her head to indicate the fighting.

"Yeah. Who's the girl trying to send Remy to Tartarus?"

"His ex," Izzy said then glanced at Kim. "Remember?—he'd visit her on weekends until a year ago when she broke it off. Let's tell the guys to join us. Whatever mind control you threw at these people might last for a long time and they need a break."

"I don't know," Kim said, studying Remy, then Sykes. "They seem to be enjoying themselves."

Izzy ignored Kim and telepathed Remy and Sykes. They looked up at the same time. Distracted, they didn't see their attackers. Sykes got hit in the chest, propelling him back into someone's stick, while Remy literally got swept off his feet. They both teleported at the same time, landing on top of us in a tangle of arms and legs.

"Ouch," Izzy protested.

"That's what you get for cheating," Sykes said, moving to a different seat.

Kim pushed Remy off her. "Get off me, you oaf."

Remy chuckled and plopped on a chair, his chest rising and falling. "How long have you been up here?"

"Just a few minutes," Izzy said.

Kim grinned. "Five."

"I'm going back," Sykes said. "I need to teach Lucien a lesson." He disappeared.

"Who's Lucien?" I asked as Sykes reappeared in the mix as though he hadn't left.

Remy rotated his neck. "His childhood best friend, now his nemesis."

Izzy and I laughed.

"How juvenile," Kim said. "I bet it was over a girl."

"What else?" Remy turned and studied us. "Let's finish this."

"Party pooper," someone murmured, Izzy or Kim.

"We attack from outside, surround them. Lil, start from the entrance. Izzy, you're opposite her. Kim, take the south end while I plow them from the north."

We teleported back into the fray. Maybe it was the rest that did it or the fact that we were more mentally prepared, but we had them on the run this time. Still, it was a relief when Master Haziel called out, "Enough."

The SGs staggered to the nearest chairs while we stayed standing. We even helped up the ones on the floor. Master walked to where I stood.

"What was that?" he asked.

I gave him an innocent smile. "We improvised."

"Sloppy execution," he snapped. "You should have done it smoothly, affecting everyone at once, not a few at a time." He turned and indicated the seated Guardians, who were watching us with puzzled expressions. They probably didn't understand how we had defeated them. "These are members of Xenith Security Unit, or as they are usually called, Security Guardians. They are our guests for as long as it takes. More will be arriving this evening."

"Why?" Sykes asked, his gaze going to a curly-haired guy he'd been fighting—Lucien.

Master Haziel's eyes narrowed. "They are here to offer us support. Unless you think you are invincible."

"Depends on who our target is," was Sykes' cocky response.

Master Haziel pursed his lips and nodded. "You are going to need that confidence." He glanced at all of us. "Your team is good, but you are not there yet. Maybe in a few decades. Still," he smiled and glanced at me, "you must always find a way to defeat your enemies. Do you know why I made you do this little exercise?" he glanced at us, then the SGs. "Anyone?"

"Because you have a wacky sense of humor?" Sykes said with a deadpan expression.

"And a mean streak," Izzy added.

Master Haziel didn't crack a smile, though we smiled while the SGs stared with shock. They probably couldn't believe the bold responses w e'd given.

"No," Master Haziel retorted. "Your enemies will not wait for you to notice them before they attack. They will swoop down when you least expect them. I want you to be vigilant at all times." He turned his attention to the SGs. "The Tribe practices both physical and mental warfare. You never ever let an opponent get inside your head. It does not matter how powerful they are. The Tribe did that to Lil and she just did it to you. Yes," he continued, pacing, "she used her power of persuasion and compelled you to turn against each other and ignore her team, and it worked brilliantly."

What happened to 'sloppy execution'? My face burned when the SGs focused on me. I expected resentment from them, but all I felt was approval after the initial surprise.

"You did not really think they overpowered you so easily when you outnumber them and are more experienced fighters?" Master Haziel continued. "She saw an opportunity and used it. She learned from her mistake. In the next few days, you will learn how to fight back against the paralysis that follows a mind-blend with a member of the Tribe. Warm up is over. It is time for some serious work."

"Master Haziel?" Izzy called out

He scowled. "What is it?"

"Who's guarding Xenith if the SGs are coming here?" she asked.

Master Haziel frowned. "A few will be left behind, though there is really no need. The portal will be destroyed by sundown."

Gasps came from my friends.

"You were not supposed to know about this until later today. Now back to work. Get practice swords." Daggers and swords floated from the wall. "Hand-to-hand combat that way." He pointed to the area near the door, then the other end of the arena. "Sword sparring over there."

I caught a sword and started across the floor, but I couldn't help overhearing the conversations among my friends. They were planning on going home to see their families immediately after the morning training session.

With the fear and anxiety came determination. We worked hard. The more Master Haziel pushed, the more we gave him. Still, there was a collective sigh of relief when he called out, "That is enough for today. Lil, stay behind."

I joined him in the booth, where he poured water in two glasses, offered me one and gulped down his. I knew the water would be lukewarm as usual and didn't bother to drink it, though I politely accepted the cup.

"How are you feeling?" he asked, studying me with a frown.

I shrugged. "Okay."

He nodded with approval. "Good. I talked to your grandfather this morning. Do you have any questions?"

"When will the Goddess need me? For how long?"

Master Haziel shook his head. "I do not have all the answers. I am sure she will let you know when she is ready."

"Does everyone know about me?"

"That you are the Chosen One? Yes. That the powers of the dagger are inside you because you are the Goddess' vessel? No. That is between us and the Cardinals." His eyes sharpened. "I assume you already told your friends?"

I made a face. "Wasn't I supposed to?"

"No, but what is done is done. If you have questions, concerns, or just need to talk, I am here for you."

"What if I want to vent?"

He straightened to his full height, which was several inches shorter than mine. "My students do not vent. They protest forcefully, object vehemently, or show their disapproval passionately."

I laughed. Master Haziel *did* have a wacky sense of humor.

"Come on. I want you to meet your new team." He started for the booth's entrance.

"New team?" I placed my glass on the table. He pointed toward the floor of the pit, where four SGs—two guys and two girls—were talking.

"Why do I need them?"

"They are your backup. You are going to L.A." Master Haziel indicated we should join the others, but I didn't move.

"To do what?" I asked.

"Bran needs your help with something."

"You talked to him? When? Is he okay?"

"Yes, I talked to him a few minutes ago and yes, he is okay," Master Haziel said impatiently.

Relief washed over me. "Why can't I go with Remy and the others?"

Master Haziel sighed, then pinned me down with narrowed eyes. "They are going home to see their families before the portal is sealed. *They*," he indicated the SGs with a nod, "will be your backup team until your friends return. You *must* learn to work with other Guardians, not just your regular team."

"Why? No, let me guess," I added quickly. "It is part of my duties as the Chosen One to be flexible?"

"I always knew you were a quick learner. Come along."

The four SGs stopped talking as we drew closer. I recognized Sykes' old buddy Lucien. From their black hair pulled back in ponytails, pale skin, and brown eyes, to the moles by their left eyes, the two women were carbon copies of each other. The other man had a thin moustache and a goatee. Although it was hard to guess the age of most Guardians, he appeared older than the twins, who looked like they were in their mid-twenties.

"This is Esras," Master Haziel pointed at the bearded guy, then nodded at the twins, "Lunaris and Solaris. They are heads of sectors."

I had no idea how many sectors were in Xenith, but only the best of the Guardians made sector heads, like my grandfather was the head of the Senior Guardians.

"And this is Lucien," he indicated the curly-haired guy with twinkling topaz eyes, "an enterprising young man who might prove to be useful." There was pride in Master Haziel's voice, but he leveled the young man a warning glance before looking my way and adding, "You will take the lead on this." He paused as though expecting the others to say something. When they didn't, he continued. "Do not take too long. Help Bran and come straight home. The security team is monitoring the area for the Tribe, and so far they have not spotted them since the attack on the island. Should you encounter them, do not engage them. Find a way to lose them and head home. Questions?"

No one spoke, but everyone grew tense at the mention of the Tribe. I didn't like the idea of going anywhere with four Guardians straight from Xenith. What did they know about fighting demons? On the other hand, Bran needed my help.

"What is Bran's mission and how are we going to help him?" I asked.

"Find him and find out instead of wasting time asking questions." Master Haziel dismissed us with a wave, then teleported.

Releasing a breath, I turned and faced the SGs. They stood with their hands behind their backs, legs slightly apart, body straight, and eyes locked on me as though I were a drill sergeant and they were recruits waiting for instruction. Resentment mixed with curiosity hung around them. The resentment came from the twins. What was their problem? They didn't like me in charge? Too bad. I thought I caught a twinkle in Esras' eyes, but I must have imagined it because when I looked him straight in the eyes, he didn't blink or crack a smile. Lucien's topaz eyes shone with anticipation. I liked him already.

"Okay. Let's relax and get to know each other better now that the taskmaster is gone," I joked, surprised when my voice came out confident when I wasn't.

Lucien grinned. The twins and Esras didn't relax.

"I know this is your first time here, so feel free to ask me anything," I said.

"Are we going to fight demons, Cardinal?" Lucien asked.

I grinned at his enthusiasm. "I don't know. Our objective is to find Bran, help him with whatever he's doing and come straight back. If demons get in our way, then yes, we'll deal with them. Please, call me Lil."

Lucien's grin widened. "We heard that your team uses neutral demons as informants and are friendly with them. Can we stop by their den? I'd like to tell my friends back at home that I visited one."

"No," Solaris, or Lunaris, said, disgust written on her face. "We don't associate with demons."

I studied her, not surprised by her attitude. The Guardians' innate hatred for demons was homegrown. When I first met Remy, Sykes, Kim, and Izzy, they'd felt exactly the same way. Bran had cured them of such prejudices.

"We do things democratically around here, Lunaris," I said firmly.

"My name is Solaris," she snapped rudely as though insulted I couldn't tell them apart. She jerked her thumb and indicated her twin. "*She* is Lunaris."

I kept my cool when all I wanted to do was snap back, but I was leading this mission and that meant keeping my cool, just like Remy or Bran would. "We usually go with what the majority decides, which means we vote."

"Then I vote we don't fraternize with any demons, active, neutral or whatever you want to call them," Solaris said.

Her sister nodded. The two were angry about something, though I wasn't sure what. Esras' gaze moved from me to the twins and back to me again, but he didn't speak. I had a feeling he was one of those guys who just watched and listened without intervening.

"That's going to be interesting, because we are going to Jethro's Bar and Jethro is a demon, a Neutral to be specific," I said with just a tiny bit of glee. "And if you didn't already know, Cardinal Bran is considered a Souled Demon by some."

The twins looked at each other and made faces. Their attitude was beginning to piss me off. Lucien raised a finger to get my attention. "Yes?"

"Can we eat at Jethro's since it's getting close to lunch time?"

"No," the twins said, in unison this time.

Esras shook his head, too.

I gave Lucien a sheepish grin. "Sorry, we've been outvoted. We'll probably be back here by lunchtime anyway. If we are not, we can eat at a restaurant owned by a Guardian."

Lucien was disappointed, even though he tried to cover it with a smile. "Is Jethro a member of the Outcasts?"

"It's an insult to use the term 'Outcasts'," I corrected him impatiently.

He blinked, his smile waning. "I didn't know."

Feeling bad since he was the only nice SG in my unwanted new team, I gave him a smile. "They are called the Brotherhood of Guardians or just the Brotherhood. And no, Jethro is not a member. He is a neutral Hermonite." From the corner of my eyes, I caught the glance and eye rolls the twins exchanged. Grinding my teeth, I added, "But that doesn't mean he didn't go after human souls at some point. What matters now is he doesn't do it anymore. He supplies us with information on demonic activities that our Psi-dar can't pick up. We, in turn, offer him protection." I glanced at my watch. Eleven o'clock. I gave them a sweeping glance. "Do you know where the weapons room is?"

"Yes, Cardinal." Esras frowned. "Master Haziel showed us around."

"Did he give you hunting coats to conceal your weapons, too?"

They all nodded.

"Good. Wear them and let's meet outside the weapons room in thirty minutes. Oh, and Esras?" He glanced at me. "Don't call me Cardinal. Everyone calls me Lil." I waited until they teleported, then sighed. This mission could turn disastrous if I didn't watch my temper.

- 13 -

UNEXPECTED ANSWERS

The alley behind Jethro's bar was filthy, as usual. Leading with Lucien, I slowed down our teleport until I found a spot away from the icky puddles, then rematerialized.

Lucien grinned. "That was cool. How did you slow down?"

"A trick I learned recently," I said absentmindedly, reaching under my trench coat to touch my lower back. It felt warm and tingly, like an itch that wouldn't go away. Not sure what it meant, I ignored it and focused on Bran.

A quick scan told me he wasn't at Jethro's, which was packed as usual. I still didn't understand why he chose to sleep at Jethro's when it took less than a second to teleport home.

The twins appeared, one after the other. They looked around with disgust. Once again, I couldn't tell them apart until they spoke.

"Where are we?" one asked. Her voice was gentler, which meant she was Lunaris.

"L.A. warehouse district. This building belongs to Jethro. The bar's entrance is that way." I pointed toward the front of the building.

"Yeah, I can feel them," Solaris said in her high-pitched annoying voice. "Demons," she added, reaching for the ninja stars she'd placed in sheaths around her waist when we were in the weapons room.

"No weapons, please," I warned. Her eyes narrowed as though she wanted to defy me, then she backed down, her hands dropping to her sides and forming fists.

"Where's Esras?" I asked when the Guardian didn't appear.

"Master Haziel came to the weapons room right after you teleported and needed to have a word," Lunaris answered.

"He'll miss the telegate if he's not careful," I warned. A telegate was a trail of energy disturbance left behind when one teleported. "One time, when we teleported here, only two of us made it while the others ended up across town."

Esras appeared just as I finished speaking. He was red in the face, uneasiness pouring from him.

"Is everything okay?" I asked.

"Yeah," he said and tugged the collar of his shirt. The fact that he couldn't meet my eyes told me his nervousness had something to do with me. If he didn't want to talk about it, fine. I couldn't take any more mess directed at me. What bugged me more was the twins' antagonistic attitude toward all demons. They had grumbled while we chose weapons, and I was sure they wouldn't stop.

"Before we go inside the restaurant, you need to know it is packed. Don't do or say anything to antagonize them, because we are not here to fight. In fact, Jethro has a policy against many things, including fights and teleporting, in his bar. If a demon makes a sudden move, don't assume he or she is about to attack. If you have to respond, just subdue them."

"This is not right," Solaris murmured.

"Solaris," her twin warned.

"You know I'm right," Solaris snapped. "He did this on purpose. He knows how we feel about…about…" she glanced at me and lifted her chin, "about being friendly with demons." I had a feeling she meant to say something else.

Lunaris sighed and glanced at me. "I apologize for my sister—"

"You don't need to apologize to *her*."

The way she said "her", I might as well be something that crawled from the sewer.

"What is your problem, Solaris?" I asked, working hard to control my temper. "If you feel so strongly about them, why did you volunteer to come with me?"

"We didn't volunteer. The senile old fart told us to come," Solaris said.

Something inside me snapped. "Don't call Master Haziel names. He's many things, but he's not senile or a fart, whatever that is. I'm sure he had his reasons for choosing you."

"Of course, he does," Solaris snapped. "He is playing head games with us, as usual."

My eyes narrowed. "What is that supposed to mean?"

"He knows how we feel about demons because they killed our parents," she snarled.

I blinked at the hatred in her voice. "Oh, I didn't know."

"Why should you? It happened thirteen years ago during the demonic raid," she answered, her eyes flashing. "You were only three."

Oh, no, not that again. Did they know my father was behind it? Would I ever put what he did behind me? My father had gone on a murderous rampage while searching for my mother and me, but no one had ever made me feel guilty for his actions until today.

"I'm sorry," I said.

"You should be," Solaris said with so much venom I cringed.

"That is enough," Esras interjected.

"You stay out of this, Esras," Solaris snapped.

Solaris, her sister warned her telepathically, but somehow I heard her. *It is not her fault.*

Of course it is. He was searching for her.

Was this the purpose of this mission? To see if I could work with people who hated my guts?

Solaris continued to glare at me. "Your father—"

"Is in Tartarus," I said with as much venom as I could master, which was easy because I was now pissed.

"No, he's not. He's been seen more than once the last two weeks."

My stomach hollowed out. "That's crap. My grandfather defeated him during the battle on Jarvis Island, and anyone who claims he's alive is calling my grandfather a liar. I'm sorry you lost your family, but I lost my mother and grandmother, too. *And,* I am not responsible for Valafar's actions."

Solaris opened her mouth again, but her twin grabbed her arm and marched her to the back of the building. I didn't bother to listen to their exchange. I took some deep calming breaths, then glanced at Lucien and Esras.

"You handled that very well," Esras said. Lucien nodded.

I shook my head. The very thought that Valafar could be alive filled me with dread. My feelings toward him were still conflicted. Part of me wished he wasn't suffering in Tartarus. He had once loved me enough to raid Guardian enclaves while searching for my mother and me. The other part of me wished he would just disappear forever. He'd been ruthless and ambitious, and if by some remote chance he'd survived Jarvis Island, he'd come for me again. Even giving weight to Solaris's rants pissed me off.

"Are your feelings going to get in the way of this mission?" I asked when the twins rejoined us.

"Of course not," Lunaris answered and I could tell she was telling the truth.

Solaris glowered instead.

I cocked my eyebrow, but she still refused to speak. "If you can't be objective, Solaris, then go back to the valley and report to Master Haziel."

A flicker of uncertainty flashed in her eyes.

"I mean it. If you can't take orders from me, you have no business being here."

"My feelings won't get in the way of my duties, *Cardinal,*" she said through clenched teeth.

"Good because rule number one is never let personal feelings get in the way of getting a job done." I glanced at Esras, then Lucien, before coming back to the twins. "If any of you have a problem with me because Valafar was my father, put it aside for now. You'll have plenty of time afterward to continue hating me. Jethro may be a Hermonite, but he's an ally. His customers are our allies too. You don't attack anyone unless I say so."

Silence.

"Is that understood?"

"Yes, Cardinal," the four said in unison.

This time, I didn't tell them not to call me Cardinal. We'd wasted enough time talking. "Let's go."

No one spoke as we sidestepped puddles of grey muck and walked toward the entrance. Valafar alive? What utter nonsense. We exited the alley and entered the road running in front of hulking warehouses. The parking area in front of the bar was packed with bikes.

Like most of the warehouses in the area, the exterior needed fixing. In fact, it looked exactly the same as the first time I saw it. The green and black canopy above the metal railing was faded, the chairs and table were chipped and paint was falling off the surface. The only new additions were the ancient words scrawled on the glass window.

"Ready?" I asked before opening the door. Lucien and Esras nodded right away. The twins took their time, but they eventually did.

The aroma of freshly brewed coffee mixed with spicy foods greeted us when I opened the front entrance. The tingle and heat at the base of my spine slowly spread upward and outward as though someone had injected something hot into my spine. My fingers grew warm and for one brief moment, my vision blurred then sharpened as I glanced around.

I recognized faces in the crowd, but the usual nods and smiles were missing. There was a mass transformation as the shape-shifters reverted to their human forms. Scales smoothed out and body hair shrunk until skins were human-like. Horns, tails, and claws retracted. Cat and dog-like ears shifted. Lizard-like tongues stopped lapping at bug soups. Then there was mass teleporting from the tables near us to the far walls, Hermonites tripping and bumping against each other.

They'd never run from us before. Maybe it was the new faces. I glanced back and was surprised when they all stopped walking and stared at me like I'd sprouted two heads. When Lucien's eyes went to my hands, I looked down and gulped. My hands were glowing. Why?

The ancient texts were visible on my wrist and the back of my hand, and it hit me. I was a human lethal weapon. The Kris Dagger's powers had sensed the demons, just like they had with Dante and Kael a week ago. Chances were I was already emitting rays harmful to everyone in the room. No wonder they'd teleported away as soon as we stepped inside the restaurant.

I glanced around and fought panic. Jethro's customers stood near the walls and watched us warily. The tingle along my spine and arms intensified, and the glow around my hands grew brighter. If I didn't control my powers, I'd flood the room with the Kris Dagger's death rays and kill every Neutral in the room.

I focused hard on staying calm. It was one thing to control my powers when I sparred at home and quite another when I faced demons. *They're not my enemies…they're our allies…they're not my enemies…they're our allies…*

Flashes of past scenes zipped through my mind—Jethro welcoming us with open arms, giving us information, riding in a motorcade, eating, playing a game of pool in the next room, listening to Karaoke singers. Some of the memories were hazy, possibly because I couldn't remember when they happened, but being in the bar brought them back.

My hands grew dimmer. The more I focused on the Neutrals' past goodness, the dimmer the symbols grew. After a few more seconds, the glow disappeared, though the buzz along my spine remained. I glanced at the other Guardians, who were watching me with a mixture of concern and awe. Even Solaris forgot to glare at me with hatred.

Let's go, I telepathed them.

Eyes followed us as we approached the counter. One of the bartenders teleported, leaving behind the one I recognized from a few months ago. He'd helped us locate a Nosferatu demoness. Because of my messed-up memories, I didn't know how often our paths had crossed since.

A wave of fear and resentment flowed from him, his gaze shifting from me to the others then back to me again, but he didn't bolt like his friend.

"We need to talk." I could see the Neutrals watching us from the corner of my eyes, so I kept my voice low. "Privately."

He nodded, then appeared on our side of the counter. I must not have been emitting the harmful rays because he didn't appear to be in pain. We followed him across the restaurant, eyes drilling holes in our backs. I had no idea where the resentment came from. It couldn't be because I'd become a demon's worst nightmare. From what I remembered, Jethro's customers had always liked having us around.

Before we left the restaurant floor and the narrow hallway leading to Jethro's office and private quarters, I glanced back. The Neutrals watched us like hawks.

"Esras, you come with me. The rest of you keep watch out here. If anyone approaches, stop them and find out what they want. If they want to talk to me, ping me. If they attack, knock them out."

They nodded, even Solaris. Her attitude had undergone a dramatic change, but I knew it wouldn't last.

"I'm an empath, so I'll know if you need our help," I added, then followed the bartender and Esras down the hallway to Jethro's office, which was a lot more spacious than I'd first thought.

The once dreary room had undergone some changes—several bunk beds and a dresser now replaced the piles of newspaper that had taken up most of the space. The lumpy sofa Bran had used when he'd lived with Jethro was still there along with the desk.

I faced the bartender, who kept his distance as though he expected me to hurt him. "Where's Jethro?"

"He is missing because…because…" He swallowed.

I frowned. "Because of what?"

"His association with you guys…the Guardians," he finished in a rush, his face flushing.

"What makes you say that?" I asked.

"Two nature-benders came looking for him last night after he left for a meeting with the Cardinals. They knew he was meeting with you. Not *you,* Cardinal Lil. I mean the older Cardinals, who picked him up. The nature-benders vowed to come back. As soon as the Cardinals brought Jethro back, they reappeared and took him. I didn't know what to do, so I contacted the Hermonites out there." He slanted his head to indicate the bar. "They organized a search party. Most of them spent the night searching for Jethro. Some are still out there."

That might explain the resentment toward us.

"What did the nature-benders look like?" I asked, hoping they were Dante and Kael.

"Tall, big, long, curly brown hair. They looked like twins."

Definitely not Dante and Kael. "Have you seen Cardinal Llyr?"

"He was here an hour ago. As soon as I told him about Jethro, he left to search for him, too. He thinks whoever took the others has Jethro."

"The others?"

"Young Hermonites have been disappearing for several weeks now. There are rumors that the Guardians kidnapped them."

"What would we want with demons?" Esras asked.

"To turn them into Guardians, like you turned Cardinal Llyr," the bartender said.

I sighed. How many times did we have to go through this? "Bran chose to be with the Guardians. No one turned him. And we have nothing to do with their disappearances," I added firmly. "I'll talk to the Hermonites before we leave."

"Do you think that's wise?" Esras asked.

"They are our allies, Esras. Of course we have to calm their fears or they could turn against us. With Jethro gone, that seems more likely than ever. " I turned my attention to the bartender. "Did Cardinal Bran sleep here?"

"No. He was in and out of here yesterday during the day. He told Jethro he was searching for his brother. He came back an hour ago, changed his clothes and was about to leave again when I told him Jethro was missing." The bartender pointed at a scrunched-up black T-shirt and pants at the foot of the couch.

I picked them up with the tips of my fingers. They were filthy and smelled. Beside them were a plastic bag and several price tags. I glanced at Esras. "What do you think?"

He lifted the shirt, then the pants. "The dirt covers the front of his shirt and pants, which means he was on his stomach, either lying down or crawling." He sniffed them. "Smells like sewer."

If Bran had spent the night in some rat hole, it might explain why I'd tossed and turned all night long. I'd felt his discomfort. I glanced at the bartender. "Did Cardinal Bran say where he was headed?"

"No. Are you going to find them?" the bartender asked hopefully. "Jethro means a lot to us. This bar is a refuge for my kind, and half the people in the bar have called this home, just like Cardinal Bran has."

"I know. Why don't you go back to the bar and tell them I want to talk to them? They have to know we would never hurt them or turn our backs on—"

Several pings hit me at once. *What is it?*

A demon is here, and he insists on talking to you, Solaris telepathed.

I stepped into the hallway and frowned. All the three Guardians had their weapons pointed at…Gavyn? Dressed in white slacks and a matching blazer over a light blue shirt, his silver hair cropped in layers, he looked like he'd just stepped out of a country club.

He smirked and waved like we were best buds. The tingle at the base of my spine shot up my spine.

"Hey, little sister," he said. "What are you doing in this dump? With the Tribunal's army hunting your kind, I thought you'd be hiding with the rest of the Guardians."

Tribe…Tribunal? The two words sounded almost alike. Did they mean the same thing? I had no interest in asking Gavyn because he'd only gloat and piss me off more. Already, I wanted nothing better than to wipe the smug smile off his face, but Bran would never forgive me.

I struggled to calm my mind and bring my powers under control. It wasn't working. The power pulsing up and down my spine needed an outlet.

"What do you want, Gavyn?" I called out, fear of hurting him keeping me in the doorway.

"You and I need to talk. Alone. Tell your new minions to," he wiggled his fingers, "move out of my way."

"I don't think so," I said, aware that Esras had followed me. He stood protectively behind me, tension shooting from his body.

"Scared to be alone with me, little sister?"

"Yeah, scared for you, and I'm not your sister."

He cocked his brow. "What? You're not going to be mated with my brother? Last time I checked, the sun rose and set on him. You even saved my life from your malevolent sister. That's the kind of thing you do for family, or family-to-be. By the way, I never got around to thanking you for that." He touched his chest and bowed. "Thank you."

No matter how annoying he was, I had to remember he was Bran's brother. I focused on controlling my powers until the tingle on my back receded.

Meanwhile Gavyn lowered his head to peer into Solaris's eyes and whispered, "How do you feel knowing your precious Chosen One is the reason you are being hunted, sweetheart? Why do your people have to suffer because of her? First Valafar and his raid, and now the Tribunal and its, uh, what do you Guardians call its army again? Yeah, the Tribe, the mighty Guardians' worst nightmare."

Seriously? He was like a child sometimes. When he didn't get his way, he threw tantrums by saying the dumbest things. Solaris didn't need him egging her on. "Let him pass."

Instead of obeying, Solaris hissed out a breath. "What are you talking about, demon?"

He smirked. "Wouldn't you like to know? Move aside like a good little Guardian."

"Only the weak and incompetent summon more powerful beings to fight their battles," she snapped, then shifted closer to him. "And if you ever call me sweetheart again, fiend, I'll send you to Tartarus so fast they'll be picking pieces of you off the walls for centuries." She threw a look at me over her shoulder. "He's all yours, Cardinal." Then she stepped out of his way.

For one brief moment, Gavyn leered at her. "I hope you and I meet again, *sweetheart*. I'd love to show you a thing or two that would make your head spin." He sauntered past Esras and me. "Stay here, old man. My business is with the lovely Lilith."

Esras hesitated and glanced at me.

"I'll be fine," I reassured him. Gavyn's arrogance was annoying, but he only ever acted cocky when he had the upper hand. *He knows where the Summoners are,* I telepathed Esras. *Just give me a minute with him.*

He nodded, but he didn't like it. I hurried after Gavyn.

"Scram, minion," he ordered when he entered Jethro's office and saw the bartender.

"You shouldn't be here," the bartender snarled. "Jethro doesn't allow your kind in here."

Gavyn smiled. "My kind? I thought this," he waved, "was a sanctuary for all Nephilim, good or bad."

"Except bottom-dwellers like you," the bartender retorted.

Gavyn's eyes flashed. He studied the bartender, his lips curling up. "You know what I miss? The old days, when we tied traitors to rocks and set vultures on them for eternity."

"And soul-suckers were sent to rot in Tartarus for eternity," the bartender retorted.

In a fraction of a second, Gavyn's hand moved and a sizzling, red energy ball materialized above his palm.

"Enough. You," I nodded at the bartender, "go back to the bar."

He scurried out of the room.

"He was being insolent," Gavyn said, the energy ball fizzling out.

"What's wrong with you? You know the rules. You can't touch Neutrals under our protection, or all bets are off."

He smiled though his gray eyes remained cold. "You'd test my brother's loyalty by attacking me to protect that nobody?"

"He's not a nobody, and Bran would understand."

"Would he?" Gavyn's eyes glistened. "I don't have time for this. I have things to do, places to go." He glanced over his shoulder at Esras. "Do you mind?" The he flicked his finger and the door slammed shut on Esras' face.

I frowned. His energy powers seemed to have grown stronger. First an *omni* energy ball, now a show of telekinetic ability. "What do you want, Gavyn?"

Gavyn's eyes narrowed as he studied me, his head cocked to the side. "There's something different about you."

What? I wanted to ask, but I hated discussing anything personal with him. Besides, there was enough weirdness that came with my new powers I really didn't want to know. "Where have you been? Bran's been looking for you for two days."

"And he almost got killed, thanks to you. I'm getting strange vibes from you that are very intriguing. What have you been up to? I know we haven't seen each other in a while, but the changes in you..." his eyes narrowed and he added slowly, "I can now see what my little brother sees in you."

Ew. The thought that Gavyn found anything remotely attractive about me made me want to throw up. "Why is it my fault Bran almost got killed?"

Annoyance flashed in Gavyn's eyes. "He was in trouble, I contacted you but you chose to ignore me. But that's yesterday's news. He's okay, for now. In fact, he was here earlier. I can still feel his energy."

"I don't like being accused of things I haven't done, Gavyn."

"This time, you're guilty as charged, but I'm in a good mood and would rather talk about you and this new vibe—"

I waved my hand without meaning to and sent him upward and backward until his back slammed the door and his feet dangled several inches off the floor. "I'm not in the mood for your stupid games either, Gavyn. Start talking."

Furious didn't begin to describe the expression that flashed on his face. "Put me down!"

"Tell me what you're talking about. What trouble was Bran in? When did you contact me?"

"Don't be hotheaded, Lilith. You touch me again and you, your minions, and everyone in this building go poof. You didn't think I'd come here alone, did you? Put. Me. Down."

I did a psi scan to confirm his words. There were demons outside, on the ground and on the roof of the building. I wasn't sure whether they were regular demons or the Tribe, but I refused to show Gavyn that his threats worried me.

I guided the power buzzing on my back to move to my right hand, just like Master Haziel had taught me. My fingers tingled as the ancient writings appeared on the surface of my skin. Then my hand started to glow.

"What in Tartarus is that?" Gavyn asked.

"Start. Talking."

Uncertainty flickered in his eyes, but then his smugness returned. "Go ahead. The Tribunal will only bring me back," he bragged.

There was that word again—the Tribunal. What did it mean? "No one returns from Tartarus."

"That is where you are wrong, little sister. Not only will I come back, but I'll be stronger. On top of that, you'll have to explain to my brother why you sent me there in the first place."

Bran. If only Gavyn wasn't his brother. I let him go. He landed on the floor like a cat, adjusted his blazer, and brushed off his shoulder. Another smug grin touched his lips.

"What is this new power you have?" he asked, staring at my hand.

I willed the writings from my hands. They disappeared along with the glow. I took a step away from Gavyn. "I think you should leave now."

"Okay, if you insist on knowing the truth," he said flippantly, "I put your phone number through your human medium and sent you some text messages."

My mind raced as I tried to recall what was in the messages from Kylie.

Are you with Bran? The first one had said. Kylie often checked if I was alone before asking me over to her place. I'd responded with a "no". I hadn't read the next two messages because of the meeting.

Get over here now, I need your help… The last text had sounded so much like Kylie, I hadn't bothered to finish reading it. It never crossed my mind to wonder why she hadn't used abbreviated texts like she usually did.

"Why couldn't you be clearer? I thought they came from Kylie, and she thought her brother sent them." I was yelling by the time I finished.

"Clearer? What part of 'get over here now, I need your help stopping Bran' wasn't clear," he snapped, losing his cool too. "Or 'Bran needs you'?"

Guilt washed over me. I shouldn't have ignored the rest of the message, or the previous ones. "What happened?"

"Oh, now you want to know?"

"Just. Tell. Me."

He made a face. "He pissed off a few club owners while searching for me, got into a few fights. I couldn't help him because I was in the middle of an important meeting, so I contacted you. By the time I finished, which was a few minutes ago, I learned he wanted to meet me, which as it happens works perfectly with my plans. I want to see him too. " His expression grew serious. "In fact, I have a proposal for the two of you."

I rolled my eyes. "Really?"

"Listen first before you blow me off. Join me."

"Excuse me?"

"You and Bran should leave the Guardians and join me."

He had lost it if he thought we could ever do something so stupid. "Why would we do that?"

"It is the only way to stop the Tribe."

Maybe he wasn't crazy. "What do you mean?"

"All this mess would have been avoided if Bran had done the right thing and accepted his responsibilities as the leader of the Hermonites." His voice dropped. "The truth is out, Lilith. The Tribunal knows how he 'won' the battle on Jarvis Island."

The hollow feeling I hated settled in my stomach. A little over four month ago, Valafar had staged a fight-till-death combat on Jarvis Island and told the demonic world the winner would become their leader. At the same time, he had manipulated us, dangling the list of the humans who'd sold their souls to Bran until Bran signed a contract and joined the combat to win it back. I did not remember the details of that night, but Bran had filled me in. I had had no choice but to help him win. My participation, a secret among the Cardinals, had been known by only three demons—Valafar, who was dead, my sister and Gavyn. Even though Gavyn hadn't been able to attend the event, Bran had told him afterward.

"How could you use what Bran told you in confidence against us?"

"I didn't." A weird expression crossed his face. "I mean, I did it to help you. Besides, that was just the first evidence *we* presented to the Tribunal. There's more. You and your grandfather brainwashed Bran and made him switch—"

"Bran chose us," I snapped. "I'm getting tired of your people saying we influenced his decision."

"That's your opinion. The fact remains that the switch is a first in the history of the Nephilim. The Tribunal wasn't sure how to deal with that, until we told them about the Specials. Those children will cause an imbalance of power in the Guardians' favor. And last, you decided to help soulless degenerates from the human cesspool. There are rules, Lilith. When humans sell their souls, they belong to us. You are not supposed to give their souls back."

I couldn't come up with an argument against the things he'd said. We were guilty. No wonder the Goddess wanted us to find the Summoners to avoid annihilation.

"Who summoned the Tribe? The Order? Can we meet with it?"

"Those feeble-minded members of the Order cannot agree on anything, let alone a historic moment as the summoning." He smiled smugly. "I formed a new council and summoned the Tribunal. Then the Tribunal sent its army to fix things."

I swallowed, refusing to panic. "Fix how?"

"Hunt you guys down and make Bran take his rightful place with us. If he can't, then *you* must take his place. You both won, so technically you should be co-rulers. The Specials must be returned to us. However, if you and Bran join me now, the Guardians can keep them. Oh, and no more helping humans. We've recovered our losses over the last two weeks and even acquired new ones, so we are even. The bottom line is if we get you and Bran, we can ask the Tribunal to rescind its orders and send the Tribe home."

He was nuts. There was no way I'd ever willingly join the dark side. On the other hand, if Bran were in danger… Unfortunately, he would do the same to protect me. There had to be a way to stop the Tribe. But what if Gavyn was lying to manipulate me?

"When do you want an answer? I mean, can we sit down and discuss the details with your council?"

Gavyn chuckled. "Nice try. You can meet the council *after* you agree to join us."

"Where? Mount Hermon?"

"The assistant manager who gave you that name is in Tartarus. Don't worry about the details. I'll finalize them with Bran."

"With both of us," I corrected him. "Did your council kidnap Jethro?"

He cocked an eyebrow, the gesture so like Bran's it annoyed me to see it on his face. "You ask way too many questions, Lil."

"Did you?"

"We didn't kidnap anyone. They volunteered. You have your army of Guardians willing to die for the cause, and now we have ours." He smirked as though he knew his words would shut me up. "One little personal piece of advice, Lilith. That new ability you have can be very tempting to a power-hungry demon, so be careful who you show off to, especially when you meet my council."

I stared after him, surprised. He'd just warned me. Now why would he do that? He opened the door and disappeared out of view. I thought I heard him say something to the others, but I was busy replaying the conversation I just had. It was crazy, yet everything made sense, especially the way the Tribe only came after us, never the senior Cardinals.

I released a breath I didn't know I was holding, my gaze meeting with Esras'. Behind him stood Solaris, Lunaris, and Lucien. They slowly entered the room.

"You heard?" I asked them.

"Everything," Esras said. The other three nodded.

"Are you going to consider their offer?" Solaris asked. "Take one for the Guardians?"

I shot her an annoyed look. "Of course not. You can't believe anything Gavyn says. He's mean and manipulative."

"What if he was speaking the truth?"

"Not now, Solaris," Esras warned.

"Why not? The CT ordered the portal closed and hundreds of SGs are being asked to put their lives in danger for something her team did. What if she and Llyr can stop this nightmare?" She faced me and raised her brow.

Put that way, it made sense to give in to Gavyn's diabolical plan. "I don't know, Solaris. Maybe we will. I have to talk to Bran and my grandfather about all this before…" I cleared my throat, refusing to give in to my emotions. I hated Gavyn Llyr.

"So who really won the battle on Jarvis Island?" Solaris asked.

Part of me wanted to blow her off, but another realized the truth would eventually come out. “Bran did, but I helped him during the last fight.”

“So it’s true, the two of you won?” she continued

I shrugged. “Something like that. Let’s go. I have to talk to Jethro’s Neutrals.”

The others started out of the room, but Solaris wasn’t done. “So the demon wasn’t lying. You two are co-rulers, king and queen of the Hermonites.”

“Shut up, Solaris,” her sister snapped from the doorway. “I swear, sometimes I wonder what goes on in your head.”

“We now know why they are after us and *we* will stop them,” Esras said. He shot Solaris a glance. “Cardinals don’t run or throw their own under the bus, Solaris. We find out the Tribe’s weaknesses, and use them to our advantage.”

“One thing still doesn’t make sense,” Lucien said. “Tribunal means court, right?”

Esras and Lunaris nodded. Solaris didn’t bother to respond. She was probably thinking up another line of attack.

“Why would a demon court decide our fate?” he asked.

Silence followed his question, but with it came another possibility. “If they have a Tribunal who decide their cases, then we probably have one too,” I said. “We could have a rebuttal for the accusations leveled against us.”

“Maybe the Senior Cardinals have answers,” Lunaris said.

“Master Haziel, not the seniors,” I said.

“Then let’s go home. I’d like to know if a Tribunal can really bring people from Tartarus like he claimed,” Solaris added. “It might explain why a Guardian saw Valafar. Maybe their Tribunal brought him back.”

I inhaled, then exhaled slowly. Of all the things Gavyn had said, that worried me the most. No one was supposed to escape from Tartarus, yet he had said their Tribunal could bring demons back.

“We can’t go home yet,” I said. “We must find Bran before Gavyn does.”

Solaris eyes narrowed. “Why?”

“He’s likely to do exactly what you want—sacrifice himself.” To save me.

- 14 -

NO SERVICE, GUARDIANS

"Why didn't you tell them the truth back there?" Esras asked when we left Jethro's bar.

"That Jethro joined a demonic faction run by Gavyn and his evil friends?" I shook my head as I led the way back into the alley. "He didn't. He wouldn't. Gavyn might act like he has all the answers, but he's a manipulator."

"You promised to bring back Jethro and the children Gavyn's new council kidnapped," Lucien said.

"We will, Lucien. I always try to think positive." I stopped when we reached the back of the alley. "There are two places we can search for Bran. There's a restaurant we usually hang out when we are in town. It is lunchtime now, so if he stopped to eat, he should be there. It is owned by a member of the Brotherhood."

"Lead the way," Esras said. He'd become more talkative since the meeting with Gavyn, while Solaris had grown more quiet. I liked it.

I teleported inside Keiran's office and found him behind his desk, eating. He looked up, violet eyes widening underneath thick lashes. "Lil? What are you doing here?"

"Looking for Bran." The others appeared beside me. "Lucien, Esras, Lunaris, and Solaris." I indicated the restaurateur. "Keiran, a member of the Brotherhood. His restaurant is the best in L.A."

Keiran put his plate down and stood. "I'm sorry we're meeting under these circumstances, Guardians. I would have loved to welcome you with open arms. Unfortunately, I can't."

I blinked. "What?"

"Guardians are officially *persona non grata* around here."

"Since when?"

"Since last night."

Great! The day couldn't get any worse. "Does that mean Bran hasn't been here today?"

"Oh, he has…was here. He stopped by for breakfast and said he'd be back for lunch at," he looked at his watch, "noon. It is five to. If you want to wait for him, sit." He waved toward the chairs around the room. "I'll even get you something to eat."

No one moved.

"But you just said we are not allowed here," I said.

"In the restaurant. This is my office," Keiran explained, flashing a lopsided grin. "Besides, I choose my friends, not my leaders."

I glanced at the others and indicated the chairs. Lucien was the first one to sit, but his fascinated gaze stayed on Kieran. He'd never met a member of the Brotherhood before. Not that they were really different from us. I grabbed a seat, too. Esras and the others had no choice but to sit.

"So? Why can't we eat here anymore?" I asked.

Kieran perched his butt on the edge of his desk, crossed his arms and legs, and shrugged. "Last night, we got a visit from the senior Cardinals. They brought us the news about the arrival of the Tribe. Our leaders asked the Cardinals if they could offer sanctuary to our young, the Specials, and our elderly until the situation with the Tribe was resolved. We'd hoped they'd take them to Xenith or at the very least, hide them at one of your High Council Headquarters." He sighed and shook his head.

"They refused?" I asked, even though his scowl answered for him.

"This morning Cardinal Hsia brought us the news. Your leaders in Xenith said no. So as of today, no Cardinal is allowed in our compound or at any business run by a member of the Brotherhood. Officially, we've gone back to being neutral. Literally." He grinned and placed a clairvoyant crystal on his table. "So what would you like to eat?"

I shook my head. "We don't want you to go against your leaders, Keiran. We can eat at one of the Civilian-run restaurants."

"No, you can't. Every restaurant and business run by your Civilian Guardians is closed. They all have *Will Re-Open Under New Management* signs on their doors. I was going to ask Bran what's going on."

"All Civilians were told to head back to Xenith," I explained.

"Of course." Keiran waved a hand over the crystal, activating it. "Order something while you wait for Bran. It's on the house."

Despite his words, no one moved. I caught the furtive glances between Esras and the twins and focused on them. Their guilt hung thick in the air.

"You knew about the Circle's refusal to help the Specials," I said in an accusatory voice. No one answered. "Esras?"

"Yes, we knew about the orders," he answered.

"And you're okay with them?"

He shook his head. "We've been taught to always follow directives given to us by the CT, Lil. When we heard about this, we knew there was nothing we could do to change things."

"Besides, you know the Specials on a personal level," Solaris added. "We don't, so we're not really emotionally invested."

And…the bitch was back. "What about logic, Solaris? Does sealing the portal and leaving behind helpless children make sense to you?"

"Helpless?" Solaris asked. "The Specials have more powers in their little fingers than hundreds of Guardians in Xenith combined. We don't know where their loyalties lie, and as nature-benders, they might be more useful here than in Xenith."

"Shut up, Solaris," I snapped. "Every time you open your mouth, you say something that makes me want to zap you to the last millennium. For starters, the Specials and the Brotherhood are our allies. Maybe not yours, but definitely ours. My grandfather will not bail on them. Second, Keiran said there are Brotherhood children and the elderly who need shelter, too."

The silence that followed my outburst was eerie. Keiran grinned. Lucien's eyes were wide with, I don't know, shock. Esras kept a straight, a face while Solaris sputtered with indignation. Lunaris was staring at her hands, so I couldn't tell her reaction.

"You can't talk to me like that," Solaris said belligerently.

"I just did," I said. "Third, the Specials are children, not warriors. We are not supposed to decide for them which side to support in this endless battle between us and demons. That will be their decision when they turn sixteen."

Solaris opened her mouth to speak.

"I'm not done. Fourth, we are the ones who left them defenseless when we killed their parents and destroyed Coronis Isle. But my team did the humane thing—"

"We're not human," Solaris retorted.

"Yet it is our humanity that makes us different from demons. My friends and I rescued the Specials from demons when they were being forced to do despicable things. How's the CT's agenda different from the demons? Why should the shriveled old goats sit in their hidden world, destroy the only portal, and ask children to save them from the worst demons we've ever encountered? Where's their moral high ground?"

"You shouldn't talk about our leaders like that," Solaris warned. "Xenith is our home. Of course, we must protect it."

"You know what? I was born right here, so my leaders are right here on Earth, the ones I battle demons every day to protect. I've never met the CT, never been to your precious Xenith, and from what they're doing, don't ever want to visit it, so protecting *your* leaders and their perfect world is not *my* problem. If I were to choose between defending them and the Specials, I'd choose the children."

"They're hardly helpless," Lunaris cut in, repeating what her sister had said.

"So?" I shot back. "No matter how powerful they are, they're not ready to battle demons like the Tribe."

Solaris's brown eyes flashed. "Maybe we should give them back, along with you and Bran, and get the Tribe off our backs once and for all."

Now I understood why they only let Cardinal Guardians fight demons. These SGs were wimps. "You know what? I'm done arguing with you. Cardinals don't give in to demons, and they don't run away. If SGs are taught to act cowardly in the face of danger, then you should head to the valley right now, pack your things, and go back to Xenith."

Another silence followed. From the look on Solaris's red face, she wasn't backing down. Neither was I. If she opened her mouth again and spouted more nonsense, I was going to reduce her to a blabbering idiot forever. The others avoided eye contact. Keiran continued to grin.

I marched out of the room, barely resisting the urge to slam the door. Burying my face in my hands, I slid down the wall and sat on the hallway floor. Me and my temper. It didn't matter that the CT's decision was callous. I shouldn't have said the things I did. Of course, I wanted to visit Xenith, see where my grandfather was born. That I've never been invited rankled me a bit.

"Somehow I knew you weren't told about the Specials," Keiran said from behind.

I glanced at him. "I was awful."

"You were brilliant."

"I shouldn't have said anything. They're scared, that's all."

Silver flashed in his violet eyes.

"Of a bunch of children?" he asked in disbelief.

"No, of the Tribunal," I said.

He winced. "Don't say that name out loud."

I glanced at him. "Why not?"

"It is how they are summoned. The council warned us against calling out the name."

Interesting. "Yeah, a court made up of demons. No wonder they were impartial."

"No, Lil." He slid down the opposite wall and joined me on the floor. "The Tri-whatever is made up of both demons and Guardians…dead ones. They mediate Nephilimic matters. When the Brotherhood wanted recognition as a legitimate subgroup of the Guardians, neutral to the war between demons and Guardians, my people summoned the Tri… the Nephilimic court. We lost the petition, but we still went ahead and formed the Brotherhood anyway. Whoever summoned them this time has a grudge against the Guardians."

Or felt they were cheated out of a leader and powerful children. What if Gavyn had spoken the truth? It meant there had been a trial and we'd lost, except the verdict was unacceptable and so out there, I couldn't begin to imagine leaving the Guardians to live with the demons. Whoever had represented us had to be a freaking Guardian Law School dropout. If such a school existed.

"What else do you know about the Tribe's powers?"

Keiran shook his head. "Our council was stingy with those details. We were hoping you'd fill us in."

"We?"

"A bunch of us believe we should fight with the Guardians regardless of the CT's decision. I want you to talk to them, convince them that you'll have our backs if we are attacked."

"Me?"

He nodded. "Yes, you, Lil. You are the Chosen One."

Not again. What would he say if he knew the Tribe was after us because of what we did?

"We'll have your back. The decision not to offer shelter to the children and your elderly came from the CT, not my grandfather and the Cardinals."

"The Cardinals will do what the CT tells them. That's what Darius said. We'd rather have a pact with you and the junior Cardinals. Meet us at Club Zero, talk to my friends, and convince them you are our allies."

"When?"

"Tonight. We'll be there from ten to one."

I nodded. "The others will be back by then." I slanted my head and indicated his office. "Did they order lunch?"

"The men did. The women didn't." He got to his feet. "I'll ask them again. You want the usual?"

"I'm not really hungry. I'll have a drink…the usual. Whatever that is."

He chuckled. "Oh, I forgot about your memory loss. Kim mentioned it. One tall glass of strawberry-lemonade slushy coming up. And you usually a prefer shrimp salad sandwich for lunch and oven-baked chicken pasta for dinner. If you change your mind, let me know." He disappeared into his office.

Kim must have shared quite a bit of Guardian business with Keiran. Not that I was complaining. Love made us do all sorts of crazy things. I leaned against the wall and sighed. I wasn't sure how long I sat there before Keiran returned with my slushy. "You sure you don't want the salad?"

I smiled. "Thank, Kieran. I'm okay."

He disappeared back into his office and I went back to my thoughts and my drink. Noon came and went, but Bran didn't appear. Refusing to worry, I put my empty glass down, then sat straighter and slightly forward, closing my eyes and letting my mind go blank. I took deep breaths, held and released.

Pranayama often calmed my mind, but it wasn't enough this time. I forced myself to replace the images with more loving ones. Bran. Grampa. People who loved me regardless of what I did, what I was, who would face anything to keep me safe.

As though I'd pushed a switch, calmness rushed over me. Reasoning returned. Instead of getting worked up, I realized I had to talk to someone from the inside—Kael and Dante. They'd know about the Tribunal and their verdict.

I gave Bran fifteen more minutes, then got up and went inside Kieran's office to join the others.

Esras and Lucien were chatting with Kieran, but stopped when I walked in. The two empty plates on a tray said only the guys had eaten. The twins must have declined Keiran's offer. Their loss.

"Thanks for lunch, Kieran, but we have to go," I said. "If Bran stops by, please tell him to wait here. We'll be back in a few minutes."

"If he asks where you guys are?"

"Tell him we've gone to see Kael and Dante."

His brow shot up. "The two nature-benders?"

Someone protested, Solaris or Lunaris, I didn't check or care. Instead, I focused on Lucien, who didn't bother to hide his excitement. "Follow me."

We materialized on the rooftop helipad on U.S. Bank Tower. While the others peered at the buildings around us, I studied the sky. There was a heavy haze over the city and a few planes heading to LAX, but there was no sign of the cloudy mass hiding the Tribunal's army.

"How are you going to contact them?" Lucien asked from behind me.

"By sending a signal, but first there's something you need to know. Don't threaten them in any way because they'll react and you won't like it."

"But I heard they were loyal to us," Lucien said, his voice rising.

"To me, not all Guardians." Even as the words left my mouth, I worried. Our last meeting hadn't been fun. The monkey on my back was calm now, but I knew the tingle would begin when Dante and Kael appeared. "When attacked, they'll defend themselves."

He swallowed. The others stared at me as though they weren't sure whether to believe me or not. The twins were having a heated telepathic argument about me. They were so loud I couldn't help overhearing them.

Arrogant? Unfit to lead a mission? That rankled. Hadn't I offered to feed them? Put up with Solaris's snarky comments? It wasn't as if they were model Guardians either.

"Ready?" I interrupted them rudely.

"Not yet," Solaris said.

"Listen, you can discuss my shortcomings later. We need to do this now." The sky was still murky, but at least there were no planes. I focused on a position, then willed a bolt of lightning to appear above the city. It went straight into the air, then split in four different directions.

Lucien's murmur of awe was cut short by the appearance of Kael. Seven feet tall with black slacks, matching shirt and a leather duster, and wraparound glasses which made his short, blond hair appear even lighter, he looked fierce.

He ignored the others and bowed toward me, a frown furrowing his forehead. He also kept his distance. Just as well, since the energy on my back was dying to be released.

"What's wrong?" he asked.

"Jethro is missing and Bran is searching for him. Can you help us find him?"

"Sure."

I fought to control my powers, thinking of all the times the nature-benders had helped us. "Where's Dante?"

"He's checking the perimeter." Then he nodded at someone behind me.

I turned to find Dante had materialized, diamonds glittering on his ears, bat-like wings closing behind him like a cloak. He watched me warily. My gaze went to his arm even though it was covered with his coat.

"It's okay," I reassured him, smiling. The power was responding to my thoughts and reducing in intensity. "I have everything under control."

He cocked his brow.

"Okay, almost," I amended.

"Good, because we need to leave. Now."

"But you just got here. I have questions—"

"They'll have to wait." He glanced at the sky, then cut me a censuring look. "You were supposed to send a subtle signal, not give them a beacon to follow. It won't be long before they get here. Let's go."

"We're not…we can't…" Solaris stuttered.

Dante's head snapped toward her. "Do whatever you wish, Guardian. Lilith is leaving. Come on. I can feel them."

"So can I." It was the same energy I'd sensed at Mrs. Watts', only stronger. Despite the tug on my energy, I didn't see any lightning clouds.

"I'll go with you!" Lucien called out, teleporting to my side.

I glanced at Esras, then the twins. They were busy glancing around, searching for our would-be attackers. Esras already had two daggers in his hands. "Come on, guys. Master Haziel warned us not to fight them. We have to leave now."

"Then you shouldn't have sent that signal," Solaris retorted.

"Follow me," Dante ordered and teleported.

"Go, Lucien. I'm right behind you," I fibbed. As soon as he dematerialized, I reached for my dagger. "Okay. We have a thing about not leaving our people behind, so if you stay, I'll stay."

Surprise flashed across the three Guardians' faces.

"You can't stay," Kael protested. "You're not ready to fight them."

"That's beside the point now. You should leave, Kael. I release you from your oath." There was no point in having him die because of a bunch of idiots.

The first cloud popped up to our right as the words left my mouth. My heart dropped. Ready or not, we were fighting. Civilian Guardians, even the ones trained to guard Xenith like Esras and the twins, were no match for demons, but there was no time to whine about it.

A second and a third demon appeared in quick succession

"Don't let them get inside your heads," I warned, my grip tightening on the hilt of the dagger. "Think of things and people you love, happy memories."

My eyes widened when I saw the daggers in Esras' hands shimmer and shift as they elongated until he held swords. He tossed one to Lunaris, who caught it with her left hand. An alpha energy ball appeared above her right. Solaris held a wire-tipped whip and an energy ball, too.

Security Guardians? I didn't think so. Only Cardinals had the abilities to manipulate elements. By the time I glanced back at Esras, he had a sword ready for me.

"Catch." He threw it.

I sheathed my dagger and plucked the sword from the air. Adrenaline shot through my veins, my heart pumping with dread at what we were about to face, and with it was relief that Esras and the twins weren't SGs after all. Why hide the fact that they were Cardinals?

"Leave, Kael," I yelled, even though I wished he would stay. "This is not your battle."

"I disagree, princess." He pulled out a stick of some kind and pressed a button at its base. Three blades with serrated edges shot out, then coalesced together. "I took an oath, and a Prime never goes back on his word."

"True," Dante said from behind me, having reappeared without our knowledge. I grinned with relief. Our chances kept getting better. "I knew something was wrong when you didn't follow us," he added and looked up at the three demons. "How long have they been circling?"

"They just appeared," Kael said.

"Think happy thoughts or mentally go to your happiest memories. No matter what, don't let them get inside your heads or they'll make you see your worst nightmares."

"I know," Dante said and drew out a long, serrated dagger. "Get ready to attack when I give a signal."

"No," Esras interjected. "We can't do this now."

"It's too late," I snapped. "You chose to stay, so we fight."

"It's never too late to regroup, Cardinal," Esras said quickly, his gaze swinging from Kael to Dante, but the two nature-benders ignored him, their gazes on me.

"Lil!" The twins snapped.

I glanced at them. They didn't look so confident anymore either.

Order them to get us out of here, Solaris telepathed me.

I was tempted to ignore her, but they were right. We weren't ready. "Can we make it out of here, Dante?"

He exchanged a glance with Kael. "If one of us leads you away while another plays decoy."

"I'm not leaving you behind to fight them alone," Kael snapped. "You won't survive."

Dante shrugged. "I'm not fighting them. We know this world, they don't. A lot has changed since they were last here. Loop and meet me at our building in ten."

Their hands brushed. It happened so fast I thought I'd imagined it, until I felt the flow of intense emotion between the two. Who said demons couldn't love? These two had something good going on.

Be safe, Kael warned him, then glanced my way and ordered, "Follow me."

Before we could leave, a high-pitch sound vibrated the air around us. I blocked my ears, but it was useless. I retreated to a place where nothing could touch me, a place of love and happiness with people I loved. The sound receded as though I'd lowered its intensity.

I let go of my ears and looked around. The others were blocking their ears too, except Dante and Kael. Before I could remind them to think about their loved ones, the roof shook and I turned to find its source.

For a moment, I was too blinded by the brilliant light coming from the cloudy mass to see anything. Another thud followed, then a third one. All three demons were on the roof with us. Unable to move, I watched with morbid fascination as the cloud dissolved away and the light grew dimmer, until the being at its core became visible.

My jaw dropped, the sword almost slipping from my grip.

- 15 -

UP CLOSE AND PERSONAL

Angels?

No wonder our amulets hadn't reacted to their energy. Everything made sense now. The thick clouds. The bright lights. The high-pitched sounds angels called music that shattered glass surfaces. Even their ability to harm humans and get away with it was so typical of angels.

Refusing to panic, I studied the white wings rising behind the one in front of me. They were massive. Impressive. My eyes locked with the angel's and I shivered. I'd never seen such coldness in anyone's eyes, not even a demon's. But then again, he wasn't an ordinary angel. He was an archangel, an annihilator, one of the angel hordes that had defeated our forefathers and sent them to Tartarus.

I swallowed and glanced at Dante, who was to my right. His eyes didn't shift from the archangel, though his expression was amused, which didn't make sense. Dante wasn't the smiling kind.

"Everything will be okay, Lilith," he reassured me softly.

We'd be lucky to make it off the roof in one piece. The archangels were big and buff. The blond facing me wore a white tunic like a suit of armor, along with a gold kilt-like wrap, gold sandals and a matching cape. His eyes were an indeterminate color. The sword sheathed on his side was long, the hilt golden too, but he didn't pull it out. Instead, he crossed his arms and studied me like a principal who'd caught a student ditching school.

I stared right back, realizing he was trying to get inside my head. *In your dreams, pal.* I was armed with memories, happy ones. The ones he'd tried to steal from me.

A flicker of surprise flashed in his eyes, then disappeared. My heart pounding, I glanced over my shoulder. Esras, the twins and Kael had closed in, their backs to us in a defensive stance, weapons ready. They were no longer covering their ears. The other two archangels faced them, their attitude equally condescending.

"Dante," the one in front of us said in a deep, rumbling voice that vibrated my bones. A sneer marred his perfect face as he stared at Dante. "I can't say it is nice to see you again. How long as it been?"

"A couple of centuries. Give or take a decade. What do we owe the honor of your presence, Raphael?"

"We want the girl," the archangel said without glancing at me.

"You can't have her," Dante declared.

"My fight is not with you, Dante. Not this time," Raphael said and pulled out his sword. "But I will fight you to get her. The little imp is an abomination."

"She is just a little girl," Dante retorted, stepping forward, wings flexing.

"If only that were true, but you and I know what she will become. She was never meant to be born."

Dante chuckled. "Yet here she is. Once she was, there was no stopping those sworn to protect her. How long have you been searching for her now, Raphael?"

The archangel didn't like that. His hand tightened on the hilt of his sword. "Were you the one hiding her before her powers manifested? Is that why we couldn't find her?"

"No, love shielded her. I'm just one in a line of her protectors. You can't stop her from fulfilling her destiny."

Hysterical laughter filled the air, but I didn't realize it came from me, until the archangel turned those cold eyes on me. What color were his eyes anyway? They seemed to change every few seconds.

"What is so amusing, imp?" Raphael thundered.

"You," I said, surprised at how calm I sounded. "Don't you know that love trumps hate?"

"Don't lecture me on love," he bellowed.

"As an archangel, all you know is how to follow orders. You don't understand love, not like we and humans do. It explains why you hurt all those people. Most of them sold their souls in the first place to help those they loved."

"They will understand that every action has consequences."

"How? You wiped out their memories," I retorted.

"They will have their memories back once they die, and an eternity to relive their past."

"That is what all this is about—free will. Master Haziel's ramblings about fates and my survival makes sense now. My survival was guided by love, not fate. I mean, what are the odds of a powerful Cardinal falling in love and marrying a human? Very low, but they chose to stay together and damn the consequences."

He glowered. "Your grandfather started this chain of events with his recklessness. Your leaders should have stopped him."

"Perhaps they knew the kind of Guardian my grandfather is, the kind that doesn't give up when faced with obstacles and believes in the power of love. My parents falling in love wasn't fated either. They chose each other despite the odds." Even though Raphael didn't respond, his eyes said I was right. "Are Bran and I fated to be together because of the choices those who loved me made or the choice he and I have made and will make?"

The archangel took a step forward. "You and the young man—"

"Will survive this," Dante finished, shifting, so he stood slightly between me and the archangel.

"That is the problem with your kind. Too many choices," Raphael said without any inflection in his voice. "Look at you, Dante, her champion. You are ready to die for her, yet the last time we met you were in the service of her father and believed in his cause. Fickle as humans and twice as arrogant, your loyalty is worth nothing."

Dante chuckled. "That is the beauty of having free will, Raphael. Something we have, and you don't. We can think for ourselves, make our own decisions. Like the child said, you do as commanded, without thought, questions or doubt, like a puppet on a string."

There was a roar and Raphael charged. Dante boldly moved forward too, but the clash of steel against steel didn't follow. Instead, a whooshing sound came from above, then a wing dropped on the roof between them with a sickening thud, forcing both of them to stop. White feathers floated in the air just as another wing followed. Though chopped from their bases, there was no blood, just a weird glow where flesh should have been.

We all looked up.

Bran gave a mocking bow toward Raphael, his wings flapping furiously. "Sorry for my untimely arrival. You can either continue and lose more of yourselves, or find your friend before the humans do, archangels."

"This is not possible," Raphael bellowed, pointing his sword at Bran. "How did you do this, Nephil?"

"Easy. With this," Bran raised his dagger.

"Find Samuel," Raphael yelled to the other two angels. "And get him too."

While he issued orders, Dante issued his own by telepathing something to Kael. All I managed to hear was "now", then Kael grabbed my arm. "Follow me. You too," he added to the three Cardinals.

We took off at the same time as the other two angels. The surprised look on Raphael's face was the last thing I saw before we disappeared, though I wasn't sure whether it was from seeing us teleport or Dante rushing him.

We spanned the globe—Chicago, Buenos Aires, Melbourne, St. Petersburg, Vienna, and London, then materialized on an empty floor of a building. Lucien stopped peering at the sky through the floor to ceiling windows when we appeared

"Finally," he said, hurrying to us. "I thought you were dead. He…the other nature-bender said you were in trouble and ordered me to stay put or he'd make me sorry. Where is he?"

"Making sure we got away safely," Kael snapped, then walked to the window to study the sky too. I wanted to follow him and reassure him, but first things first.

I turned to face the four Cardinals. Every conversation we'd had zipped through my mind. I'd treated them like newbies, and they'd let me. I walked to where they stood and handed Esras the sword. My voice was calm when I spoke, even thought I was furious. "Why wasn't I told you were Cardinals?"

"I didn't like the idea to begin with," Esras said, then glanced at the twins. "It's why we arrived late in the alley."

"Was this some sort of practical joke you three cooked up or another one of Master Haziel's brilliant teaching moments?"

This time, no one responded. Either they didn't want to tattle on Master Haziel or they were guilty. I couldn't look at them without feeling like a total idiot, so I turned and rejoined Kael.

"You okay?" he asked.

"I will be."

"What happened?"

The urge to vent washed over me, but I squashed it. His concern for me was instinctive, but he was more worried about Dante, who still hadn't appeared.

"Long story," I said and glanced out the window. Below us, the city spread like an oasis in a desert. Above, not a single cloud marred the vast blue sky, which meant we were safe. Was Bran safe? Just because I didn't feel his pain didn't mean they hadn't captured him. Even thinking about it made my chest hurt. I had so much to tell him and so many questions.

"They'll be okay," I said.

Kael nodded. "Of course. Dante is unstoppable, and Llyr might be reckless but he's smart."

Despite his words, he was worried. Even though the tingle on my back returned, the writings didn't shoot to my hand, so I knew it was safe to touch him.

I reached out and gripped his hand.

Kael lowered his head and studied our linked hands, then me. He smiled and gave my hand a gentle squeeze, then let it go. "You are good for the Nephilim, Lilith. I don't care what that archangel said. It will be an honor to fight by your side."

I shivered, imagining fighting the archangels. "Do you think we'll have to fight them?"

He nodded. "Yes. The Tribe never stops once they've received a directive. We'll need an army. Dante and I are not alone. You can count on us and our friends to protect you. There will be many casualties, but this time, they'll have some too. We just need to know how Bran chopped off that angel's wings. No Nephilim, Guardian or demon, has ever done that before."

"That's a good thing, right?"

"Oh yes. Angel wings are not just the symbol of their glory. They contain most of their powers. Chop them off and an angel becomes useless. All they can do is ascend, if they are strong enough even to do that. In most cases, they stay in their physical form until one of their own finds them and helps them ascend."

"Is that why they cut off our forefathers' wings?" Lucien asked from behind us. I hadn't realized he'd joined us until he spoke. I want to tell him to go away, but there was something cute about him. He didn't have the edgy ruthlessness of the other three, who were smart enough to keep their distance.

Kael nodded. "Yes, young Guardian. Before the Principalities were banished into the abyss, they chopped off their wings first, making it impossible for them to ascend or use their powers. The lucky ones escaped with their wings but lost their feathers, making them more powerful than the average Nephilim, but still not as strong as an archangel. That is what makes Dante and Bran very unique."

Maybe that explained Bran's ability to chop their wings off.

"If we can't defeat them, can we summon the Tribunal?" I asked.

He winced. "Don't use that name."

"You believe *it* can hear us?"

"It does. Say it often enough and loud enough, and the court will convene right here." He looked behind us and concern flickered in his green eyes.

I turned to find Dante had appeared and was busy inspecting one of his massive bat-like wings. It had a fresh wound, as did his right cheek. A hollow feeling settled in my stomach even as Kael and I rushed to his side.

"Where's Bran?" I asked.

Dante looked around and frowned. "He was right behind me."

A quick scan and I swallowed. I couldn't detect Bran's presence.

"When did you last see him?" I asked in a high-pitched voice.

"We teleported together, dodging their lightning bolts." A horrified expression crossed Dante's bruised face. "They must have destroyed the last telegate."

My heart sank. Blasting a telegate was like lighting a fuse line attached to fireworks. The path of destruction followed whoever was teleporting, instantly killing them and leaving nothing behind.

"We have to find him," I said.

The cardinals nodded. They still had their swords out.

Dante jerked his head. "The last teleport was in—"

Bran's sudden appearance cut him off. Still high on adrenaline rush, he had a broad grin on his lips and a sparkle in his emerald eyes, dimples flashing. His wings, shirt, pants and coat were muddy, but he had no bruises I could see or feel. Relief left me weak.

"Hey, sunshine," he said, then sauntered toward me at the same time as I ran across the room.

"What happened?" Dante asked sharply, not masking his irritation.

"They blew the telegate with me in it. I had to get off and loop my path like crazy before coming here. Good thing you told me where you were headed. Locking onto Lil's energy helped pinpoint your exact location." He pulled me in his arms and held me tight.

I'm okay, he reassured me.

I thought they got you.

Me too. I'm okay. Really. For a moment, he just held me, until I stopped shaking, then he kissed my temple, leaned back and studied my face. "That was some signal you sent. I thought the Tribe got you."

"They almost…because of them," I added and jerked my head toward the Cardinals before I could stop myself. I immediately regretted it. Blaming them for refusing to leave was pointless now. "No, that's not completely true. They don't know Dante and Kael and didn't want to leave with them, which is understandable."

Bran glanced over his shoulder at Esras and the twins. "What are you doing outside the valley without the gang?"

"Trying to find you," I said. "The others went to Xenith to say their goodbyes."

He frowned. "Why?"

"They're closing the portal until this mess with the Tribe is over."

Bran shook his head. "I knew about the portal. I was asking why you were trying to find me."

"Master Haziel's orders. Did you find Jethro?"

"No. I was closing in on a lead when I saw your signal. On my way to you, I noticed an archangel circling in the air and saw the ones on the roof. He didn't see me coming. By the time he did, he'd lost one wing. He started to fall, but I was faster."

Being able to fly and having the element of surprise had helped him. Dante might use his wings to his advantage too. How many of their friends had wings? Kael was busy inspecting Dante's singed wing. They looked so cute together. Unfortunately, they also had kept secrets from us.

"Dante and Kael knew about the archangels, but didn't tell us," I said.

Bran shrugged. "Can you blame them? The archangels are scary beings."

He didn't sound remotely afraid, but thinking about them filled me with both fear and anger, which was counterproductive. "Can we go home now?"

"Sure. What's wrong?" Bran asked, frowning.

"We'll talk later." I incline my head toward Esras and the twins. "Tell them we're leaving while I say goodbye to Kael and Dante." Bran's gaze followed me as I walked toward the two nature-benders.

"Hey," I said to draw their attention. "Thanks for helping us escape Raphael and his warriors."

Dante's wing folded behind his back like a cloak. "Thank us when they are gone. I want to show you something." He took my arm and led me to the wall. "Do you know where we are?"

"Las Vegas."

"Treasure Planet Casino to be precise," he corrected. "It is our building on the Strip. We will be open for business in a few weeks, but whenever you need to contact us, come to this floor. As soon as you teleport in, we'll detect your presence. No humans or demons will be allowed on this floor, except you, Bran, and your Cardinal friends." He glanced over his shoulder at the Cardinals. "The other ones," he amended. "If you need us, come here. No more sending signals."

I studied his face, then Kael's, who'd moved closer and now stood by his side. "You guys knew we were dealing with archangels when we mentioned them last week, didn't you?"

Dante frowned and exchanged another glance with Kael. "Our paths have crossed before. We had to be sure it was the same horde of archangels."

"Just how old are you?"

"Old," Dante said with a finality that didn't invite more questions. "We're still searching for the Summoners, but we know they are the ones kidnapping young demons. We don't know why."

"To start an army. Gavyn, Bran's brother, told me," I added when they scowled. "He also said that he and his friends summoned the Tri…the Nephilim court. He said other stuff too, which I'm beginning to believe might be true after what that archangel said."

"Don't take anything Raphael said to heart," Dante said reassuringly. "Most archangels resent the fact that the Principalities rebelled against the prime directive, and chose free will and love. The thought that you could unite the Nephilim and start our path to ascension bothers them. I don't know what verdict the court came up with, but Raphael is running his own show, so be very careful. Any time you leave the safety of your enclave, make sure you let us know. Stop by here first, or send someone to inform us."

"Okay. Since you know more about them than we do, do you know if they or the court can bring back someone from Tartarus?"

Dante's eyes narrowed. "They are the ones who put the Principalities there to begin with, so that is possible, but I've never heard of anyone coming back. Why do you ask?"

"Just something Gavyn said. Could they…do you know if Valafar is alive?"

Dante shook his head. "Of course not. Your grandfather defeated him and sent him to Tartarus."

"Who told you Valafar is alive?" Bran asked from behind me, his voice deceptively soft. I hadn't realized he'd joined us. "Gavyn?"

"No, Solaris," I said, turned and realized my mistake when his emerald eyes grew stormy. "Bran—"

"You what?" He was by the twins' side by the time he finished the question.

Solaris cringed.

"I…I, uh…" Solaris stammered.

"What did you tell her?" Bran snarled through gritted teeth. Esras opened his mouth and started to speak up, but Bran silenced him with a look. "Home. Now. Follow us."

He was back by my side before I could protest his attitude. I didn't need him fighting my battles. Worse, he was humiliating the Cardinals in front of Dante and Kael.

"Bran," I protested.

"She had no right to screw with your head like that, Lil. Not right now with all the crap we are going through. I'll be in touch." A nod at Kael and Dante and we teleported.

He looped our teleport before we ended in the foyer of my house. Along the way I tried to reason with him, but I might as well have been talking to a wall. The others appeared behind us, not giving me a chance to calm Bran or lecture him on his high-handedness.

He rounded on Solaris. "Start talking."

Fear paralyzed her. Lucien distanced himself from her as though her guilt might rub off on him. Esras wore a resigned look.

"Our parents were killed during the nature-bender's raid and we wanted Valafar to pay when we heard he was alive," Lunaris said. "We'd been searching for several weeks when we heard that Cardinal Falcon had killed him."

Bran's eyes narrowed. "So you decided to mess with Lil's head, while we are in the middle of a crisis, by saying he's alive."

"We were told he was alive," Lunaris said.

"Told by whom?"

"A Civilian Guardian saw him in Buenos Aires," Solaris finally spoke up. "I set off with my Cardinals to investigate. There's a group of Werenephils in the Amazon. They are hiding a powerful but aging demon."

Bran cocked his brow. "And?"

"They were gone by the time we got there."

"That is because Valafar is dead and trapped in Tartarus for eternity. I was there. I watched him die," Bran said. "The two nature-benders who helped us today were his men. Dante was his right-hand man, Kael one of his senior guards. They betrayed Valafar by helping us. Do you know what he would have done to them had he survived?"

The twins shook their heads.

"Used them as an example. Hunted them down and publicly punished them before killing them, so no demon would ever thinking of crossing him. He was ruthless, the kind of demon not afraid to get his hands dirty."

Silence filled the room, but in my head the conversation with Gavyn kept replaying. Could Valafar have summoned the Tribunal and sent the archangels after us, then asked Gavyn to offer Bran and me a deal? Bran stepped aside and said, "Now about what you said to Lil..."

"No, that's okay," I said. *Please, let me handle this.*

He hesitated, then stepped back.

When I glanced at him, I found him standing guard, arm crossed, legs apart, gaze locked on the twins as though to warn them to act right or else.

Please, wait for me in the kitchen.

His eyes narrowed and he appeared ready to refuse, then he nodded and left. I waited until he disappeared, then faced the Cardinals. "Tell me again what you learned about Valafar."

Surprise flashed across the twins' faces.

"It's just like I said," Solaris said, for once her voice not belligerent. "We had a lead, a den of Werenephils in the middle of the Amazon guarding an aging, powerful Lord that fit Valafar's description. That lead turned cold. We were about to give up when one of my Civilian Guardians spotted him in Buenos Aires again. Before we could confirm it, the Damned Humans in our sector whose contracts we'd canceled were being attacked and their fortunes reversed, and young demons started disappearing. We even thought our inquiries had led to the attacks. Then the incident on the island happened and we were put on lockdown." Lunaris gave me a look I couldn't explain, like she felt sorry for me and wasn't too happy about it.

The hated hollow feeling settled in my tummy again. "You heard what Gavyn said about the Tribunal bringing back demons from Tartarus. There could be a connection."

"Can we trust anything he says?" Lunaris whispered.

I shrugged. "I don't know. I'll ask Dante and Kael to look into it after we're done with the archangels." If *I* survived.

They nodded.

"Okay. I'll see you guys around." I turned to head to the kitchen.

"I'm sorry, Cardinal Lil," Lunaris said, stopping me in my tracks. "We shouldn't have brought up Valafar during a mission or now when we have other things to worry about."

"That's okay."

Solaris looked like she'd swallowed a rotten egg. An apology from her wasn't going to happen. Fine. I didn't need it. "See you later, Cardinals."

"May I say something, please?" Esras said. He'd been so quiet I'd forgotten his presence. Lucien's too.

Why couldn't they just leave? I was sure they had to report to Master Haziel or something. "Esras, I've a lot on my mind, so please make it quick."

"I'm sorry if you feel we misled you about our identities," he said.

"I don't *feel* you misled me, Esras. You misled me. Whether Master Haziel put you up to it or it was your brilliant idea to test me is now pointless. Are you a Cardinal too, Lucien?"

Shoulders hunched, the younger man shook his head. "No. Master Haziel asked me to…to…"

"To what?" I asked impatiently.

Lucien swallowed visibly. "To be his, uh, 'eyes and ears' is how he put it. He wanted to see if the four of you, all sector heads, could work together. He said you could learn a thing or two from each other."

Yeah, I learned something all right, how to be a jackass. "My grandfather heads this sector, not me," I reminded Lucien.

"But you will be the leader when your grandfather retires," Lucien said.

Sure, if I survived the archangels. I was too tired to argue with him. "Thanks for having the guts to tell me the truth. I did learn something from you guys, so all in all a successful mission." I turned to leave, but the Cardinals didn't move.

Lucien looked confused. "But Master Haziel expects all of us back in the pit."

"You guys go ahead. I'll see him later."

"But—"

"Go," Bran barked from behind me.

Lucien teleported, but Esras and the twins stayed.

"Before we leave, I have something to say." Esras moved closer, his gaze intense. "Let's start over. I'm Esras, son of Fearghal, head of Southeast Sector, headquarters Melbourne. Master Haziel was right. There's much we can learn from the way your team operates and the alliances you form. It doesn't matter whether they are with demons or Neutrals, they come in handy. We would not have made it out alive today if it weren't for your friends."

He smiled, but I wasn't ready to forgive him yet.

"It is true Master Haziel told us not to say anything," Esras continued. "I wasn't happy with his decision, but I was trained to never question orders from my superiors."

"Funny, my team is the opposite. We question everything and break rules often."

He nodded. "We've heard. Maybe we will learn to be more… spontaneous with time. All I know is Guardians should stick together."

Tell that to his two companions, especially Solaris.

"To make up for this afternoon's fiasco," Esras continued, "I'd like to invite your team to our house for dinner tonight. The rest of my team will arrive this evening after visiting their families in Xenith. We're staying at Cardinal Hsia's until this crisis is over."

"We're staying with Cardinal Moira," Lunaris said. "I head Northeast Sector, headquarters Brussels."

"Southwest Sector, Buenos Aires," Solaris said. "We're staying with Cardinal Janelle."

Bran lived with Aunt Janelle too. From his scowl, he wasn't too thrilled by Solaris's news. I'd hate to have a twin and live away from her just because of my powers. I wondered how often they saw each other.

"Is the dinner for all the Cardinals or just us and Esras' team?" Bran asked.

Esras glanced at Solaris and Lunaris. "You should all come, so we can get to know each other in a relaxed environment. So? How about it?" He glanced at me.

I didn't really want to deal with a roomful of Cardinals who knew so much about us while we knew next to nothing about them. On the other hand, we had a common enemy—archangels—to defeat. We had to learn to work together.

"I'll talk to my friends as soon they return and we'll let you know," I said then started for the kitchen.

- 16 -

PHEROMONES

"I still don't like them," I said as soon as the Cardinals left. "Especially the twins."

Bran chuckled, following me into the kitchen. "I've hunted with them. They're not so bad."

"They deliberately misled me about where they were from. Solaris and her sister even refused to eat at Keiran's," I made a face, "which was so insulting because we can't use his restaurant anymore, yet he offered us food."

"I know. The Brotherhood is pissed at the CT because of the Specials' situation."

"Your Cardinal buddies didn't seem to care."

"They're not my buddies," he protested, though the corner of his lips lifted and a dimple flashed on his cheek.

"It's not funny. They're stuck-up. I never thought I'd say this, but I miss Kim. In fact, I can't wait for her and the others to come back."

"I don't know about that. I like having you to myself." He wrapped his arms around my waist, lifted me, and placed me on the kitchen counter. He moved closer, his expression serious as he studied my face as though he hadn't seen me in weeks.

"The archangels are after me, Bran," I whispered.

"They'll have to go through me first to get to you," he said confidently. "And through your grandfather, the Cardinals, the Brotherhood…I don't know if Keiran told you, but he and his friends are with us. Then there's Dante and his nature-bender friends, Jethro's Hermonites. No one is touching you."

Feeling a little better, I pushed my fingers through his hair, held his head in place, and leaned forward until our lips touched. I gently rubbed my lips across his. "You need a haircut."

"Are you offering to trim it?"

"Maybe."

He chuckled and mashed our lips together, taking me to that special place where want, need, and acceptance met, where nothing else mattered. No Tribunal, no archangels, no annoying brother. Our breathing came out faster and faster, hearts beating at the same pace and threatening to burst free of our chests.

He eased back and pressed his forehead against mine. I opened my eyes to find him studying me intently as though memorizing my face, his emerald eyes fierce. "I couldn't sleep last night."

He frowned. "Nightmare?"

I shrugged, not wanting to bring up Goddess Xenia and the vessel thing. "You must have slept in a hard, bumpy place."

"Sorry about that. I found the Order's new quarters, an old hotel in Detroit. It is being renovated on the outside, but all the action is in the sub-levels. After they refused me entrance, I used the back door."

"Filthy underground sewer?"

He cocked his eyebrow. "How do you know?"

"I saw your shirt at Jethro's, and you still smell awful."

He chuckled. "The funniest thing was they didn't seem to care about us. Not once did any of them think or mention the Tribe or the archangels."

"That's because they aren't the ones who summoned the Tribunal, uh, the court."

He cocked his eyebrow. "Tribunal?"

"We have a lot to talk about."

"Just a minute." He dropped a kiss on my forehead and stepped back. "Do you have anything to eat around here?"

"Sure. We have some cold cuts. I can make you a sandwich and—"

"No, I'll do it." He stepped around the counter and went to the sink to wash his hands. He knew where everything was. "I overheard what you told the Cardinals about Gavyn." He spoke calmly, but the way he scowled said he wasn't calm.

Wishing I could spare him the heartache, I said slowly, "I, uh, didn't mean for you to hear that until I explained everything."

"Then explain away." He got busy making his sandwich.

"Gavyn was in high spirits when he came to Jethro's," I started. Bran went chalk-white as I talked. He came around the counter and sat on a stool, his sandwich forgotten.

"That's a load of crap. For starters, no one convinced me to change sides. Second, the contract I signed to fight on Jarvis Island was a fake. It was between me and Damien, but since he doesn't exist, the contract was null and void. I'm no more the winner of that stupid combat than you are." Angrily, he turned and grabbed his sandwich.

That thought had never crossed my mind. Hope stirred deep inside me as I continued to talk while he demolished his sandwich. His eyes flashed dangerously when I explained Gavyn's claim that the Tribunal could bring a demon back from Tartarus.

"That's explains why you think Valafar is alive. Yeah, I overheard your conversation with Solaris. Tartarus is the end of the line for demons, Lil. There's no coming back until time stops. Who represented us in this cockamamie court? Either they weren't prepared or they were just incompetent." Bran blew out air, ruffling the hair sloping over his forehead. "Did Gavyn ask about Celeste?"

I shook my head.

"It doesn't make sense. He knows this place," Bran said. "If he and his new friends summoned the Tribunal, why didn't he give the archangels our location?"

"I don't know. Maybe he wants you and Celeste out of harm's way first. Remember, he wants to see you."

Bran grunted. "I'm tired."

"You can nap here. I'm sure you don't want to deal with your sour-faced guests."

He chuckled. "I meant I'm tired of Gavyn's bullshit. I've given him chances, always hoping he'd change only to see him blow it." He got up to make another sandwich. "I thought Celeste would make him change, but his hatred for the Guardians keeps growing instead of lessening."

"So you're not going to see him?"

"No. I don't want to listen to any more of his excuses for betraying me."

This was what I'd wanted to hear since I'd fallen in love with Bran, yet now it made me angry. Gavyn was a poor excuse for a brother and always managed to drag Bran down. This time he had gone too far.

"What about Celeste? She loves both of you."

"I'll go see her before they destroy the portal. Want to come?"

I wrinkled my nose. He was lucky he got a free pass to go whenever he pleased after the CT proved he was Tariel's grandson. "No, thanks."

He paused in the process of removing another slice of bread and cocked his right brow. "The CT never said you can't visit."

"They never said I could, either."

"You just want the red carpet, marching bands, and confetti," he teased.

That he could find humor now was so amazing. "Why not? I'm the wielder of the Kris Dagger. We took out Coronis, stopped the demons from electing a leader, and rescued the Specials. I should get a hero's welcome."

"Not going to happen. Instead of marching bands, we have archangels gunning for us."

And we were back to my nightmare. I sighed. "Actually, they're gunning for me."

"You mentioned that before and I went with it. Why are you so sure about that?"

I explained what Raphael had said. Bran's eyes darkened the more I talked. He piled meat on top of the slice of bread absentmindedly. "What if there's a connection between Gavyn's rants and what Raphael said? According to Dante, the Chosen One will unite the Nephilim and lead them down the path to ascension. What if it's already happening? Without me, you would never have switched sides or fought on Jarvis Island. Without me, the Specials would still be with the demons and Coronis would still be alive. Without me, Dante and Kael might not have found love."

Bran shot me a skeptical look. "What?"

"They love each other. It's really cute."

"Are you sure about that? It doesn't matter. The archangels won't win. Like I said, we won't let them. *You* won't let them." He rounded the counter to rejoin me, another sandwich in his hand. He paused instead of taking his seat and added, "Once we talk to your grandfather, you'll see that I'm telling the truth."

I should have stopped talking right there, but I couldn't. "What if Valafar is alive?"

Bran scowled. "I'm beginning to hate this game. You know, when you say 'what if' and I come up with an answer."

I pouted. "It's not a game. I'm serious. What if he survived the attack on Jarvis Island?"

His green eyes darkened. A shrug followed. "Then wherever he is, he's too weak to do anything. The last time we saw him, he was a shriveled old man. A shadow of the powerful nature-bender he once was."

"Physically, yes, but mentally…" I shook my head. "He could be behind this mess."

Bran shrugged and asked, "How are your powers?" His attempt to change the subject was pathetic.

"We have to explore all possibilities, Bran. About Valafar, the archangels, Gavyn's agenda."

He pushed back the hair from his forehead, his expression angry. "What do you want me to say? That there could be some truth to what Gavyn said about Valafar and that the thought of losing you to the archangels is already haunting me? Or that I blame Gavyn for all of the above? Is that what you want to hear?" he asked sharply.

"Yes," I snapped right back. "I need to know exactly how you feel, so I know I'm not the only one feeling like this. I'm scared, Bran. Terrified. I keep thinking that this time we won't win. That no matter what you or anyone says, this is it." My voice was shaking by the time I finished talking.

"Come here." Bran put his sandwich down and pulled me into his arms. "You drive me crazy, you know that?"

"I know."

"But I love you anyway."

"I know."

"You are never alone, and we'll find a way to beat them," he vowed.

Should I tell him about the Goddess using me as a vessel? No, that would be too much information for now. There was always the chance that I'd ascend and escape the archangels once she was done with me.

Not liking my thoughts, I stepped away from Bran's arms. Even though he picked up his sandwich and bit into it, his eyes stayed on me. I started making my own sandwich, wishing I'd eaten something at Kieran's.

"How's your headache?"

"Gone."

"Your powers?"

"Steady for now."

He nodded. "That's good."

"Do I look different since the attack?" I asked when he continued to watch me.

"You mean other than the glow and the sparkle in your eyes, or the fact that you're the most beautiful girl in the entire world? Because that's not different."

Heat rushed to my cheeks at the compliment. "I'm serious, Bran. Something happens to me every time my powers are off. My heartbeat shoots up, I get hot and—"

"Release lots of pheromones," he finished.

"Phero…what?"

He chuckled. "The chemicals that make humans act like idiots around us. Nephilim release them. It's what makes us so irresistible and," he licked the mustard off his finger, "gives us a higher sex drive."

Everything that happened after the attack rushed back—the way we'd made out in my room, Remy's stare, Gavyn's disgusting fascination with me. This was something I didn't want to deal with now.

"Never mind." I scooped up the bread, even the sandwich I'd started making, and dumped them in the fridge, then retrieved a bottle of water. "I have to report to Master Haziel."

"Whoa, stop." Bran blocked my path. "This is nothing to stress about. Most of us start releasing at eighteen. You started early. The attack may have something to do with the sudden spike in pheromones."

"Then it can't be good."

"No, it is. We almost made it to third base."

His words were slow to register. When they did, I smacked his chest. "Did you just use a baseball metaphor? That's so Sykes."

Bron made a disgusted face. "If I can handle your pheromone overload, so can you. Without feeling embarrassed. I'm the one who must fight even harder to resist you."

I wasn't worried about him. He could control himself in any given situation. "Do the others know?"

"I don't think so, but they'll eventually figure it out."

I made a face.

"You know why?"

"I don't want to know." I twisted the cap off the water bottle and took a sip. I didn't like the look in his eyes as he went back to his sandwich and took a bite. "Okay. Why?"

"When you're tense or excited, you release more. When you panic or get pissed, any drastic change in emotions triggers them."

My eyes narrowed. "Now you're just making stuff up."

He gave me a wide-eyed innocent look. "Would I lie to you?"

He would if it meant making me forget my other problems. I wrinkled my nose.

"I stink, I know." He pressed a kiss on my nose. "I'm hitting the showers, then heading to Xenith. Don't mess with some poor guy's head while I'm gone."

I rolled my eyes. "We're having dinner with your Cardinal buddies, so hurry back. And tell Celeste I said hi."

He stopped smiling. "Okay."

I called Kylie as soon as he left. When she didn't pick up her phone, I sent her a text message.

HQ was so quiet now that the Civilian Guardians were gone. Things changed as I crossed the Academy's foyer and got closer to the pit. The clang of metal reached me. I shivered, remembering the archangel's sword. I reached up and touched my neck. What happened to Guardians when they died?

I tried not to gape when I entered the pit. Master Haziel was sparring with Lucien, their swords colliding, lifting, and thrusting. I had never seen Lucien spar before, and he was pretty good for a SG.

They stopped when they saw me. Lucien walked to the wall to return the practice weapons. Master Haziel waved me over and headed to his observation booth.

"What happened?" he asked, pouring water in a glass.

"The others didn't tell you?"

"I am asking you."

I could tattle on Solaris, but it wouldn't earn me any brownie points. "We didn't exactly accomplish our mission, since Jethro is still missing. He's probably in the secret hideout of the Summoners being tortured or something." Master Haziel didn't even bat an eyelid. "But I guess you already know that. Bran is home and will soon leave for Xenith."

"He and I will talk as soon as he gets back. How did thing go between you and the other Cardinals?" he asked, watching me intently.

I gave him a toothy grin. "We got along splendidly. In fact, we're having dinner tonight."

"Same story as the others…interesting," Master Haziel said. "Lucien's version was even briefer."

So no one had tattled. There was hope for them yet.

"Anything else?" he asked.

"What do you want to know? What Gavyn said or Archangel Raphael's mission in life?"

"I have no time for that young demon's schemes or a cold-hearted angel's rants. I am more interested on whether or not he got inside your head. The other Cardinals said they made no attempt to invade their thoughts."

Another proof that I was the target, not the others. "He tried, but I resisted him."

"Archangels are very good at finding people's weaknesses and using them. Lucien?" he called out.

Lucien looked up. "Yes, Grandfather?"

Grandfather?

"Go home. We are done here."

"But—"

"Now," Master Haziel added.

"He is your grandson?" I asked after Lucien left the pit.

"Great, great, great grandson."

"And you are okay with him being here now? With the Tri-whatever and the archangels and all? Aren't you scared he might get hurt?"

His leathery face scrunched. "The boy is eighteen, free to choose what he wants. At the present, he wants to be here. What is this Tri-whatever?"

"The Nephilimic court that sent Raphael and his archangels to get me. We're not supposed to say their name or they'll appear like that." I snapped my fingers. "So how loud do I have to yell to summon the court? I have a bone or two to pick with it."

Master Haziel went still. "Summoning the Tribunal has nothing to do with how loud you yell. It is about your convictions."

Cryptic as usual. "Meaning?"

"You must *need* to meet with them."

"Oh. Like right before Raphael chops off my head with his angelic sword?"

He chuckled. "I am happy you still have your sense of humor."

"Yes, well, if Raphael wants me, he'll have to catch me first. What else do you know about the Nephilimic court? Can it bring back a demon from Tartarus?"

He nodded. "It has been known to happen."

"How come no one knows about this?"

"Because Guardians, like humans, tend to refuse to believe parts of history that make them uncomfortable."

So Valafar could really be back. Feeling sick, I just wanted to go home. "Okay. Well, that's my report. I'll see you later."

"Not so fast. Go home and change, then come right back."

"Why?"

"To train, of course. You have nothing to do for several hours. All your friends are gone." He angled his head, then added, "Your human friend is also out of town, so no teleporting to her house. Oh, you should not tell the rest of your team what happened today until the senior Cardinals talk to them this evening."

Why the heck had I come to see him? I could have telepathed my report. I was tempted to use the book on the Goddess as an excuse, but the thought of reading more about her after learning about being her vessel didn't appeal to me.

I was in and out of my home in under a minute, though I stopped long enough to check my phone. There was a text from Kylie. She'd be back tomorrow.

Master Haziel wasn't alone when I arrived back at the pit. He and Lucien were selecting swords. It must be hard to be the great, great, great grandson of someone like Master Haziel. He'd probably started training Lucien when he was a baby. Like Grampa had with me.

"Choose a sword," Master Haziel said.

With the arrival of the SGs, the swords were all mixed up and no longer grouped by era and civilization. Still, my favorites—the Robin Hood swords with their sloping guards engraved with stags and trumpeter angels—stood out among the sabers, katanas, and claymores.

I picked one and turned to find Lucien facing me with a katana. "Are you my sparring partner?"

"We both are." Master Haziel approached with two claymores.

Sparring with more than one partner was something he encouraged, but he'd never participated before. He was ancient and emaciated. One hit and he'd surely crumple.

"You sure about this, Master Haziel? I don't want to hurt you or anything," I teased.

"You think I am too old to fight you?" He cackled, the sound rusty like an engine sputtering to life. I rotated my shoulders then raised my sword, swinging the tip between Lucien and the trainer, my gaze moving in the opposite direction, looking for a sign of imminent attack.

Master Haziel lunged, and I thrust my sword forward to deflect his, then sidestepped and turned in one smooth motion to block Lucien's. Feint. Strike. Parry. Counterstrike. Lucien's footwork and flow was great, but he was timid. I was used to sparring with Bran, who wasn't afraid to push me. As for Master Haziel, his frail body was a camouflage. He wielded the two swords effortlessly. Like they were sticks.

I shuffled backward, blocking left and right, teleported and appeared behind them. They turned, but I was ready. A flurry of combination strikes….left…right…left…and I knocked the blade from Lucien's hand with my mind. He returned with two more.

Strike…block…strike…I saw an opening, dropped and swept my leg under Lucien. Down he went. Sidestepping, I focused on Master Haziel while keeping an eye on Lucien, who didn't connect with the floor. He teleported out of the way and came at me from behind, his shyness gone.

I guess he wasn't Master Haziel's grandson for nothing.

My usual strategy wasn't working. Lucien's and Master Haziel's brains were wired the same or something. They pulled a switch on me and controlled the fight, had me on run until inspiration hit—I locked on another Robin Hood sword and telekinetically yanked it to my hand. It didn't even things out, but it improved my chances.

"You can do more, Lil," Haziel said, scarcely breathing hard.

"Don't. Try. To. Distract. Me!" I panted between parries.

"Reduce the odds," he ordered.

I needed answers, not his cryptic comments. I locked on the swords in Lucien's hands and sent them flying. He teleported and caught them before they hit the ground. Then he was back like he had never left. I was tempted to incinerate their swords, but I could seriously hurt them.

Stop, you need rest, I projected in Lucien's head.

He didn't stop.

Ignore me. Fight each other.

They still came at me. Either Master Haziel was shielding them against my power of persuasion, or I was too tired to focus my psi energy. Coming up with a new move wasn't easy when you were evading being hit. Sweat rolled down my face and into my eyes, causing me to blink several times.

You cannot control our thoughts because we expected you to do exactly that. Once opponents know your attack operations, they will anticipate them next time you fight. That means you must always improvise, come up with something new. Archangels are smart and alert and impossible to surprise."

"Bran surprised one."

"You are not Bran. You do not have wings, but you *are* faster. You have the powers of the Kris within you. You can beat them. How?"

"By making sure they don't sneak inside my head," I said between pants. "By being faster, teleporting and attacking them from different angles and…and by having more of us than them."

"What if you are down to the last few Cardinals and you are outnumbered?" Master Haziel asked, his footwork and swordplay effortless. "What if it is only you against four or five of them? What if your arms are injured and you cannot hold the sword anymore and they are closing in on you? What if you cannot teleport home because the Guardians are gone or the Cardinals have been rendered useless? It is you against them. One person. Alone."

He painted a gruesome image, which on a good day would have scared me or pissed me off. Not today. Not after meeting Raphael and his friends. It was a possible scenario and he was just preparing me.

"Got it," I yelled, reaching the only conclusion.

"Got what?" Lucien asked.

I'd completely forgotten his presence. "If I told you, you'd anticipate it and I wouldn't defeat you."

Master Haziel chuckled.

I locked on two swords on the western wall and sent hurtling them toward Lucien. Surprised, he lost his footing and nearly ended up on the floor. Master Haziel expected it and adjusted his moves, using one sword to fend me off and the second to block the one I telekinetically controlled behind him.

Lucky for him, this kind of multi-tasking wasn't easy. Throwing knives and *shurikens* during a battle was a piece of cake. I'd done it with real demons, but swords were a different ballgame. I tried to keep them in the air while striking repeatedly and taking knocks.

The possibilities in the maneuver were endless, but the swords kept bobbing and my hold wasn't firm. More determined than ever to master the move, I pushed myself. I attacked from different angles, forcing Lucien and Master Haziel to focus less on me.

My hold grew firmer, until I could add two more. Lucien, not used to blocking so many swords at once, struggled and then teleported to the other end of the room.

"I guess it's just you and me, Master Haziel," I mocked.

"Smugness can get you killed," he warned sharply.

"Not when I can do this." I jerked my head and the swords I'd used on Lucien shot up in the air. My six against Master Haziel's two. Even though my hold wasn't strong and the swords were at weird angles, I had him surrounded. He lowered his swords, the tips touching the floor.

I let go of the swords and they dropped to the cement floor, the clang sounds mixing with the applause from behind me. I turned to find Sykes by the door, a smirk on his handsome face.

"Ganging up on the old man while we're gone?" he asked. "Shame on you."

Something was off about his smile. I studied his face as I closed the gap between us. His hazel eyes were shadowed, his blond hair mussed as though he'd run his fingers through it. "How did it go?"

His usually cocky smile cracked. "Not good. Mom took all this Tribe mess and sealed portal thing pretty hard. Dad was stoic. For once, I wished I had a sister or brother for them to focus on now that I'm out here."

That was big coming from him. He loved being the center of his parents' attention.

"Can I have a hug?" he added.

On a different day, I'd have known he was just flirting. Today, he was hurting. I tugged at my tank top. "I'm sweaty."

He took a step closer. "I don't care. I need your warmth right now."

Put that way. I wrapped my arms around his shoulders while his went around my mid-section, then crossed my upper back. His pain was real and deep. It wasn't easy being an only child. I didn't speak, aloud or telepathically. I just held him. He dropped his face on my shoulder, arms tightening around me, breath brushing against my neck.

My traitorous body reacted to his maleness, his scent and warmth. Not the way it did with Bran. With Bran, it was an explosion of sensations whenever we touched. This was purely physical. I reached up and stroked the hair on the back of his head. A tremor shot through him. Was he crying?

"You okay?"

He stepped back and gave me a sheepish smile. His eyes were shiny. "Yeah. Thank you."

"Sykes," Master Haziel called out. "Stay behind. Do not leave the valley, Lil. Cardinals' orders."

There goes the meeting with Keiran. Maybe we could sneak out. I touched Sykes' arm. "We have a dinner date, so tell Remy."

"Dinner? With whom?"

"The Cardinals from the other sectors."

He nodded, then walked backward and pretended an invisible noose was dragging him toward Master Haziel, one hand extended toward me. "Save me," he mouthed.

What a goofball. I wiggled my fingers in goodbye and took off toward the foyer. Poor Sykes. I imagined being in his shoes, saying goodbye to Grampa, never knowing whether I'd see him again. It would kill me.

Once I cleared the academy, I teleported home.

Hey, Sunshine? You ready to go?

For a moment, I was disoriented. Then I realized Bran was back and…

Oh crap, the dinner. My gaze flew to the clock. Six-thirty. *Yeah. I need to find out when we're supposed to be there and let the others know.*

Seven o'clock. I just talked to Solaris. Are we still going out tonight to meet Keiran's people?

I don't know. Master Haziel said we were on lockdown. He wants to see you, too.

Okay. See you in a bit.

I pinged and spoke with Kim and Izzy, then Esras. Lifting my gypsy skirt, I added two straps around my thighs and slipped throwing knives in the sheaths. By the time Bran appeared in my bedroom, I was putting on my sandals. He looked gorgeous in a hunter-green silk shirt and black dress-pants under his trench coat.

Heat simmered in his green eyes. "You look beautiful."

I blushed. "You, too. How did it go with Celeste?"

He made a face. "She didn't want to stay, but I convinced her."

"Did you tell her about Gavyn?"

He shook his head. "I couldn't. Knowing we were cut off from Xenith and about to face the archangels was bad enough. She begged me to protect him." He laughed, though there was no humor in his eyes. "Come on, let's go."

There was anger and pain in his voice, but I was used to getting those emotions from him whenever he talked about his brother. I slipped my hand through his and let my energy caress his. "What are we going to do about Keiran?"

He squeezed my hand. "Let's discuss it with the others after dinner."

- 17 -

A TOTAL FLOP

Cardinal Hsia's living room no longer had sofas, or coffee and side tables. Instead, long dining tables were lined up at right angles to form a rectangle, leaving space in the center. On one side of the rectangle were piles of pizza and breadstick boxes from a local pizza shop; the rest of the tables had place settings for about sixty people.

There were lots of psi energies downstairs and a classical piano tune drifted upstairs. It was verbally quiet, but telepathically loud.

"That's a lot of Cardinals," I mumbled.

"Other sectors have two or three Cardinals with the same power," Bran explained.

"How come we're shortchanged?"

"That's an insult. You have the senior Cardinals and me." He wiggled his brow.

"Show-off."

"Guess how many Water Cardinals there are in total?" he asked.

Water powers were rare. "One? You?"

"*Three* including me."

We headed downstairs, where the Cardinals were having pre-dinner drinks and mingling. Not your normal party by the looks of things. But then again, "normal" and "Guardians" didn't exactly go together.

The dress code was typical Guardian dark hunting clothes—pants and shirts, trench coats and boots, which meant weapons were hidden in sheaths and inner pockets in case of an attack. Our team dressed the way they normally did when we had a formal dinner—Remy in his signature preppy polo shirt and dressy pants, and Sykes in frayed jeans and a t-shirt with *Size Matters* written under an energy ball, while Kim and Izzy wore fashionable dresses with knee-length boots, their makeup flawless. No coats, but they were packing. They always did, no matter what they wore.

Bran and I moved from group to group. There was no warmth. No welcome. No attempt to say anything besides name, abilities, and sector. They all knew about my infamous father, but after L.A. and meeting with the archangels, I didn't care. I had more things to worry about.

The two Cardinal Water Guardians Bran had mentioned were fresh out of high school and wanted to know about his adventures with the senior

Cardinals. All their sentences began with, “Is it true you [illegible]”

You stay, I’ll mingle, I telepathed Bran.

You sure?

I could tell he wanted to stay and share his exploits. Even he wasn’t immune to hero-worshipping. *I’ll be fine.*

I looked around and smiled when my gaze connected with Solaris. She smiled stiffly back. *Yeah, right back at you, lady*. I assumed the Guardians beside her were from her sector. Going by their unsmiling expressions, she must have mouthed off to them about what happened in L.A.

Lifting my chin, I walked over and introduced myself. The false smiles set my teeth on edge, but I learned something. Each team gravitated toward the familiar, namely their teammates.

Like water, time ability was rare. Actually, it was even rarer, but Izzy found one, a super-hot guy with tawny eyes and bronze hair. The two hugged the wall, lost in their own little world. From the look in his eyes, Izzy walked on water.

“You mean you took them all at once?” he was saying just as I reached them.

“The energy surge from the Kris Dagger helped of course, but yes,” Izzy said with a saucy grin.

“I wish I’d seen that.”

I cleared my throat, but they didn’t hear me. I did the next best thing and pinged Izzy to get her attention. She turned.

“Oh, Lil. You guys finally made it. This is Solomon, Time Guardian, Northeast. Sol, Lil.”

“Lil doesn’t need introduction. Everyone calls me Sol.” His was the first genuine smile I’d seen, but his interest was in Izzy and their conversation.

I took one step away from them and Sykes slid in by my side. “Nice party.”

“If you like people staring at you like you’re the devil’s spawn.”

“You *are* the devil’s spawn,” he teased.

“And you are a jackass.”

Sykes laughed. “Hey, I’m getting frostbite from this lively bunch too and I’m a home-grown hero.” He glanced behind us. “Bran, on the other hand, found groupies and ditched you.”

I ignored the dig. “Where are yours?”

“Have you met Lunaris and Solaris?” He shuddered. “Energy Cardinals are supposed to be fun. They suck fun from the air and spit on it.”

He soon found a girl he knew from home and I continued to mingle until Esras asked people to head upstairs.

Bran materialized beside me and we headed upstairs. Sector Cardinals grouped together except Sol, Izzy’s time buddy, who sat beside her and

Bran's water duo. The pizzas had cooled down, but Esras' energy guys warmed them up, then the Cardinal Psis floated the boxes around the table so we could select steaming slices and breadsticks.

"Have you guys had a tough time dealing with humans here in the Northwest?" Esras asked and glanced over at our table.

Heads turned and eyes focused on us.

"I'm talking about Damned Humans whose souls we were trying to restore before the Tribe attacked," he added.

"We have," Remy said. "Some didn't want their souls back. Others went into hiding rather than make the decision."

"Humans are so unpredictable," another Cardinal said.

"Impossible to deal with."

"Always looking for an easy way out."

Their anecdotes about human encounters were many and varied. Others were amused. Some sympathetic, but the majority were haters. I refused to be drawn into human bashing. Guardians' lives were mapped out for them. The ones with powers over elements became Cardinals. The ones with moderate powers became part of the Civilian support team and ran the High Councils, owned businesses in various towns and provided Cardinals with support in other ways. The rest stayed back in Xenith. Humans couldn't live like that because they had free will. Free to do whatever they want, within societal norms, however stupid or mundane, and live with the consequences of their actions.

"Aren't you going to jump in and defend your friends?" Kim asked.

I shrugged. "No. The Cardinals are entitled to their opinions."

"Are your humans losing their memories or going into comas after being attacked, too?" Bran asked, redirecting the conversation.

Esras nodded. "When we left, we didn't know the 'Tribe' was behind the attack." Esras looked at me. "Perhaps you can tell us what happened to you on the island, Cardinal Lil. We really only learned that one of them attacked you."

All eyes zeroed in on me. Usually I would have felt self-conscious at the attention, but not after that afternoon. Facing an archangel, even though I hadn't fought him, changed my perception of things. I didn't need to impress or be intimidated by these Guardians even though most of them were older than I was.

Combining what my team had told me, my dreams, and what I recalled, I explained what I saw and heard.

"We," I glanced left and right to include my friends, "concluded they're doing to the humans exactly what they did to me, except I survived the excessive surge of despair. Humans are more fragile, so their minds shut down. Did anyone survive the attacks in your sectors?"

Esras and the twins shook their heads.

"We have two survivors," I said. "A woman and an old man."

"Can we talk to them?" someone asked.

"Maybe they could describe their attackers," another added.

"Or we could retrieve their memories," another chimed in. "It is hard to prepare to fight an enemy you know nothing about."

My gaze connected with Esras, then Solaris and Lunaris. *You didn't tell them?*

Master Haziel told us not to, Esras answered.

You told yours? Solaris asked accusingly.

Sheesh, why did she always believe the worst of me? *Of course not.*

"Lil already tried retrieval," Bran explained. "Mrs. Watts' memories were wiped clean."

"And the old man is in a mental hospital," Remy said. "We couldn't get inside to see him."

"Don't you use glamour or power of persuasion to get past humans?" a bearded older psi asked in a condescending tone.

Remy shrugged. "We do, but Lil wasn't with us."

"Your team splits up when you are on missions?" a Cardinal at the opposite table asked.

"If we have to," Remy answered. "But with the contracts, there was no danger of a serious attack, so we came up with a strategy that worked. Sometimes we worked together, sometimes we split."

"The Senior Cardinals approved of this practice?" someone asked.

Remy chuckled. "I don't know. They tend to give us a mission, then let us accomplish it without looking over our shoulders."

"Are you saying the Senior Cardinals weren't involved in the canceling of your contracts?" Esras asked.

"Of course not," Remy said impatiently. "It was *our* mission."

Silence followed.

At our table, we looked at each other and shrugged. I didn't need to hear their thoughts to know what they were thinking. They outnumbered us three to one in some sectors, yet we were way ahead of them on the number of human souls we'd restored.

"Lack of supervision is why they bend the rules," a familiar voice carried to us. Solaris. I'd recognize her malicious, nasal lilt anywhere.

"Why they were kidnapped and taken to Jarvis Island," someone else added.

"Hey! We kicked ass on Jarvis," Sykes protested.

"You got lucky," someone else said.

"If we had a Time Cardinal and the Kris Dagger, we would have done exactly what you did," a guy piped in.

Sykes laughed. "Don't think so, dude. You'd still be choking on our dust."

"That's right, because it is not the dagger that matters," Remy added in a mocking tone. "The wielder does, and we have the best. Besides, Izzy is not the only Time Guardian in this room."

"What is that supposed to mean?" Sol demanded. "Are you saying I'm not as good as she is?" Then he spoiled it by exchanging a grin with Izzy.

"It means we're willing to take risks while you guys play it safe."

The room erupted. Salvos flew back and forth. Izzy and Kim laughed and encouraged Remy and Sykes, who treated the entire exchange as a joke. The others didn't think it was funny. Their anger level kept shooting up.

Do something, I telepathed Bran.

Let them get the jealousy and resentment out of their systems first.

"That's not true," a female Cardinal yelled. "We take risks every day."

"Our record speaks for itself," Sykes said.

The woman made a face. "You get the best assignments."

"Have the best trainer," another one added.

"You know why?" Sykes spread his arms and made the sign of horns with his fingers. "We rock!"

The shouting got worse. Anger swirled in the room and penetrated my shield. At first I thought I'd be okay, but I was dealing with Cardinals, and the more powerful the Guardians, the stronger the emotions. I pressed on my temple, trying to ease the pressure.

You okay? Bran asked.

No. Stop them or I will.

Bran teleported to the space the tables created in the middle of the room. The shouting went down a few decibels, then blissful silence. Bran walked in circles, looking at each Cardinal in the eye.

"This is pointless, Cardinals," he said in a hard but calm voice. "It doesn't matter who accomplished what or where. The greatest accomplishment of this century was the death of Coronis, the most powerful demoness since the beginning of time, and you were all a part of it. You fought valiantly, proving that the Cardinals can come together and accomplish anything. Everything else since then is just icing."

The silence was deafening. Wide eyes followed Bran. He was only twenty, younger than half the Cardinals in the room but higher up in the Cardinal hierarchy because he hunted with the senior Cardinals.

"We are now facing a new pack of enemies, ones so powerful it made our leaders destroy the only portal in case we failed. We are on our own, Cardinals. That means we," he indicated the occupants of the room with his finger, "must depend on each other, because failure is not an option. But if we keep fighting among ourselves, we won't need the Tribe to destroy us. We'll self-destruct from within. We are all the Guardians have. Start acting as a team, Cardinals. Start acting as one unit with one objective."

The silence was eerie, but I wanted to cheer.

"Well said," Grampa said, entering the room. Despite his calm, commanding tone, his dark eyes flashed furiously. The effect on the Cardinals was immediate. Everyone sat straighter.

Behind Grampa came the other senior Cardinals. From their ceremonial robes, they had just come back from their meeting with the CT in Xenith.

"The deplorable display we just witnessed here tonight tells us that you are not ready for anything," Grampa said, his voice strangely calm. "You are not ready to fight, lead, or defend yourselves. So there's no way you can be ready for the task our people and our leaders have entrusted you with—defending them." Heads lowered around the table, the silence so deep it was spooky. I glanced at him from the corner of my eye as he walked forward and stopped before Esras.

"Dinner was a good idea, Esras, but as you can see they need a lot more than food to knock sense into their heads. It is time you all learned the truth." He paused and studied our faces. "We want everyone to teleport to the foyer of the Academy and go to the pit. The SGs are already waiting. We are going to have a general meeting."

No one spoke, verbally or telepathically, until we entered the pit, where there was a low buzz of conversation from the SGs. They appeared to have doubled in size since this morning and had taken up most seats, except the front row. The bleachers on the opposite side were still folded to create more floor space, some of which was taken up by a long table and seven chairs.

Once again, Cardinals from each sector gravitated toward their teams. The silence that followed as we waited was heavy with tension. It was as though everyone knew something big was about to happen.

When the Senior Cardinals entered, Grampa instructed Bran to sit with them then he propped his elbows on the table and leaned forward. For a moment, he didn't speak, just studied us. The seat at the end of the table next to Cardinal Moira remained empty and I wondered if we were waiting for someone else.

"Some of you are already aware of the identity of the Tribe," Grampa said, his voice echoing around the pit despite lack of microphone and speakers. "But there is more you need to know, things that are not stored in clairvoyant crystals or found in books and scrolls in Xenithian libraries." He glanced to his right. "Cardinal Hsia will explain."

Cardinal Hsia was the Time Guardian and the history guru. She leaned forward, the usual twinkle missing from her eyes. "When Goddess Xenia charged us with guarding humanity, she told us something else. From the beginning of time, it was decreed that for there to be good, there must be evil to balance it. One can't exist without the other. Even before Coronis rebelled and started her Hermonite group, there were Nephilim left behind as demons. Her group just made things worse."

She paused and looked at us.

"The Tribunal," she glanced at me, "is a special court that convenes to discuss Nephilimic matters. They solve disputes between Guardians and demons. Disputes that impact the balance between good and evil. Their answer usually involves sending hunters to correct the problem. We didn't summon the court this time, which means the demons did. The court ruled in their favor and sent a Tribe of archangels to correct the problem."

There was a ripple of murmurs through the room. Some raised their hands.

"Silence, please," Grampa bellowed. "I know you have questions and we will try and answer them in an orderly manner. Yes, the tribe we are dealing with is not made up of demons. They are archangels, and their job is to correct what they presume are mistakes we have made. This is why the humans whose contracts you canceled are either dying or are in comas. This is also why they are hunting us. We don't know why, but we're sure we'll learn the answer in due course. Any questions?"

This time, the ripple of conversation was telepathic and more hands shot up. Solaris leaned forward and glanced at me, then smiled. Her gaze not shifting, she raised her hand, too. She was going to tell them what Raphael had said—that I was the one they were after. I had planned to discuss it with Grampa first.

It's okay, Bran reassured me telepathically.

Our gaze met and clung. It *wasn't* okay. *We should tell them what Raphael said.*

Master Haziel said it was nonsense, Bran insisted. *Let it go.*

It was easy for them to dismiss everything. Their head wasn't on the chopping block.

"Yes, Remy," Cardinal Hsia said.

"What exactly have we done to make them think we could destroy the balance between good and evil, Cardinal?"

I didn't bother to look at Solaris. I was sure her hand was still up, her butt barely touching the seat in her eagerness to respond.

"I'll answer that," Grampa said. "After conferring with the CT, we reached the conclusion that killing Coronis might have been a coup for us, but it was a major blow to the demons. Stopping their plans to select a leader, and acquiring Coronis' list of damned souls scared the demons even more. They've lost hundreds of thousands of souls. Typical of them, they summoned the court and complained."

"Yes, Solaris?" Cardinal Hsia asked.

I shrank back into my seat and waited.

"When we were in L.A. this morning with Cardinal Lil, we learned there might be more than one reason why they summoned the Tribunal," Solaris said.

I held my breath and waited, my heart pounding with a mixture of dread and fury.

The senior Cardinals looked at each other, then me and scowled.

"What other reasons?" Grampa asked.

"The demons believe the Specials belong with them," she said.

Bitch. Wasting my energy hating another Cardinal was wrong, but she made it so easy.

"What if we summon the Tribunal and agree to return the Specials and the remaining contracts to the demon? Would that stop the archangels from coming after us?"

"We can't do that, Solaris," Grampa interjected, his dark eyes glistening. "That means sacrificing human souls and those helpless children to save ourselves. It is immoral and cowardly, the very opposite of everything we stand for. Once the Tribunal reaches a decision, it is final."

I grinned. Where were the pom-poms? Go Grampa! Put. Her. In. Her. Place. I caught Izzy's gaze. *What?*

What did you do while we were gone?

Long story. I'll explain later.

"The Specials, the Brotherhood, and Neutrals are our allies," Cardinal Hsia added. "We don't turn our backs on our allies."

"So we are going against the CT's directive?" Solaris asked, like an idiot hell bent on digging her own grave.

The Senior Cardinals looked at each other, but once again, Grampa explained. "The CT decided not to give refuge to the Specials, the young and the elderly members of the Brotherhood in Xenith. We make our own decisions when it involves our enclaves, which means we can offer refuge to anyone if we so choose."

Solaris open her mouth again and there was a collective groan from the Cardinals seated around her. Maybe it was their response or something else, but she decided not to continue being a pain. Tension hung heavy in the air, but more hands shot up.

Cardinal Hsia looked at Sykes and nodded. "Yes, Sykes?"

"Who are the members of this court? What are their credentials? And how dare they judge us?"

Laughter followed.

Trust Sykes to lighten the mood. Cardinal Hsia grinned as she explained. "The tribunal is made up of Guardians and demons. Six demons get free passes from Tartarus to join six ascended Cardinals."

Sykes got up and talked louder, to be heard above the questions being fired left and right. "How do we summon it? We would like to appeal its decision, because it's obvious whoever represented us never finished law school."

Cardinal Hsia chuckled as she motioned him to sit. "One question at a time. We are always represented by the same person, Sykes. Goddess Xenia. And since she was the one who charged us with the task of guarding humans, I'd say she graduated *summa cum laude*."

Laughter rolled through the room.

Sykes slowly sat down.

"The court usually convenes whenever and wherever you summon it," Cardinal Hsia continued, "which means, it could appear right here and right now."

I raised my hand. "Do we really summon it by calling out its name?"

"Yes," Cardinal Hsia answered. "When a group of Nephilim—Guardians or demons—gather and synchronize their thoughts and energy while calling its name, the Tribunal will appear, so please refrain from saying the name. If you must refer to them, use 'Nephilim Court' or the term 'The Tribe'. It is a generic term that refers to both the archangels and the court they serve."

"Has the Tribe ever had a reason to hunt us like this?" someone asked.

"Yes. They are the ones who rounded up the Principalities and later their children, our forefathers, and sent them to Tartarus. Luckily, our Goddess had already created Xenith and we relocated it *before* the attack. The Tribe is also behind the fall of every ancient civilization known to man…Egyptian, Roman, Persian, Mayan, Mesopotamian," Cardinal Hsia continued. "When the balance is in our favor and evil is at an all-time low, civilizations thrive. More inventions are made, illnesses and diseases get cured. Humanity is at its best. The demons are never happy when humans thrive and there is peace. Then, they usually summon the Nephilim Court, which sends the Tribe to reset the balance."

"How?" someone asked.

"They let out more powerful demons from Tartarus to counteract our influence."

A shiver ran down my spine. My gut said Valafar was back, that Solaris and Lunaris were right.

"Others say they undo some of the work we've done," Cardinal Hsia continued. "The next thing you know, demons have the upper hand, and they start messing with people's heads."

The door to the pit opened and in walked Master Haziel. Cardinal Hsia waited until he had crossed the room and sat on the empty chair beside Cardinal Moira.

"At the peak of every civilization, humans sit back and marvel at their brilliance," Cardinal Hsia explained. "They start to act like they are better than those who came before them or even those among them. Some go as far as to set themselves as gods. That kind of pompous attitude leads to civil unrest, wars and many deaths, and the end of another civilization. Humans are unaware of the war being waged on them by the Tribe. Unfortunately, the archangels never stay around to witnesses the chaos that follows," he added. "They leave it to us to clean up their messes."

This time, the heavy silence was longer. What was the point of battling demons when there was no end in sight? Was getting our redemption worth all this trouble? Immediately, I felt like such a traitor for harboring such thoughts. Of course it was. Everyone had a purpose. Ours was to minimize the influence of the demons and earn back our grace. Humans' was to better their world, until it tumbled down and they had to rebuild again. It was a vicious cycle.

"Do you want to add anything, Master Haziel?" Grampa asked.

The trainer pursed his lips, then said, "Junior has something to say."

Bran winced. He hated that nickname even though the older Cardinals used it because he reminded them of his grandfather, whom they'd hunted with.

Instead of talking while seated, Bran stood and gripped the back of his chair. "Over the last two days, I've been searching for the demons who summoned the court. Last night, I learned that their new council, The Order, is not behind the summoning. In the last few weeks, young demons have gone missing and they suspect that we took them, so their main concern right now is mounting an attack against us. We know that the group that summoned the Nephilim Court is the same one forcing these young demons to join them. What we don't know is their agenda. Yes?" he added and pointed at someone behind me.

"How did you find out The Order is not behind the summoning?" a woman asked.

"The Order's new headquarters is somewhere in downtown Detroit and heavily guarded, but I managed to get inside and eavesdropped on their conversations and thoughts. They held a meeting, but all they discussed were the missing children and how to mount an attack against us." Bran glanced at Master Haziel, who nodded.

"This morning, one of our allies was also kidnapped. Master Haziel sent," Bran glanced at me and smiled, "Lil, Solaris, Lunaris, Lucien, and Esras to help with the search, but before they caught up with me, they were attacked by the archangels."

There was no collective gasp or murmur. Just silence. Necks craned to look at us. Kim and Izzy glared at me as though I'd held back on them. Sykes and Remy scowled.

Later, I telepathed them.

"It was Raphael and some of his men. One was in the air. The Cardinals stood their grounds, their weapons drawn. They weren't backing down."

I fought the urge to giggle. He was such a good liar. Where were Dante and Kael in his narration?

"I surprised the one in the air. We fought and I managed to chop off his wings."

Whispers rippled through the room.

"The wings are our answer to defeating an angel. They are their source of strength, their source of power and their shield when attacked." Bran slipped his hand in the front pockets of his pants and rocked on his heels. "Without them, they are useless. Without them, they are reduced to lower ranks. It takes years to earn wings back, so they always make sure you don't go after their wings. I will work with fliers on how to attack them from the air."

Questions followed but I didn't really listen. I was exhausted, lack of sleep finally taking a toll on me. My eyelids kept drooping, until I realized Bran was no longer talking and Master Haziel had taken over.

"Remember," he said. "The only way to send them running is to disable their leader. When you identify the archangel leading them and force him to quit, his followers will leave too. From now on," Master Haziel continued, "Cardinals with like powers will train together in the mornings. Psi Team will be led by Mrs. Deveraux and the trainers from other sectors. Earth Team will have Nero and other earth instructors. Energy Team… Air Team and so on and so forth. The purpose of doing this is not only to sharpen your skills and let you learn from your peers. During a battle, you won't need to look around for one of your teammates to help you in a crisis. If you need help from a psi, any psi will help because they've learned the same moves. If you're looking for extra weapons, any Earth Guardian should know when you telepath them."

He paused and glanced around. No one spoke, though I could tell they were unhappy with his announcement.

"In the afternoons, you'll go back to your sector teams and share with them what you've learned. Occasionally, you will spar with the SGs with the same abilities. In the evenings, dinner will be served at the Academy cafeteria. Attendance is mandatory. Once again, you will sit with your new teams. This will continue until you learn to get along and think as a team. We are at war, Guardians. A war we plan to win."

The silence stretched as he studied each of us intently, then he bowed to the Senior Cardinals and walked out of the room.

"A few more things before you disperse," Grampa said after the door closed behind Master Haziel. "Keep a low profile around the valley. I don't want to hear of trouble with the locals." His gaze swept everyone and stopped on us. "But most important, no one must leave the valley. We are on full security alert. The Psi-dar is working at its maximum capacity. If there's an emergency and you feel you must leave the valley, come and talk to us first."

You think he knows about tonight? I asked Bran.

How could he?

Nothing ever escapes him, I reminded Bran.

"Any questions?" Grampa asked, drawing my attention back to him.

Silence.

"Then head to your assigned homes. Training begins tomorrow morning at six. Lil, Bran, Esras, Solaris, and Lunaris, stay behind."

Meeting at my place when you are done, Remy telepathed before he left. The room emptied fast. Grampa signaled us to move closer.

"What happened in L.A.?" he asked.

We took turns explaining, not leaving anything out including what Gavyn and Archangel Raphael had said. No one tried to reassure me that I'd be okay, that whatever Gavyn and Raphael had said was wrong. Not even Grampa.

All he said when we were done talking was, "We can't use our powers without alerting the archangels. That means doubling the amount of weapons we carry from now on."

The other Cardinals nodded.

Grampa turned and studied me. "You have a question?"

I really wanted to know if he believed I was in danger, but I didn't want to appear self-absorbed, so I asked, "Is it possible to bring the Specials here?"

Grampa shook his head. "There's no space at the Academy or the houses to accommodate them."

"There's room in our house, Remy and Sykes' place," I insisted.

"Not anymore. We'll find a solution, Lil. Go home." Grampa stood, signaling the end of the meeting. "The rest of you, stay behind."

I glanced at Bran, but his expression was unreadable. Sighing, I headed for the door. I needed to clear my head. From the foyer, I teleported outside Number 1—the house above the underground offices. It was bigger than all the houses in the enclave and was officially the guesthouse for all visiting Guardians. Kim's house was next to it.

The sun had already set, but the summer evening was warm. Most of the Guardians were indoors, lights burning bright behind curtains. Even at my house.

I pinged Remy.

Come over, he said. *We're rearranging the furniture.*

I crossed Sagebrush Drive and started downhill toward Remy and Sykes' place.

How many 'houseguests' do you have?

Just two.

Two wasn't bad, but it meant we couldn't meet at their place anymore. How many guests did we have at my house? All the rooms in our basement were empty, and the sectional in the family area could be converted into a queen bed. Having people around was going to be weird. I was used to being with just Grampa and Aunt Janelle who came and went.

- 18 -

NEW ROOMMATES

Remy and Sykes' front door flew open before I reached it. "Welcome to our new home," Izzy said.

"You and Kim are their houseguests?"

"Oh yeah." She closed the door behind me. "When your grandfather told us we were getting houseguests, we decided—"

"Rather the slobs we know than ones we don't know," Kim cut in as she walked by with a clear tote bag filled with creams, lotions, and hair gels. She disappeared inside the bedroom that had been Remy's.

"You guys kicked Remy downstairs?" Sykes already had a bedroom downstairs and didn't need to move.

"Not really. The guys chose downstairs, which is great for the nudist colony wanna-be."

"I heard that," Sykes yelled from downstairs. "I eat breakfast in the morning, so I'll still come upstairs."

"Don't care," Izzy yelled back, grinning. "Just put on some damn clothes before you do or you'll know firsthand what Kim can do with frigid air. Want to see my room?" she added softly. "Remy transported the furniture in one teleport."

The perks of being an Earth Guardian was his ability to manipulate solids, including shrinking them to portable sizes. "Your clothes?"

She laughed. "Oh, no, he didn't touch those. Or my shoes. He's good, but I wasn't taking chances."

Izzy's bedroom was right by the front entrance, like mine. It used to be a workout room; now it was a replica of Izzy's old bedroom. Done in palettes of brown, gold and jungle green, and a queen bed with a sheer golden canopy over it, it exuded warmth.

I noticed two clairvoyant crystals on her computer desk. One projected images of a family of five. I recognized Izzy in some of them. In others, she was much younger. The second crystal showed short homemade movies of a young girl about ten, her hair even curlier than Izzy's. She was a gymnast. Another one showed the same girl dancing. The images changed to show a handsome guy. Something about his expression and the way he moved reminded me of Dante.

Izzy was so private that I had never asked her about her family, but she noticed my interest. “My brother, Dominic, and my baby sister, Aria, short for Arianna,” she said with forced cheerfulness. She picked up the second crystal and smiled. “Dom is studying to be an art historian while Aria… Aria wants to be everything.”

“Your brother is handsome,” I said.

“Sadly, he thinks so too, which makes him insufferable.” Izzy put the crystal down, waved a hand over it, and deactivated the images. Her eyes were overly bright as though she was holding back tears.

“And those are my parents.” She pointed at an image of a lovely couple seated next to each other on a loveseat. I could see her brother Dom in both her mother and father.

“You look like your mom,” I said.

“I know.” She turned abruptly. “Come on, I’ll show you Kim’s new room.”

I’d never entered Remy’s bedroom before, but Kim had definitely transformed it into hers—everything was white and designer, from the dresser, to the vanity chair with a skirt, to the canopied bed, to the throw rug.

“When this mess with the Tribunal is over, Izzy and I will get our own place instead of moving back with my parents,” Kim said.

“Good to know this move is not permanent,” Sykes said from the doorway. “Aren’t you guys done yet? We want more info on the archangels.”

“Out of my room, Sykes,” Kim ordered. “You don’t waltz in without knocking or pinging me first.”

“I knew this was a bad idea from the word go.” Shaking his head, he disappeared downstairs.

Kim and Izzy looked at each other and giggled. Poor Sykes. They were going to make his life hell. We followed him downstairs and settled on the couch. By the time Bran joined us, we were done dissecting everything, down to Gavyn’s use of Kylie as a medium.

“Are you going to tell her what he did?” Izzy asked.

“Yeah. She’s out of town right now.”

“Now can we discuss Keiran and tonight?” Kim interrupted impatiently. “We won’t be able to meet with them.”

“Or any other night until the Cardinals lift the lockdown,” Remy added.

Kim sighed.

“Why not just call him and explain the situation?” Bran asked. “He’ll understand.”

"He doesn't have a phone," Kim explained. "His customers use telepathy to make reservations. If we don't meet with them tonight, they'll believe we don't care about them."

"The Cardinals promised to find a way to help the Specials and the older members of the Brotherhood," Bran explained.

"But they always take forever to decide on anything," Kim said and sighed again. "By the time they agree on what to do, how and when to do it, it would be too late."

"Let's just sneak out and make the meeting," Sykes suggested.

"No way," Izzy protested. "The Cardinals will have our heads on a platter."

"Just a second, Izzy." Kim's gaze didn't leave Sykes. "How can we sneak out undetected?"

"Do what?" Remy asked, reappearing with drinks on a tray, which he placed on the coffee table.

"Sneak out of the valley," I said, not believing what they were planning.

Kim cut me a quick look. "From your tone, I take it you're out."

"I think we should be careful because Raphael and his men are waiting for us out there," I retorted. "Even the senior Cardinals decided they won't use their powers anymore because it could alert the archangels. The only thing stopping Raphael from finding us is the shield over the valley."

"After the attack on the island, I doubt the shield is that effective," Izzy added. "They can still sense us."

"So let's not use our powers," Kim insisted. "The Brotherhood will believe we don't care about them if we don't make the meeting."

"Don't you mean this will screw up things between you and a certain violet-eyed guy?" Sykes mocked.

"That's not it." She bit her lower lip, then looked at Bran. "We must contact Keiran and let him know what's going on."

My gaze volleyed between Bran and Kim. Before I could protest, Bran nodded. "Okay, I'll do it."

"What?" I squealed.

Before Bran could respond, Sykes spoke. "How do you plan to accomplish this amazing feat without us? I know you're the hero of the moment, but the Psi-dar is on alert mode. You teleport anyway, the remaining security team will be on your tail."

Bran chuckled. "I'll tell the Cardinals I have to meet with my brother."

"I thought you were going to use the other route," Sykes said in disappointment.

Bran cocked his eyebrow. "What other route?"

"You know, sneak to the canyon's Wind Caves and teleport from there, therefore outsmarting the Psi-dar."

There was a collective groan.

"The security shield doesn't cover the cave?" Kim asked curiously.

"You're not thinking of using it, are you?" Izzy protested.

Kim shot her an annoyed glance. "Of course not. Tell us about the cave, Sykes."

"It's a blind spot in the almighty Psi-dar's all-seeing eyes. I discovered it years ago. You can teleport in and out without the Psi-dar picking up your energy."

"Until they decide to do a psi energy count," Izzy said.

Kim glared at her. "Negative much?"

"No one is sneaking out of the valley," Remy said firmly. "There's a time to break rules and a time to lay low. Bran can try and ask the senior Cardinals' permission, and see what they say."

Bran smiled. "I agree." He glanced at Kim. "If you need to tell him or give him something, I'll pass through here before I leave."

"You really think they'll let you go?" Kim asked.

Bran nodded.

Kim grinned, then did something so out of character that we stared. She kissed Bran's cheek. "Thank you."

As soon as she teleported upstairs, Bran grabbed my hand. "Come with me."

We teleported to my bedroom. Voices filtered into the room through the closed door, but their energies weren't Grampa and Aunt Janelle's. Our houseguests must have been settling in.

"Do you really have to go? The archangels probably know your energy signature by now."

"I *have* to go, Lil."

"Why? Is it Gavyn? Are you going to see him?"

Bran sighed. "I'm not supposed to tell you this, but the senior Cardinals want to contact the Order and tell them what we know about their missing children. We can't afford to have them target us while we are still figuring out how to defend ourselves against the archangels."

That made sense. "They want you to go alone?"

"No. Cardinals Moira and Seth are coming with me. They won't be happy about a detour to the Brotherhood, but…," he shrugged.

At least he wasn't going out alone. "Be careful." He grinned, not in the least worried. "And if you guys run into trouble, go to Dante's. We have an open invitation."

Bran chuckled. "Yes, worrywart. I'll be back in a few, so wait up for me."

"Tell Angelia I'll visit her as soon as I can." I gripped Bran's shirt, pulled him closer, and kissed him. "Please, be safe."

"Promise." He teleported.

Releasing a breath, I debated whether to go and introduce myself to our new houseguests or head back to the guys' home. Despite Kim and Izzy's moving in, the house would always be Remy and Sykes' to me.

Kim was still in her room when I arrived, probably making a recording for Kieran. The others were watching an animé on TV.

"Is our hero gone?" Sykes asked.

I smiled. "If you mean Bran, no. He's gone to talk to the senior Cardinals first."

"How come they let him leave and not us?"

"You're turning green, Sykes," Izzy teased.

Sykes chuckled and stretched. "Nope. I just think he doesn't know how to have fun. Rules are boring." He patted the area of the sectional beside him. "Sit by me, Red, and let's break some."

"You really need to stop messing with me."

"Chicken," he muttered.

I sat beside Izzy. She and Remy had their eyes glued to the screen, where a dark-haired girl with red eyes was busy ferrying a boat through a misty lake with floating lanterns.

You know he only flirts with you because he knows you aren't available and to push Bran's buttons, Izzy said. *Flirt back and he'll run.*

I don't think that's going to work. What are you guys watching?

An animé series the guys like. This one is actually interesting. It is about revenge and how you lose your soul when you seek it. Another episode is about to start. Izzy glanced at me and added, *ignoring him hasn't worked either. Go over there, kiss him, and scare the heebie-jeebies out of him.*

Somehow I didn't see Sykes running. Besides, I didn't want to kiss him. I continued to watch the introduction to the next episode, though I could feel Sykes' eyes on me. Getting irritated, I glared at him. He winked and patted the seat beside him. I made a face and turned my attention on the screen.

Bran came back sooner than we'd expected.

"Well?" Remy asked.

"It's a go. Cardinal Moira and Seth are coming with me. Where's Kim?"

"In her room. I'll get her." Izzy teleported and Bran took her place.

I sank against his side. Knowing he wasn't going alone was a relief. Bran could handle himself in most situations, but the archangels were a mean bunch.

The animé was interesting, but all the training and not getting enough sleep because of the nightmares had drained me. My eyelids kept dropping, no matter how hard I tried to stay awake. Finally, I gave in. Just a few seconds of sleep was all I needed.

Something tickled my nose. I swatted at it. It flitted across my nose again. I protested and tried to turn my face away. A familiar chuckle followed. My eyes flew open and my gaze collided with Bran's.

"Why are you tormenting me?"

"We need to talk about the Specials."

"Oh, yeah, tell Angelia I'll visit…" A feeling of déjà vu rolled over me. I'd said that before. My eyes widened. I was in my bedroom, not at Sykes and Remy's. "Did you already leave and come back?"

He nodded. "Move over."

The clock on my bedside table said it was nine-thirty. "I fell asleep?"

"Yep. Before I left. I came back and you were still out." He kicked off his shoes and snuggled beside me.

I settled on my stomach, so I could see his expression. "So how did it go? Did you talk to the Order? What's wrong with the Specials?"

"Everything is okay with the Brotherhood. They know we have their backs. The Specials, on the other hand, are scared out of their minds."

I sat up. "Darius told them about the archangels?"

"That's the problem. No one told them anything, but with their abilities, they feel the others' fear. At least, the empaths in their group do. They know something is not right and they want to see you, especially Angelia. She made me swear to take you to them, but the Cardinals overheard us, so no sneaking out."

"And the Order?"

"Refused to talk to us. They insisted on talking to you—the Chosen One."

"No," Grampa said firmly.

After giving his verdict, the matter of meeting the Order was all but forgotten. I didn't get to visit the Specials either, which worried me. Angelia would think I had abandoned them. Grampa's stance didn't change despite my arguments. I even begged, which earned me a long lecture on priorities. Apparently mine were to train, train, and train some more. He promised to visit them instead.

My next visit with Kylie, the day after we met Raphael, didn't exactly go as I'd hoped. Everything went downhill as soon as I mentioned the archangels.

"Please, mind-blend with me. I have to see *him*," she begged.

"Did you hear anything I just said? Gavyn used you to find my cell phone number, Valafar might be back *and* the archangels want me dead."

She shrugged. "I don't care if Gavyn used me, and Valafar is a total loser, so whether he's back or not, he'll never convince you to join him. As for the archangel," she giggled, "even saying the word fills me with, I don't know, a shiver. The way you described him…"

Annoyed, I reminded her, "Cold eyes? Mean? Hates us and humans? *And* he wants me dead."

"Oh, I know, but you are…the Chosen One. You have the powers of the Kris Dagger and the entire Guardian army behind you. The archangels won't win. Please, show me."

"No." I got up from her bed, too annoyed to stay. "I can't even link with Bran to get my lost memories because I'm scared of messing up his energy. There's no way I'm going to link with you."

I didn't hear from Kylie for days. Just as well. Our houseguests, six female SG instructors, monopolized my time at home. They were nice, if I looked past their need to share every story about Xenith and make me watch homemade clairvoyant movies. It was like dangling something I really wanted in front of me, but keeping it out of my reach. So many times I just wanted to say "enough". But I couldn't be rude.

The first time we met, I'd entered the kitchen to find them making breakfast. I took a step back, wanting to teleport back and disappear in my room until they were done, when the one standing by the stove had turned and smiled.

"Join us, Lil," she'd said with a smile. "Unless you'd rather not."

How could I refuse?

Watching the Guardian children frolic in the water and chase butterflies at a park in Xenith made me wonder what my childhood would have been like growing up there.

"Those little girls could easily have been me," I told Bran when were alone after another long training session.

"Do you feel cheated?" Bran asked absentmindedly, his concentration on the pad he was sketching on.

"Hmm, no." My childhood had been complicated. First living with Grandma's circus tribe, then later moving from place to place with Grampa as he tried to keep the promise he gave my mother—keeping me safe from Valafar. My relationship with my grandfather was special because of the years we'd spent together. "I wouldn't trade the years I spent with Grampa or my Gypsy relatives for anything."

- 19 -

THE TEAMS

Our training became mentally, physically, and psychically draining as the week progressed. Each power team took over a classroom, while the SGs used the pit. Evenings, we ate together. The Cardinal Guardians sat in one corner of the cafeteria with our regular/sector teams, while the SGs took over the rest of the tables. They outnumbered us five to one.

The first two days were a nightmare. The Psi team focused on telekinetically controlling suspended swords while wielding one or two with their hands. Lucky for me, Master Haziel and I had already started working on the routine. The others hadn't. They grumbled and whined, and drove Mrs. D nuts.

I began to bond with a quiet guy with wavy brown hair and gray eyes. I didn't even know his name, but he was determined to master the move and seemed the nicest. I'd hoped his niceness would rub off on the rest of the Psi team. It didn't. Their attitude toward our team was like poison that seeped into everything they did.

On the third day, Master Haziel walked into the psi training room just as we were warming up with wooden staffs. He and Mrs. D spoke in low tones and kept glancing at us.

"Are you sure they are ready?" Mrs. D asked, her voice reaching us.

Master Haziel answered, so quietly that we could not hear, then left.

"Today, we are using the pit, Psi Cardinals," Mrs. D announced. "Grab your preferred swords and let's go."

The other Psi Cardinals looked at me for answers. Considering how they'd treated me with distain the last two days, I gave them a blank stare.

There were eight in total. Two of them—a black girl with red-streaked hair and a guy with pitch-black hair—came from Esras' team. The guy was either a full-blooded Nosferatu—or at least half, he was so pale. The other six were split evenly between Solaris and Lunaris' sectors. One had all guys, a redhead and two obnoxious dweebs. The last group had the nice, quiet guy I liked and two girls— a bubbly girl with freckles and a Werenephil with yellow cat eyes. Mrs. D's eyes only shifted when she was angry, so it was interesting to be so close to a pure Werenephil. The first time she caught me staring, she'd glared and hissed. I wondered what other unusual features she had. As for Mrs. D, after two days she was getting frazzled by the animosity in the room.

Ask him what's going on. Someone telepathed me, without pinging first, which was totally rude. I recognized the voice as Onora's, the girl with streaked hair. After two days, she was the only one I knew by name because the Nosferatu from her sector tended to defer to her.

Why can't you ask him yourself? I shot back.

Because you are his favorite, she retorted.

Who cares what he thinks? one of the obnoxious guys said. He had pale blond hair and a perpetual sneer. *He's senile.*

And bitter because he'll never be a Cardinal like us, his curly-haired friend added. *Trainers are expendable.*

We should tell the CT he's incompetent, the blond finished.

Cat-eyes and Freckles giggled. Onora's Nosferatu partner and the other two guys caught my gaze and looked away. I was sure my fury was visible. Mrs. D, waiting by the door, shook her head in warning, but I was too pissed to care.

"You stupid, pretentious morons," I said through clenched teeth.

They backed up.

"Lil," Mrs. D called out warningly.

"Master Haziel is not senile, bitter, or incompetent," I continued. "He is wise," I pressed a finger for emphasis, "he's strong, and he's a saint for putting up with all of you. He's trained more powerful Guardians than you'll ever be, and he takes pride in all the Cardinals' accomplishments."

Mrs. D clapped to get our attention. "Cardinals!"

"Powerful Guardians?" the curly-haired guy whispered, but I heard him. "Think she's talking about herself?"

"Must be," his blond buddy answered. "No modesty whatsoever."

I wanted to zap them both. "I'm not talking about me, you idiot. I meant the Senior Cardinals."

"Lil," Mrs. D called out again. She sounded pissed and closer.

"Listen to your Psi teacher, Lil," Onora mocked.

"Why don't you try listening, Onora? Maybe you might learn to lift multiple swords without whining. We could be attacked any moment while you play stupid mind games."

"I hope we are," the blond said. "Then we'll see how ridiculous the trainers' ideas are."

"What does he know about fighting demons anyway?" Onora said with a sneer. "He's never faced one, and if he did, he'd probably hide behind us—"

My hand shot up toward her, my reaction so instinctive I didn't stop to think of the consequences. I sent her flying across the room. Lucky for her, the foam blocks and mats were piled against the back wall and cushioned her fall.

"Lil Falcon!" Mrs. D snapped as she appeared beside Onora.

Onora refused Mrs. D's help and scampered to her feet. "You saw that. She," she jabbed her finger in my direction, "used her powers against me. It is against the rules—"

"To disrespect your trainers, Cardinal Onora," Mrs. D finished. "That alone is enough to put you on probation."

"Probation? Since when?" Onora retorted.

"Since now," Mrs. D snapped.

"I'm a Cardinal Guardian. You can't order me around."

"You have a perfectly capable, younger Cardinal Psi in your team." She waved toward the Nosferatu boy. "We are in the middle of a crisis and I will not tolerate your shenanigans anymore. How you do things in Melbourne," she glared at Onora, then cocked her head toward the blond boy and his curly-haired friend, "or Brussels is none of my business. But when you are in our sector, you will behave like Cardinals. You will listen to your trainers. And for the love of Xenia, keep your poisonous opinions to yourself. Your behavior the last two days has been unworthy of Cardinals. From now on, you listen, train, and master whatever Master Haziel throws your way. Without mouthing off."

"But—"

"Do…you…understand?" Mrs. D cut Onora off, her voice deceptively calm.

Onora swallowed and nodded. "Yes, Mrs. Deveraux."

Mrs. D turned, faced the blond and his sidekick, and cocked her brow.

"Yes, ma'am," they said in unison.

"Good. Now move. Wait by the door. Lil, stay behind."

Onora glowered as she walked away. I waited until they left the room. "She had no right to say the things she—"

"That's enough," Mrs. D snapped.

I blinked. She'd never spoken to me like that before.

She started to pace. "What she said was wrong and I didn't intervene at first because I thought you could handle the situation. Not by attacking her. Not by yelling, but by calmly explaining how we do things here."

"Reason with them? After the way they've been acting the last two days?"

"That is beside the point. You know better than to use your powers against a fellow Guardian. What if you'd shot lightning bolts and killed her? Do you know the consequences for killing another Cardinal?"

I sighed and stopped short of rolling my eyes.

"A dead Cardinal would bring the wrath of the Circle of Twelve on your head. Do you know why? They were forced to ascend early, leaving no energy and consciousness behind to feed the Psi-dar. I know you occasionally use your abilities while goofing around with your friends, but you cannot act the same way with other Guardians. There are rules we all must follow or there will be chaos."

"But you heard them, Mrs. D. They were disrespecting Master Haziel."

"I understand, but that doesn't give you the right to lash out like you just did," her voice softened. "You may be the youngest in the group, but you're the most powerful. You could hurt them quite easily."

Great! I defended my teacher and *I* was the bad guy. "They are impossible to train with. You've seen the way they act. Why do they hate our team so much? We are on the same side. Who cares about accomplishments?"

Mrs. D sighed. "They don't hate you. They fear and envy you. Most of them only know you by your reputation. Once they get to know you better, they'll see what we see—a humble young lady. Give them a chance."

I rolled my eyes this time. Fear? I didn't think so. Curiosity, resentment, envy, yes. "I've tried."

"Try harder. Spending more time with them might help, too. Invite them over for video games or a movie. They don't have such things at the guesthouses. Or go downtown for coffee or something."

No way. I already had to train with them for three hours in the mornings.

"Come on," Mrs. D said. "Let's not keep Master Haziel waiting."

The others were waiting for us outside the pit. This time, I was the one who avoided their probing gazes. Mrs. D waved and the door flew open.

About a hundred men and women were warming up inside the pit, some using jump ropes and freestanding punching bags while others jousted with wooden staffs or sprinted around the pit, which was now five times its usual size. It had been completely gutted out, all the seats and the booths removed to create more space. More Guardians training meant more weapons, which lined the wall.

The other Cardinal Psis smiled and waved to the Guardians they knew. Growing up on Earth meant I'd never had any contact with the SGs in Xenith while all the Psi Cardinals, like Remy, Sykes, Izzy, and Kim, hadn't moved to Earth until they turned sixteen. Before, I would have been envious of them. Lately, I'd come to appreciate my unorthodox upbringing.

I made eye contact with men and women I'd only seen from afar in the cafeteria, until I saw a familiar face—Lucien. He waved enthusiastically. I smiled and waved back. Two more familiar faces jumped at me from a group on my right. They were the SGs I'd met on the island the day I was attacked. They smiled and nodded.

"Guardians," Master Haziel barked, "I want half of you on this side of the pit," he pointed to his right, "and the other half on this side." He pointed left. "Grab a wooden staff."

The room split, leaving a clear area in the middle section.

"Cardinals, put your swords away and move to the middle of the pit."

We did as Master Haziel instructed. Now there were two empty areas between us and the SGs. Just wide enough for a combat zone, except the Guardians had weapons and we didn't.

As though he heard me, Master Haziel added, "Cardinals, use whatever means of defense you can to stop them. There are about one-hundred fifty of them and nine of us. Let me know when you are ready, Cardinals."

I looked at the other Cardinal Psis from the corner of my eyes. They looked worried as they studied the SGs.

This is bull, the blond whiner telepathed.

Shut up, dude, his curly-haired friend snapped. *We need to come up with a plan.*

We need weapons, the blond insisted.

We are the weapons, I wanted to correct him.

Then he would have given them to us, the quiet member of the trio said. He rarely said much. Our gazes met. *What do you think, Lil?*

I shrugged. *We use all our abilities to win this.*

Uh, please, Onora said. *It's obvious he wants us to use the move Mrs. Deveraux has been teaching us.*

But we haven't mastered it, Cat-eyes griped.

We'll do the best we can, Onora said, glancing at everyone except me. *Let's stand back-to-back, four facing one group and four the other. Lil can fight both sides.*

I was tempted to let them take a beating, but Mrs. D's words kept ringing in my head. My gaze collided with hers. She stood near the door, arms crossed and narrowed eyes locked on me. Opposite her, near the weapons on the wall, was Master Haziel. His eyes were closed as though he was meditating. He didn't fool me.

Onora opened her mouth to signal him, but I cut her off. *We are not ready, Onora.*

Her eyes narrowed. *Excuse me?*

Just listen without interrupting, okay? I glanced at the others. They were all looking at me with suspicion. *I know how Master Haziel thinks. This little jousting thing is a test or a lesson, and you won't like the results if you treat it as a joke. Nothing happens in this enclave without his knowledge. He knows about the dinner fiasco and that we are not getting along, and this is his way of telling us to start acting like a team or else.*

They continued to stare at me like I had two heads. *Do you want to double your training hours?*

They shook their heads.

So what do you say we surprise him by joining forces and doing this right?

Why should we trust you? Onora asked.

Because I have nothing to lose while you do.

What do you mean? the blond asked.

You have former teachers, childhood friends, even relatives in this room. When you fail, guess who will be humiliated?

Silence followed my question. I didn't expect an answer anyway.

We are Cardinal Psi Guardians, guys. We don't get defeated by the very people we're trying to protect. So let's knock them on their butts. Play games with their minds. Use your power of persuasion to turn them against each other. And when they are down, let's place swords as a barrier between us and them.

Chuckles and nods followed.

Like Onora said, four face one group and four the other.

And you? Onora asked.

I grinned. *I'm not going to let you guys have all the fun. Just remember, we are to disarm them, not seriously injure them.*

She nodded, then turned to face the other side.

"Ready," I called out.

"Forty-five seconds," he snapped, looking up. "If this was a real battle, we would all be dead."

How did he do that? He didn't even own a freaking watch. "Next time we'll have a plan *before* we come to the pit," I said.

He humphed. "Start in three, two, one…go."

The SGs charged, but we were ready.

We were still laughing when we left the pit and headed back to the Psi classroom.

"Did you see Master Haziel's face when we had half the guys fighting each other while the others pinned to the wall with the swords?" Cat-eyes asked.

"That's the most fun we've had since arriving here," Onora added.

"Do you think he'll make the others go through something similar?" the annoying blond asked.

"I hope so, but we can't tell them," his curly-haired buddy said. "I want to watch Haakon get taken down."

I frowned, following their conversation. "You want to see your friends fail?"

"Like an escapee from Tartarus." They laughed and bumped fists. "Haakon is one of the Earth Guardians in our team. He believes their ability is superior to ours," Curly-hair added.

All Guardian abilities had their pros and cons. I'd seen Remy rip apart a wall of steel like it was nothing, then reduce it to something so light you could blow on it and watch it float away. But he had to physically connect with an object. The strong winds Kim created could move anything, yet they were useless in a confined place. Energy turned everything into dust, yet it was so lethal Sykes rarely used it during sparring. The same could be said of water abilities. Water Guardians sucked moisture out of anything, mummifying live things in a matter of seconds. Stopping time wasn't something Time Guardians did often, because it drained them and they then had to speed up time to make things right. However impressive, they were nothing compared to psi abilities. The mind was the most powerful of all organs, yet it was also the easiest to manipulate.

We entered the classroom, but it was empty. Where was Mrs. D? For a moment, we stood around awkwardly.

"Thanks for coming up with a plan back there," the redhead said out loud, though he stood right in front of me. "If you hadn't, we would have been crushed."

I shrugged. "There's no need to thank me. We're a team."

"I know we didn't really introduce ourselves." His face grew red as he offered me his hand. "I'm Kent."

I grinned. "Like Clark Kent?"

"Who?" he asked.

"Son of Krypton…red-blue blur," I tried to clarify, but he still looked puzzled.

His blond sector mate draped an arm around his shoulder. "Kent here is more into books than comics or TV, so you have to very specific with him. She means Superman." He extended his arm in the air for emphasis. As if possible, Kent grew redder until his cheeks matched his red, unruly hair. He appeared much younger than his teammates.

"I'm Nioclas, but everyone calls me Nio," the blond said, drawing my attention back to him. He turned and beckoned his curly-haired friend forward. "He's Sim, short for Simiel. The three of us are from Brussels, Northeast Sector."

"Yuki," Onora's partner, the one I was convinced was a Nosferatu, said and moved closer.

"Eva," the cat-eyed Cardinal from Buenos Aires said then introduced the rest of her team. "Fiona and Oscar."

Once again, I found myself staring at Eva's eyes. "Nice to officially meet you guys."

"So what are we going to do now that we've made nice?" Nio asked, rubbing his hands. "The teacher is gone and Master Haziel is nursing bruised egos in the pit. Is there a cool hangout joint around this valley? And why did you guys choose this place as your base? Why not New York or L.A., somewhere with entertainment and nice restaurants?"

"We don't like our Cardinals distracted, Cardinal Nioclas," Mrs. D said from the doorway. "Besides, those so-called entertainments are only a teleport away. I've some news I need to share before we go back to practice."

No one complained about going back to practice, though I felt their disappointment. We moved closer.

"Master Haziel was so impressed by your performance he's decided to make it part of our daily routine, which means coming up with new ways to beat the SGs. You know what they say about using the same move…"

"You opponent expects it and comes up with a countermove," I said, repeating Master Haziel's words.

"That's right," Mrs. D said. "Also, from today, you will spend more time together, which means you will sit together during lunch and dinner." She paused, giving us time to protest.

Once again, no one spoke, though I read mixed feelings from them—relief, disappointment, excitement. I usually looked forward to having dinner with my friends, but since we met afterwards at Sykes and Remy's, I didn't mind.

"You understand what I just said?" Mrs. D asked. "No more eating with your sector teammates."

"Yes, ma'am," we said in unison.

Mrs. D frowned. "What have you done with my disagreeable Psi Team?"

We laughed.

She chuckled. "Okay, back to work. You might have won the first joust, but we have more work to do."

We trained for another hour, the rest of the team slowly warming up to Mrs. D as they realized her occasional sharpness wasn't an attempt to belittle them. She had high expectations, just like Master Haziel.

"She's not that bad," Onora said as we left the Academy.

"What are your trainers like?" I asked.

"Intimidated by us most of the time," she answered. The others nodded.

"Who can blame them? We're superior," Nio said.

"Shut up, Nio," Sim told him. "We are stronger Psis, that's all. With that comes responsibility. Why do you think Lil warned us during the match? We could easily have hurt the SGs."

Nio flipped him off.

We teleported once we reached HQ hallways. Even with the students and the Civilians gone, we still didn't teleport from the Academy. At home, I got in the shower. I was getting dressed when I heard movements coming from the kitchen. A quick scan and I grinned. Grampa was home. I'd missed him. I didn't see much of him anymore, since it seemed like all his time was taken with teaching or searching for the Summoners.

Removing the towel I'd wrapped around my head, I left my room and followed the sounds to the kitchen. He stood in front of the stove, stirring something. His hair seemed to have turned gray overnight.

"Whatcha cookin', Grampa?" I asked, walking to his side.

"Cream of potato soup." He dropped an arm around my shoulders and dropped a kiss on my temple. "How's training?"

"Gruesome. We took out half the SGs during a mock attack."

He chuckled but appeared distracted.

"Where's Aunt Janelle?" I asked.

"She'll be here shortly. Would you like to share our soup?"

I hated potato soup. "Sorry, I can't. I have to join the other Cardinal Psis for lunch."

He leaned back to study me, his craggy eyebrows raised. "Have to?"

"Mrs. D's brilliant idea to make us one big, happy family. Whether it works is another story." I leaned against the counter and studied him. This would have been the perfect time to bring up the Specials again, but he looked exhausted. His eyes drooped with fatigue and his emotions—he was frustrated and concerned. His beard had grown longer and whiter, too. "So? How are things going?"

"The same."

"Are you still trying to find the Summoners?"

Instead of answering, he looked at his watch. "Shouldn't you be heading to the cafeteria?"

In other words, he wasn't going to discuss anything with me. "Do you know my birthday is coming up?"

"Already? With everything happening, I totally forgot."

"Grampa!"

He chuckled. "It is in three days, I know. We'll have a small celebration with your friends."

I sighed. My birthday was the one day I reconnected with my Gypsy relatives. We always watched a special performance by my grandmother's Kalderash circus.

"Can I visit my cousins after we defeat Raphael?" I asked.

A look I couldn't define crossed his face and my heart sank.

"We *are* going to defeat them, right?" I asked.

"Of course. Oh, and taking charge of the situation like you did during the mock attack was very good. No matter how disagreeable your teammates are, when your plan is sensible, they'll always listen to you."

I laughed. Like Master Haziel, he always knew everything that happened around here. I reached up and kissed his cheek. His beard tickled my nose.

"I love you, Grampa."

I teleported and appeared in the hallway outside HQ offices, then raced toward the Academy's cafeteria. Everyone was already seated, a low buzz in the air. Onora and Nio waved me over to the Psi Team table at end of the room. Eating in here the last two days had been torture. Our team had received glares from the other Cardinals as soon as we walked in. Today, everything seemed brighter. Smiling, I started across the huge room.

A moan came from my right followed by, "My back."

When two more echoed it, I slowed down and glanced at the table. It was occupied by the SGs. One by one, they clutched parts of their body and moaned as though in pain. A second table picked up the cry of pain. Then the third.

I stopped and the moaning ceased. I studied the SGs' serious expressions, lowered my shield, then grinned. They weren't hurt. They were just messing with me. The walls of the pit weren't padded and we hadn't exactly played nice during the mock attack, but no one had broken anything. They had all been on their feet when we left. Besides, their bruises had been superficial and easily self-healed.

Grinning, I continued walking. The fake cries picked up and, like a wave, moved from table to table, perfectly synchronized with my walk across the room. My cheeks grew hot. One thing was for sure, they were not going to quit until I said something. But what was I supposed to say?

I stopped again, bit my lower lip and studied them. Some were grinning, while others still wore the fake grimaces. "Do I need to apologize for the Psi Team?" I asked.

"Yes," the SGs yelled in unison, as though their performance was staged.

"No," the Psi Team called back from their table. They were on their feet, waving and shaking their heads.

I glanced at the SGs and shrugged. "Sorry, Guardians. I must side with my team. After all, that was just the first round," I added jokingly.

The SGs nearest me started murmuring, "Rematch…rematch…rematch…"

The rest of them picked up the chant, about three hundred men and women, half of whom hadn't even been in the pit.

The Psi table whistled and yelled, "Bring it on…bring it on…bring it on…"

The chanting echoed around the cafeteria. My gaze connected with Sykes' at the Energy Team table. He looked confused. Remy and the others also wore puzzled expressions

What's going on? Remy telepathed.

Let's meet after lunch and I'll explain. I continued on to my table and was surprised when everyone raised their hands to high-five me. I sat beside Kent. "What's going on?"

"We're going to crush them again," Nio said and bumped fists with Sim.

"We thought you abandoned us," Onora said as soon as I sat.

"Why would I do that?" There were serving bowls of salad and soup in the middle of the table, along with platters of fruit and sandwiches. I floated my plate to the salad bowl and served myself. "My grandfather was home, and I hadn't seen him in a while."

The conversation around our table was lively. They wanted to know about my childhood, growing up with the Gypsies, being on the road with Grampa. I did my best to answer, but my gaze kept going to the senior Cardinal Guardians' table. It was empty. A quick scan indicated Bran wasn't in the valley. Cardinals Seth and Moira were missing too. Grampa, Aunt Janelle and Cardinal Hsia were at my place. Where were Bran and the other two Cardinals?

I finished my salad and was reaching for an apple when Nio asked, "Can you take us downtown sometime?"

"Sure. When?"

"This afternoon?"

"Oh yes, please," Onora piped in. "We've been cooped up here for three days straight with nothing to do but play games when not training. Cabin fever is starting to kick in."

Since the junior and mid-level Cardinals were houseguests of the senior Cardinals, their houses didn't have electronics. "Give me an hour to arrange something. We'll probably need cars and drivers. A good thing the Civilians left their cars behind."

"Why do we need cars?" Eva asked.

"Yeah, why not just teleport there?" Sim added.

I shrugged. "Because we're not allowed to. We drive. Don't you?"

"No, but I could learn," Nio said. "How hard can it be if humans do it?"

Was he serious? I cocked my brow at the others. They shook their heads. "You're kidding. You *do not* drive?"

"We have no need for cars," Onora said.

"How do you get to school, blend in with the other students?" I asked.

"We've all graduated; before, Civilian drivers drove us to and from school," she said. "As for humans, we didn't interact with them."

"We still don't," Nio added. "To blend in, we just observe and imitate their behavior." He grabbed Kent's arm. "Kent can learn how to drive in seconds if you have a manual. He's something of a super genius."

The guy blushed.

"I don't have a manual, but we'll figure out what to do about drivers." I stood. "I'll ping you guys when I have everything set."

Sykes, Remy, and Kim caught up with me as I left the cafeteria. Izzy was still having a heated discussion with Sol.

"What mind control did you use on them?" Kim said when we cleared the entrance.

"Not here," Remy warned.

"I don't care if they overhear," Kim snapped. "My team has the most arrogant and meanest bunch of Cardinals I've ever met. They make snide remarks at everything, have no respect for the trainers, and don't follow instructions. I was this close," she indicated with her finger and thumb, "to slapping one today."

"I kind of did," I said.

"Is that what did the trick?" she asked as we left the Academy behind.

"Not here," Remy added again, shutting her up this time though she glared at him.

At their house, everyone plopped on the sectional couch, their faces long. I didn't feel sorry for them. Kim had been a total bitch toward me too when I'd first joined the program.

"Tell us what you did," Kim said with a sigh. "Because I can't take it anymore. It's been three days of pure torture."

I explained what had happened during training and the mock attack inside the pit, and our impending trip downtown.

"That would not work for us," Sykes announced, then slid lower on his seat and propped his legs on the coffee table. "I have Solaris *and* Lunaris. Enough said."

"You finally met women you can't charm," I teased.

He made a face as though he wanted to throw up. "Wouldn't try to charm those two if you paid me. Half the time I want to slowly..." he curled his fingers and imitated strangling. "The problem is they might ascend, then come back and haunt me."

"Esras is not so bad, but the competitiveness between the sector subgroups is killing him."

Kim stood. "I'm going to invite my team to go downtown, too. Where are you guys going, Lil?"

I shrugged. "I don't know yet. We need to go for group activity, so it's either movies or bowling at Fun Park. Anything is better than having them at my house." All the electronics were in my room, which meant they'd have to spend their time there, leaving me with no privacy.

"If we agree to meet at Fun Park, can we have a bowling match?" Kim asked.

"Sure. Tell them the Psi Team has issued them a challenge. That should unite them long enough to make them feel like a team. "

Kim laughed. "I agree. What time do we meet?"

"Three o'clock? I'll call and reserve lanes."

Sykes chuckled. "Make it two lanes. We'll challenge the Earth Team."

"Challenge accepted," Remy said. "And the two winning teams can have a showdown, so make sure we have the lanes for two to three hours."

"What showdown?" Izzy asked, having appeared behind us unnoticed. "We'll keep time and make sure no one cheats." she added once we explained the plan.

"Oh come on," Sykes griped. "What's the fun without using our powers? And what do you mean by 'we'?"

"Sol can time with me. Unlike you guys, we Time Guardians get along. So how are we getting there?"

- 20 -

BONDING

"Not a good idea," Aunt Janelle said after I explained our plan to drive Remy's SUV to Fun Park so Cardinals could use it to teleport in and out through. She and Grampa were lingering over their lunch in the kitchen.

"Don't you think the locals will notice that many people coming out of such a small car?" Grampa asked.

"Fine. Then we'll walk or take the local transit bus."

"All of you walking down the hill or taking the bus will draw attention too," he insisted. "Don't worry, we'll get you proper transportation and make the necessary arrangements."

Their reluctance was annoying. It was obvious they didn't like the idea of us going downtown. It took them three days to 'plan' the whole thing. They reserved the bowling alley for an entire afternoon, set up an account, and asked for certain drinks and snacks to be served. I was surprised they just didn't demand the owners to close it down for us. The bowling alley was part of a complex which included an arcade, an inline skating rink, and a play area for children.

Of course, during those three days I had to deal with my team bitching about our enclave. How boring and quiet it was. I had no choice but to invite them to my place.

"I have a desktop and a laptop computer, TV and a gaming console," I picked up the remote from my dresser and passed it to Nio. "The controllers and video games are all down there," I pointed at the pile under the console. "I'll borrow more from Sykes and Remy's if you don't like my selection."

Kent took the computer chair, but instead of rebooting the desktop, he reached for my stash of books. The rest of the guys settled on the floor, leaving the lounge for the girls. Fiona took the lounge, but Cat-eyes Eva knelt by the guys and started talking video games as they flipped through my collection. I grinned when they chose my favorite. It was one of the two games my mother had designed before she died. She'd worked for a software company in Seattle before she'd hooked up with Valafar.

"Are these your parents?" Onora asked, lifting the electronic frame from where it usually sat on my dresser. I hadn't noticed her nosing around until she spoke.

"Yes." The flip side of playing hostess was dealing with overly curious people. I took the frame from her and slipped it facedown into my drawer. I hope she got the message to stay away from my things.

It didn't stop her. I decided to put away my photographs before they came over next time. Bran didn't seem to mind hanging out with them. I, on the other hand, missed my time with Izzy and the others.

The day of bowling couldn't come soon enough for me. The excitement hung thick in the air during training and at lunchtime. I was the one in a crappy mood. No one remembered it was my birthday. Not Grampa. Not Bran. Not Kylie. I knew the senior Cardinals were busy tracking down Gavyn, who'd disappeared again. Still, that was no excuse.

We piled in the bus the Earth Cardinals had made out of an SUV and took off toward town. Ironically, the bus had Guardian Tours plastered on its side. The first person I saw inside Fun Park was Kylie's boyfriend, Cade, playing one of the arcade games. He waved and indicated the entrance to the laser tag room, which meant Kylie was in there. She'd been gone a lot since I refused to mind-blend with her. Either she was still pissed at me or she'd really been out of town.

"Mr. Falcon's party?" a woman asked before we reached the bowling counter.

"Yes," I said. "The others are right behind us." While the woman led my team to tables near the lanes, I went to talk to Cade.

"Kylie is playing laser tag with Amelia and Nikki," Cade said, his eyes on the screen as he blasted alien invaders. "So how long is your friend going to study bats?" he asked.

"What?"

"Your blonde friend. Kylie's been driving her to and from Whistling Caves every night for the last week. Since we're supposed to take her tonight again, I wondered how long she has to do this."

"I don't know," I said slowly, but my mind raced. Kim must have been using the cave to teleport out of the valley undetected. She'd needed someone to pick her up at her house and take her back. Other than the housecleaning company, Kylie was one of the two humans who came and went inside our compound without arousing suspicion. The other one was my other human friend McKenzie, who was in Europe for the summer.

"Why can't she ask one of you to take her?" Cade asked.

I shrugged and said the first thing that popped in my head. "It must be a surprise for one of us."

Cade made a face. "Bats?"

"Yeah, they make good pets. Oh, there's Kylie." I hurried away from his side before I could tell another senseless fib to cover the last one. Who kept bats for pets? I didn't give Kylie a chance to go to Cade. After

I hugged Nikki and Amelia, I grabbed Kylie's hand and pulled her toward the bowling area.

"You've been keeping a secret from me," I whispered.

She grinned. "I keep lots of secrets from you. You have to be more specific."

I glared. "Kim and the cave."

Kylie exhaled. "Oh, I'm so happy you know. You have no idea how much I wanted to call you and..." She stopped and studied me with narrowed eyes. "You read my mind? After you promised not to?"

"She can do that too?" Cade asked from behind us, making me jump.

"Of course I can," I said with a false smile. "All Gypsies do."

He grinned and asked, "What am I thinking right now?"

"You want to buy pizza and drinks, but you're not sure you have enough money for the three of us."

Cade looked like he'd swallowed a fly.

"You don't have to buy me anything. I'm here with friends."

"I'll have a slushy." Kylie giggled and pulled her boyfriend's arm until he gave her a kiss. Then she gripped my arm and pulled me up the ramp to the bowling side of Fun Park.

Cade was still watching us when we reached the counter overlooking the lanes. Regular people were being turned away, so the stools were unoccupied. The Guardians were still pouring in, but most of them went straight to get their bowling shoes, then to the seats by the scoreboards.

"Do you think he's buying the Gypsy angle?"

Kylie laughed. "Oh yeah. It would never cross his mind that you are anything else. It never crossed mine."

"Good. Now back to you. Why are you getting mixed up in Guardian business?"

She rolled her eyes. "Kim told me about the lockdown, which you forgot to tell me, you meanie."

"I would have if you'd bothered to call me back. I thought you were out of town again."

"I was, then I came back. Is it true they destroyed all the portals and you have, like, a gazillion Guardians secretly training at HQ?"

"Hundreds," I corrected.

"Gazillions sounds more urgent and exciting."

"There's nothing exciting about it." I was a bit jealous of Kim. Okay, not a bit. A lot. Kylie was my friend, and *I* was supposed to tell her Guardian news, not Kim. "They closed the only portal. When did Kim have the time to tell you all this stuff?"

"While I drove her to the cave," Kylie explained. "The first time she texted me to pick her up, I thought *you* were in trouble or something. Once she explained about how you guys are secretly training and everyone was depending on you, I knew I shouldn't bother you."

"So you're not mad about the mind-blend thing?"

She snickered. "No. I, sort of, understood why you couldn't do it. You'll get around to showing me everything after your powers are stable, right?"

"Right. Did she tell you why she needed to sneak out?"

She looked toward the food counter to check on Cade, who was talking to Nikki and Amelia near the food court. "I told Cade that Kim was studying bats, but she told me she was carrying messages back and forth between you and your allies. So, is it true about the secret training?" Kylie leaned forward, her eyes wide.

I was tempted to tell her the truth, that Kim had gone to see her boyfriend, but I couldn't do that to either of them. Kylie wanted a chance to help us, even though there never seem to be anything for her to do. And Kim was in love.

"Yes, we are training, but all the Cardinal Guardians are here." I indicated the chairs near the lanes that were filling up fast.

Kylie's eyes popped. "How many in all?"

"Sixty. We're going to have a bowling game."

She made a face. "Bowling? That's boring."

I laughed. "You should sit with us and watch. You'll change your mind about what is boring and what isn't."

She blinked. "They'll…you'll let me sit with you guys?"

"Of course, silly." Lucien appeared at the entrance of the room and looked around. Since we were only nine in the psi team, I'd invited him. Plus, I sucked at bowling and he'd said he was good. Apparently, bowling was a pastime in Xenith. "Come on, I'll introduce you to Lucien, Master Haziel's great-great-great-grandson, and my Psi Team."

She followed my gaze over and her jaw dropped. "Whoa, he's hot. They all are. Is the really pale one with black hair a Nosferatu?"

"Yes, but don't worry, he won't combust in the sun or feed on anyone."

For a moment, she just stared at the group. "Thanks for the invite, but I think I'll pass. Cade, Nikki, and Amelia are waiting for me."

"Chicken," I called after her, then started around the long counter toward the others.

The Air Team had fifteen members in all, nine men and six women, and from their expressions they still weren't getting along. Sykes winked at me, but kept his distance because of Lucien. They had to make nice. It was hardly time for old feuds. Remy's Earth Team was the largest. The tension within the other teams hadn't disappeared, despite the fact that Master Haziel had pitted them against SGs like he had with the Psi Team. Maybe the fact that there were fewer of us made it easier to get along.

We paired up, each team using six of its members for the first round–Psi against Air, Earth against Energy. Lucien and the two Water guys, who arrived with Remy, joined our team to even out the teams. The extra Cardinals opted to be timekeepers and subs. Even though we had four lanes designated to the teams and left the remaining eight empty, no humans were allowed to bowl. Warm-up was fun, with a lot of teasing.

At first, everyone used their normal skills, which wasn't exceptional by human standards. Then suddenly a ball veering off-course changed directions. A gust of wind shot past a bowler and made the ball move so fast it was a blur. Balls rose in the air without being touched, and spun as they raced down the lane, or rolled at never-before seen angles. My personal favorites were the smoking balls that left behind charred lanes, which Earth Guardians fixed.

Each team tried to outdo each other, with Izzy and her timer friends awarding higher points for more spectacular moves. People started to line up along the wall surrounding the lanes. Others moved closer. The glamour had to be working still, since no one else was pointing.

"Do you wonder what they see?" Onora asked.

"A bunch of serious players," I said, watching Sykes. He had an energy ball the size of a grapefruit. He pressed it against the bowling ball, making the red decorations on the ball glow. Then he walked forward and took aim at the pin. The ball shot off toward the pins like a rocket, charring the wooden lane for a moment before Remy repaired it. "With the majority of us dressed the same, they probably think we are some kind of a bowling team."

The games became more competitive and loud, with opposing teams doing whatever they could to stop the ball from reaching the pins. The drinks kept coming. Then pizza. The crowd watching us grew bigger and bigger.

Then the people walked away, went back to their video games and playing pool. Only a powerful psi could influence an entire room like that. Even as the thought flashed in my head, Grampa appeared.

I checked my watch. It was seven. We'd lost track of time, and going by his expressions, he wasn't happy.

"I'll take care of the bill," Grampa said. "Go home, change, and head to the cafeteria. Stay with your group."

The SGs and all the senior Cardinals, including Bran, were already in the cafeteria when we arrived. The tables and chairs had been moved to leave an empty area in front of the room.

"What is going on?" Eva asked.

"I don't know, but the senior Cardinals love to hold unexpected meetings around here. It's usually over something bad." The SGs had stayed behind this afternoon, but after a week of training, I was sure they needed some R and R too. "Or maybe we have some kind of entertainment."

"No, I vote for bad news," Onora said as she sat across from me.

I shrugged. She was such a glass-half-empty person.

"Maybe this is about your human friend," she added. "The one you were talking to at the bowling place."

I frowned. "What about her?"

"Her psi energy is larger and brighter than in most humans," she said.

"She could see through the glamour," Nio added. "I heard her thoughts."

"Don't you mean you read her thoughts?" Onora said and chuckled. "I saw you checking her out."

"Did not," he said with disgust as though he wouldn't be caught fraternizing with a human girl. He had just sunk lower in my book. "She's a medium."

Nio looked skeptical. "A real medium, not a faker like most human psychics?"

"Or Gypsies," Onora teased.

I hoped she was teasing because my Gypsy relatives were pretty magical people. Before I could respond, Grampa stood and everyone's attention shifted to him.

"Today is a special occasion," he said, glancing around the room before finding me. "My granddaughter turns seventeen and we have a family tradition we've honored since she was a child. Because of the crisis with the Tribe, we have decided to do things differently this year. So with great pride, allow me to introduce you to the amazing…Stromboli Circus. "

I covered my mouth and fought tears. He remembered. After all the bitching I'd done, he had not forgotten my birthday.

Lights dimmed. Beams from four clairvoyant crystals converged at the front of the room and an image of a man appeared. He looked splendid in black pants and shiny matching boots, white shirt with a bowtie, a red and gold embroidered jacket and a sequined black cape. He wore white gloves and carried a bowler hat and a sparkling walking stick.

The moustache didn't fool me. I knew the twinkling eyes, cocky swagger and wiggling fake eyebrows belonged to Anton Kalderash, my cousin three times removed or second cousin twice removed. I could never tell the difference. By the time he started to spark, tears had filled my eyes.

"Ladies and gentlemen, boys and girls, today is a very special day because one of our very own is celebrating her seventeenth birthday.

Tonight's performance is dedicated to my great niece, Lil. Wherever you are, *ves'tacha, sastims*!" he added, using the Roma term for 'beloved' and wishing me 'good health' the Romany way. "This is your day."

- 21 -

GUARDIANS DON'T RING DOORBELLS

After the acrobats, the trapeze walkers, the clouds and all the wonders that made Stromboli Circus so great, they sang "Happy Birthday" and the Guardians joined in. The applause as the lights turned on was thunderous.

Two Academy cooks wheeled in a tiered birthday cake and brought it to our table.

"Make a wish…make a wish…" the room erupted.

I studied the grinning faces around the hall through teary eyes, made the wish, and blew out the candles. The cooks cut and distributed pieces of cake, but I couldn't eat. I left our table and walked to Grampa's.

"Thank you, Grampa," I said, kissed his cheek and gave him a hug, which brought on another round of applause.

"I didn't do anything. Junior organized everything," he said, his voice carrying. A few chuckles followed. He really should stop calling Bran Junior.

Bran sat at the end of their table, grinning. I wanted to run to him and show my appreciation with a kiss, but I couldn't. Everyone was watching.

Blushing, I started toward him. He got to his feet. Oh, forget the others. I ran straight into his arms and wrapped my arms around his neck. He lifted me up and laughed. We didn't kiss, not in the traditional way. Our energies caressed and melded, which brought on a whole different kind of sensations. The applause didn't surprise me, and I was sure my face matched my hair.

He leaned back and chuckled. *I give you your birthday wish and you cry?*

I hadn't realized I was crying until he mentioned it. *I'm not crying.*

He wiped the wetness off my cheeks. *Of course not. Let's get out of here.*

We can't leave while everyone… I turned and realized people were already leaving, most of them carrying their slices of cake.

"How did you do it?" I asked as soon as we left the Academy behind us.

"It was nothing."

How like him to downplay his role. "It couldn't have been easy. They move a lot and are suspicious of strangers."

"A little? Even after I showed them pictures and talked about working with your grandfather, they didn't believe me. They kept saying you wouldn't break the family tradition."

"How did you convince them?"

He pulled me closer and chuckled. "That is my little secret."

It didn't matter how he did it. He was the best boyfriend ever. I hugged his arm as we continued toward the tunnels. "Let's go to my place and shut the world out."

"Not yet. Your friends have planned something for you."

"Really? What?"

He laughed, dimples flashing. "Always impatient."

I loved surprises. "Come on."

"At least pretend you are surprised when we get there." He covered my eyes with his hands before we entered the basement. We walked into the room and stopped. "Ready?"

There was no sound, but I felt the others' presence. Bran's hands dropped. I looked around and laughed. The room was decorated with birthday balloons and streamers, and everyone wore silly birthday hats. I loved it. Izzy blew a kiddie horn while Remy pressed a drink in my hand.

"Guys, you shouldn't have."

"Ahoy, matey," Sykes called out by the wet bar, where bags sat side by side on the counter. He wore an eye patch and a glove with a large hook. Lifting one of the bags with the hook, he added, "Me found you some booty over here."

On the coffee table were drinks and one of Remy's special cakes.

"Where is Kim?" I asked.

"She'll be here," Izzy said. "She's talking to your grandfather about the housing situation."

Bran picked up one of the hats and placed it on my head. I plopped one on his head too, then picked up a horn and blew so loud he covered his ears. We danced, ate and acted silly, until the sound of the doorbell intruded.

Guardians didn't ring doorbells. I performed a quick scan and jumped up. "It's Kylie. She's here for the party."

We all teleported upstairs, hurried to the door and opened. "You got here right on…" My voice tailed off when I noticed her expression. She was scared. "What is it?"

"Kim is missing."

We pulled her inside and closed the door. She kept wringing her hands, her eyes bright with unshed tears. "I took her to the cave tonight. She said she'd only be gone for half an hour, so Cade and I waited. Then the two kids appeared. I think one of them is that kid…Angelia." Her gaze stayed on me. "They want to talk to you, Lil."

Everyone starting talking at once.

"How did they find us?" I asked.

"How long has she been sneaking out?" Sykes added.

"If the Specials can find us, so can Raphael," Remy muttered.

"If Kim's been taken, we need to tell the senior Cardinals," Bran said.

"No," Izzy said. "She wouldn't want them to know she's been sneaking out to meet Kieran. We have to get her back without them."

"We need weapons," Bran said.

"I'll get them," Remy offered.

"No." Bran gripped his arm before he could teleport. "A single person in the hallways will draw attention, and if you get caught, our plans will be blown. We all go. Sykes and Izzy take the west hallway. Be loud and your usual obnoxious self, Sykes. Izzy, do your best to shut him down. Lil and I will take the East hallway and walk towards the Academy. If anyone appears, detain them. We want Remy to get everything we need because once we leave the valley, we can't use our powers."

"Me? Obnoxious?" Sykes asked.

"Yes, you are," Izzy retorted as the two headed downstairs to the secret door in the basement.

"What about me?" Kylie asked, biting her nails.

"You stay here," Remy snapped. "What were you thinking, driving her out there in the first place?"

Kylie's eyes grew big and she visibly cringed.

"It's not her fault, Remy," I warned him. "Kim fed her a story and she fell for it. It's not your fault, Kylie. Kim should have known better."

"She shouldn't be involved in Guardian business in the first place," Remy retorted, following us downstairs. He disappeared inside his room and came out with a satchel.

"How long have they been doing this?" Bran asked as we entered the tunnel leading to HQ.

"About a week," I said. "Cade let it slip when we met at Fun Park this afternoon."

"Why didn't you tell us?" Remy asked.

I glanced at him over my shoulder. "Tattle on her? I don't think so. Besides, isn't our motto, 'Don't confess unless you are busted'?"

"You of all people should know things are different now," Remy snapped. "Archangels are just waiting for one of us to screw up and lead them back to the valley. You should have told us."

"I found out this afternoon, Remy. You guys live with her. How could you not know she wasn't in the house every night?" I retorted just as we reached Izzy and Sykes.

Remy shot me a nasty look. "We can't all close our eyes and find the exact location of people's energies."

I blinked. Where did that come from?

"Ease up, man," Bran cut in. "We are all worried about her, so there's no need to turn on each other."

"I'm with Bran on this," Sykes said. "You need to chill, dude. Because if we are passing blame, I shouldn't have told her about the caves."

"Damn right." Remy turned to Izzy. "You knew about them too?"

Izzy's eyes narrowed. "Don't you give me that nasty look. I tried to talk her out of it several times, but no one tells Kim what to do."

"You should have tried harder," Remy said through gritted teeth and stomped ahead of us.

"What crawled up his pants?" I heard Sykes ask as Bran and I followed Remy.

"You know how protective he gets," Izzy said. "He'll probably blame himself if something happens to her."

No, Remy's behavior went beyond that of a team leader. Could he have feelings for Kim? He disappeared into the short hallway leading to the weapons room.

"He's kind of overreacting," I said.

Bran shook his head. "I don't know. He's been in a crappy mood since they graduated. Sykes said he needs some girls."

Or maybe just one. "When did Kim start dating Keiran?"

"The beginning of sum…oh, you think Remy *likes* her?"

"It's possible. His reaction right now was over the top, very unlike him." We reached where the hallways met and branched off to the Academy and the Psi-dar room. The lights were blazing on the Academy side, loud cheers reaching us. They must have been re-watching the circus performance.

The wait was hard. Any second, I expected us to be caught. I sighed with relief when Remy reappeared in the hallway with the bulging satchel and hurried toward Izzy and Sykes. Once he was in the clear, we followed.

Back upstairs, we found Kylie pacing. She was a hot mess.

"We can't suit up here," Bran said when Remy unzipped the bags. He had brought our hunting clothes, including boots. "If anyone sees us, we will look like we're going hunting."

That made sense. I'd worn a Gypsy skirt and ballet flats to go bowling. Remy could have transformed them easily, but we couldn't afford to use our powers.

"I'll drive," Remy said, still sounding pissed. He stuck out his hand toward Kylie, who quickly handed him the truck keys.

We snuck out of the house, looked up and down the street to make sure no one saw us, and piled inside Cade's truck. Bran and I shared the front passenger seat while Sykes, Izzy, and Kylie piled into the back. Tension hung in the air as we took off. Any moment, I expected a Cardinal or Master Haziel to appear in front of the car and stop us.

The tension eased a bit when we reached Mountain Road without being stopped. We barreled down the hill, cut through the Island and headed toward First Dam. "So you left the Specials with Cade?" Izzy asked.

"I had no choice. The girl did something to him," Kylie said. "He kept asking who they were and where Kim was. The girl was so rude. She told him to shut up, waved her hand and Cade fell. I don't even know if he's okay or not." Her voice shook to a stop. "Then she ordered me to get you if I valued my friend's life. She was so scary."

The Angelia I knew was sweet. She often listened to Daryl, who was the oldest of the Specials. Another long silence filled the car as Remy raced past First Dam and hit Highway 89. The canyon road meandered, but he didn't slow down as he took the corners. No one complained.

The parking lot near the Wind Caves was empty when we screeched to a stop and jumped out. "Where are they?" Izzy asked.

Right on cue, Daryl and Angelia materialized. Cade wasn't with them.

"Where's Cade?" Kylie asked in a screechy voice.

Daryl pointed toward the cave. "He's up there. Asleep. We'll bring him out."

Despite his words, Kylie stared toward the cave and chewed on a nail.

My gaze swung from Daryl to Angelia. She usually couldn't wait to give me a hug. This time, she stayed by Daryl's side and glowered.

"How did you find us, Angelia?" I asked.

"We followed Cardinal Kim's telegate," Daryl answered, his silver eyes eerie under the truck's headlights.

"What happened to Kim?" Bran asked.

Daryl reached out and took Angelia's hand. Her lips were still scrunched up and her eyes narrowed.

"Angelia?" I moved toward her. She took a step away from me, her hands fisted. Frowning, I stopped. "Did something bad happen to Kim?"

"You lied to us," Angelia hissed.

I blinked. "What are you talking about?"

"You destroyed our home and killed Coronis," she yelled. "You killed our mommies and daddies."

My heart dropped. We'd defeated Coronis and her followers nearly a year ago, but I'd dreaded the day she would learn the truth about what happened.

"Angelia." I took another step toward her.

She launched herself at me, catching me unaware and nearly making me lose my balance. Punches rained on my arms, stomach and chest, anywhere she could reach.

"Why did you do it?" she yelled. "Why? You are one of us."

Too shocked to grab her wrists and stop her, I just stood there and let her vent.

Someone plucked her up from behind and lifted her away from me. Bran. Without speaking, he marched with the kicking and screaming Angelia to the other side of the parking lot.

I didn't realize I was shaking until Izzy put her arms around me. She said something I didn't catch or didn't want to, I don't know. Tears welled in my eyes, but I blinked rapidly. This was no time to cry. We had to take Angelia and Daryl home before the Psi-dar detected their presence, the find Kim and bring her home before the security team noticed we were gone.

Across the narrow parking lot, Angelia continued to struggle against Bran. We were too far to hear his words, but his mouth opened and closed as he talked to the little girl, then she went limp and slumped against him.

Shrugging Izzy's arms aside, I swiped at the tears and focused on the conversation between Daryl and Remy.

"...wanted to know what's going on, why everyone's so scared," Daryl said. "Cardinal Seth and the Council talked about where to hide us until the hunters were defeated. They wanted to take us to the Academy in South America or Europe. Someone asked about Coronis Isle."

"And?" Remy asked when Daryl paused.

"Cardinal Seth said there was nothing left after you destroyed it and sealed the portal. We all heard them." He turned his head as though to glance at Angelia. She and Bran now sat and faced each other. Whatever he was telling her seemed to be working.

"Angelia thinks you are a bunch of liars and killers," Daryl added in a whisper, adding to my guilt. "She's the one who suggested we follow Kieran and see if he could lead us to you. She wanted to hear the truth from you. Tonight, we got lucky."

It didn't matter that Coronis and her followers had been evil or that, for centuries, the Cardinals had tried to find the portal to the island with little success. No one wanted to tell Daryl his parents were killed because they were evil. Worse, strong psi readings ebbed and flowed from the cave, indicating he and Angelia hadn't come alone. I tried to get an exact reading to see how many Specials were in the caves but couldn't.

I felt a tug and peered at the road in the direction we'd come from. We were not alone. My eyes met Remy's.

What is it? he asked.

We are not alone. There are more Specials in the cave and we have Guardians shadowing us. I indicated the road with a nod.

He turned to look, just as a car zipped past without stopping, and its headlights lit another car parked on the shoulder of the road.

Remy nodded toward the road. *Sykes, see who they are.*

"Where are you going?" Izzy asked him softly.

"To take a leak."

She made a face. "You are so gross."

Sykes just laughed and disappeared in the shadows. He had explored this valley and the surrounding canyons, and he could sneak up on whoever was spying on us before they knew he was there, unless they were Psi.

"Look, Daryl," Remy said, placing the palms of his hands on his knees and bending until he was eye-level with Daryl, even though the gesture was wasted on the blind boy. "What happened on Coronis Isle couldn't be helped. Coronis was evil and had to be stopped. I'm sorry your parents died too."

"Goddess, Remy," Izzy swore. "What happened to being subtle?"

"That was subtle," he retorted. "I focused only on Coronis."

"It's okay, Cardinal Isadora," Daryl said, sounding mature for his age. He was fourteen and the oldest of the Specials in our sector. "My father and mother were Primes, but because I was blind and not very big, they thought I was not perfect. They dumped me at the institute with the other Specials when I was four. Five was the minimum age for admission. They didn't care that I wasn't being trained, that I was often used as a guinea pig and sent to fetch things for the other Specials. They were ashamed of me, but Coronis had a need for children like me. My powerful hearing abilities meant I would one day be a power source for her, to be drained when she needed an energy boost. You could say my life sucked, but now…"

Suddenly, his bravado disappeared. His chin trembled and his eyes filled with tears. He shoved his hands in his pockets, mentally controlling himself.

"My new mom and dad are nice," he continued. "I don't want anything to happen to them. I don't want to leave them behind, especially my mom. She doesn't have powers like the others." He looked toward the cave and frowned. "We don't want to go to the Academy in South America or Europe. We want to stay here with you."

There was no room in the valley for the Specials. Not in the Academy or our homes. We also had no Civilians to keep an eye on them while we trained.

"You must protect us," Daryl added. "You owe us."

"You are blackmailing us?" Remy asked, not masking his outrage.

Daryl grinned. "Yes. You protect us, or else we'll go all over your valley and use our powers. We'll do things, good and bad, to make sure the people see us doing them."

A giggle drew my attention to Kylie. I'd completely forgotten her presence.

"It's not funny," Remy reprimanded her, then glared at Daryl. "There's nowhere for you to stay in the valley and you cannot threaten us."

"Then we won't tell you where Cardinal Kim is or who took her," Angelia said from behind me.

We whipped around to face Angelia. Bran's hand tightened on her shoulder, and from the way she tried to shrug it off, she didn't like it.

"You are holding her hostage?" Remy asked in an outraged voice.

Angelia made a disgusted face as though Remy's suggestion was beyond dumb. "N-no."

"Tell them," Bran ordered.

She shot him a mean look, then mumbled, "Demons took her."

"Which ones?" Izzy asked at the same time as Remy. "Were they hiding in a cloud mass?"

"Was there lightning?" I added.

"There were no clouds. Is that what everyone is scared of? Lazari?"

"Back to the question, Angelia," Izzy said impatiently. "What kind of demons?"

"They were a mixture of Nosferatu, Werenephils, and some nature-benders," Angelia spat out. "Kieran and his friends fought them two nights ago and he said they were from the Order of Hermonites."

We sighed with relief. Demons we could deal with. The Order had asked to meet with me, but Grampa had said no. Could this be their attempt to get our attention? "Where did they take her?" I asked, my glance moving from Angelia to Daryl then back to Angelia.

She ignored my question, even refused to look at me. I sighed. The Brotherhood was doing what they were supposed to do—raise the Specials neutrally—teaching them about our history without labeling Guardians as good and demons as bad. If we had had time, I would have broken the rules and explained to her about Coronis and why we sent her to Tartarus.

"Lil asked you a question," Bran reminded Angelia.

"I'm never talking to her. Ever," she added, shooting me a mean look.

"Fine. Pretend she's not here," Izzy snapped through gritted teeth. "Where did they take Kim?"

Angelia sneered. "I don't like you either."

"You know what? Right now the feeling is mutual, brat," Izzy retorted.

"Behave," Bran cautioned, though I wasn't sure whether he was talking to Izzy or Angelia. "Tell us everything."

She jerked her shoulder from his grip and moved to Daryl's side. "We followed Kieran and his friends when they left the compound tonight, because we knew he was meeting Cardinal Kim. We materialized at the same time she did. Then the demons attacked. They didn't give the Cardinal time to use her powers before they grabbed her and teleported. Kieran and his friends followed. I followed them, while Daryl used the Cardinal's telegate to find your enclave."

"He followed a telegate backward?" Izzy asked.

"He's the best tracker we have," Angelia bragged. Trackers could detect trace amounts of Psi energies and follow them. If Kim followed protocol, she made several stops before her last teleport, which meant Daryl was really good. "I followed the demons to their den, then met Daryl at home," Angelia continued. "You let us stay and we'll tell you who took the Cardinal and where she is being kept."

I glanced at the others. Their expressions were grim. We all knew why Kim hadn't fought back. Using her powers might have alerted the archangels.

Bran's gaze swung between Daryl and Angelia. "You two are going home or I'll tell Darius what you've been up to. Lil can retrieve the images of the demon's den from your heads."

"If she knows what's good for her, she won't try it," Angelia retorted.

"Come on, Cardinal Bran," Daryl added. "Do you really think we would let you take away our bargaining chip?"

Izzy laughed. "We are being blackmailed by two prepubescent kids."

"I'm fourteen," Daryl said, sounding insulted. "The clock is ticking, Cardinals. So what is it going to be? Cardinal Kim's life or a sanctuary for us?"

They had the upper hand and knew it. As children from Coronis' evil breeding program, they had powers we didn't even know about. I had no idea what I'd face if I mind-blended with Angelia.

"We have to find a place for them to sleep tonight," I said.

"Lil," Bran and Izzy protested at the same time.

"You're not going to let her guilt you into helping her again," Remy snapped.

"I'm not. If they were just the two of them, I'd say to take them back, but they're not." I looked at Angelia. "Tell the others they can come out now."

She hesitated as though to defy me.

"Do you want me to do it?" I asked.

She shook her head, then looked at Daryl.

"No teleporting," Bran warned.

Meekly, they walked up to the cave and disappeared inside. Within minutes, they reappeared with Cade, telekinetically carrying him. He was still out. Kylie ran to his side and cradled his head.

The others Specials followed, like a line of ants. Some carried backpacks, others their favorite toy. It wasn't just the two dozen Specials we rescued months ago. They were accompanied by their adopted sisters and brothers, mothers, aunts and grandmothers—a total of nearly sixty children under the age of sixteen, and about thirty women.

"Tartarus' pit," Izzy mumbled, eyeing them with wide eyes.

"Okay, Angelia, we've agreed to your terms," Remy said, not masking his impatience. "Where is Cardinal Kim?"

"Lord Valafar took her."

- 22 -

WE MEET AGAIN

My stomach roiled. It couldn't be true. The conversation with Gavyn and Solaris flashed in my head like a nightmare. Despite the twins' claim, I hadn't really believed my father could still be alive.

"Are you sure?" Bran asked in a harsh voice.

Angelia nodded. "The demons who took her said so. They took her to an old hotel they're fixing up."

"Where?" Bran said.

"I don't know. It was an old hotel with the words 'Lee Plaza' on the front."

"The Lee Plaza. That's in Detroit." He glanced at me. "It's the Order's headquarters. Did you go inside?"

"No way," Angelia said. "As soon as I heard the guards say, 'Lord Valafar will be happy. Now he has leverage.' I got out of there. I don't know what 'leverage' means, but it sounded bad."

"This changes everything," Izzy said, shaking her head, curly ponytail swinging back and forth. "We have to tell the senior Cardinals. Kim might not want them involved, but we're dealing with the devil's spawn. Sorry, Lil."

"No," I said.

Izzy's eyes narrowed. "No?"

"I know Valafar is evil and unscrupulous, but I meant, no, we can't tell the senior Cardinals. My grandfather is not going to let me go anywhere near Valafar, and when he takes that position, everyone will think he's throwing Kim under the bus to protect me. Worse, we go in with the others and there will be fighting and killing. We use powers, and the archangels will find us. *I* have to do this."

"I know what you are planning, and I'm not letting you do it,' Bran said, emerald eyes flashing.

"You are acting the way Grampa would," I shot back. "I'm the one he wants. Not Kim. I will not allow him to hurt her to get to me." I glanced at Izzy and Remy. They didn't meet my gaze. "You all know I'm right. I have no intention of staying with him. As soon as Kim is safe with you guys, I'll escape."

No one spoke, but their refusal to agree or disagree said a lot.

"You are not meeting with him without us," Bran vowed.

"Of course not." Somehow I had a feeling Valafar was behind Gavyn's invitation to join them. Would he listen to reason? Maybe agree to call off the archangels if I agreed to have some sort of a relationship with him?

"What do we do about *them*?" Remy asked, slanting his head toward the Specials and their entourage.

One of the women detached herself from the group and approached us. "I am Aurora, Daryl's mother," she said. "We didn't know you hadn't offered us sanctuary. The children..." she glanced at Daryl and blinked. "If you want us to leave, we will leave."

With them back in the Brotherhood compound, we wouldn't have to worry about them. Unfortunately, Angelia already believed we were liars. Sending them home now would only confirm it.

"No, you don't have to leave," I said just as a familiar black SUV pulled off the highway and onto the parking lot. Sykes stepped down from behind the wheel. The passenger doors opened and out stepped Esras, Lunaris, Solaris, and Lucien.

"What are they doing here?" Remy asked.

Sykes raised his heads. "Don't worry—everything is under control. Master Haziel sent them. He ordered them to help us."

No one bothered to ask how he'd known.

"Cardinal Sykes told us about Kim being missing, but not them." Esras indicated the children and the women with a nod.

"We'll explain later," Bran said. "Right now, we have to get them out of here and indoors. The glamour won't hold for long." His gaze followed a car as it zipped past us, then he glanced at Remy. "They can't teleport or the Psi-dar will lock on them. Any ideas?"

"I'll get transportation...buses. Esras, come with me," Remy said.

"Where are we getting buses at this time of night?" Esras asked.

"The local transit bus depot," Remy said impatiently. "We'll *borrow* two. Lil, we'll need drivers. Ask Kylie and Cade. We'll take their truck and leave it by the grocery store next to the depot. They can pick it up when they return the buses. If they say no, compel them. We. Need. Them." He nodded at Sykes. "Find a local hotel that can accommodate all of them. Each room can have an adult and two children. The teens can room in groups of two or three. Come up with a good cover story."

That was the Remy I knew. Confident. Decisive. Unstoppable.

Sykes snapped his fingers. "Already got a cover story. They are exchange students from Europe touring the country with their parents, and the valley is their next stop."

"Good. We'll be back in a few." He and Esras took off in Cade's truck.

"I need a cell phone," Sykes said, looking around. "Anyone got one?"

My eyes connected with Bran's. I'd felt his gaze on me ever since we discussed Valafar. He wasn't too happy with my decision, but he knew there was no way out.

How are you holding up? he asked.

I'm trying not to think about it. "Kylie might have a phone," I said and moved away. She still held Cade on her lap and watched me with a weird expression as I drew closer. "How's he doing?"

"I don't know. Can you wake him up or something?"

"I will. Just give me a second. Can we borrow your cell phone?"

She pulled her cell phone from her jacket pocket and shoved at me. "Then come back and take care of him, Lil. We are going home. This…" she looked around and shook her head. "We didn't sign up for this. I want out."

I should have seen that coming. Despite the fear of what was to come, namely meeting my father and negotiating Kim's release, it annoyed me that she was bailing out on me. "Okay."

I took the phone to Sykes. Bran had taken over where Remy had left off and was issuing orders. It was amazing how well they worked as co-leaders.

"Lucien, you'll go with the Specials and keep an eye on them until we return. The rest of you," Bran nodded at Izzy, Solaris, and Lunaris. "Reassure the children. They're scared."

"Just because we are women doesn't necessarily mean we're better equipped to deal with the children," Solaris grumbled.

"Then don't do anything until we get to Detroit, Solaris," Bran said without any hint of anger. Then he nodded at Aurora. "Gather the women. I need to talk to them."

Everyone got busy, even Solaris. I made my way back to Kylie's side.

She stared at me with sad eyes. "I know you are not going to like this, Lil. I thought I could be in your world, help even, but tonight I learned I'm not ready for this. I want us to stay friends, but you must ask your grandfather to erase everything I know about you and your world."

Things would never be the same between us. Not for me. "And your abilities?"

She was silent for a long time, and I was sure she wouldn't answer. "If I'm meant to be a medium, I'll tap into my powers again."

"Could you do us one last favor?" I explained about the buses Remy and Esras had gone to get, and needing drivers. "Remy said he'll park your truck by the bus depot, so you can pick it up when you return the buses."

She blew out a breath. "Okay. But what if we get busted?"

"We'll bail you out, expunge your records, and erase the cops' memories."

"You can do all that?" Cade mumbled in awe.

I looked down. When had he regained consciousness?

"You're okay," Kylie said, touching his face, then she helped him to his feet.

Cade looked around. "Who are these people? And don't tell me Gypsies. I regained consciousness earlier in the cave and saw those children create balls of light out of thin air. They did something to me again and knocked me out. Again."

"Energy balls," Kylie corrected him, then stared at me with saucer eyes. "What are you going to do?"

I had no idea. Telling her the truth about us had been necessary because she was a medium. Cade was just your average teenager with an active imagination and a truckload of curiosity.

"Tell him what he needs to know for now," Bran said from behind me. "Remy and Esras are bringing two buses, which means we'll need both of you. Lucien is not used to dealing with humans and will need your help too."

"Humans?" Cade asked with a weird inflection in his voice.

"Yes, humans," Bran said impatiently. "Lil, you want to explain?"

I shook my head. Once was enough. Despite understanding Kylie's reasons for bailing out on me now, I was hurt and disappointed in her.

What happened? Bran asked, studying me.

Kylie wants out. Explain everything to Cade. I'll go and see if the others need help with the children.

No, stay. Bran gripped my arm and moved closer to Cade, eyes narrowed. "We are entrusting you with something sacred, Cade. No humans around here know who or what we are, except Kylie. And even she can't handle it and wants out. If you tell anyone about what I'm about to tell you, I will make your life so miserable you will kill yourself to escape me." He paused. "No, I will teleport you to a Nosferatu den and let you be their blood supply for a year. Do you understand?"

Cade nodded. "What is a Nosferatu?"

"Vampires," I explained, then glared at Bran. "Don't."

"No, he needs to understand why keeping our secret is important and the consequences if he doesn't. We are Guardians, Cade. Half-angel and half-human. We have been called different names by humans, been worshipped and revered. The evil branch of our family is what you guys call demons. We are the good guys. They are the bad guys. They want to take over the world and be worshipped again. We couldn't give a rat's ass about such things, so we hunt them down. Some kidnapped Kim and we are going to get her back. Questions?"

Cade shook his head, but I'd never seen a man so scared. I gave Bran's hand a squeeze. Valafar's return had him more rattled than it had me.

"Good. The rest isn't important," Bran said then focused his attention on Kylie. For one brief moment, I thought he was going to be mean to her too. Instead, he exhaled and said, "You have been a true friend to Lil this past year, Kylie, and an ally to all of us. For that, we'll always be grateful. You want out, it's your choice and Cardinal Falcon will see that you get your wish. In the meantime, do you think you could help Lucien when you get to the hotel?"

Kylie nodded. "Sure."

"Thank you. Sykes will give you the name of the hotel and the group's reservation number. You and Lucien will stay with the Specials and their parents until we get back." Bran glanced at his watch, then his glance volleyed between Kylie and Cade. "If we are not back by morning, keep an eye on the Specials while Lucien goes to the enclave to talk to Lil's grandfather."

Kylie gave him a wobbly smile. "Okay."

"I'll check on the others." Bran squeezed my hand, then walked away.

"I've never seen him so…intense," Kylie said.

"Did he mean what he just said?" Cade whispered. "About making me kill myself and the vampires?"

"Every word," Kylie said, sounding a little shaken too. "They don't hurt humans."

"Thanks, guys." I gripped their hands. "I'll talk to Grampa about the memory thing."

Kylie nodded. "Later. Right now focus on finding Kim. I hope she's okay."

"Me too," I said. "My father should know better than to kidnap a Guardian."

Kylie blinked. "Oh, Lil."

I gave her a tiny smile and walked away.

"Her father?" I heard Cade ask.

I joined the others just as Esras and Remy pulled up with the buses. We got busy helping the children into their seats. The last to go in were Daryl and his mother, who had her arm on the skinny boy's shoulder. Angelia was already inside the bus, her face pressed against the window as she stared at us. Her anger had lessened but she still couldn't look at me without glowering. I wished there was something I could do or say to make her happy. I tried to catch her eye, but she stuck her chin in the air and ignored me.

"She'll come around," Daryl said from beside me. "Bran explained to her and she understands, but . . ." he shrugged.

She felt I had betrayed her by not telling her myself. Sighing, I smiled at Aurora, Daryl's mother. "We will be back before dawn, but if you need anything—"

"Lucien and your two human friends will help," she finished. "Cardinal Bran told us. We have credit cards and some money with us, so don't worry. You go and rescue your friend." She cupped my face, surprising me. I had thought she would hate us for refusing to give them sanctuary. "Thank you for rescuing our son from Coronis Isle."

Daryl rolled his eyes. "Come on, Mom."

Within minutes, the buses pulled out. No one spoke until they were out of sight. We left the SUV in the parking lot and trekked up to the cave. Despite being a local attraction, the inside was dark and dingy. Sykes created energy balls so we could see clearly. Solaris and Lunaris added more.

"Did you guys bring weapons?" Bran asked, his gaze moving from Esras to Solaris and Lunaris.

"Just the usual," Esras said, pulling a dagger from his boot. Solaris removed a whip. The tip was split into two with jadeite metal tips. Lunaris had a set of knives.

We changed, piling our regular clothes and shoes in the satchel Remy had carried. Then we slipped weapons into hidden sheaths under our coats and boots. Esras and Remy turned some of the knives and sheaths into swords and scabbards. Even though the Kris Dagger was inactive, Remy had brought it. He must have remembered what I had told them, that Master Haziel had insisted I must always carry it.

"Remember, we are going to talk, not fight, which means you don't attack unless you get attacked. And no matter what they do, don't use your powers. The last thing we need is Raphael and his tribe descending on us."

"I don't get it," Solaris said. "They have one of our people and we're going to talk?"

Our people? Her tune had changed.

"Valafar has her, Solaris," I said. "The Specials told us his men took Kim to the Order's den in Detroit."

A strange look crossed her face. A mixture of anger and excitement, I thought, but I could have been wrong.

"Let's pair up," Bran said. "Lil and I will take the lead. I know exactly where the Order is holed up. Sykes—"

"I'm with Izzy," Sykes said, taking her hand. He still couldn't stand the twins and didn't care who knew.

Bran nodded at Remy and Esras. "Take the rear, guys."

"What if Valafar doesn't agree to a trade?" Solaris asked.

Bran glared at her. "There's not going to be a trade. We'll get Kim and we'll all come home." Talking only seemed to make him angrier. He grabbed my hand. "Let's go and get this over with."

We appeared in a field of some kind, across the street from a hulking, abandoned building. Street lights showed three arches with columns framing what once had been a grand entrance. Bricks now replaced the large, lower glass windows, while the ones on the floors above it gaped vacant like unseeing eyes. Above the smashed cinder block door were the words, "The Lee Plaza".

Sirens resounded in the distance and loud music blared as an occasional car zipped past on Grand Boulevard. The tingle on my lower spine kicked into gear as we started toward the building, our amulets lighting up like stars.

"So this is the abandoned city," Solaris said.

"Not for long," Bran said. "Demons are moving in. Although they are adding sub-levels while doing very little to the surfaces."

As we moved closer to the building, the warning tingle on my back went crazy, sensing the humming energies of demons. Inky writing etched under my skin before the two dozen demons surrounded us. I controlled my powers with some difficulty.

"We are here to see the Order," Bran said.

"Why?" a woman called and stepped forward, the street light bathing her pale face.

Whatever hopes I had of the meeting going smoothly disappeared when I recognized Lottius, a Nosferatu girl with a bad attitude and a powerful father. We'd tortured her for information months ago. Dressed all in black like her gang, her black hair no longer had a streak of white in it.

"Lottius, you have a Cardinal Guardian and we're here for her," Bran said.

"Nice to see you again, Llyr. I see that being hunted like animals hasn't humbled you yet," she said, walking toward us.

"They have to catch us first," Bran retorted.

"Be careful what you wish for, gorgeous." She glanced at me and her eyes flashed. "The princess returns. Are you going to give yourself up and stop this madness?"

"We are here for our friend," I said, refusing to be drawn into a discussion about me.

“My father is the head of the Order,” Lottius said, “We are part of security now, so before we can let you through, we must discuss [illegible]”

Bran was behind her, a sickle wrapped around her throat before she finished speaking. “We’re done discussing,” he said rudely. “Take us to your father.”

“Do you have a death wish? A signal from me and the guards will finish your team.” She tried to push his hand, but he pressed the dagger into her skin. “Unhand me.”

“No, walk and lead us to the entrance,” Bran snarled. He could be such a badass, and he’d been in an ugly mood since we’d learned of Valafar’s existence. “Any move from any of you,” he added without glancing at the demons, “and I’ll show you how sharp this baby is.”

The demons stopped, then fell back as we moved toward the building. The wall shimmered and disappeared to reveal a wide, arched hallway filled with debris. The elevators lining the arched hallway were all unusable, except for the one that suddenly appeared to our right, its steel doors new and shiny.

You sure you want all of us down below? Esras asked. *Shouldn’t some of us stand guard?*

We stay together until we find Kim, Bran said.

The elevator door opened to reveal mirrored walls and a burgundy carpeted floor. Soft music played in the background. The demon guards glowered as the door closed on their faces.

“The atrium,” Lottius said.

The elevator descended. Lottius glanced at me from the corner of her eye and shifted away. She was more scared of me than the knife at her neck. The power radiating up and down my back couldn’t be the cause. I had it under control.

Had I turned her? During our last meeting, she’d tried to kill me after we released her, and to punish her, I’d compelled her to fight evil—a death sentence for any demon.

“Let her go,” I said.

Bran frowned. “Why?”

“She won’t try to escape or hurt us. Isn’t that right, Lottius?”

Lottius rubbed her neck. “You cursed me.”

“I compelled you to do good, hardly a curse.”

“I’ve had to hide how I feel, sneak behind my friends and family to help humans,” she said through clenched teeth. “If my family finds out the things I’ve been doing, I will be banished. Remove your voice from my head, Guardian,” she spat.

“It’s called a conscience, Lottius, but I will remove it if you do us a favor.”

"I'm not helping you in my father's…" She scrunched her face, as though battling herself, then snapped, "Fine, what is it?"

"Teleport to the top of Treasure Planet Casino and tell Dante and Kael we need them."

Her eyes widened. "They'll kill me before I open my mouth."

"Then you'd better talk fast when they appear." The elevator door slid open to reveal the guards from upstairs. Under their watchful eyes, we stepped into a hallway. Gold accents, plants and chairs along the hallway, chandeliers and light sconces, it was a replica of the decaying hallways upstairs.

We followed Lottius to the atrium and paused to gawk. There had to be hundreds of demons, all dressed for some kind of a ball. Music played in the background and trays of champagne and finger foods floated around.

"They kidnap one of us and celebrate?" I said through clenched teeth.

"Un-freaking-believable," Sykes muttered.

"Not everything is about you guys," Lottius retorted.

"They just spoiled 18th-century fashion for me," Lunaris threw in.

The females wore flowing gowns and fancy upswept hairdos while men actually looked dashing in waistcoats, embroidered frock coats, and stockings. I wondered if the swords on their sides were real or part of their costumes. Was my father hiding among them? The masks and wigs made it hard to tell. Not that I expected Valafar to do something so mundane. He was too arrogant to dress up for a masquerade party. Besides, their psi energies said these were mainly mid-level demons, mixed with a few upper ones.

The ones closest to us noticed us first and silence fell like a wave across the room. The music stopped. The tingle near my spine reached a fever pitch, but I held it back through sheer will, my heart pounding with the effort, sweat starting to run down my back.

"This way," Lottius mumbled.

Eyes followed us, Lottius, and her guards across the rectangular indoor court. It looked nothing like the hotel lobby above. It was huge, about half the size of a basketball court. A set of grand stairs coiled to the second floor, then to the next ten floors. From the glass doors and walls, and the wide patios with potted plants and flowers, this wasn't a business establishment. This was their home. The ceiling had a huge painting of the sky with a few clouds adrift, giving the illusion of outdoors.

We appeared to be headed toward a double door with wicked etchings. It reminded me of the doors to the Guardian Academy, except it was twice as big and twice as wide. They opened to reveal a large room with a vaulted ceiling, dominated by a large round table with twenty-four chairs at one end. Half of the chairs were occupied.

The room pulsed with demonic energy. The arrogance on the faces of the seated occupants indicated we were in the presence of the Order. None was my father. Disappointment washed over me. Annoyed with myself, I tried to remind myself that he was behind Kim's kidnapping.

Unlike the demons with masquerade masks, the members of the Order made no attempt to hide their faces or hair. Horns, cat eyes, pointed bat-like ears, hairy or scaly faces looked almost comical against their outfits, which were similar to those of their guests. At the end of the table was a tall, pale man with pitch-black hair tied in the back.

Lottius walked to edge of the table. "Father."

"Thank you, daughter. You can leave us now."

As she walked away, my gaze connected with her father's. He didn't offer us seats, just watched me with cold yellow eyes.

"You should not be here," he said.

Bran stepped forward, "Gabreel, we—"

"Silence!" the demon hissed. "You don't speak until I give you permission." He turned his attention back to me. "And you can address me as Lord Gabreel."

I didn't respond.

"We gave you a chance to make a deal with us, Lilith, but you ignored it. Why?"

"*We* are here now." The door closed with a loud click, bolts sliding into place. We reached the same conclusion: a trap. Hands reached for waists and thighs, and came up with daggers, sickles, knives, and a whip. Heat shot up my back then down my arm, the writings etching themselves under my skin. I'd expected that. The surprise was that they flowed to the Kris Dagger, which began to glow. My gaze connected with the others. They were all grinning.

The Kris Dagger was back!

The scraping of chairs on the floor filled the room as the members of the Order scrambled to their feet and tried to put distance between them and my dagger. Gabreel grew paler. Our grins probably made us appear crazier than the Mad Hatter.

Lord Gabreel cleared his throat. "Lilith—"

"*Cardinal* Lilith," I corrected him, slipping the dagger into its sheath. I tried to release the hilt, but it clung to my palm, the writings racing from the blade back to me. Weird. The flow of power had changed. "I believe *Cardinal* Bran was about to explain why we are here, *Lord* Gabreel. Oh, and if you think you can trap us in here…" I turned and pointed at the door. Blasting it with a lightning bolt would have proved my point, but that would have drawn the archangels. I opened it, turned, and faced them.

The demons walked back to their seats.

"We are here for Cardinal Kim," Bran explained.

"She is not here," Lord Gabreel said.

"I think you misunderstood my words, Lord Gabreel. We know she is here, so bring her out or we're burying all this," he indicated the building, "along with every demon in it."

Mocking laughter resounded in the hall from behind us and we turned to look as a woman entered the room. Wearing tight leather pants and high-heeled boots, black hair cascading behind her like a waterfall, and bright red lips, I'd recognize her anywhere.

Solange. My half-sister.

- 23 -

THE DEAL

"No humility even in defeat," Solange said, then threw a disdainful look my way. "Little sister, nice to see you again."

"I hardly think we are defeated," I said, recovering. I'd known we would meet again. I just hadn't spent time thinking about it.

"Wait until you meet the archangels," she said.

"Already did," I shot back and grinned. "Raphael is quite the character, but I wasn't impressed."

Her smile faltered. "You are lying."

I faked boredom, even pretended to study my nails, which was childish, but Solange rubbed me the wrong way every time our paths crossed. Why couldn't I have gotten a nicer sister?

"Believe what you want, Solange, but we kicked ass. Bran even clipped a few wings."

Gasps came from the occupants of the table. Solange's eyes narrowed suspiciously, as though she wasn't sure whether or not to believe me. I went for the kill.

"Isn't funny how every time our father comes up with a diabolical plan, you are always at the center of it? When are you going to understand that you will never please him?"

"Oh, but I have. Without me, the Tribunal would not have brought him back. Without me, the archangels wouldn't be after you now."

I wanted to wipe the smug smile off her beautiful face. "Yet, as soon as he returned, he came looking for me. No matter what you do, he'll always need me more."

"He doesn't need *you*. He needs your dagger and the power that comes with it."

"Not from the message I received through Gavyn. He's willing to summon the Tribunal and ask them to rescind the orders given to the archangels if I agree to join you."

"That's a lie," Solange yelled. "We presented our case and the Tribunal ruled in our favor. The archangels will come for you and the Kris Dagger will be ours."

I shook my head. "Oh, you are about the dumbest daughter ever. The dagger belongs to us, and it always will."

A snicker drew my attention to the other Cardinals. I'd completely forgotten their presence. A flash of amusement flickered in Bran's eyes. Sykes smirked while Remy's scowl hadn't changed since we left home. Esras looked like he'd landed in the Twilight Zone. Guess he hadn't heard of my evil sister. Solaris…

"Watch out, Lil," Solaris yelled.

I whipped around, instinctively knowing that the threat came from Solange. A knife whipped through the air, the blade glistening. I froze it a few inches from my neck. Her aim was good. Pissed, I flipped the knife around and…someone grabbed my arm. It was Remy.

Don't. We need her, he said.

No, we don't.

Silver flashed in his gray eyes. *She knows where Kim is.*

She tried to kill me. That I couldn't do anything about it pissed me off. I jerked my arm from Remy's hand, reached out, and closed my hand around Solange's knife. Her eyes widened when it burst into flame.

"You are such a freak," Solange said, the sneer marring the perfection of her face. "No wonder no one wants you to live. Your presence is destroying the balance between good—"

"Already heard the speech from Raphael," I cut her off. "Where is Kim?"

"With our father of course." She moved closer and sat at the edge of the table, one booted leg resting on a chair, her back to Lord Gabreel and the members of the Order. She studied us, one at a time. "All you have to do is hand over the Kris Dagger, and I'll get her."

Remy inched closer to her, the expression on his face saying exactly where he'd like to send Solange. "Do you think we are that stupid? That we would trust you to keep your word?"

"I have the upper hand here, handsome. That means I call the shots." She glanced at me and sneered. "So what is it going to be, little sis? The dagger or your friend?"

That was a no-brainer, but I now understood why the Goddess Xenia had transferred the powers of the dagger to me. She'd known Solange and her minions would come after it. Had she also known they'd kidnap Kim?

"You can have it." I pulled the dagger out and stopped the power inside me from connecting with it, rendering it useless.

Bran gripped my arm. "No. We will meet somewhere neutral for the trade. Away from humans, her followers, or the Order."

"That's out of the question," Solange said. "I take it now or you forget your friend ever existed."

Remy growled.

Solange studied him. "What? Is she someone special to you, or do you just hate me?"

"I wouldn't waste an emotion on you, Solange," Remy retorted. "You touch a hair on her head and you are mine."

Solange faked a shudder. "I can't wait. I haven't had fun with a Guardian..." she winked at Bran, "since our time together. If my memories are correct, it was exciting."

Now I was the one vowing to hunt her down. How dare she bring up her past relationship with Bran!

"You have fifteen minutes to bring Kim to the old train station or we are coming for you, your father, and his army," Bran added.

Solange laughed. "Now who's underestimating the other? First, you have no idea where *my hideout* is. Second, I'm not walking into a trap. Third, we don't have an army." Solange threw a hasty look over her shoulder at Lord Gabreel and his cronies, then stood. "I'll mingle with the others in the common room while you discuss my terms, then do as I say."

But we had seen her reaction and reached the same conclusion.

Bran chuckled. "They don't know about your little army, do they?" He glanced at the demons behind Solange. They hadn't said a thing since she arrived. "Do you? She and her renegade friends are the ones kidnapping your children."

"Is this true?" Lord Gabreel roared.

Solange glared at the demon. "No, it's not. Why do I need an army when I have Coronis' Athame?"

Bran blocked her path when she started for the door. "Or maybe it is not an army you are after. Maybe an unlimited supply of power is what you and your father need. Living in the pit can be a bitch when you can't self-heal. Does he have blistered skin from being vanquished? Maybe the flesh is falling off his skin from infection?"

"You don't know what you are talking about." Solange gripped the hilt of her dagger and backed up.

Bran followed her, reckless with his taunts and his life. I inched closer in case my crazy sister forgot we were in the room and did something stupid. The others positioned themselves around the room, keeping an eye on the Order in case all this was staged.

"How many demons does he drain a day?" Bran asked. "The young men and women you rounded up just don't cut it anymore, right? He needs the unlimited power of the Kris Dagger, and you, his dutiful daughter, decided to get it for him."

"He doesn't need anyone's energy," Solange said with a sneer. "He's stronger than ever, and the wielder of the red Athame is the one that drains psi energies. *I* am the wielder, not him." She pulled out the dagger, the blade glowing red. "I could drain your powers where you stand, Bran Llyr," Solange threatened in a cold voice, her eyes changing color until they were the color of her blade.

The monkey on my back leapt and shot toward my right hand. I didn't care if the archangels locked on us when I used my powers. The Red Athame was a leech, a life-sucker, and my sister wasn't using it in my presence.

Contain your powers, Bran warned me.

I got them under control, but one false move and she's dead.

A smile flickered in his emerald eyes. *I got this.*

"No one forced those demons to join us. We offered them a better life and leadership than they did," she jerked her head to indicate the Order. "You have your army, and so do we." She raised the dagger in the air and red light streamed from it, passing through the paneled ceiling.

"What is she doing?" Lunaris asked.

"Sending a signal," Remy ground out.

In a second, Lord Gabreel went from seated to Solange's side, his hand wrapped around her neck, his fangs elongating. For one brief moment I was sure he would tilt her head and sink his fangs into her neck. Solange must have thought the same because color drained from her face.

"My sons and daughters are your father's power source?" the Nosferatu asked, speaking slowly. "You will tell me where he is hiding." He bared his fangs. "Now."

Solange shifted into smoke form, her laughter echoing eerily in the room. Before it stopped, screams from the hall split the air, sending a chill up my spine. A loud crash followed, then the door collapsed under the weight of demons in costumes. Some still wore their masks. Others tripped on their gowns before bursting into flames as energy balls hit them from behind. I shoved the Kris Dagger in its sheath and pulled two knives from the straps around my thighs.

"Leave…go…teleport out of here," Lord Gabreel yelled to his followers as they poured into the ballroom.

"Where do we go, Lord Gabreel?" one demoness asked.

"Check into human hotels and wait for my signal."

"Bunch of sissies," Sykes said, lips curled in distaste, his hazel eyes already glowing as he switched to battle mode.

"They are not fighters," Lord Gabreel snapped. "Most of them are Civilians, and this is their home."

"Then get them out of our way," Bran called back, already moving toward the hell pit in the other room.

We followed.

"Bring me the Kris Dagger." Solange's words floated into the ballroom, and a feeling of déjà vu washed over me. Coronis had said the exact same words a year ago

Bran paused, moved to my side, grabbed the back of my head and kissed me. It wasn't a soft kiss. It was hard, merciless and an affirmation of his feelings for me under the circumstances. "I love you, Sunshine, but right now, I want you to do whatever it takes to put her under your spell. I don't care how you do it…knock her out, get inside her head, just stop her from leaving. She's the key to finding Kim." He turned and disappeared in the chaos.

Remember, don't use your powers, Remy reminded us telepathically from somewhere in the atrium. *The last thing we need is Raphael and his army finding us.*

Yelps and screams sent another jolt of disgust through me. The stench of dying demons—a mixture of rotten garbage and a sickly scent like baby powder—hung heavy in the air.

Izzy shoved something in my pocket before she disappeared. I dug into the pocket and touched crystals. Someone grabbed my arm and I responded instinctively—raising my dagger and bringing it down.

"It's me, Lilith." Lord Gabreel let go of my arm and teleported out of the way before I made contact. "We thought you had our children and we were willing to negotiate a deal for their return. We didn't know one of our own was doing this."

"Why are you telling me this now?" I asked impatiently.

"Don't trap Solange. Kill her. The more people she drains, the stronger and hungrier for power she'll become. Just like Coronis. Kill her now."

There ought to be a law against having demented siblings. Bran had Gavyn, whom he refused to kill. I had Solange, whom I couldn't touch until we had Kim. "How many switched sides?"

"They were kidnapped," Lord Gabreel corrected me.

"How many?" I snapped, not even sure why I needed to know.

"Hundreds. Between three and four."

That was a lot. I glanced at the other members of the Order. "I hope you get your children out, because no one takes my dagger."

The tingle on my spine had become an ache that needed release. So I did. The power shot to my limbs; the head rush felt like pure endorphins. I might not be able to use my powers, but *I* was a weapon, my very presence a demon's worst nightmare. I gripped my knives and lunged through the crowd, searching for Solange in a sea of black with an occasional colorful costume.

What was it with Nephilim and wearing black? The only way to tell us apart was our eyes, which tended to have the same glow as Guardian amulets during a battle. The demons' red eyes matched the red stones on their belts and the pommels of their weapons. Lottius's security team wore all black, like ninjas, but unlike Solange's renegades they had no marks on their clothes.

Demons scurried out of my way, their faces distorted in pain from the energy pouring from my pores.

"Bring me the dagger," Solange screamed somewhere from above.

I looked up to find her, but two demons braved the pain and came after me. I released the knives and sank them into their throats. The knives floated back into my hands as the demons burst into flame. Another came from my right; I feinted left, blocked his arm and kneed him. He went down and my knife followed.

Solange was gone when I looked up. Instead, I found Bran, wings out, three demons surrounding him. He whipped around, his wings slicing one in half. He then teleported and reappeared behind another, raising his dagger and bringing it down in one swift fatal blow. A well-aimed kick sent the third off the rail. Before he could land on the fighters below, Bran flicked his wrist and released a ninja star. It caught the guy between the eyes. He burst into flame.

Graceful and deadly.

I caught a flash of red from the corner of my eye and I whipped around, hoping it was Solange. A smoldering energy ball rolled toward me. I dodged and it caught a demon behind me. I hit the demon who'd thrown the *omni* ball in the chest with a ninja star.

Where was Solange? And why were some demons creeping upstairs like zombies in masquerade costumes? I teleported behind them.

Your three o'clock, Bran yelled in my head.

I turned swinging, but the demon ducked. She kicked, aiming for my ribs. I caught her foot and twisted it. She whipped around in the air, but before I could finish her off, a blade sank into her chest. I looked up and my gaze connected with the person who had thrown it.

Lottius.

She grinned and gave me a mocking bow, which would have been her last if Izzy hadn't seen the demon charging her from behind. Who would have thought we'd have Lottius and the Order's guards fighting alongside us? We were outnumbered, and more of Solange's men kept teleporting in.

I spied Dante and grinned. He caught several demons with lightning bolts, coming to Sykes' aid without him even knowing it. Sykes was busy having fun throwing ninja stars, his grin deliciously devilish. On the floor to my left, Remy and Kael stood back to back, taking on four demons. I couldn't see Izzy or Lunaris, but Solaris was unstoppable with her lethal whip, the metal tip sailing through the air and slicing demons in half.

Someone landed on me, knocking me down and causing me to lose hold of my knife. I flung them aside and jumped up, tripping over demons in costumes. Looking at their wizened faces, realization hit me like a ton of bricks—Solange was using the Athame. The zombified demons on the stairs made sense.

An older demon blocked me. He winced with pain, but still moved closer. "Your father needs you, Lilith," he begged. "Only you can help him."

"No one told him to come back from Tartarus," I retorted.

"He didn't ask to be brought back. Bring her to the island," he added.

He teleported just as an arrow pierced my left side, I sucked in a painful breath. Numbness spread on that side of my body as I searched for the demon that had attacked me. I found her reloading her crossbow.

I didn't stop to think. I just reacted and willed lightning bolts, vaporizing her on the spot.

Bran appeared beside me. *You okay?*

I could be better. Biting my lower lip, I grabbed the shaft and yanked it out.

How bad is it? he asked.

It's already healing. Watch your back.

He turned and rejoined the battle. My side hurt, but now wasn't time to cry or complain. Not using our powers sucked, but our bodies could still self-heal. The numbness was already fading away, my wound healing faster because of the Kris Dagger's powers.

A loud cackle came from the top of the stairs and I turned. Solange had her dagger pointed at the remaining half-dozen demons, red light streaming from their eyes to the tip of the dagger. Once again, ghastly memories flashed through my head—Coronis draining Bran and my friends with the same Athame before we killed her.

I sent the knife I'd dropped toward Solange. She dissolved into smoke and floated away. The blade flew back to my hand as drained demons rolled down the stairs, some of them still alive, their sunken eyes following me and begging me to end their misery.

"Sorry, can't help." Not without using my powers again. I kept an eye out for Solange. She materialized near the rail several floors up. I followed.

"Come on, little sis," she mocked when I rematerialized. "Pull out the Kris Dagger and fight me."

"That's too easy. You'll be dead in seconds." I had to catch her off-guard and set the trap. "Take a whack at me. I know you'd like nothing better than to punish me for being Daddy's favorite," I laid it on thick.

Her eyes narrowed.

"I'll give you the dagger if you beat me," I added.

"I'll just take it after I beat the crap out of you," she bragged, then shoved the Athame in its sheath. "I've wanted to do this for sixteen years."

She rushed me, throwing a punch. I feinted to the right, swung and aimed for her ribs. I got a solid hit, but she didn't even flinch. Her grin widened as though pain was her source of pleasure.

"You'll have to do better than that, little sis," she mocked and came at me with a kick, her movement so fast she was a blur.

I teleported out of the way, causing her to lose her balance. Reappearing behind her, I brought my elbow down hard on her back. She went down on one knee and shifted into smoke.

"Not bad," she said when she rematerialized.

"How about not shape-shifting?" I dared her.

"If you swear not to teleport," she retorted and lunged at me again.

I met her, trading blows, kicks and jabs. She was fast, but I was better trained. I caught her with a roundhouse kick, the force whipping her around and causing her to lose her balance again. She broke her fall and came back swinging, catching me on the still-healing spot the arrow had hit. I hissed at the pain and staggered back.

Laughing gleefully, she launched herself at me again. I side-stepped, grabbed her arm and used her weight against her, sending her flying over my head. Instead of going down, she flipped over like a gymnast and landed in a crouching position, then came at me low, barreling into my stomach.

I brought my elbow down on her back, but the effort was lost when we both went down, arms and legs tangled. She got some lucky hits before I flipped her and pressed my elbow against her neck. I reached for the crystals to trap her.

She cheated and shifted into smoke form, leaving me on all fours before she aimed a vicious kick on my side. I hissed at the pain, sure she'd cracked ribs.

A hand yanked me from the floor as though I weighed nothing. Solange laughed and dissolved into smoke form. I twisted, ready to fight my captor, and gulped. "Grampa?"

He scowled. "Stop wasting time. Finish with her and get out of here," he ordered. "We have the situation under control."

My mouth opened and closed, but I didn't ask the questions that burned the tip of my tongue. How had they found us? Was he angry we'd disobeyed them again? Too late—he was already gone.

I got to my feet. While Solange and I had been making up for missed years of sibling rivalry, I had forgotten about the other Cardinals. The battle had taken on a new intensity. Lord Gabreel and his followers had abandoned their home, leaving behind their mummified friends on the stairs. Solange's demons had changed to their real forms—hairy or scaly faces, horns and tails, fangs and rows of shark-like teeth. Nephilim powers were enhanced when they took their real shapes.

Solange surprised me, landing a blow on my chest and slamming me against the rail. Grampa was right. This was no time for games. I got inside her head before she realized my intention.

Sit down. Her legs folded and she dropped on the floor.

"That's cheating," she screeched.

"So did you." I removed the crystals from my pocket, then, with a flick of my fingers, placed them around her. Light shot out and curved above her head, creating a cage.

Solange sneered. "I'll never tell you where our father and Kim are."

"I already know. What is it with you demons and islands? Can't stand living among humans?"

"Not when we can't rule the…" Her voice trailed off and her eyes widened.

I turned to see what had her eyes wide with fear and my heart sank. "The archangels," I whispered.

Lightning flashed around the court, the surge of power knocking me backward. I skidded on the floor until my back slammed against the wall. The floor shook and a continuously fizzing, brittle sound came from behind me.

I turned to see fissures race across the glass wall and teleported out of the way, but there was no place to hide. Shards of glass rained down on us. Lights went out, leaving the angelic lightning as our only source of light.

Panic and chaos followed as the archangels swooped down the ten-story foyer, their wings causing a gale, swords gleaming under the flashing lights and reflecting their emotionless, perfect faces. How could beings so beautiful be so vicious?

- 24 -

THE TRIBUNAL

"Thanks for this," Solange said. The windstorm created by the archangels' wings had knocked away the crystals and released her from the trap. She shoved the Kris Dagger in a pouch with weird markings. I'd first seen that bag with Valafar the night I recovered the dagger. "It even allowed me to hold it. Should be easy to control."

She teleported before I could lock on the dagger. I searched for her, but it was impossible to see in the jarring flashes of lightning. It was worse than being on a dance floor with strobe lights.

Above, the sizzling clouds covering the ceiling formed an impenetrable barrier. Demons stupid enough to brave it came back down charbroiled. Below, some covered their ears to block the sound, not understanding the archangels were already inside their heads and what they were hearing didn't come from outside. Others screamed in terror, not realizing the scenes playing in front of them were false.

Solange wasn't going anywhere. The trick was to find her before Raphael found me.

Remember, don't let them inside your heads, Grampa's voice rang in my head, but I knew he was reminding all Guardians to have reruns of their happiest moments. It also meant minimal telepathic communication. The archangels could use the link to get inside heads.

Heart pounding, I tried to find Grampa. The archangels had a glow around them, which helped pinpoint their locations. Bran and the other flyers were in the air, battling several of them. I counted at least a dozen more hacking down demons and Guardians like they were weeds, not caring who they killed.

Screams of death filled the air, the demons' burning bodies mixing with flashes of light as Guardians died. How many would ascend? Or were they doomed to end up in Tartarus because they had gone against the archangels?

I spied Solange drifting toward the ballroom. I teleported after her, delaying my reappearance until I saw her aura. She wasn't alone.

There's a secret passage behind this wall, she telepathed her partner. *We can use it to avoid the archangels' shield.*

Are sure you have the right dagger? someone asked.

I recognized the voice of the old man who'd begged me to help my father.

Yes. See? The pure energy of the Kris Dagger appeared as Solange pulled it out of the bag with demonic writings. I locked on it and willed it to fly to my hand as I rematerialized.

Solange and her friend whipped around, but the dagger was already bonding with me, the writings appearing like slithering snakes on the blade. In the darkness, my skin glowed, the writing coiling and gliding. I didn't have to look in the mirror to know my eyes were glowing too.

"I told you, the dagger belongs to me," I snarled in a voice I didn't recognize.

"Lilith, your father—"

The old man didn't finish his words. A thud came from behind me and I whipped around. Raphael. He couldn't even give me a moment to savor outsmarting my evil sister. Big sparkly wings outstretched, cold eyes narrowed, he sauntered toward us like he knew he had already won.

Mewling sounds came from behind me. I turned to find Solange and the older demon on their knees, gripping their heads. Then they dropped like sacks of potatoes. *Call for backup*, the irrational part of my brain screamed, but telepathy wasn't an option. Besides, I had trained to take this bastard down.

Instead of panic, an eerie calmness settled on me. I assumed a fighting stance and waved the dagger. Compared to his sword, which he hadn't bothered to draw, my weapon was puny, but it glowed with the brilliance of stars.

"So, how do you want to play this?" I said, going for cocky and liking how calm and confident I sounded. "My head on the guillotine?"

Surprise flickered in his eyes. "That would be nice, but since we don't have one, why not just come with me?"

I laughed. "Right. Like, I'm not going to make this easy for you."

He scowled. "I'm trying to avoid fighting you, Lilith."

"Why? Scared?"

"If you give up, my warriors will stop killing yours."

I considered the offer for about a second. "Sorry, but if I die, and that is a big if, I want to go down like a Cardinal Guardian. Fighting."

"Silly girl." He pulled out his sword. It was huge, light bouncing off its blade like stars. He moved closer. I shuffled backward, searching for an opportunity.

"Do you think you stand a chance against me?"

"Hmm, let me think. Me and my dagger against your sword and those deadly wings, I think we are about even."

He moved so fast, the sword arcing toward my neck before I raised my dagger. I barely managed to teleport out of the way.

"Do you know how many battles I've waged this millennium alone?" he asked.

"If you feel you have to brag…"

He rushed me again, moving so fast he was blurry, but I was ready. I pointed the dagger and blasted him. The force propelled him backwards, the look of utter disbelief on his face comical.

I grinned. "You thought you neutralized the only weapon that can send you back home."

Lightning bolts shot from somewhere near him and singed the air as they raced toward me. I battled bolts with bolts, causing the room to light up like fireworks. Temporarily blinded, I felt rather than saw him move and teleported. Slowing down, I watched him move around in circles, searching for me. It wouldn't be long before he sensed my energy.

I rematerialized behind him and brought the dagger down on his back, aiming for the base of his right wing. The dagger cut deep. Instead of blood, light poured out of the wound, blinding me.

Next thing I knew, his other wing slammed into me like a ton of bricks and sent me flying across the room. I hit the table, pain radiating up my side. I scrambled to my feet and searched for my dagger.

"You dared to cut my wing?" he bellowed.

Where was my dagger?

He closed in on me. I zapped him with bolts of lightning but they bounced off him like ping-pong balls off a table. He had a shield protecting him. *Now, Goddess. If I'm meant to be your vessel, use me now.*

Instead of the Goddess, Remy appeared beside me and shoved a sword into my hand.

"Find Grampa," I told him.

"No, I'm not leaving you with him."

Raphael swung his sword wide arc and brought it down fast. Remy blocked and turned, but the archangel had already disengaged his blade and attacked again. I came at him from the other side, but he was fast and a better fighter than both of us put together. Nothing we did seemed to slow him down. In fact, I had a feeling he was toying with us.

Remy swore. "Damn, he moves like…,"

"A dancer," I griped.

"Like his sword is a freaking extension of his arm," Remy said.

"Starting the party without me?" Sykes asked, appearing behind the archangel.

Raphael smiled without looking his way. It was a cold smile. Cruel. Mean. "No, waiting so I can to dispatch all of you to Tartarus with one blow."

"We don't go to Tartarus, bonehead," Sykes said.

While Remy kept him busy, his sword changing shape every few seconds, I slammed the archangel's right side with lightning bolts while Sykes pelted him from the other side with energy balls. The bolts and energy balls didn't hurt him, and I realized why. His wings were wrapped tight around him and acted like a shield. They were protecting him.

Remy noticed too and upped the ante of the attack, hoping to give me an opening, but he miscalculated. Raphael turned, his injured wing slanting at a weird angle. The tips caught Remy across the chest and he went down, bleeding.

Remy! I yelled, becoming distracted. I felt rather than saw the wing move toward me. It caught me across my arm before I teleported out of the way, leaving behind a nasty wound.

Pissed, I telekinetically lifted Remy's sword and mine and continued to attack Raphael. At the same time, I tried to zap him again. He redirected my lightning bolt toward Sykes. The force threw Sykes across the room, where he hit the wall and came crashing down with a sickening thud. If the fall hadn't kill him, I was afraid that the burn from the light had.

"If you killed them…," I warned, lifting my hands.

"It will be your fault," Raphael said. "I gave you an offer, which you turned down. Now, it's just you and me. No more of your friends to distract me."

"That's where you are wrong, Raphael," Grampa said from the doorway and he wasn't alone. Bran was beside him. Both of them had bruises on their faces and torn coats. "It's over. Stand down."

"I have my orders," Raphael said.

"We're summoning the Tribunal. You and your warriors must stand down."

"Until I receive different orders…"

Grampa and Bran teleported at the same time. They reappeared behind Raphael, each of them grabbing a wing. Raphael tried to shake them off, his wings whipping up and down, left and right, but his injured wing slowed him down.

"Now, Lil," Grampa yelled.

I willed all my power, mine and the Kris Dagger's, from deep inside me. Heat rose and suffused my body. My body tingled and started to glow. Not just my arms. My whole body. I raised my arms, redirecting the powers. Above the glow, my eyes met Raphael's. He couldn't protect himself with his wings trapped. Fury distorted his flawless face as a flood of bright light shot out of my hand and hit him square in the chest.

"You are going to wish you agreed to our deal, young Guardian," the archangel bellowed just before he exploded.

The force flung me across the room. Disoriented, my ears ringing, I just lay there, waiting for my breathing to slow down, wondering how many bones I'd broken. My body felt like I'd been stepped on by an elephant.

Slowly, the pain ebbed. Were Grampa and Bran okay?

I turned my head and saw Bran getting up, his back feathers singed and reduced to stubs. Grampa, already standing, offered him a hand, and the two walked toward me. The lights were back on, the broken bulbs repaired. Way to go, Earth Guardians.

I sat up and grinned. It was over. We had won.

"Stop whining. You'll both be fine," Cardinal Hsia's voice reached me and I turned.

She held a hand over Remy, sparks leaping from her palm to his chest, and the other over Sykes. Remy was busy grimacing at the gaping wound on his chest, but Sykes smirked when our gazes connected. I looked at his chest and my stomach roiled. His entire upper torso had deep burns. It was hard to tell where his singed clothes ended and his charred skin began. Still, I was relieved they were okay. I looked at my arm. The wound inflicted by the archangel's wing was already healed.

How many Guardians had survived?

"They're not going anywhere," Izzy said, and once again I turned and sighed with relief. Her face and hair were a mess, but she didn't appear injured. Then again, as a healer, she self-healed faster than most Guardians. She and Solaris were setting crystals around Solange and her minion. "You can interrogate them now."

"Are you okay?" Grampa asked.

I stood and hugged him tight, tears stinging my eyes. Bran gripped my hand, his emerald eyes searching my face for visible signs of pain or maybe he was worried about the archangel's threat. Raphael's words still rang in my ears, but I didn't want to think about them. We'd won, and that was all that mattered.

"Are we really going to summon the Tribunal?" I asked.

Grampa stepped back and patted my cheek. "We have to, because Raphael will keep this up until he accomplishes his mission."

"Which means he'll bring back more archangels," I said, feeling tired just thinking about fighting him again. We had barely managed to send him and his tribe home.

Grampa nodded. "And we'll keep fighting them. You did great tonight, but you should have contacted us as soon as Raphael cornered you. We were searching for you when we heard his bellow." Grampa shook his head and chuckled. "You nearly chopped off one of his wings."

Nearly wasn't good enough. "What happened to his warriors?"

"We clipped a few wings, injured some."

"How many did we lose? Will they ascend?"

Grampa's expression grew sober. "Quite a few, mostly SGs, a few Cardinals. And yes, they will ascend, but we are more united now than we've ever been. Guardians. Demons. Neutrals. All fighting to protect you. When the archangels come back, we'll be ready for them. In the meantime, help your friends, then join us. We must start the summoning. Solaris, we'll get all the information from those two later." Grampa teleported.

Left with Bran, I studied the bruises on his face, his wings. I reached up and touched the cut on his forehead. The bruised skin disappeared.

"Your wings," I mumbled, touching a stubby feather. It slowly filled out.

He gripped my hand, then placed it on his cheek, his gaze on my face. "My wings will be okay. Why didn't you telepath me when he attacked?"

"You were busy and I didn't want you distracted."

"Come on, Lil," Cardinal Hsia called out. "We are only four healers and there are many Guardians with more serious injuries than Bran. Finish with these two. Izzy, come with me."

I rolled my eyes. "We just sent an archangel and his warriors home," I whispered. "You'd think we'd have a hero's moment."

Bran laughed, cupped my face and gave me a sweet, but oh so brief kiss. "We'll have our moment after this. What deal was Raphael talking about?" he asked as we walked toward the others.

"He'd asked me to surrender and his warriors would spare the Guardians. Maybe I should have."

"You heard your grandfather; they'll ascend, and we are more united than before. Tonight we fought as Nephilim against a common enemy. The Brotherhood, Dante and his nature-bender friends, Lottius and her demons were all united because of you."

And so many were dead too, because of me. "But when the archangels come back—"

"We will fight them again. No one is surrendering. Where's your dagger?"

I looked around. "It's in here somewhere, but it's only active when I touch it."

"I'll find it." Bran ran his knuckles along my jaw. "Don't ever think of surrendering. You wouldn't want to leave me behind, would you?"

No, I wouldn't. I turned and hurried to Remy and Sykes's side.

"What deal is Bran talking about?" Remy asked.

I explained Raphael's offer.

"Self-righteous prick," Sykes muttered. "Doesn't he know our motto?"

"We have a motto?" I asked, placing my hands on their wounds.

"Yeah. 'Live, Love, and Die in Glory', meaning live and love like it's your last time and if you're going down, take as many douchebags with you as possible. And I'm not talking about demons. Archangels just replaced demons at the top of the 'douchebags' list."

Remy chuckled. "That's a good one."

They bumped fists. Remy's wound had already closed up. His torn shirt and coat repaired themselves and the blood that had caked them floated away. Sykes' burns had disappeared too, leaving behind his singed shirt.

"Want me to fix that?" Remy asked.

"Nah, this is a collector's item." Sykes hopped to his feet. "I'll donate it to the Xenithian museum. The title will read," he pretended to read a headline, "'Superior Cardinal Energy Guardian Triumphs Over Inferior Angelic Fire'."

"Mouthy," Bran said. He had found my dagger.

"Works for me, bro. You could even sell a few of your stubby feathers. Do you guys realize we just made history? We can even rewrite the Guardian history. Does anyone know how the seniors found us?" Sykes asked

"Lucien," Izzy answered, having reappeared beside us without our knowledge. "He went straight to Master Haziel after dropping off the Specials," she said impatiently. "The summoning has started and the seniors want you guys center stage. Lil, Master Haziel wants to see you first."

"He's here?"

"Of course. Come on." She grabbed my arm just as a murmur filled the air. "Tribunal…tribunal…tribunal…"

We hurried toward the hall as the chant rose and increased in intensity. Hundreds of voices raised, demanding to be heard. "Tribunal…tribunal…tribunal…"

Then there was silence.

I stepped over broken furniture and shards of glass. Scorch marks spotted the carpet and walls, telltale signs of energy balls and dead demons. Guardians and demons stood on opposite sides of the room. I followed their gazes and frowned. There was nothing up there. Where was the Tribunal?

"This way," Izzy said, dragging me away from the gathering and toward the area under the stairs.

"But the Tribunal…?" My voice trailed off when I noticed Dante. He stood apart from everyone, his expression furious. He wasn't staring up. "Dante?"

He looked at me as though he didn't recognize me. A bad feeling washed over me. "Where's Kael?"

"He's gone." Dante's voice was rough.

"Gone where…no," I shook my head, tears rushing to my eyes. "Not Kael."

"He died with honor, fighting for what he believed in—you," Dante said harshly.

I saw through his harshness to the pain. It was so deep and vast, so heart-wrenching. I closed the gap between us. "I'm so sorry."

"It's not your fault."

It was. Every life lost tonight was on me. Dante stiffened when I touched his arm, and I wasn't sure whether he feared I might burn him again or he just didn't want my touch. Demons weren't big on hugs, but it didn't matter. I wrapped my arms around him, pressed my cheek against his broad chest and squeezed. He stood there stiff as a board, his pain increasing instead of lessening.

"I'm so sorry. I wish I could bring him back for you," I whispered.

He didn't relax, but he patted my back. "Enough with that. Go. The Guardians need you."

I stepped back, my hands dropping to my side, and searched his face. There was so much pain and rage. "I don't want you to be alone, Dante. Join us. I mean, come live with us. You don't even have to be a Guardian. You can be Neutral or whatever."

The look he gave me was unreadable. "I can't do that, Lilith. I must avenge his death."

Of course. "Which archangel killed him? Raphael? I will fight with you and together we will clip his wings."

"No. He was betrayed by one of us."

Guardian or demon? "Who?"

He shook his head. "You'll have enough to deal with in the coming months and don't need to worry about this. This vengeance will be mine."

"But will I see you again?"

"We will meet again, Lilith. This is just the beginning." He bowed and pressed a fist to his left chest, then teleported.

The beginning of what? My suffering. No matter what anybody said, the archangels had come for *me*, not the others. Yet I was still alive and they were gone. Kael would end up in Tartarus, where the other demons would probably get high on torturing him because of me. If Raphael's offer was still open when he came back, I was taking it and stopping these endless sacrifices.

I wiped the wetness from my cheeks and said. "Let's go, Izzy."

But Izzy's eyes were glued to something behind me. I turned, then looked up and blinked. Astral images of thirteen men and women on ornate chairs hovered in the air to our right.

The Tribunal.

Only the top halves of their bodies were visible, I noticed. Six wore hooded white robes and smiled down at the Guardians while the other six, dressed in black, snarled. Even in death, demons were mean representatives. Despite the obvious differences, they were all old, with grey hair peeking from under their hoods. The men had long, shaggy beards and moustaches.

The thirteenth member of the Tribunal interested me more. He was younger, with no beard, no hood and no hair. In fact, he looked like a monk. Even his red robe was different from the others. He must have been their leader, or the judge.

"Who summoned us?" he said in an eerie voice, the sound ebbing and flowing as though he spoke through a mist or a long tunnel.

"We did," Grampa said from somewhere in front of the Guardians.

"You need an advocate to address this court, Cardinal Falcon," the leader said.

- 25 -

THE SACRIFICE

"Let's go." Izzy pushed me in the opposite direction. "Master Haziel said he must talk to you about something before you face the Tribunal. Don't ask me what. I'm just the messenger. I think he doesn't have long to live."

I frowned. "What do you mean 'he doesn't have long to live'?"

"He's dying."

My heart dropped. "He can't."

"I tried to heal him, but he wouldn't let me."

"We'll see about that." I refused to lose another person I cared about.

At first, all I saw was Lucien on a chair by a couch that looked like someone had redesigned with a blowtorch. Moving closer, I saw Master Haziel reclining on it, his eyes closed. As though he sensed my presence, he opened his eyes and tried to sit up. My interest in meeting the Tribunal disappeared as I stared into his wise eyes, felt his pain and heard his thoughts. He was ready to die.

Tears filled my eyes again as I knelt by his side. "Don't try to sit up, Master Haziel. What happened? Where does it hurt? And how could you come to fight the archangels?"

A gurgling sound came from his lips and I realized he was laughing. "How could I not? You think I should have stayed home to watch over the Specials while you have fun? No, this was our battle. I did not call you here to discuss what is done or to heal me. It is my time to go."

I shook my head. "You can't die. I still need you."

One gnarled hand gripped mine. "You do not need anyone. I saw you fight Raphael. You were fearless. Fast. A bit cocky," he added and chuckled, the sound dry and hollow, "but it was necessary today to disarm him. That does not mean you should do it again. You are more than ready."

If he had seen me fight the archangel, why hadn't he told the others? Not that it mattered now. I had to help him. I pulled back the sleeves of my coat and willed the power to move from my core. The ancient writings appeared on my skin and my hands started to glow. I moved closer.

"No, Lil," he said harshly. "There will be no healing." He patted Lucien's hand. "Leave us, son."

"But Grandfather, if she can heal you—"

"She cannot. We have said all that is needed to be said, Lucien. Go. Tell the family I will watch over them."

Lucien's topaz eyes swam with tears as he gave Master Haziel a hug. Izzy, who hadn't left, had tears racing down her face too.

"Go, go, you do not want to miss this historic moment. You too, Izzy. Tell all the junior Cardinals I will keep an eye on them, so they had better stay sharp." Lucien reluctantly got up. Izzy hugged Master Haziel one last time, then the two of them left. Master Haziel waited until they were gone before speaking again. "Look at me, Lil, and listen very carefully. No matter what happens, do not reveal the dagger's powers in you to Valafar or his men."

I frowned. "Why would I do that?"

"Things will become clear with time. Also, whatever decisions the Goddess makes, accept them without question or arguing. All is and will be as they are meant to be." He faded briefly, his body becoming transparent.

"Master Haziel," I cried out.

"My time here has come to an end, but I have prepared you for what is about to happen. This is just the beginning."

Not again. First Dante, now him. "The beginning of what?"

Instead of answering, he patted my hands. "I will miss our time together, dearest child."

"Me too." The air around us buzzed with energy as though a strong current zinged through the air, but when I looked, there was nothing there. "This beginning you all keep talking about—"

"Do not keep the Goddess waiting," he cut me off and smiled, face puckering. "Get up and receive her."

I looked around. "Where is she?"

Something touched my forehead and, as though a veil lifted from my eyes, an outline of a woman with massive wings, bathed in light, appeared. Mesmerized, I watched as the light faded, until she stood before me. Goddess Xenia. She was glorious, her eyes luminous and skin radiant as though tiny lights danced under her skin. Her wings, white and dazzling, lifted gently behind her, and her silky white dress flowed to her sandaled feet.

Not sure whether to stand up and bow, drop on my hands and knees or even speak up, I gave her a tiny smile. She offered me her hand instead, a charge shooting through me as I took it and stood. I was surprised my legs could hold me upright.

Then I realized something—she wasn't alone. Guardians hovered behind her. Dead Guardians. I recognized Lunaris. I had no idea she hadn't made it. Solaris would be devastated and blame me. My gaze connected with Cat-eyes Eva, then the obnoxious Sim, both from our Psi Team. There were a few more Cardinals from the other teams and a lot more SGs, whose faces I recognized though I couldn't remember their names. They all wore white robes like the Goddess' and floated several feet above the ground. If they had been wounded during the battle, it didn't show on their clear, glowing skins.

Then Master Haziel appeared beside the Goddess, looking ethereal like the others. A quick look over my shoulder confirmed that his body was gone.

"Once again, Coronis will speak for the Hermonites," the Tribunal leader called out from the other end of the room. "Who will represent the Guardians?"

It is time, Lilith, the Goddess said in a soft melodic voice.

No, not yet. I ignored Master Haziel's horrified expression and looked into the Goddess' kind eyes. *I lost many friends tonight, but I don't see one of them with you. Can you help him? Please. He was a loyal friend and died protecting me.*

The nature-bender Kael has been very vigilant in watching over you. How would you like me to repay him? She asked sounding neither pleased nor angry.

Watch over him and don't let him go to Tartarus.

A thoughtful expression settled on the Goddess' ethereal face. *I'll see what I can do.*

Thank you. I'm ready now.

She opened her arms. I walked into them and sucked in a breath at the powerful invasion. It felt like I had been zapped by a thousand volts. Heart pounding furiously and my breathing labored, my vision dimmed, then sharpened. Everything around me appeared brighter, their auras enhanced.

I looked down and blinked. The light from my skin penetrated my dark hunter clothing, and even though I couldn't see the rest of me, I was sure my eyes were luminous just like hers had been.

Let's go.

The words echoed in my head and sent a jolt through me. I wasn't sure how this vessel thing worked, whether she planned to take over my mind, body, and powers or if I just spoke on her behalf. Already her grief and fury at the loss of so many Guardians was overwhelming my senses.

The Goddess, someone whispered as I approached the gathering and the word buzzed through the rest of them. They turned and stepped back, leaving a path for me to pass. Some reached out and touched my arms. Other smiled, tears in their eyes.

I will speak to my people before we join the Tribunal, the Goddess said. *Repeat my words and do exactly as I instruct you.*

"I am so sorry for the pain you have endured tonight and the senseless loss," I said, but the soft and musical voice was nothing like mine. "Your beloved daughters and sons, sisters and brothers, uncle and aunts are now with me." I reached out and touched a face here, a shoulder there, a hand, an arm.

The Cardinals standing in front of the Guardians turned. The Goddess' feelings and thoughts receded, allowing mine to dominate as my gaze connected with Grampa, then Bran. My hand brushed Bran's and lingered as I walked past him. I traded smiles with Sykes, Remy, Izzy, and the other junior and mid-level Guardians. A sharp pang of relief shot through me when I noticed Kieran standing behind Darius and some of the Brotherhood Guardians. At least they'd made it. Solaris glowered, probably blaming me for her loss. I didn't blame her. I was responsible. Nio was sure to miss his buddy Sim too. I fought tears and remorse again by the time I stood beside my grandfather.

Grief and loss are part of our existence, Lilith, the Goddess said, her soft voice soothing.

Does it get any easier? I asked

No, but you will learn to grieve as you move on.

What if it is my fault?

You think tonight is your fault? Tonight is just the beginning. It is something neither you nor I can control.

The beginning of what? I asked, hoping I'd get an answer this time.

The beginning of your journey, something your father and Coronis hope to stop. Look at them.

Across the hall, Valafar stood beside Solange. He was dressed in his trademark black pants and tunic, a red sash wrapped around his waist and a cloak with red lining over his shoulders. He looked a few pounds lighter, but he appeared healthy. No skin falling off or anything gooey. I really didn't want to care, and couldn't explain the relief that washed over me. Maybe my heart was wired differently, so I loved him even though he would do me harm.

Solange wore a triumphant grin, the red Athame clenched in her hand. Fury coursed through me as I recognized Coronis' energy inside her. I wasn't surprised that my sister was Coronis' vessel. She could already wield her dagger.

"Guardians?" the red-robbed leader of the Tribunal asked.

"I will speak on behalf of the Guardians." The voice that came out of me was firm and commanding, the sweetness of minutes ago gone.

"We recognized Xenia as the Guardians' advocate," the leader said. "Proceed."

"Before we start with the proceedings," I said, repeating the Goddess' words, "we demand the return of the Cardinal Kim whom Valafar and his followers kidnapped."

Across the hall, Valafar and Solange conferred, then he disappeared. Within seconds, he reappeared in the middle of the floor with Kim. She looked disoriented, her hair a mess and her clothes filthy, but she seemed fine. An excited murmur rose among the Guardians as her uncle teleported to her side and hugged her, then led her back to the Guardian side. It was the first time I'd ever seen Cardinal Seth show emotion.

I focused on the Goddess' next words. "We also demand the return of the old Hermonite they kidnapped. His name is Jethro."

"He chose to join us." Solange spoke in Coronis' annoyingly screechy voice.

"I refuse to take her word for it. Jethro must make an appearance before this court and talk to us. He's the leader of his group of Hermonites and cannot be dismissed callously."

"We already asked him, and he chose not to waste the Tribunal's time with such a trivial matter," Solange insisted.

"We get to decide if a matter is trivial or not," the leader said. "Next item on the agenda."

"When you convened a meeting a few weeks ago, I was unavailable to defend the Guardians against the vicious lies concocted by the demons," I said.

Solange laughed before I could continue, bringing back memories of Coronis cackling as she drained the powers of Guardians. Other memories came from the Goddess—hateful pranks perpetuated by Coronis, jealous tantrums over their father's affection. It was as though my relationship with Solange was a replica of hers and Coronis'.

"It is not our fault your second in command is incompetent," Solange said, her voice harsh and malicious.

"Tariel needed a vessel and his grandson volunteered, then fed him lies about their family," I continued. Tariel was Bran's grandfather and a former Cardinal Water Guardian. Coronis had kidnapped him, drained his energy and mated his only son, Bran's father, to a demoness. Obviously, Gavyn wasn't above duping his grandfather.

"This is another trivial matter that cannot be changed," Solange retorted.

"I concur. Next," the Tribunal leader ordered.

I couldn't read the Tribunal, which sucked, but the Goddess didn't seem worried. "The first case presented to this court was the hypothetical unfair advantage the Guardians have over the demons, which could tip the balance between good and evil. I don't see it."

"Without Valafar," Solange said, "the demons will not have a strong leader who can stand up to the Guardians and stop them from dominating and destroying humanity."

Tell them you concur, the Goddess said.

Why?

Because I know what I am doing, Lilith. Repeat my words.

Why Valafar? Why not some other nature-bender?

Lilith, she warned, her voice rising.

"I concur," I said through gritted teeth.

"Could you repeat what you just said?" the Tribunal said.

"I concur," I called out. Even if it was the dumbest reasoning I'd ever heard.

You know I can hear you, the Goddess said.

Good, I retorted before I could stop myself. When she didn't speak, I wondered whether I had gone too far. The problem was that Grampa had raised me to stand up for what I believed in.

She chuckled. *You remind me of myself at your age. Impatient, impertinent and stubborn. Do you understand about the balance between good and evil and how it helps humanity to thrive and give us purpose?*

Yes. But why him? There must be other powerful demons lounging in Tartarus.

There is a reason for everything that is happening right now, so be patient.

I hated the bitter taste of defeat, but I clammed up. The reason had better be a darn good one.

"Next," the Tribunal spokesman said.

"Second," I continued, so pissed I spoke through gritted teeth, "this Tribunal was made to believe that the Guardians influenced Bran Llyr's decision to change sides. This is not true. We have witnesses that will testify to the fact that he made this decision on his own."

"All of them Guardians," Solange retorted. "Whatever they say will be biased."

I glanced at Grampa and nodded. Darius stepped forward. "Darius son of Palizur is not a Guardian," I said. "He's a Neutral."

"Yet he and his group fought alongside the Guardians today," Solange retorted.

"So did the Order," I snapped. "It doesn't mean they are on our side. They just hate you more."

"There is no need for him to testify, move on," the Tribunal said.

That wasn't good. I exchanged a look with Grampa. Was he worried about the way the proceeding was going too? "The second witness is Jethro. He is not a Guardian or a Guardian sympathizer. He will testify that Bran sought his help to find the Guardians."

"Bran Llyr needed the Guardians' help to rescue his sister, but he stayed only after he met Lil—your vessel, dearest sister," Solange said with a sneer. "If it weren't for her, Bran would not be a Guardian."

The Goddess started to speak, but the Tribunal interrupted her with, "We will take everything you've said into consideration when we make our final decision. Next."

Solange consulted with Valafar. "You should take one more thing into consideration before you make your verdict," she said. "Bran Llyr won the battle on Jarvis Island, which makes him the rightful leader of the Hermonites."

"He was lured to Jarvis Island the night of the mortal combat under false pretenses," I snapped, speaking quickly to keep up with the Goddess. "The contract was between him and Damien, a person that doesn't exist. As a result, he didn't win the combat and is not the rightful leader of the demons."

We waited for Coronis to object, everyone holding their breath.

The members of the Tribunal stared at her too, then the leader said, "Next item."

Everything fell into place when the Goddess gave me her next orders. "With Valafar's return, we want the orders given to the archangels to be withdrawn."

Silence followed. All the other requests had been foreplay, nothing compared to this. The members of the Tribunal glanced at Valafar and Solange again.

"Any objections?" their leader asked.

Solange conferred with Valafar before she looked up. She didn't look happy. "We agree to withdraw—"

A loud cheering came from the Guardians. Some hugged. Others laughed. No more Raphael and his tribe shadowing us. My gazes locked with my friends. They were laughing too. I couldn't. The Goddess wouldn't let me. It was as though she knew more was to come and it wasn't good.

"Hold your applause," the Tribunal spokesperson ordered. "She is not done speaking."

Everyone stopped talking as though someone had flipped an off button.

"On two conditions," Solange continued. "One, we want the children the Guardians stole from us. Some of their parents are alive. Is it not a parent's right to raise his or her child?"

"It is," the Tribunal leader said, and the rest nodded. "What is the second condition?"

"Valafar was denied a chance to be a parent, too. He wants a chance to change that. We ask that Lil should live with him for exactly the same number of years she has lived with her grandfather. If, by her thirty-fourth birthday, she wants to return to the Guardians, she can be free to do so."

The silence was deafening, the shock absolute. Panicking, I waited for the Goddess to object or something. For the first time since she had possessed me, I couldn't read her or come up with a snarky comment. Then she spoke, but I had a feeling it was all for show.

"The requests are ludicrous," I repeated her words. "We don't have the Specials. They are being raised by the Brotherhood. When they are old enough to decide, they can choose sides. As for the matter of Lil," I continued, speaking quickly as the Goddess dictated. "She *did not* choose to be raised by her grandfather and therefore cannot be held responsible for the years she spent with him. She didn't even know Valafar existed until she turned sixteen a year ago. A year has passed since she decided to stay with her grandfather and the Guardians."

"There's nothing ludicrous about our requests," Solange yelled. "This is about a father who was denied his rights. Just like the Specials—those parents who are still alive want a chance to mold their children, Valafar deserves this. Lil lives with the Guardians because that is all she knows. Maybe after living with Valafar she might decide she prefers to stay with him."

"She already heard what he had to offer her and chose to be a Guardian," I retorted.

"Enough," the Tribunal leader bellowed. "Move on to the next item."

"We are done," Solange said.

The Tribunal looked our way.

For a moment, I couldn't speak, fear blocking my throat. "We are done."

"We will adjourn and come back with the verdict." Their astral images disappeared.

The silence that followed was heavy, then telepathic buzz filled the room. I refused to turn around and look at my grandfather, Bran, or my friends. I didn't need to. I heard their thoughts. They were willing to fight the archangels again and sacrifice more Guardians rather than let me live with Valafar. Seventeen freaking years. Stomach churning, my gaze connected with Valafar's.

Why was he doing this? Did he really think he could turn me? From the smug look on his face, he believed it. He also knew he'd won because he knew exactly what I planned. I couldn't live with myself if more Guardians died to save me.

Are you willing to do this? the Goddess asked, having heard my thoughts.

Do I have a choice? I snapped, so pissed I didn't care about being polite.

Yes.

No, I don't. Living with him is the only solution.

You are willing to sacrifice yourself for the lives of your people. That is one test you already passed. Be strong and stay true, Lilith, and all is and will be as it is meant to be.

The conversation I had had with Master Haziel flashed through my head. The warning not to show my powers to Valafar and the orders to go along with the Goddess' decision. He'd known this would happen. *What in Tartarus' pit does that mean?*

It means that things that are meant to happen are happening, which will shape the future. I will leave you now, my child.

Why? They haven't given us their verdict.

Their verdict will not change anything. You've already made your decision. Be strong, my child. I'll always be with you whenever you need me.

Vertigo hit me and my knees gave away as she left me, but strong arms wrapped around me. Grampa's earthy warmth enveloped me and mixed with Bran's fresh pine scent as his hand wove into mine. Two men who loved me implicitly and who were willing to fight till death for me, yet they were helpless to stop the verdict the Tribunal was about to deliver. The problem was they weren't the only ones. No one could save me but me.

The Goddess hovered to my right, her expression serene. The Tribunal reappeared and silence fell in the room again, eyes lifting.

"The verdicts read as follows." Their leader unrolled a scroll and started to read. "First, Jethro will be released immediately, so he can return to his people."

No one spoke or cheered.

"Second, no one influenced Bran Llyr to *join* the Guardians. He made that choice, so this matter should not be brought before this court again. Third, he is also not the leader of the Hermonites because the contract he signed was fraudulent."

I glanced at Bran. His expression was dark, body tense, hand like a death grip around mine.

"Fourth," the judge continued. "The orders given to the archangels will be rescinded effective immediately."

Once again, no one cheered. I couldn't breathe, my heart pounding so hard I was sure I'd faint. I gripped Grampa and Bran's hands, and studied the faces of the members of the Tribunal as though their expression would give me a clue. They weren't smiling.

"However, the matter of the Specials will be revisited at a later date. We will observe them first before making a decision." He paused then continued. "As for the sensitive matter of Valafar's request, Lil will not live with her father for seventeen years. It is an unreasonable request."

The hall erupted in applause, but I heard the unsaid "'but." Stomaching churning, I waited for him to continue.

"Silence!" the Tribunal spokesman bellowed. "However, it is reasonable to have her live with her father for one year, the same duration she has lived as a Guardian."

I exhaled, fighting tears. One year wasn't bad. My gaze flew to Grampa, then Bran. They were furious. Sykes and the others were shocked.

They can't do this, Bran ground out.

One year is not bad, I reassured him.

It's a lifetime. I will find you, he vowed. *I don't care what they say, I will.*

Bran had never had an off switch when it came to me, so I knew he meant every word. Unfortunately, to pull off such a rescue, he would put himself and everyone I loved in danger. *No, I will find a way to escape,* I vowed.

"After one year," the judge continued, "she will choose whether to stay with her father or return to her grandfather. Once she chooses a side, her decision will be final and recognized by this court. The Guardians must not attempt to 'rescue' her or the deal is off." The judge leaned forward and pinned us with a glare. "When I say 'the deal is off', I mean she will stay with her father for *seventeen* years. If she attempts an escape, the deal is off too. On the other hand, Valafar must not mistreat her or harm her in any way, or she will be removed from his care and returned to the Guardians. This verdict is final and will not be brought before this court again."

The silence was deafening. Whatever plans Bran and I had had just gone down the tube. After our encounter with the archangels, I knew the Tribunal's punishment would be swift and merciless if we disobeyed them. Tears prickled the back of my eyes, but I fought them back. This was not the moment to cry and indulge in self-pity.

I clung to Bran and absorbed his warmth, his love, let his energy blend me with mine and take me to that special place where nothing could hurt me. When I tried to lean back, he refused to let me go. Tears threatened to flow again.

Promise me you will not come after me, Bran.

Don't make me promise something I won't keep, he warned. *You have no idea what Valafar is capable of.*

I can handle him, and it is only a year. Please, don't go against the Tribunal.

We are mated, Lil. No one, not your father or the Tribunal, will ever keep us apart.

Then wait for me, I begged.

He didn't say anything, his arms tightening around me, both of us shaking.

"Lilith Falcon, cross the floor," the judge ordered.

Someone rubbed my back. I knew it was Aunt Janelle without looking. Over Bran's shoulder, my gaze met with Sykes, then Remy, Kim, and Izzy. They moved closer, their expressions so easy to read; they were ready to declare a war. I knew then they'd do something stupid if I cried or indicated I needed their help.

This is bull, Sykes said.

Damn right, Remy added. *We are willing to take on the archangels again.*

You can't. This was meant to be, I reassured them. *The Goddess said so.*

The lead judge said something and Bran stiffened. Grampa put his arms around us both. "It is time, Bran," he said in a voice that wasn't steady. "You have to let her go."

I will be at our spot in Maui every day, Bran vowed, then kissed me. Branding me. Giving me something to think about for the rest of the year then he stepped back. I was still reeling from the effects of the kiss when Grampa hugged me.

"You will do this and come back stronger than ever." Grampa's voice broke.

A tear escaped and I swiped at it. "No matter what happens, I'll always be a Guardian and I'll always love you, Grampa."

He stepped back and Aunt Janelle took his place. "You will make it, *Luminitsa*."

"I know, Aunt Janelle. Take care of him for me," I whispered. "Bran too."

One by one, I hugged the Cardinals, even Cardinal Seth, then my friends. Izzy cried. Kim had a better grip on her emotions. Remy and Sykes made vows I couldn't afford to acknowledge. I don't remember whether I walked or teleported, but one second I was having a group hug, the next the Goddess was leading me away.

Every step that took me away from my loved ones was like a stab through my heart. I shivered even though I wasn't cold, wept though no tear rolled down my face.

Look at me, the Goddess commanded.

I did, but all I saw was Grampa's face. He didn't look sad anymore. He was smiling. Or maybe I wanted to remember him smiling.

You'll be fine, sweetheart. Imagined words or not, I believed him. His face was replaced with Bran's. My heart contracted and tears rushed to my eyes. I loved him so much and would miss him with every breath I took.

Yours always, mine forever, he vowed. Again, whether imagined or not, I heard him and my heart ached.

Yours always, mine forever, I repeated his words, then made the trek to my father's side.

THE END

ACKNOWLEDGMENTS

Thanks go to my girls, Jeanette Whitus, Catie Vargas and Katrina Whittaker for taking time to read and give me wonderful feedback on the raw and unpolished version of this book. Your honesty, constructive comments and generosity is astounding. I couldn't have asked for truer friends and supporters.

To my teen beta-reader, Morgan Leishman, thank you for not cursing me out when I sent you chunks and kept you waiting for the next installment. To Merab, who continues to feed me information and listen to my crazy ideas, your insight into how teens think and act are invaluable as always.

To my agent, Leticia Gomez, you are truly my champion. Your enthusiasm and ability to fight for me is humbling. To Kate Kaynak and her team of editors at Spencer Hill Press, thank you for believing in my work and investing in me. Rich Storrs, my very humble and insightful editor, we make a formidable team, don't we? Your input always put a smile on my face. You are a funny guy. The final package would not be perfect without you.

Last, but not least, thanks to my family for their infinite patience. Your love and support means everything to me.

Life has been hell for seventeen-year-old Emma since she moved from sunny California to a remote Alaskan town. Rejected by her father and living with the guilt of causing her mother's death, she makes a desperate dash for freedom from her abusive stepfather. But when her car skids off the icy road, her escape only leads to further captivity in a world beyond her imagining.

Angela J. Townsend

Amarok

Having poison running through your veins and a kiss that kills really puts a dent in high school.

Kelly Hashway

Touch of Death

ABOUT THE AUTHOR

Ednah Walters grew up reading Nancy Drew and the Hardy Boys and dreaming of one day writing her own stories. She finished her Ph.D. in chemistry, married the love of her life, and decided to be a stay-at-home mother. She now lives in a picturesque valley in Utah with her husband, five children, and two American short-hair cats. When she is not writing, you can find her doing things with her family, reading, traveling, or online chatting with fans.

Awakened, the prequel to The Guardian Legacy series, was released in September 2010 by Pill Hill Press with rave reviews. She's currently working on the next book in this YA fantasy series. You can visit her online at **www.ednahwalters.com**.

When not writing about the Guardians, Ednah writes romantic suspense under the pseudonym E. B. Walters. She has released four books in this genre. You can visit her at **www.ebwalters.com**.

Made in the USA
Charleston, SC
09 February 2013